Dangerous LIES

ANNA LOUISE LUCIA

Medallion Press, Inc.
Printed in USA

DEDICATION:

For Paul Lucia 1936-2007 Who first told me stories of
"dawn runs on hard sand," and "picking fossil seashells
off the Sahara's ancient seabeds," and who helped turn
me into a storyteller.

Published 2009 by Medallion Press, Inc.

The MEDALLION PRESS LOGO
is a registered trademark of Medallion Press, Inc.

Printed in the United States of America
Typeset in Adobe Garamond Pro

ISBN# 978-193475508-2
10 9 8 7 6 5 4 3 2 1
First Edition

ACKNOWLEDGMENTS:

Thank you to Emma Wayne Porter, who coaxed and coached me, and said, "If you fill the plot holes, you get to keep the voice." Thanks to Dad, for maps and memories. Thanks to Mum, for being outraged at rejections and overjoyed at the sale. To P-J, for technical advice. Kate Walker's timeline advice, Jennifer LeBreque's revisions guidance, Julie Cohen's critiquing, and Brigid Coady's encouragement were invaluable—thank you, ladies. Special thanks to my Romantic Novelists' Association New Writer's Scheme reader, who finally convinced me this story was not dead in the water at all. Julie, you were saying that all along-I'm sorry I didn't hear you! And always and ever, thanks to my husband, Ian, for patience, encouragement, belief . . . and for the champagne.

prologue

The sun was a beast, a curse.

He was used to it. But today, at this time, it was hard even for him. Too hot for thought, too hot for sweat. The desert air parched his throat and seared his lungs. It seemed impossible that the dust and sand under his feet should not fuse into glass, that the mess of limp tents and abandoned vehicles ahead should not have simply melted away under the sun's attack.

Here, off course, deep into Western Sahara, there were three tents, two Land Rovers. He'd noted that at a distance, then thrown a camo net over his own vehicle while the dust was still settling, and jogged in on foot. It was too hot for haste, too, but he had no choice. The light wind turned a collapsed awning into a banner. A broken tent whipped like a loose sail. The yellow dust streamed around rocks scattered like broken pottery on the flat ground.

No dunes here. No glimmering oasis, no lone camel, no robed figures. Only three tents, two Land Rovers, and five bodies.

They were staked out in front of the largest of the tents—two locals, three Westerners. English, to be precise. He knew their names, the names of their families. The name of their employer, tucked away demurely in rural Kent. The security guards there, he knew, stopped the traffic on the main road for the ducklings to cross.

It was a world away.

He knew their faces, too, but the file photos weren't much use. They'd been beaten before they were tortured, and he approximated their identities from details of height, weight. Even their hair colour was indistinguishable, becoming the yellow-grey-brown of the desert here.

He didn't stop. There was no point searching them.

He looked, instead, for the sixth man. The man their enemies had missed. A rapid search located him some two hundred yards away, curled up on his side behind a cluster of rocks that might have offered a little shade for a few hours in the morning at least. The heat of the last two weeks had baked him dry, but he was largely untouched.

The scavengers in this part of the Sahara were mostly human.

The dead man was holding a laptop, clutched to his chest, his whole body curled around it protectively. The laptop itself was fried, but that didn't matter. What he was looking for was still in the drive, just like they'd said it would be.

He retrieved it, dropped the laptop beside the dead man, and left him.

It was what they paid him for.

It was what he did.

chapter one

She shouldn't have come.

There were doves in the courtyard, snowy white and silent. They slept on ledges and in niches, on the roof above the pointed Arabian arches, even on the bowl of the broken fountain.

In Marianne's mind's eye, and in her grandfather's photograph, the arches, the walls, and the fountain were bright and blinding white. Nearly seventy years ago they would have been, but now they were grey and peeling, and here and there a dirty orange stain showed where some elaborately carved bracket had rusted into memory.

Marianne folded the map she held with careful fingers, and stowed it in her shoulder bag. For years she'd dreamed of visiting Morocco, the country her grandfather had loved so much. He'd only lived here for a few years, but the place had burrowed itself into his soul, and woven its thread into the stories he told her years later at home in England.

When her father's death had dealt her grief and freedom

in equal shares, Marianne had taken that rare and precious commodity in both hands, packed new clothes and a new courage, and booked her flight before she'd changed her mind.

Sighing, she stepped forward out of the shaded doorway into the courtyard proper, the rough render catching at the long sleeve of her tunic. In that cherished photograph, the decorative tiles around the fountain lay in a neat order that contrasted with the wild exuberance of their design.

Now they were cracked, lifted, and scattered underfoot. But the black-and-white print could not have shown the depth of the cerulean blue that dust and debris were working hard to conceal.

It was like the photograph, and it wasn't. The false memory that picture and her grandfather's tales had painted for her hadn't anticipated the decline, but it hadn't shown the colour, either. Hidden good, concealed evil.

She nudged one loose tile with the toe of her cork-soled shoe, absently settling it back into its place by the fountain's weed-covered plinth. Her movement startled the sleeping birds, who rose in flustered and flapping cooing, swirling the dust with their feathers, and clapping away into the sunlight. With them gone, the space was dead and still, smelling of hot dust and a little of guano. It was a forgotten space, abandoned. Decayed.

It was a mistake, though, to think that the house had been left empty when her grandfather had left. The agents, eagerly anticipating an impulse buy from a gullible tourist, had told her the dwelling had stood empty only for a year or two.

"More like five," she sighed, running a wary hand down the pillar of one stately arch. The rust stains and broken tiles told of a neglect even older than that.

She tipped her head back, letting the sun's heat brand her face. Her skin was pale, the sun was strong. She'd stayed in the shade at the hotel pool, and even now she wore a wide-brimmed hat and sunscreen. *I am sensible*, she thought, *even when being reckless*. She didn't much like the notion.

The doves had settled somewhere out of sight. Their cooing floated down to her, and her mind conjured the soft sound of water playing in the fountain, which now stood dry.

The water was long gone. Her grandfather had died years ago, before her mother. And her father . . .

"Damn." She flicked sudden tears off her chin with fingers that shook. "Damn."

She shouldn't have—

"Should you be here?"

She spun on one foot, half tripping on the loose tiles, and steadied herself with one hand on the fountain edge.

The man who had spoken stood in the shadows of the doorway, and for a moment the contrast made him appear dark, as Arabic as any other resident of Rabat, Morocco. Then he stepped forward, and the sun claimed him as her own.

He was fair . . . no, he was golden, gilded, bright. Tall, slim, with a grace of movement that made her stomach clench. His hair was short, tousled, but his grooming was impeccable. Blue eyes, a face lined in the shape of a smile, even now, as he frowned at her. Surfer dude meets the City of London. The debonair beach bum.

She'd seen him around the hotel, here and there. She'd felt his eyes on her, too. Once she'd thought he might have approached her but he didn't.

She frowned.

He smiled. "Are you lost? I couldn't help see you come this way, and I was wondering—"

"The agents know I'm here," she snapped, more breathlessly than she'd have liked. She tightened her grip on her bag and edged towards the doorway. "So does the hotel."

His brows went up, but he was still smiling. "That's good. Good precautions." He gestured towards the street outside, turning a little so he stood sideways in the doorway. Blocking it and yet not blocking it. "But this is still not a good place for a lone female tourist. You're well off the tourist trail here."

"I wasn't sightseeing."

"But you are a tourist?" The blue eyes were open, his gaze straight and honest. The mouth was smiling, the posture was nonthreatening. But her steady heart rate had gone the way of her breath and the sun beating down on her head, hat or no hat, made her light-headed. At least, she chose to blame that light-headedness on the sun.

"I think I should get going," she said, squaring her shoulders, and making an obvious move towards the entrance.

"Ah," he said, shaking his head a little. "I'm being dense. I should introduce myself. I think you've seen me at the hotel? I saw you—"

I saw you. She closed her eyes for an instant, bathing in the illicit, tempting thought that he meant that how it sounded. That he'd really *seen* her. But, then, there wasn't anything to see.

I saw you, too, she thought.

"—by the pool," he continued, "although we never spoke." He held out his hand, steady and strong. "I'm Alan. Alan Waring."

Marianne stared at his hand from a distance of six feet and tried to come up with a plausible reason not to touch him. There was a roaring in her ears. Was he coming on to her? Was he dangerous?

How was she supposed to tell?

A bitter sense of inexperience and uselessness almost swamped her, but the anger in its wake propelled her forward two steps to take his hand and shake it briskly. "Marianne," she said.

The look in his eyes said he'd noticed the withholding of her surname. But he didn't press the issue. "It's a pleasure to meet you, Marianne. What brings you to Morocco?"

The words and delivery were smooth, the mouth still smiling, but at the end of the sentence, his gaze slipped away, his head tipped a little to one side as though he was listening to something outside.

"I, um . . . a holiday. What about you? Business or pleasure?"

She blushed on the word, horrified, when his head tipped back towards her and a laughing smile curved his beautiful lips. "Right now I wish I could say pleasure, but sadly I'm here on business."

Suddenly she caught what he must have been listening to. The distant roaring that wasn't in her ears. "What is that?"

He half turned away from her, his smile fading a little. "A demonstration."

Marianne frowned. The roaring ebbed and flowed. It was still far off, but it sounded angry, tense, pent-up.

"But the hotel said it was a peaceful demonstration."

"One is."

"One?"

He glanced back towards her, and he looked faintly apologetic, slightly ashamed. As if Rabat was his hometown. "Whenever there's a march in support of reform, there's usually another one rejecting it. They're making progress, but . . ."

"Isn't the march a long way off, though?"

His mouth twisted. "Yes. But although the peaceful march is over there"—he waved a hand down the street—"the troublemakers usually amass over there"—his other hand waved in the opposite direction.

"Um. Are you saying we're in danger?"

"Yes and no." He glanced swiftly around the courtyard and then his gaze settled on her, rueful. "Today it's about the laws governing women's rights and protection. I'm just a Westerner. You're a Westerner and a woman."

She swallowed. "I should be getting back to the hotel."

His brows raised. "Which way?"

"I'm sorry?"

"Are you going to head towards the march, where trouble is going to erupt, or away from the march, where trouble is going to start?"

She bit her lip.

He smiled again, then said, "Have you seen much of the city?"

"What?"

He held out his hand. "Let me show you some of the little-known areas."

She frowned. "You'll take me back to the hotel?"

"Yes." He nodded. "But we'll take the scenic route." He had a nice smile. It made the skin around his blue eyes crinkle.

"No, thank you," she said.

She thought for a moment that the smile was going to become a frown, but it only deepened. "You can trust me."

"It's very kind of you, but I'm not doing anything wrong, and I'm decently covered, they—"

"In theory," he interrupted, "not in practice."

"What do you mean? They said cover my legs and arms, wear a hat . . ."

He smiled. "There's covered and there's covered, and you could still be the spark that lights the powder keg. Come on." He held out his hand again, looking impatient to be gone, beckoning her with his fingers when she hesitated.

She was mad. She had to be mad, to be thinking of taking his hand, and taking him at his word. But she *had* seen him at the hotel, and he was polite and charming, and . . . and . . . And she wanted to.

Marianne took a breath, and took his hand.

"Let's go," Alan said.

❀ ❀ ❀

Her hand was cold.

A ridiculous thing to be fixated on, but there he was. He might have noted the slimness of her palm, or the softness of her skin, but no, he had to record the inconsistent details . . . Alan shook his head at himself, holding her hand in a light grip and taking the second alley on the north side, which appeared to finish in a dead end but did not.

On this typically hot Moroccan day, Marianne was swathed to the neck, shaded in a big sun hat, and smelling of coconut sun cream, but her hands were cold.

Low blood sugar? A chill? Anxiety? He had no idea. And he had no idea what he was doing here, self-appointing himself protector to some lost tourist. *Decently covered*, Alan thought.

Well she was, in point of fact.

She was covered. But cover a woman like Marianne in a bin bag and she'd still get attention. She wasn't what he'd call beautiful, precisely. Just . . . eye-catching? No, not even that. Something about her . . .

And he'd be damned if he'd stand in some dilapidated backyard explaining the meaning of allure to her while she frowned down at herself and plucked at the hem of her tunic.

"What were you doing there, anyway?" he asked, drawing his silent companion round a blinding white-painted building. "Don't tell me you were property hunting."

"No."

Hardly. Westerners went for new apartments in the modern quarter of Rabat, or seafront flats in Casablanca. Not some dilapidated house invoking dusty images of old Morocco like a half-forgotten dream. He smiled at her sidelong. "Looking for the real Morocco?"

"No, I . . . someone I knew used to live here." She wasn't out of breath yet. But chances were she soon would be. Alan slowed his pace a little, turning up a narrow street winding up over irregular, shallow steps.

"You're trying to find them?"

She shook her head. "No, it was a long time ago, I think . . ." She hesitated, in speech and step, and he halted for a moment to look at her. Dark eyes watched him, as if trying to figure him out from the lines on his face.

Good luck.

She shook her head slightly, as if discarding a fanciful idea. "I think it was a mistake to come," she finished.

"How—this way," he said, sending her before him through a gap between two buildings, "—how so?"

"The image is better than real life," she said, and either she was starting to lose her breath, or she wasn't sure she wanted him to hear that.

"I can understand that." Boy, could he. "Sometimes the picture is cleaner . . . safer." Sometimes the lie was so much easier to live with than the truth.

Sometimes the truth changed your life.

"Turn right," he said, harsher than he intended, as she stepped into the next street. He took her hand again and stepped up the pace.

What in heaven's name was he doing?

He'd been in the neighbouring quarter for a meeting that had not gone well. He should have been thinking through the implications of that carefully negotiated meeting going so wildly awry. He should have been solely concerned with getting back to the hotel, reporting back to HQ, hiding the small thing that even now burned a hole in his back pocket.

Instead, walking swiftly down that narrow, discreet lane, he'd caught a glimpse of her through the doorway, standing in the courtyard, a still part of a decaying tableau of Moroccan life. Dark hair, dark eyes, but a skin so pale, so luminous against the cream linen she wore that there was no mistaking her for a local, not even for someone who came here regularly.

And there was something else, too, some thread of a mood that had caught his eye. Whether it was the emptiness of the house, or the still sadness of the woman, he did not know, but there was an air of melancholy, of . . . loneliness?

He almost snorted. Ironic.

Even then, he should have walked on. It was only an impulse of kindness, the type that HQ disapproved of so intensely, but had to acknowledge added a depth to his cover. Alan, the charming, helpful English businessman. Good manners and good conversation. He'd never leave you in a fix. Never take you for a ride.

Never rob you blind, and leave you for the desert to kill.

That was the inherent difficulty with covers. They had to be consistent. Especially when drawn from life.

Which had left him at square one. One foot in the road, and one in the doorway, half listening to the rising baying of the hounds of dissent, and simply incapable of abandoning a woman in danger.

He glanced down at her as they crossed a silent street in two strides—well, four for her—and disappeared into a covered alley that stank like a toilet. She was flushed—he wasn't moving slowly—and definitely breathless now. Her hat was crumpled in her other hand, and he could see where wisps of hair were curled and darkened by sweat on her temple and cheek.

His heart, steady in pursuit, steady when pursued, skipped and settled into a harder rhythm.

Definitely something about her.

Marianne was lost in seconds.

Alan took them down streets, lanes, through squares,

courtyards . . . Once or twice it seemed as though he was taking them through someone's home. Once he pulled her swiftly through the tables of a café. It seemed to her that he wasn't heading in a straight line, but weaving like a fox would to run the hounds ragged.

Half-running down a steep, narrow lane, they spilled out into a wider street, and Alan swore.

Down the road a knot of men were gathered, talking and shouting, clustered by the entrance of a blue-painted building. They were all veiled to the eyes.

But Marianne didn't have to see their faces to recognise the anger radiating off them, and see it in the sharp, jerky movements of their arms, and the line of their shoulders.

A shutter slammed beside her, making her jump. Across the street another shopkeeper dragged piles of brown and blue pots inside, and hurried to shut the door.

She hadn't really been scared before, just wrong-footed and unsure, with all the fearful associations that *not knowing what she should do* traditionally held for her. But when Alan caught her by the arm and dragged her behind him, her stomach lurched and her knees weakened. *Oh, God . . .*

There weren't many of them. Marianne peered around Alan's arm and saw twenty, maybe thirty. They were intent in themselves, arguing, ranting, building each other's outrage and indignation to fever pitch.

Alan's grip pinched her skin, but she said nothing, trying to remember to breathe, in spite of the heat and the dust and the twist of dread. Moving slowly, Alan started backing away, pushing her behind him as he went. Craning over her shoulder, one steadying hand on Alan's back, she saw the street turned sharp right a few short yards away.

Then the noise from the men swelled, shouts of greeting, of exhortation, as another man, face uncovered, stepped out of the building and joined the group. She thought she felt Alan go still for a second, but he was moving again so shortly afterwards, she couldn't be sure.

The new arrival turned their way, staring for a moment, then waving an arm at the others. A few more heads swivelled in their direction.

One man took two, short, angry steps towards them. Another joined him.

And the new man bent very, very slowly and picked up an empty bottle at the side of the road.

Under her hand, Alan's back was utterly still.

He's not breathing, she thought. Then, *neither am I.*

When it came it was more of a sigh than a roar. The men wavered, stumbled . . . and then surged forward like a beast made of a multitude of parts, and each of them hungry.

Without fuss, without exclamation, Alan spun on his heel and started to run.

Her feet slipped in the dust, she staggered, off-balanced by surprise and Alan's hold. Somehow she dragged her feet under her, hauled in a breath, and pushed forward, drawing level with Alan as he turned back to look.

"*Move,*" he hissed, and she did, not daring to look behind as he did, her whole back crawling with the anticipation of a blow.

Alan skipped behind her, swapping arms and switching sides. He flung a hand out as they reached the bend, catching hold of something on the corner of the building, and sending them swooping round ninety degrees in a cloud of dust and an ungainly skid. He let go the building, and pushed her on.

There was grit in her shoes, sand in her eyes and the mob and her blood roaring in her ears. *We can't outrun them,* she thought, *we can't—*

"In here." Alan flicked a latch on a narrow gate of planks, paint peeling red and green, and pushed her through it ahead of him. It was little more than a narrow space between two houses. Not even wide enough to earn the name alley, just a gap, with a wavering channel running down the centre, where water would run in the rains.

He crowded in after her, bending close to the gate to close it, one palm braced on the splintering wood, one easing the latch into place silently. The mob passed, a shadow at the gate, a shouting and thundering, shivering a skein of sand from the back ledge of the gate.

The noise outside went away, the noise inside was only their breathing, her feet shuffling on the ground as she tried to edge her way to some personal space, somewhere she could breathe.

She was immediately half-blinded in the shadows and half-stifled in the still, hot air. She braced one hand on the rough-rendered wall opposite. With her back against the other wall, she couldn't even straighten her arm. She dragged in hot, dusty air, choking on the racing of her own heart, and tried not to panic.

Looking around, she saw that the other end of their hiding place was blocked by piles of something like boxes. *Oh, God.* "Where—"

Alan whirled on her, plucking her close, wedging her between his chest and the wall, one arm immobilising her, one hand hard across her mouth. Outside there were shouts, a distant cacophony, unreal and distorted.

Everything was unreal. The shafts of light piercing the rickety door were like golden blades. The dust motes that danced on them were gods and angels, djinns and genies. She was blinded with light and dazzled with darkness in one breath.

In the stuttering dark he was a wall of heat, pressing her back, holding her in place. Adrenaline surged in her, heightening her senses, making her want to shout against his hand, making her want . . .

One of those golden blades sliced across his throat, where the collar of his pale shirt was undone. It gleamed on his damp, tanned skin, and glinted on the bead of sweat that was travelling—now fast, now slow—down the rough stubble underneath his jaw.

Her breathing had steadied, but her heart was still racing. There was no sun, now, on which to blame her light-headedness.

He was golden, gilded, bright.

His palm against her mouth smelled of him, and of spice and heat. She dragged the scent in, her eyes fluttering half-closed. His skin would taste of salt, she knew . . . It would taste salty and hot and intense.

It would taste . . .

She put out her tongue, half-dizzy, half-dreaming, and tasted him.

His body jerked against hers. His eyes were glowing in one of those brilliant beams from the broken door, all white and blue, like a clouded summer sky. They fixed on her, holding her more effectively in place than the hands that gripped her and the body that pinned her.

He ducked his head. The hair at her temple snagged on the roughness of his jaw, and his breath spilled down her neck. "Mari," he whispered, a word of warning, but his grip on her changed, gentled. His thigh brushed hers, his chest pressed against her breasts. Outside, distantly, a crowd roared, but the sound of her blood drowned out their hate.

She tasted his skin again. He snatched his palm away.

She was afraid. But this was the other reason she was here, wasn't it? In fact, if she was honest with herself, following in her grandfather's footsteps was the excuse for this . . . meeting men, a man, finding out . . . Eight years, more, of the most contained, confined life that life could deal you, willingly, if not gladly, caring for her father . . . and now.

Now the most gorgeous man she'd ever seen was

pressed up against her in the dark, and her head was spinning with recklessness. She arched her back and pressed closer.

Infinitesimally, his position changed, his body somehow cupped around hers, not the position of a guard and a captive, but the pose of a man encompassing a woman. She lifted her hands. They weren't hers. Not when they brushed against his shirt to feel the way his chest rose and fell with his breathing. Surely they weren't her hands, those hands that tested the tension in his arms, tracing the bulk of bicep and shoulder, that touched the skin of his neck where the sunlight stroked it.

The points where they touched were the only parts of her that existed. Breast to breast, thigh to thigh. His hands on her waist. The brush of his jaw against her skull. It was as if she was a join-the-dots picture. For a wild, irrational moment, she felt that if he touched her everywhere, she would burst into being. If all of him touched all of her, she would come alive.

There was a heat in her that beat back the sun. The bead of sweat on his neck trickled down to touch her fingers and at that hot, wet touch, she raised her head, turning, reaching for, longing for his mouth.

His hands had moved. They cradled her head, spiking through her hair. Her eyes were open, but she couldn't see. There was only the touch of his body, the stroke of his breath across her lips, a heat that was almost flesh.

Almost his mouth. Almost a kiss—

And then he moved, a moment of disorientation, his

hands dropping to her waist again, his head sliding away.

⚘ ⚘ ⚘

"This is a catastrophically bad idea," Alan hissed, close to her ear, trying not to breathe in the sweetness of her, and failing. He felt her shiver, couldn't miss it, the way she was plastered to him—the way he was plastered to her, to be fair. Goose bumps rose on her arms, under his hands.

He backed off, just enough, and shook her, knowing— none better—the drugging that adrenaline could do. "There are people outside who would love the opportunity to hurt you, just for being female, and visible. Do you really think they're going to give up and go home if they find you kissing a stranger in public?"

She was stiff and shaking against him, now, eyes wide and shocked.

And that wasn't fair, because it wasn't her fault. *It wasn't you*, he wanted to tell her, but he didn't dare.

The moment Tahir had stepped out of that blue building into the mob of his own making, Alan knew those much-maligned generous, kindly impulses had let him down for once.

Marianne would have been perfectly safe in her courtyard, in her alley.

In his company, she was far, far more at risk.

He shifted his weight, straining to hear beyond the sound of his breathing, and hers. Outside, the street was quiet. Farther off, the sounds of protest still drifted.

Now, now he had the kind of *complication* HQ deplored. And here, half in his arms, completely under his protection, this woman Marianne believed a Moroccan had taken one look at her and hated her enough to kill.

It wasn't you. It was me.

But he couldn't say that. That was only the half of it. And even that half was not his to share.

Oh, God. Give me the desert, he thought, *and the choices that are all about heat and water and air and dust. This oasis, this well, this night, this trail.*

Marianne took another shivery breath, and his anger turned suddenly. What the *hell* were HQ doing? Why was Tahir, a man Alan knew by sight as a local troublemaker, by repute as a hard case, and by briefing as his contact, stirring up trouble in the wrong quarter, instead of meeting with Alan at a prearranged location?

But it wasn't Mari's fault. He glanced down again, caught by those big, shocked eyes. "Do you have any idea what you're doing?" he pressed. Because it was rapidly becoming apparent that she hadn't a clue.

Her lip trembled.

No. No she didn't. He eased back a little more, as much as the space would allow. "It's alright, Marianne. I'm not going to let them get to you."

She blinked, her eyes flicking to the inadequate door to his left. She looked confused, disorientated.

She *was* scared because of the riot, right? Not because

of what she—he—*they* had felt?

Bloody hellfire. He swallowed.

It was quieter outside already. Distantly he registered sirens and blare of loud hailers. Order being restored. Slowly, not wanting to startle her, he brushed her hair back from her face, tucking stray tendrils, stiff with dust and sweat, behind her ear. "Not, I hasten to add, that I'm not sensible of the honour." He smiled. "Another place, another time . . . another less murderous crowd . . ."

The intention was to make her laugh, not to make her slightly cross-eyed as she tried to focus on his face. Still, silent, she was not getting the joke.

"Mari." He settled his hands on her shoulders, stroking softly. "They're going. We'll give it a while, and then head back to the hotel. And then—" he paused deliberately.

She looked hunted, wary. "And then what?"

He smiled, putting everything into it. "And then I'd very much like to take you out to dinner."

chapter two

Alan took her to a place he knew tucked away in the back streets. He'd hate to inspect the kitchen too closely, but the food was impeccable. He knew the owner, slightly, and not by name, but the young man's eight-table restaurant was on his list of potential bolt-holes.

He wondered, then, why he'd chosen that place exactly, when mixing business with pleasure was not his style, and he usually kept any amusements strictly to those tourist haunts that would never be of any use to him.

Odd, he thought, ushering Marianne to a table in the corner and seeing her comfortably seated, while the waiter lit the dribbled candle under the beaded shade with every appearance of delight at their first customers of the evening. He bobbed and smiled and Alan slipped comfortably into Arabic to argue out the important matter of food. There wasn't much point consulting Marianne—he doubted she'd be able to read the menu.

They'd talked a little longer on the walk back to the

hotel. Nothing personal, nothing threatening. Just enough to bring the colour back to her cheeks, and calm the tremor in her fingers.

Just enough to find out she was delightful.

Was it her unsophisticated style, the straight look from those dark eyes? Or was it that allure, the allure he couldn't quite describe, when his living depended on measuring people in one look, recording all the information in one glance?

He didn't know.

He'd been careful to tell her that he'd take her out where Western dress was acceptable. He told himself that was so *she* would be comfortable, and carefully ignored the warm appreciation that ran through him when she met him in the foyer wearing a pale green strappy dress that swirled about her knees.

She could certainly while away the hours, days even, while HQ decided how they wanted to exit him from Morocco.

Well, there were worse places to be stranded for a while. Of all of North Africa, Morocco was about his favourite, particularly when he got the chance to get off the beaten track, so to speak. Which he did, of course. Frequently.

She sat there staring at him, clearly a little uncomfortable.

"Relax," he smiled. "If I'd wanted to eat you, I wouldn't have taken you to one of the best kept culinary secrets of Rabat."

"Oh."

"Oh?" he smiled. She was sitting on her hands, chewing on her lip. Maybe this wasn't such a good idea—it looked like she wasn't even capable of sustaining a conversation.

"I'm sorry," she said then, surprising him. "I'm being silly. But I hardly know you, and I hadn't expected to venture out of the hotel much, you see." She frowned sharply, staring down at the shabby tablecloth. "I sound stupid."

"Not at all."

The waiter came back then with two glasses of mineral water. Marianne took a sip of hers immediately. He played with his glass, watching her, wondering what impulse, exactly, had brought him here.

The candle flickered as the kitchen door swung shut, painting shadows and light over the creamy skin of her throat and the first hint of shadowed cleavage.

Ah. He acknowledged the frisson of desire wryly. *Ah, yes, I remember.*

But that didn't exactly do him justice, either. Frustrated as he was being stranded here while HQ dithered, he was still, amazingly enough, prone to the odd selfless impulse. And this one was odd. Take a holidaymaker under his wing because she was alone and there was a whole resort full of men he didn't want to take advantage of her loneliness.

"So who was it you were looking for?"

She frowned. "At the house?"

He nodded.

"Oh, I—" Worried eyes flicked over his face. "My grandfather used to live there."

He raised his brows. "You visited him there?"

"Oh no," she shook her head. "It was long before I was

born. Before my mother was born, actually. He lived there, I think, for about five years, and then came home, married Grandma, and they had my mother soon after."

"What brought him out here in the first place?"

"I don't know. But he used to talk about it all the time. Not . . . not specifics, you know? Just a feel, a love for the place."

She wasn't looking at him now, just playing with her glass, one arm lying on the table, her voice dreamy and becoming more relaxed. The love in her voice, for a man he guessed was long gone, was as clear as if she'd painted it on the whitewashed walls.

"We used to sit in the garden, under the apple tree," she continued, and Alan concentrated on not distracting her, "and he'd tell me stories. Just things he'd done, where he travelled, what he ate, what he laughed at. He had a photo, too—just one. It showed that courtyard, a black cat sitting by the fountain, and a woman in the shade. The cat was called Euphrates."

What was the woman called? he thought, watching the young woman opposite him with the pale English skin and the dark Arabian eyes.

"I knew from what he said which quarter it was in, so . . ." Her voice petered out, and she shrugged.

A pilgrimage, he thought. And wondered how soon he could get back to the desert. "So you thought, since you were here, you'd check it out?"

She gave him a funny look, guarded and wary. "Kind of."

So she was uncomfortable talking about herself again.

Easily dealt with. "You say you hardly know me. Shall we amend that?"

"Oh, I didn't want to pry . . ."

And he usually spent most of his time *avoiding* questions. He must be mad.

"Not at all. What would you like to know?"

"Well"—she grinned then, and effortlessly added charm to allure—"you said *business* this afternoon. What business?" She was sweet, and he'd been lacking sweetness.

He grinned back, kept it easy. "I work for a company that specialises in electronics and IT for emerging markets. I'm in sales—establishing new contacts and contracts." The old lies slipped easily off the tongue. "But you're on holiday?"

"Oh, yes," she said quickly, her eyes flicking to his face and away. "I've never been abroad before. It was time I got out a bit."

"Why Morocco? Isn't that a bit extreme for a first try?"

"Yes. I suppose it is. But I wanted somewhere exotic, you know. Popping across to Calais would hardly have done the trick, would it?"

Since she hadn't said what "the trick" was, he couldn't comment. She wanted a break, he thought. An adventure.

Why?

"So why Morocco, still? You could have gone to"—he waved a hand—"Barbados, Thailand, New Guinea . . . why here?"

She didn't quite meet his eyes, her cheeks a little pink. "Ah, I see. The grandfather was why?"

"Yes." A smile curled her lips, but it was forced, and gone too soon. "It sounds stupid, I know."

"No, it doesn't." But it did sound a little odd. Who travelled hundreds of miles to spend half an hour in a derelict house, just because a relative had lived there, decades before?

Only a very, very disconnected person.

All of a sudden, keeping the smile showing, the shoulders loose, the jaw unclenched was becoming more and more an effort of will.

"He spent a lot of time in the Sahara when he was young," she said quickly. "He told me tales . . . magic. I've always wanted to go."

"But you're not going anywhere near the desert, are you? Not the desert proper— you said yourself, you didn't intend to leave the hotel, even."

The consciousness, embarrassment vanished. "Well, I've got to start somewhere, haven't I?" she said indignantly. "I think I'm doing well even to get here!"

"And so you are," he said smoothly as the salads arrived.

"What about you? Why do you do the travelling thing? Don't you miss being home—" She broke off. "You're not married are you?" she asked, wide-eyed, a piece of tomato halfway to her mouth.

"No."

"Involved?"

"No."

"Why not?"

"I've not had any . . . urge"—*use*—"for long-term relationships. But that's hardly an interesting topic of conversation. Why don't we—"

"Why not?"

He almost choked on his salad. He coughed, drank a
little water, and sat back in his seat to frown at her. She was
tucking into her salad, the "closed subject" signals going
completely over her head.

She just had no concept of that sort of social interac-
tion, he realised, and suddenly felt very old. Which was
ridiculous, because he was only thirty-five.

"How old are you, Mari?" he asked, and was suddenly
scared of the answer.

"Twenty-four." She was still picking over the salad,
almost oblivious to him. He relaxed a little. She was still
ridiculously young, but not quite as young as she might
have been.

"And you didn't answer my question."

Perhaps not so oblivious. He chewed, swallowed, and
smiled at her again. "Are you usually this persistent?"

"I'm not usually this anything," she said, and he had to
bend in to hear the softly spoken words. She set down her
fork, and he saw her square her shoulders before meeting
his eyes with a sort of rueful resolution. "It's all new to me,
Alan. Everything is."

He thought he began to understand. "A sheltered

upbringing, Mari?"

"Something like that. And you still haven't."

He took a mouthful of water, watching her. "Haven't what?"

"Answered the question." And not to be underestimated. It seemed it was a lack of experience that made her this way, not a lack of intelligence.

"I'd forgotten it."

"Why no urge for long-term relationships?"

This evening was taking on a certain surreal quality. Usually he'd be more successful at avoiding questions, more successful at having his own answered without his companion even realising it. He wanted to laugh, but he certainly didn't want to offend her. Instead he hid twitching lips in his glass of water again.

He set the glass down again and finished his salad while she watched him. He kept a gentle frown on his face, intending her to interpret that as careful thought. Truth be told, he was just as likely to be analysing a problem behind an apparently open smile.

"I'm not sure," he said when he had finished and laid down his fork. Marianne was picking at crisp lettuce with her fingers, nibbling on the pieces. "I've never really thought about it."

She opened her eyes wide. "Never?"

He met her gaze deliberately. "Not until now."

She looked at him confusedly. "Why now?"

His eyebrows climbed his forehead. Good grief, she

didn't even get that. "I'm flirting with you, Mari. Have a heart."

Thankfully, the waiter returned as she opened her mouth. He whisked away the salad plates and laid heaped dishes of couscous—chicken for her, fish for him—before them with the air of an emissary making an offering of gold and jewels.

"They say," he said easily, sifting the fragrant grains with his fork. "That to get really good couscous you need to order ahead. Here they cook this fresh, every day, no matter what. It's fabulous. Try it."

Mari was staring at her plate, sitting on her hands again.

"Trust me," he said, propping his head on his hand. "It's delicious—you'll like it."

Her head jerked up, "Oh! Oh, I didn't mean . . . I wasn't worried about the food. It looks lovely." She took a forkful to prove it, and went, "*Mmmm,*" dutifully, before she could possibly have experienced the true flavour.

Then a startled look flashed across her face, she went to say something else, choked on her mouthful, and went slightly purple. He handed over her water, and then his napkin, and waited, thoroughly amused, till she subsided.

"It *is* good," she gasped eventually.

"Well, I did tell you," he said, with a hint of reproach.

She was busy, working her way through her meal with enthusiasm. He shook his head, and addressed his own plate.

It was almost empty when Mari seemed to lose her

enthusiasm and start pushing a chunk of chicken round her plate with her fork. "What you said earlier," she hesitated. "About flirting? Why?"

She was full of questions. And his stock of answers was suddenly empty. "It seemed like a good idea at the time," he said, leaning back in his seat.

"Oh."

"Why does a man flirt with a woman?"

"Oh, but I'm not—"

"A woman? I find that hard to believe."

"No. I mean yes. I mean, I'm not the sort of woman a man flirts with."

"But I just did, Mari."

"Marianne."

The evening wasn't turning out to be the light diversion he'd been seeking.

But he wasn't being fair on himself, either. He had had altruistic motives. He'd honestly stopped to speak to her because he knew she could be in danger. And he'd asked her to dinner because . . . because . . . Because nobody that lonely should be alone.

He wondered then if she knew she broadcast such a level of tragic loneliness, and then if it was only he who was receiving.

He set his knife and fork together with a click.

The waiter came and cleared the dinner things, on the edge of Alan's notice, because he was watching Mari. He looked down and found their dessert sitting in frosted glasses.

"I was flirting with you because you're pretty, I like you, we are together here tonight, and I wanted to make you smile. And blush."

That much honesty was scary. Liberating, but scary.

She stared at him, and her eyes said, *you like me?* which made his mouth twist and his fingers shake, just slightly. It was like feeding a starving kitten, and he wasn't sure if that made him a benefactor or pathetic. Ridiculous to lose your breath over a dinner conversation.

Then she surprised him. She made a little fist with her hand and beat the table, scowling.

"What?"

"I don't know what to do."

"About what?"

"About you! About this! I don't have the . . . the skills to know."

He interrupted her, as much out of kindness as embarrassment. And *that* feeling, turning his stomach, twisting his heart, was pity, he knew. "Just relax. Enjoy yourself. The food's good, I'm not an ogre, and you're safe. Calm down and enjoy yourself."

She looked at him, big eyes in a lovely face—neat nose, sweet mouth, flawless, natural skin—and he wondered what the hell he was supposed to do with her.

Ah, yes.

He took a few mouthfuls of the sharp, sweet syllabub and took himself back to the alleyway in his mind. Deliberately, resolutely running over again her heated, unspoken invitation and the burst of dazzling desire it had conjured in him.

And then he made himself remember the fear in her eyes, when she found herself out of her depth. Truth be told, he should have known. It was all there, the hesitancy, that fear, the feverish plunge headlong into something that needed more nerve than you could summon.

Even now, if he was honest, he had no intention of letting her get away from him without having a little more of that. You didn't find a thing like that and let it get away. You didn't find someone like Marianne Forster —a little discreet enquiry at the front desk had easily elicited her surname—and willingly wave goodbye.

But there were . . . complications. His work, her reticence. But mostly what it was that had made her so inexperienced in the first place. Was it just that sheltered upbringing? He could hardly conceive it. If he'd known Mari as a rampant teen, he'd have stormed a citadel for one kiss.

He set his spoon down and pressed the napkin to his lips. "You never did get around to telling me how it is that you are travelling"—he paused, twisting his glass of water on the tatty tablecloth, glancing up at her as he did—"alone."

She watched him guardedly over her syllabub, spoon poised. "No," she said, "I didn't."

He couldn't help smiling at that—it was so very Mari. "You can trust me, you know," he said. "This isn't about any hidden agenda. I really would like to know more about you."

This time the look was downright suspicious. "Why?"

"A generous impulse?"

She snorted. He laughed. He didn't think he'd ever taken someone out for a candlelit dinner who snorted.

"No, really. I don't know of any good reason why I shouldn't help you if I can. Is there one?" He sipped his water, watching her delicately taste the smooth dessert. Her tongue slipped out to catch a smear of cream, and he couldn't help tracing that movement with his eyes, even while it made it harder to concentrate.

Much harder.

She swallowed, and so did he. "No. I suppose there isn't. I still don't know why you would want to, though."

"Look, Mari, I like you. I think you've got guts. You're pretty, good fun, and passionate." He paused, watching her blush in the warm candlelight. She really was pretty. But he couldn't resist teasing her. He flicked a glance around the room—still empty. "And if you're a bit temperamental, it's only to be expected—"

"Temperamental!"

It was only a small table, and she was already leaning on it with her elbows. Swiftly, he wrapped a hand around the back of her neck and pulled her close, landing his laughing mouth on her outraged one. She squeaked when his lips pressed on hers, but she whimpered when his tongue traced her sealed mouth. Something changed then, from a light-hearted tease to something hotter, heavier, more suited to the fragrant darkness. Her fingers found their way to his collar and he felt her convulsive grip, there, against his skin, as he moved his mouth against hers.

He pulled back a fraction. Her eyes were closed, dark lashes a soft veil against pale skin made rosy by sunshine. He slid from his seat, still holding her, and dropped to his knees beside her chair. "Open your mouth, Mari," he breathed, and her rose petal lips trembled and parted.

He kissed her again, sliding his tongue into her mouth and tasting the tang of lemon and the smoothness of cream.

And there it was.

It wasn't a fluke. The heat, the shiver, the *need*. A gut-wrenching, breath-stealing desire.

Bloody hell, he wanted her. Somehow, anyhow, here, now, whatever. He wanted to peel her out of that little dress and take a much more leisurely examination of a sweet waist, smooth hips and breasts that begged his mouth.

He fought to stay gentle. He wanted to crush her mouth under his, thrust his tongue inside, but he didn't. He kept it light, teasing, a taste, a touch, a tantalising of the senses. He lifted his mouth slightly, and she gasped, her brows drawn tight in a small frown, her hands tugging him back down to her. He kissed her with a smile, sucking on her lip, letting his tongue take just a little more of what he wanted.

His hand was on her leg above her knee—how had that got there?—he inched the hem of her dress a little higher and stroked her thigh with his palm.

The door to the kitchen went. He jerked back,

disorientated, automatically defaulting to work mode, where an unexpected interruption might mean discovery, disgrace . . . death. But as he glanced quickly in that direction, the door swung closed again. It had only been the waiter. He must have withdrawn tactfully when he saw they were . . . occupied.

He took a deep steadying breath, which didn't do much to steady him anyway. Marianne was watching him, eyes wide, that little frown marring the arch of her brows again, her lips softly parted, wet, red.

He gently withdrew his hand from her leg and stood, looking down at her, wondering what the hell to say, when words were usually the most accessible weapon in his armoury.

🟣 🟣 🟣

What now? Marianne thought, wildly. Alan was staring down at her in silence, looking grim and a little white around the mouth. Was she supposed to say something? Or nothing. She dragged the napkin off the table and into her lap so she could twist it to death unnoticed.

Her lips were alive. They tingled and felt slightly swollen—she'd never been this aware of her mouth before. She looked down, sucking on her lower lip, trying to capture the sensation. And that wasn't all. There were other tingles, all over. She could still feel his hand on her thigh.

Thank heaven for small mercies.

"I should apologise," he said in a low voice.

She lifted a hand, still clutching the mangled napkin, but he continued before she could tell him, *no, please, don't say you're sorry.*

"But I'm not going to. I wanted to do that, Mari." He sat down again, but if he'd wanted to kiss her he didn't look very pleased with the result.

Oh, God, what did I do wrong?

The waiter crept back in then, so she couldn't ask him.

Alan ordered coffee, in a soft, even voice, turning a language she'd thought guttural into something enchanted. She closed her eyes to listen, and when she opened them, the waiter was gone and Alan was watching her with hooded eyes. He smiled slowly, and some of the tension lifted. She was starting to adore that smile, all several hundred watts of it.

The waiter returned, then, with tiny cups of a rich, fragrant black coffee that was as searing as it was soothing. And Alan, sipping his own coffee with the appreciation of the connoisseur, told her about Morocco, about the places she should see, where she could relax, where to be careful. He was entertaining, knowledgeable. And completely impersonal.

Remembering that kiss, she wondered how on earth he managed it. She could never be impersonal with him again.

⚕ ⚕ ⚕

Alan had never found it harder to make simple conversation. What was it about this girl that made him want to ask real questions, about things that mattered? Or worse, made him want to tell her things. Things he had no clearance to share.

He walked her back to the hotel—it wasn't far, and the evening was warm. He told her what he knew of the streets they passed and the shadowed bulk of larger buildings, farther off. He carefully avoided saying any of the things that teased his mind, right until they made it back.

He caught hold of her hand as they reached the door to her room. "What are you doing tomorrow, Marianne?" he asked.

And then wondered what he was thinking of. Tomorrow he had to move about the city resurrecting some old contacts and setting up a Plan B. And C, and D, and so on. Just in case.

Just in case what, Alan?

There were two shallow steps up to her room. She opened the door, turned on the top step, and faced him, even then not quite high enough to see him eye-to-eye.

"I hadn't thought. I was going to—"

He spared her the necessity of finishing the sentence. "I wondered if you might like to come to the beach with me? There's a little place I know, quite deserted most of the time."

What if the vibe was right? What if something wasn't quite right at HQ? He would need an alternative route back both for himself and, potentially, if things really got messed up, for his cargo. He needed to use tomorrow to set that up.

"I'm not . . ."

"No hidden agendas, Marianne, remember?" He swung her hand back and forth a little. "Just for fun."

He wasn't here to be having fun. They weren't paying him for fun. But, for God's sake, he was *bored*. His was a straightforward job, most of the time. When it got ridiculously cloak-and-dagger, he got frustrated. Restless. Bored. No one could hang him for wanting to spend a little recreational time with a pretty woman.

She stared up at him, still uncertain, and he found he was holding his breath.

She swallowed, looked away, looked back. "Okay," she said. Then, belatedly, "thank you."

He smiled, and watched her blush. "You're welcome."

She backed up into the doorway, pulling a little at her hand. He chose to interpret that as her wish to pull him along and came up another step himself.

I wonder . . .

She was staring somewhere in the middle of his chest now: he could see the top of her head, the tip of her nose, and the wispy ends of her fringe hiding her brow. She smelt sweet, an indefinable flowery scent that was somehow nostalgic. The urge to kiss her was a detached thing, like someone watching them, thinking, *That man looks like he's going to kiss that girl.*

Odd.

He was too tense. It was the delay getting him out of

Morocco. It wasn't usual, it wasn't routine. And there was no one watching them.

As he watched, Marianne shivered. Just once, just a little, but it was enough.

The urge to kiss her wasn't detached anymore. But he'd become angry with himself somewhere in this weird conversation. He could feel it now, chipping at his good humour and patience.

For a breath or two, he wasn't sure if anger was going to push him forward or back, and he did wonder, of course he did, what Mari would make of the kiss that he might give in anger.

But it was late, and he was just disgusted enough with himself to paste a smile on his face and usher her into her room. "I'll come up to your room about ten, if that's okay," he said easily, holding the door open beside her. "Don't forget your sunscreen. You look like you burn easily."

She slipped through the door smartly and turned to face him. "Yes, I do," she said, with a look of seriousness. "I do burn easily." Then she took his hand from the door, and gently closed it in his face.

He paused in the corridor, irrationally annoyed with himself, with circumstances, with his HQ contact's dithering, with timid little Mari growing the resolve to attempt to warn him off, however subtly.

He dug his hands in his pockets. He'd head up to his room, call room service for coffee, and later get in touch with Stuart again. There had to be some decision from HQ by now.

He hoped it didn't interfere with tomorrow's beach trip, though. He found he was irrationally obsessed with seeing Marianne in a bikini.

Alan sighed, irritated with his mind's wandering. However much he had a bad feeling about HQ's lack of decision, it seemed like his job's power to hold his attention was waning.

And Marianne's influence was waxing.

He headed for the stairs.

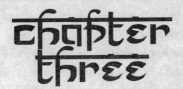

chapter three

Alan ditched his jacket and unbuttoned his shirt as soon as he reached his room. He headed to the window—no matter how often he opened it, the maid always shut it tight when he was gone. The night breeze was cooling. Outside, the old city—half exotic, half modern—was sleeping the sleep of the virtuous.

Lucky city.

He loosened his cuffs, rolling the fine cotton up to his elbows. He went to the bathroom and let the cold tap run till it was truly cold, then splashed water on his face, thinking about nothing in particular. At least, trying to.

Lifting his head, he stared in the mirror as the water ran down his face and dripped off his nose and chin.

He'd had to fight for work in this part of the globe. Tall, blond, and blue-eyed men were not your first choice for undercover work in the area of the Sahara. HQ had always preferred to place him in the Scandinavian countries, where Saxon might easily pass as Viking.

But it had only taken one trip, covering for a wounded colleague, and he was sold, his soul forever pawned for the sake of one lonely, barbarically magnificent sunrise.

He closed his eyes to recall it. The bright, unashamed colours, the silence that was somehow a better fanfare than half the world's trumpets. And the rising heat, that *don't mess with me* warning, almost singeing the skin. *Don't underestimate me, child*, the desert sun said. *I could kill you in a moment, without thought or remorse.* Every day he'd survived on that trip felt like a year of living. Every small success like a great victory.

Alan opened his eyes. His face was dry again, but his eyes were moist. He grinned derisively at himself and turned to the combined bath and shower behind him. The bath panel came free easily, as it had the first time he'd identified his first-choice hiding place. His laptop was inside a semi-rigid plastic sleeve, taped to the underside of the bath. He reached past it and checked that the small thing from his back pocket was still safely stowed, taped to the wall side of the bath, in its magnetic shielding. It was. His fingers stroked across the small, square package—it hadn't been tampered with. It was a smart card, a tiny chip loaded with information.

According to his contact, HQ were very, very keen to take a look at it.

He shook his head slightly, leaving the smart card alone, pulled the laptop free, and replaced the panel, then took it through to his bedroom.

It was quick enough to log in to the secure zone only accessed by himself and his contact. While he waited for any messages, he checked his e-mail. The account which managed his UK identity contained a message from Brian Keys, his business manager.

Brian managed a medium-sized landscaping business that ostensibly made enough money for Alan to employ three staff, including Brian himself, and finance his frequent, wandering trips abroad. On average he spent six months of the year in England. In truth, he was little more than a sleeping partner. The business made enough to keep his staff comfortably paid, and any surplus went into securing him a future for when, inevitably, he was no longer in his prime.

Contact from Brian was rare enough for Alan to open the e-mail immediately. But it wasn't that important. Just a fairly minor staff changeover. He added a couple of amendments to the contract and suggested a wage review for all staff, which would allow them to hire better qualified people in the future and retain staff better. He added that he was exploring the Norwegian Fjords and expected to be home sometime next month.

You think you saw Alan Waring in Morocco? Must be some other Alan Waring...

Which prompted him to send one of his rare e-mails to his sister, Jenny, and her family. He hated lying to her. Perhaps that was why he was such an infrequent correspondent.

When he was finished, the other window was blinking.

The laptop screen winked at him.

:- Message for Courier

He entered the appropriate access code and waited.

:- Courier—Party are aware package is in Morocco. Representatives of Party have been seen in Rabat. Caution advised.

Excuse me?

Alan shifted on the bed, tucking one foot beneath him and balancing the laptop between his knees. He just wasn't in the mood for the spy crap. He tapped out his response.

:- How in the hell do they know the information is in Morocco, Stuart? If they know that, they must be looking for me.

:- Negative. Cover is intact. HQ tracing information vector. Must remind Courier of directive 74, advising against the use of . . .

:- . . . personal names in communications. Yeah, I know. What now?

:- HQ advise hold position. Instructions for exit to follow. In meantime Courier should take advantage of any opportunity to process the package to England.

Any opportunity? Alan reread the line, although he didn't need to.

:- Elaborate "Any Opportunity."

He waited, unease stirring in him again. *What's going on?* he thought. *Talk to me.* He'd always found his HQ contact, Stuart Bristow, a little nervy, a little too in love with procedure. But then he'd always found him reliable and conscientious, too.

:- You are authorised to become physically separated from the package, according to your professional judgement, should the opportunity arise. Relay any arrangements to HQ Contact with due urgency.

Woah, there.

That was highly unusual.

And that was an understatement.

He couldn't understand HQ's edginess lately. But he had put it down to the reshuffle of a related department. He'd heard it said that might cause problems. Alan still veered towards the opinion that this was a storm in a tea-cup. HQ were prone to fits of over-caution, in his experience. He wouldn't be surprised if it was just an error arising from the reorganisation. Stuart was being slightly stuffier than usual, too. Alan rubbed a hand round the back of his neck, surprised at the tension he found there.

He liked this job when things were straightforward. He even liked complications when they were something he could directly deal with. But these delays and cryptic warnings were annoying.

He acknowledged the instructions, signed off, shut down the laptop, and concealed it again.

Then he flopped back on his bed, cradling one hand on his chest, and throwing the other one over his head. The ceiling fan spun lazily, stirring the air just barely.

He was restless. He'd usually be back home in England by now. God knows, he wasn't needed there. His "other" business back home was little more than a cover, and basically ran itself, but something in him needed to rest and recoup back home in York, or lose something of himself.

He never stayed for more than a few months. The house was big and empty, and before too long he'd find himself thinking in sentences that used words like "alone" and "lonely," and that was a matter of choice. No use fretting over something he couldn't, wouldn't change. Something he was born to do, it had turned out.

Shifting onto his front with a sigh, he started thinking about that "Any Opportunity" thing, and about Marianne. Tomorrow was going to be fun. He needed the relaxation.

And he was still curious about her.

Before long his thoughts met and melded, running away on their own paths. The second time he snorted himself awake, he shuffled off the bed, stripped, and slipped between the covers.

He slept—and dreamt of lemon syllabub and big, scared eyes.

Alan was kindness itself.

Marianne hugged her knees, looking out on a brilliant blue sea. It was a perfect picture—sea and sand and sun—timeless and beautiful. Beside her on another brightly coloured beach towel, outside the shading of the parasol,

Alan was propped on one elbow munching grapes.

The beach was small, deserted, entirely theirs. They'd swum first—shyness sending her plunging into the cover of the water despite the fact that she hadn't been swimming since she was a child. And it hadn't escaped her that . . . well, that her inexperience in this, too, hadn't escaped *him*. Alan had stayed close, laughing, joking. Never once had he acted the lifeguard, even though they both knew that was the role he was playing.

They were silent now, listening to the waves, but it was the first time they'd been quiet for what seemed like hours. It was so good to talk—about everything and nothing—with someone who listened. Who even seemed to care about the answer. It made her feel secure, almost intelligent. Cared for.

Her father hadn't talked much in the last months. Sometimes she thought he'd stopped listening years before. Immured in the big house in some of the remotest countryside in England, she'd talked to herself more often than not.

She was a terrible listener, too.

But Alan . . . Alan looked at her while she talked, as if it mattered what her face was saying, as much as what her mouth was. They'd talked without stopping. Except to eat, of course. He'd been the perfect host, there, too. The picnic he'd brought along had been magnificent.

And because he was kind, and because he'd been so nice to her, she tried not to wonder about *why* he was being so kind, and *what* he wanted for being so nice.

There was another thing, too. Uneducated she might be, but she was not always stupid, and although she'd chatted forever about food and films, books and how she found Morocco, it hadn't escaped her that he had hardly told her anything about himself.

He had a sister. She was married with two kids. He was a salesman, investigating emerging markets for IT. When he was home, he lived in York, but work kept him travelling about half the year. That was about it.

But turnabout was fair play, and though nice he might be, and kind he was certainly being, she wasn't about to heave her sob story up over him, and give him enough material to make him sorry for her for the rest of his life.

Oh no. Not that. She'd had enough pointless pity from people who were strangers and people who should not have been. It was funny, really, how people could actively pity you, but not even pick up the phone to lighten your load.

She wrinkled her nose, feeling that slight tug of skin close to burning. Flopping back in the shade, she closed her eyes, shuffling her feet across to move them out of the sun. Her toes brushed Alan's leg.

"Sorry," she mumbled, without opening her eyes.

His rumble of laughter was as soothing as the sound of the surf. "Be my guest. Comfortable?"

"Mmm. Very."

"Good," he said, softly, and she could hear the smile in it.

That smile. *Mmmm.*

Drugged with food and sunshine, soothed by the sound of the waves, Mari slept.

🏵 🏵 🏵

She woke with a shuddering breath, to see Alan bending over her, his face inches from hers. The fingertips of one hand hovered near her cheek where the trails of tears tracked cool lines.

"What were you thinking about?"

"My father," she said, without thinking, before waking, before she remembered not to quite trust him.

"Tell me about your father."

All at once, it was easier to tell him than not.

"He's dead."

"I thought he might be." The rough pad of one fingertip stroked her cheek. "You were crying in your sleep."

"I'm sorry."

"Sorry? Don't apologise, Mari."

"Marianne," she corrected, automatically.

"Tell me. When did he die?"

"Four months ago. And eight years ago."

Alan looked a question.

She sighed, moving her legs, but more uncomfortable with her thoughts than her position. "Eight years ago he was diagnosed with multiple sclerosis, the primary progressive form. He thought he was dying ever since."

Alan settled down beside her, propped up on one elbow,

his shoulder touching hers. He was so close, but she felt comforted. "Did he really see it like that?"

"Not always. I know I'm not being fair." She closed her eyes, still feeling the sick aftereffects of the dream that were so much like raw grief. "But sometimes it feels like I've spent my whole life waiting for him to die, and dreading every day that brings it closer." And waking up every morning wondering if she was alone.

"You were sixteen?"

"Fifteen. I managed to stay at school until exams. Well, mostly. Mostly I worked at home and did what I could. I didn't get many passes, of course. And from then on he needed me more and more."

"Didn't he have any nursing care?"

"We lived in an isolated area, not many people. There just wasn't the money. Well, he could have sold the house and moved to a home, but it was Mother's, you see, and he didn't want to leave home. He refused a lot of treatment, anyway. He didn't want to live that way."

"But he didn't mind his daughter sacrificing her youth for him."

She looked up at him, shocked. "I didn't grudge him it! He was my father. Why shouldn't I have cared for him? Who better?"

He stroked the hair at her temple with a touch infinitely tender. "I'm sorry. I shouldn't criticise him."

"I miss him. I woke up one morning after the funeral and realised I was nothing, knew nothing, had done nothing. I just," she shook her head slowly. "All I knew was the house, you know? I wanted to get away."

"Find yourself?"

"I don't think there was a *myself* to find. It never had a chance to grow. Create myself, maybe."

"So." His hand rested against the side of her face, warm and rough. "That's why you're here."

"Yes." She stared resolutely past his ear, hating that he knew now, but hating more the impulse to tell him all the horrible details. All the little things that had hurt her, from the first day she knew her father was going to die, to the last day and that mockery of a funeral, standing in the rain with two impatient, duty-bound mourners.

"But why were you crying?"

"It was just the dream. The grief's not bad, really. I get used to it. Only . . . sometimes at home I'd find myself getting up to do something that had always been done at that time, and realising that there wasn't any need. That he'd gone and all the things I took for granted had gone, too."

※ ※ ※

Alan understood that feeling. The sudden disconnection. The need to build a new life when everything changed. He'd got himself a new job, bought his house in York, created a new life. But Mari . . . had she even had a home to rely on?

"Did he leave you anything?"

"Oh, the house was mine. And there was plenty of money, too, as it turned out. The solicitor found it, tied up in shares and things. Funnily enough, thinking about it, there was probably enough for private nursing, it turns out." She shrugged. "I didn't know. I'm sure Dad didn't either."

Alan had his reservations. "But the dream."

She shivered, and he held her. "It was nothing. Silly."

"Tell me."

A couple of shaky breaths later, she did. "I was going round the house, opening doors. It's a big, old, Victorian thing, loads of rooms, big gardens. Every room was empty, really empty—it was horrible. And every time I opened a door and found it empty, I left a piece of me behind in the room—it was like I faded—until I was staggering from room to room, empty, all empty, and I was nothing but a shade, a whisper of shadow, lamenting."

"Ah, Mari," he said, aching for her grief, tucking her in close to him as she began to cry again. He couldn't quite comprehend a girl, not even a woman, suddenly having to assume the care of her father, when she should have been out having fun with kids her own age. He heard so much that she didn't say, guessed that she'd been something of a loner even before her father had been ill. Heard of the complete lack of people to help, to even give her an afternoon off to go out for herself.

Her small frame shook with sobs she was trying to stifle, half on the towel, half on him. He swallowed, hard, absurdly wishing he had been around when she was a child, to take some of that burden from her.

He ran a hand down her side, feeling the smooth skin ripple and shudder as she choked on another breath.

"I'm sorry, Mari."

He wrapped that arm around her, turning her, and tugged her to him so that her head rested on her other arm and her back was snug and secure against his chest. She was warm from the sun. She was still shaking.

"Shhh," he said, feeling her tears wet and chilled against his upper arm. "It's okay, I'm here." He tucked his arm tight around her, cupping her waist in his hand where it pressed against the towel. "It's okay, Mari, really it is."

✿ ✿ ✿

Marianne was mortified beyond belief. Grief was a wild thing that seemed to strike with no warning, but she hadn't wanted to make a fool of herself.

But Alan wasn't laughing, he wasn't bored, and he wasn't angry or embarrassed. He was comforting her like he wanted to, like it mattered to him. Like he cared.

She turned her head on the pillow of his arm, staring up at his face, only inches away. Her eyes were blurred with tears, and the sun shone strongly behind his head, turning his wind ruffled hair into a brilliant halo, shadowing his features. He blocked out the light.

"Why do you care?" she asked him, knowing she didn't have to explain herself.

The muscle under her head jumped, the arm about her waist tensed convulsively.

"Because," he said, and ducked his head to kiss her.

Every part of him that touched her was hard, tense, so Mari wasn't expecting gentle. She went rigid herself, seeing him swoop down on her, setting ineffectual hands to his big shoulders. But gentle was just what she got.

His lips stroked across hers, warm and giving, learning the shape and texture of her own. She felt his breath, hot on her cheek, the sweep of his hair across her temple. She felt his tongue, too, just tasting, teasing. Making no effort to take more. Her own breath shuddered in and out of beleaguered lungs and a knot in her stomach—a knot she'd never even known existed until now—loosened and melted away like liquid sun, burning and giving life.

"Alan?"

"Shhh."

He smelled of the sea. He tasted of it, too, when somehow between her own burning and melting, and the skilful instruction of his mouth, her own lips parted and welcomed the taste of him.

It was just enough to tease, just enough to hint at something more. Enough to turn that delicious melting into an aching, making her press closer, flicking her tongue out in instinctive response.

Rearing back from her, he watched his own hand pass over her hip and down her leg, slowly, down, down, and then back up again, sliding possessively over the front of her thigh.

In answer, she ran her own small hand over his back. The skin was warm, no, hot. Summer hot and live beneath her fingers, here and there a dusting of sand to break the smoothness. Only now did she appreciate quite how broad his back was. Now she noted the width of his shoulders, the hard muscles bunching on his back.

His hair was bright as the sun, his eyes blazing blue as the sky. "You look like a sun-god," she said, without thinking.

Alan laughed, rolling her onto her back, coming over her in a rush. He nudged her thighs apart with one knee and settled between them, pressing forward in a slow thrust that left no doubt as to his state of mind. Or body. "No gods here, Mari."

She should have felt panicked, half-crushed under him, his hips pressed so intimately against hers. But she didn't. She wondered at it with a tiny portion of her mind. With the rest she welcomed him. The hardness that pressed so insistently against that ache felt so perfect, so *right*.

She'd done that.

Oh my.

She slid her hands down his back, either side of his spine, down into the dip of his lower back, till her fingertips slipped just under the band of his swim shorts. Her own boldness amazed her.

Her restraint amazed her.

She looked up at him, saw how his blue eyes blazed, his

lips set. He rocked against her once, and his back heaved with his harsh breathing.

Biting her lip, experimentally she rocked back.

"Ah . . . Mari?"

She rolled her hips again, her heart racing with the excitement of discovery.

He groaned, ducking his head, but her sharp little surge of triumph was obliterated by sensation when she felt his lips brush her skin just above the edge of the swimsuit. His breath was hot, his jaw rasped against her. She could barely breathe.

He lifted his head. "You—"

She reared up, kissing his collarbone, licking the salt from his skin, then lying back to check the result.

His eyes were closed, his brows contracted, his lips twisted in a look almost of pain. She went perfectly still.

What had she done wrong?

Eventually his breathing steadied a little and he opened his eyes.

"I'm sorry," she whispered.

"Sorry? Ah, Mari, you have no idea . . ."

Well, exactly.

Hurt and suddenly uncomfortable, she tried to shuffle out from under him, but he held her down easily.

"No, no," he said, "Mari, stop it. You didn't do anything wrong. I don't think you could if you tried."

Her lip was trembling. She hated it. "You mean, I don't know—"

"I mean you did everything right. You feel right, Mari. You feel . . . incredible."

She fought hard not to say, *really?*

He answered her anyway, with a smile, with a soft kiss to the bridge of her nose. "But the beach is not exactly the best location in which to take this to its logical conclusion."

"Excuse me?" she squeaked.

"Oh, hush," he said, on a laugh. "Don't look so outraged. All I mean is we're not doing it on a beach, Marianne."

She blinked at him. "Oh."

"There's too much bloody sand," he said.

That was the pattern of the next few days. She laughed, and talked, blossoming under his eyes. She kissed him back when he kissed him, too, and there were plenty of kisses. He couldn't get enough of her, laughable as it was.

Delighting in her company, putting aside all thoughts of work, Alan took her anywhere he thought she'd like to go.

Except the desert.

She asked him, one night, when they dined on the terrace of a small French restaurant, under a pergola lit with a thousand white fairy lights. She sat back in her chair, smiling at him, and dropped her napkin onto her half-finished main course.

"Beaten?" he asked, smiling at her look of chagrin.

"Completely. I'm stuffed!"

He chuckled, charmed by how incredibly un-charming she could be when relaxed and trusting. He blinked a little at his wine glass at that thought. Trust. Such an emotive word. Many people in his life trusted him.

He lied to them all.

"Alan?" Her voice was uncertain.

"Mmm?"

"Are you . . . are you alright?"

He lifted his head and smiled at her. "Quite. The cuisine has beaten me, too, if it's any consolation. I forgot how large the portions were."

Mari was faintly flushed from the wine, her eyes bright. She was beautiful, too. Had he once thought her only pretty? They'd been out and about all day—her hair was tousled from the hot wind, her cotton dress was a little crumpled. She looked . . . real. He thought, an odd fancy, that if she were to disappear now, she would leave a Mari-shaped hole in his world.

"You've known every restaurant we've been to."

"So I have," he drawled, spinning the crimson wine in its bulb. "I'm in this area a lot. I know it well."

She leant forward a little, nibbling at her lip. He watched the movement, suddenly finding a worthy successor to the pleasure of the wine.

"So, you've been to the desert proper?"

He smiled. If she only knew. "Once or twice."

She licked her lips. His smile faltered.

"Well, would you . . . I mean could you—"

"Spit it out, Marianne."

"Will you take me out into the desert? Please?"

She leant forward, eager, waiting for him to say yes.

How could he take her out into the vast Sahara? Easily. There was nothing to hurt her out there if he was with her. But there was plenty to hurt him. Not least the inevitability of discovery. How could he pretend not to love that place, not to know its every mood? How could he bring lies to the only honest place in the world?

He couldn't. She'd take one look at him in the setting he'd come to think of as his soul's birthplace and see right through careless, smiling Alan. Or worse, he'd pollute the desert with pointless, selfish deceit.

"No," he said.

It was the first thing he'd refused her, and he watched the damage of that one, short word with something approaching panic.

Mari subsided, her mouth falling open a little. Then she shut it, shifted a little so that she sat in her seat straight and prim. She dropped her eyes, but not before he'd seen the flash of hurt, and the horrible, awful fatalistic look that followed it. Like the refusal was only to be expected, only what she deserved.

He found his lip had curled of its own volition, and twisted his mouth into an alien smile. "You wouldn't like it, Mari, trust me."

There's that trust word again, Waring, Alan thought.

"Better to keep your dreams," he said softly, and had

to fight to keep that smile, alien as it was, when he saw her own pathetic attempt.

God, what a mess.

She looked up, her face ostensibly calm, when he'd loved spending time with a Mari who was far from calm. "I thought my dreams were real, you see. Will you excuse me?"

She went to get up.

"Mari—"

"It's Marianne, Alan. I've corrected you enough times."

He rose, lifting a hand to her. She stopped, one hand on the back of her chair, showing a poise he'd given her, that he'd never wanted her to use. She lifted her brows, coolly questioning, and then, at that moment, he'd have given her a thousand miles of desert, and more besides, just to have back again the smiling, relaxed woman of a moment before.

"I'm sorry. I'll take you. Of course I'll take you."

She stared back at him, a little pale, studying his face with a little half-frown. For a breathless moment he thought, stupidly, somehow she could read his panic. Then she took a deep breath and smiled sadly.

"No, I don't think so."

"But, Mari—"

"I wanted to. Now I don't. Perhaps you're right, and it's better to keep the dreams."

🏵 🏵 🏵

She was still stiffly upright when they got back to the hotel. He watched her clutch the wrap he'd bought for her in the Medina—an endless stream of blue silk—tightly wrapped round her shoulders. She went before him up the steps, passed through the door he held open for her without a word or a glance.

He was torn between admiration and irritation, and it was perhaps the fact that admiration was winning that made him say, softly into her ear, "Are you sulking, Mari?" His fingers brushed her neck, deliberately provocative, a calculated reminder of every touch they'd shared.

Her head came up, her eyes blazed, and suddenly he was caught in a blast of awe that left him, astoundingly, speechless.

Marianne turned and studied him for a moment and he swallowed, absurdly panicked, again, at what she might see.

"I don't sulk," she said, evenly, and he remembered, then—too late—the life she'd led and the burdens she'd assumed willingly, and felt utterly ashamed.

She must have seen that remembrance in his face—God help him, she might have seen the shame, too—because she gave a tiny but decisive nod, swivelled on her heel, lifting the trailing ends of her wrap in one hand, and left him behind.

She walked across the gleaming granite tiles like she owned them, like she owned the whole hotel, the whole world. Her head was high, her hips swayed, her footsteps were placed with consummate assurance *just so*.

It was as if he watched her in slow motion. The sinuous sway of her hips, the way she held her head, the elegant line of her shoulders, the perfect angle of her arms, elbows close to her narrow waist, defining the curves of her slender body.

He could hear the music from the streets again, down in the cafés where the locals drank. Drums like a heartbeat, pumping in the blood, backing the yearning, exultant voices.

Out of the corner of his eye, he saw there was a party at the reception desk, a mixed group of men and women of all ages. They all watched her, the men with open admiration and curiosity, the women with narrowed eyes and pursed lips.

Alan wanted to cheer.

Mari lifted one hand a few inches, letting the wrap play out between her fingers. The silk rippled past her hip, slip-shimmering as it slid around the curve of her behind.

He hadn't the breath to cheer anymore.

They reached the lift: he pushed the button. He was breathing hard, as if they'd run the last few yards of polished floor.

The lift was on the sixth floor. He almost groaned.

He saw her clearly, the sweep of a pale golden shoulder, the slope of a breast beneath the dress, the flash of dark eyes, the set of her delicate jaw. He felt off-balance, disorientated . . . and at the same time elated.

"Alan?"

He had to swallow before he could speak. "Yes?"

"Will you come upstairs with me?"

He swallowed again, throat dry. She wasn't asking for an escort. She was asking for a lover. He could read it in her eyes. *If you won't give me the desert, give me this . . . one dream or another . . . I was looking for adventure . . . Be my adventure . . .*

"Are you sure?" in spite of the cool sweetness of the hotel air, his voice was desert-dry.

She turned her head and met his look with a steady gaze that was, if not truly unafraid, then completely resolute. One end of the wrap slipped entirely from her grasp and lay on the floor like a pool of sky.

"I'm sure."

The lift arrived, and he held the door for her while she stepped past him, trailing the blue silk. He moved past her in the small space, leant back against the lift back, and pulled her with him. She fell against him with a gasp, looking up at once.

He reached past her to hit the button for her floor, waited for the door to close before he slid one hand down to cup her backside, and ducked his head.

"Marianne," he breathed against her lips. "I'd be honoured."

chapter four

Marianne was dimly aware of the lift moving, but the lurch of greedy gravity only made her head swim all the more. Alan's face was a blur, hovering close. Burning blue eyes and sun-darkened skin, his breath on her mouth, his hands on her body.

She rose on her toes, sliding against him, making that breath catch for a moment, then sigh out again, hotter. Straining to close the gap between them, she lifted further, just brushing her lips against his. Her senses were wild and alive. She felt the drag of his stubble against her chin, the soft pressure of his lips. She tasted his breath and breathed in his scent and thought, crazily, *I didn't know you could smell sunshine.*

He didn't take over the kiss, didn't duck his head, didn't move his hands. She smiled against his mouth, nipping his bottom lip lightly, and laughed to feel his hands clench on her. She leant back a little to tease him about it, looking into those blue eyes, with the smile lines beside them, pale skin in the little creases . . . And then she heard the word he wasn't saying.

But.

I'd be honoured, but . . .

He wasn't saying it. But it was there in his eyes. Regret. Restraint. And, worst of all, the slightest hint of pity.

The lift went *ping*.

She peeled away from him, moving stiffly, feeling frozen. They both bent to retrieve her wrap, but she got there first, whisking the silk away under his hand, gathering it into an awkward crush of cloth.

Staying a pace ahead of him, she walked swiftly down the corridor to her room, wanting sanctuary, needing privacy.

"Why did—"

"I don't—"

They broke off.

"After you," Marianne said, turning her key card over in her hands, conscious of the tremor in her fingers. She wanted to get inside, get away. But more than that, worse than that, she wanted him to kiss her again. More than kiss her. Every breath reminded her of his touch, even the movement of her dress reminded her, here clinging, here slipping softly against her skin, there—oh, *there*—rubbing against her nipples.

Alan gave her a wry look, took the card from her and opened the door. Leaning back against the jamb, he slid his hands into his pockets. "Normally I'd insist that you go first, but I suspect what I have to say is safer."

"Safer?" Her voice was level. Amazing.

"More sensible, perhaps."

Her heart raced, knowing now that the unspoken *but* had matured into a *no*. How mortifying.

She licked her lips. "Maybe I don't want to be sensible."

The wry grin faded, his eyes narrowed. For a moment she thought he was angry, then with new insight realised it wasn't anger he was feeling. Not at all.

Then his mouth twisted in a crooked smile, and he brushed back a lock of hair at her temple. "One of us has to be," he said lightly. "For all you make me want to be reckless."

It was praise, of a sort. More than she was used to. But then Alan was more than she was used to, in every way. She smiled back, in spite of it all, loving how he made her feel. Like she was special, clever, beautiful . . . capable of anything.

She loved . . .

Her answering smile faltered, but she held onto it, just, while her stomach dropped like a stone. A cold sweat prickled between her shoulder blades. *He musn't see!*

"Well, then," she said, proud, deeply proud of the way her voice sounded teasing and relaxed. "I'll cut my losses and say goodnight." She stepped neatly past him in the doorway—at least, she tried—but his heat and his scent radiated like a force field, and he stood in the door, so she had to squeeze close by him . . .

She blinked. Somehow while she hesitated Alan had manoeuvred himself out of the way without even touching her, and was standing seemingly at his ease in the corridor.

"Will you let me take you to dinner tomorrow? A farewell dinner?"

Just dinner? "I have to pack."

"There's time."

She had to be alone. She had to think. She shook her head at him. But she said, "Yes."

"Goodnight, Marianne." He still smiled, but there was a twist of something in his eyes, a shadow, a pain.

She straightened her spine, conjured a smile, wished him goodnight, and closed the door on him. Then she sat on the bed, and dropped her head in her hands.

What had she done?

You've fallen in love with Alan Waring, that's what.

It was mortifying to discover the person she had been trying so hard not to be was the person she really was.

No amount of running around holiday resorts with drop-dead gorgeous guys was going to change that. In fact, it had only reinforced how pathetic she was. Alan had offered her the perfect vacation, hinted at the perfect affair. And what had she done? Gone and fallen in love with him. And now that she was in love with him, she just couldn't face the thought of . . . of making love to him if he didn't feel the same.

It was ridiculous.

It was pathetic.

But it was true.

A few seconds ago, she'd thought her happiness hanged on getting him in her bed. Now she wanted him nowhere near it.

Or rather, she did. But not under the terms he offered.

I don't know of any good reason why I shouldn't help you if I can.

Her cheeks burned. What a mess. He was just being kind, that's all. She used to think all she wanted was a little kindness, a little company.

How wrong could she have been?

⚜ ⚜ ⚜

He'd thought the disorientation would pass, out of her shining influence.

He was wrong.

And he must have been mad, surely, to turn down what she was so clearly, and so triumphantly, offering. That mix of reckless bravado and barely conquered trepidation was so utterly, so bewitchingly Mari. How had he resisted?

Why had he resisted?

Alan realised he'd been standing in the corridor, staring at the door to his room, for a full minute. He shook his head, and went in.

The truth was, he'd intended to take her up on it, he mused, heading for the bathroom. Was heady, breathless, with the thought.

And then . . . then he hadn't liked himself very much.

His face felt tight as he slipped the bath panel free again, and pulled out the laptop. He took it to his bed, booted up, and logged on.

Nothing.

And that silence from HQ should matter one whole lot more than the remembrance of those wide dark eyes, hurt, but holding on to pride.

Alan shook his head, sharply, shut down, and concealed the laptop again.

Time, finally, to set up that "Plan B" he'd been intending to create for days.

Time not, really not, to think about Mari alone in her room, and the decision he'd made and still didn't understand.

  ⚘ ⚘ ⚘

A day without Alan was more horrible than it ought to have been. But somehow the space gave Marianne the nerve to be with him again, and not fear that she'd blurt it out, tell him . . . tell him . . .

I love you.

She dressed with care that evening. She'd bought a new dress the previous afternoon in the Kasbah des Ou-whateveritwas. Alan had told her the name, but she kept forgetting it. The dress was patterned with swirls of subtle shades of amber, long and close-fitting. The neckline was softly draped, seductive. She *felt* seductive, and was careful not to examine her motives in this almost ritual preparation.

There were butterflies in her stomach. She smoothed the dress down carefully, struggling to ignore them. She was almost ready, and she was early.

$$\text{\Large ⬥ ⬥ ⬥}$$

If he wasn't careful, he'd be late.

"Plan B" had suddenly come through that afternoon, and Alan just about had time to get to meet his chosen contact, and then take Mari out afterward. He was half-dressed when he remembered he ought to report the meeting he'd set up, the potential transfer, to HQ. He'd hiked the laptop out from under the bath quickly, and set it up there in the bathroom while he shaved.

A quickly typed message had received an equally quick response from Stuart Bristow, a calm and colourless acknowledgement. He elaborated, explaining there was suggestion that his contact might have an alternative route out of Morocco for Alan's cargo, that he was meeting him at the address in a small street in the Medina, at 19:15.

Shutting down, Alan glanced at his watch again. He was going to be late, but hopefully not significantly so. His felt his mind shifting into work mode, enjoying the heightened sensation, making his preparations almost by rote. He gave Mari a quick thought as he left the hotel, and paused at the desk to give the concierge a message, half his mind still on work.

"I have to go out," he said, mentally tracking his route through the Medina. "An urgent meeting. Will you inform Miss Forster, please?"

Mari put the phone down and sat on the bed. She tucked her hands under her knees and sat there, staring blankly ahead.

There really wasn't any reason why he shouldn't cancel, was there? It wasn't as if she was important. Or exciting. An awful, crawling feeling of insignificance came over her, and she swallowed hard round the lump in her throat.

"It could be worse," she said aloud. It didn't help. She had been so looking forward to tonight.

In spite of her best efforts, the tears began to fall.

The man was dead.

Alan was not a doctor, but he didn't need the utter stillness of the dusty passage to tell him that the figure propped up against a sack of flour wasn't breathing. The gaping wound under the chin, grinning like a second red mouth, was a clue.

A dead giveaway, thought Alan. *If you'll excuse the pun.*

In any case, there was the smell, too.

In the kitchen behind him, food sizzled and pans rattled. In the outer room beyond, insistent drums led a Berber courting song, beating down the laughter of the performers.

The man had been searched. He'd been partially stripped, and the pockets of his trousers were torn. The frayed flaps of cloth were soaked with blood now, but there were no bloody finger marks anywhere. He'd been alive when they'd searched him.

And when they hadn't found what they wanted, they'd slit his throat like a goat in the slaughterhouse.

Alan watched the great wet-dark stain growing, the edges feathered in tiny right angles, following the weft of the trouser cloth. There was no more to come from the wound, but the blood they'd spilled hadn't set.

There were no flies yet, either.

I'm late, Alan thought. *I'm half an hour late.*

He unpeeled his fingers from the door handle, wiped it clean with the cuff of his shirt, passed down the corridor in three strides—careful to avoid the blood—and exited the back door.

He moved just fast enough to create an illusion of purpose, but not urgency, and didn't stop until he was almost a mile away.

Half an hour ago, that man had been alive. Alan stopped, closing his eyes for a moment and leaning against the post of an awning, breathing deep. Two breaths only, and up again, and walking, strolling like a tourist taking the air.

Bloody hellfire.

It was not unknown for one of HQ's precious plans to go wrong. If it was straightforward, they wouldn't send him, after all. And he'd dealt with more colossal balls-ups than this. More bodies. More blood.

His mind ran back to the smart card's origin—the seismographic team they'd sent him after a couple of months ago—the one he'd found dead two hundred miles from where they should have been. Or before that, the source who'd lost his head . . . and *lost his head*. When intelligence—both definitions—was patchy, work was risky.

HQ always made sure Alan knew as little as possible. And he approved. Find this man, fetch that report, deliver this dossier. These were the instructions that he worked to, nothing else to give away, no one else to betray.

He worked alone, and with the minimum information.

But he knew this: that meeting, that contact, hadn't been one of HQ's.

It had been one of his.

Grim-faced, Alan took a turn that would lead him back to the hotel.

His mind worked, running fast, jumping ahead. His enemies, whoever they were, had known about the meeting. From the dead man? From another?

He, Alan, had not yet been directly approached.

In recent months, HQ had taken to talking at length

about his "reputation" in northwest Africa. Alan hadn't been fooled. It wasn't the reputation of Alan Waring, businessman, they were banking on. It was the reputation of the "unnamed agent" who had the uncanny ability of retrieving information, items, even people from the desert and then vanishing without trace.

They knew *of* him, but not who he was.

But with the dead man compromised, he had to assume they at least had a clue, if not a name. It was only a matter of time before they caught up with him.

Bloody hellfire.

He kept moving, checking behind him as he went.

Alan swept his hotel room. Ten minutes' swift work had secured him what he needed. His luggage was sacrificial. It would tell no one anything useful about his work. He slung his laptop bag and his flight bag containing the smart card over his shoulder and opened the door.

He was glad, now, that he hadn't slept with Mari. It would be easier for her, when he disappeared.

It didn't feel much like "easier" to him.

A concierge was walking down the corridor. It was the same man—about five foot nine, slim build, very short dark hair, neatly trimmed black moustache—Alan had left the message for Mari with.

"Ah, Mr. Waring," the man hailed him. "Miss Forster

was asking for you."

"She was?" *Dammit.*

There was something in the concierge's face, a pursing of the lips, the faintest hint of disapproval behind the courtesy.

What?

Alan tugged the straps of his bags into a more comfortable position, using the action to cover a quick scan of the corridor. No one else. "Did Miss Forster go out to eat, do you know?"

"I believe Miss Forster is still in her room. She was . . . concerned that you were unable to join her."

Concerned? Alan allowed a rueful smile to touch his mouth, and ran his hand through his hair. "She was angry?"

"Upset."

Damn. He remembered Mari's tears on the beach, how he'd wanted so powerfully to shield her from that, and other, hurts. And now he was causing them.

The corridor was too narrow, the ceiling too close, the lighting too dim. He needed the expanse of the desert, and light that left no shade. It was time to go.

Mari will get over it. He knew though, in spite of that assertion, that there would be some small part of her that never would.

Better tears on her face, than her blood on his hands.

"Ah. Well, thank you." He dug out a note, meaning to tip the man unobtrusively, but the concierge backed away a step, making it impossible. Alan half-turned away towards the lifts.

"You will go to her, sir?"

"No, I—" He had to relocate, go to earth, contact HQ from another location and arrange . . . he looked up. The concierge was no longer trying to hide his disapproval.

They did not know who he was. Yet.

They had not waited to ambush him.

Mari goes home tomorrow.

The priorities of the evening had shuffled and reorganised themselves. How had he come to place Marianne so low on the list?

Why was she important enough to be higher?

Alan swallowed. "Yes."

The smallest of smiles twitched the black moustache.

When the knock at the door came, Marianne hesitated. But it must be someone from hotel, after all. Something about her bill? She tightened the belt on the white bathrobe, gave her face another swipe with the overlong sleeve, and opened the door.

It was Alan. His face was just a touch too pale, the lines finely drawn. He looked tired, tense . . . still gorgeous.

"I'm so sorry, Marianne," he said. "Are you okay?"

She was horribly, furiously conscious of the state of her face, red and swollen with tears. "I'm fine," she said shortly, and went to close the door.

He stuck his foot in it.

She gaped in outrage.

"Wait, Mari—"

She opened the door a little, and he smiled his approval. The skin around his blue eyes crinkled.

She slammed the door on his foot.

He howled and moved so quickly she wasn't quite sure what happened. But the door was bouncing off the wall and ricocheting shut, he'd dropped his bags against the wall, swearing blue murder, and suddenly he was right there in front of her, touching her, catching her by the arms.

Expecting him to yell at her, she glared up at him, but his mouth was tightly closed, his face tightly controlled. Only his breathing was ragged.

With pain, she hoped.

She opened her mouth to tell him she wanted him to leave, but it suddenly seemed such a colossal lie, she choked on the words. She didn't want him to leave.

But very soon she would be on her way home.

Once, wandering with him in the streets of Casablanca, on a day trip he'd organised, she'd fretted about how to ask him if she'd see him again when he returned to England. Now she was miserable to be leaving, and desperate to get away from him, all in the same breath.

She twisted against his grip, and he let her go, his hold gentling to ensure her balance before he stepped back. "I meant it," he said. "I *am* sorry, Mari."

"Right."

"Didn't you get my message?"

"Yes," she said tightly, making space between them, and clutching the robe tightly closed at her neck.

She could feel his eyes on her, scanning her face. She turned away.

"Uh . . . I didn't realise you . . ." He stopped. A pause. "Something came up really suddenly, Mari . . . business . . . It couldn't be helped."

Out of the corner of her eye, she could see him grimace at his own words.

"Mari, I'm sorry. I had no idea you'd take it this way."

Her mouth twisted. "So it's my fault."

"No! No. I'm an idiot . . . I never realised. You were looking forward to this."

"But you weren't. It doesn't matter."

"I . . . I was, Mari. And it does matter. I'm sorry I left it a bit late to work that out."

The expression on his face reminded her of her father's, when he'd found something else he could no longer do. Seeing that twisted look of self-disgust, she began to feel sorry for him, and that was no help at all.

Two steps took her to the corner of the bed, not at all blind to the way Alan stepped back to give her room. She sat, found herself looking at the bags Alan had dumped by the door. A laptop bag she hadn't seen him with before, and a grey and black flight bag that looked familiar.

"We have the same bag," she said, to fill the silence.

"I'm willing," he said, in something closer to his usual voice, though through clenched teeth, "to admit I deserve the big chill, screamed abuse, even a physical attack, but don't, for heaven's sake, talk inconsequentialities with me."

In spite of herself, her lips twitched.

"If you talk about the weather now, I'm liable to fall to my knees, howling."

She sniffed. But only to prevent the smile.

She heard him move and looked up as he came into her field of vision. He crouched down at her feet, looking up at her. The twisted look was gone, but he wasn't smiling, either, only watching, taking in every detail of her face.

Marianne swallowed. "I'm sorry about your foot."

One side of his mouth tipped up. "I've had worse. You were provoked, anyway, I'm sure . . ." His voice tailed off, and then he lifted a hand and gently tipped up her chin.

"Marianne?" Alan asked. "What is it?"

She felt dull and stupid. She'd tried hard not to let all her feelings show, but obviously she'd failed. "What's what?" she tried, but his fingers were firm and warm on her chin, and he wouldn't let her look away.

"I don't mean just . . . just this. What's wrong?"

"It's only . . . it's the end of the holiday. I have to go home. It's over."

He smiled at her. "It doesn't have to be over," he said, dropping his hand and setting it lightly on her knee. She was suddenly acutely conscious she was naked under the robe.

Marianne stiffened and folded her hands in her lap,

surreptitiously taking a hold on the edge of the robe over her legs. "Yes, it does," she said, and she was proud her voice didn't shake. She'd grown that much.

Alan scowled at her for a moment, but it wasn't long before the habitual smile reasserted itself. She would miss that smile. Desperately. Always.

"Will you tell me why," he asked, "or do I have to guess?"

She sighed, her shoulders slumping. "You'd never guess in a million years."

When she looked back, she realised she was wrong. That look of solemnity was new to his face, at least within her sight. He studied her, and she didn't look away. It had been horrible hiding her feelings when she'd wanted to share them with him, along with everything else.

Why this man? What a mistake she had made.

She looked back steadily and hid nothing.

Alan straightened with a whoosh of expelled breath. He rammed his hands into his pockets. "Well," he said. "Isn't that a complication?"

"I'm sorry," she choked. She tugged at the robe again, smoothing it tightly closed, using the movement to duck her head until she could master the threat of tears.

Then she glanced back at him and saw the look in his eyes. Gentleness, kindness. Understanding.

"Oh!" She slumped, boneless, so startled she couldn't organise her words. "I thought! I mean, I expected . . . Ah, Alan, do you have to be so *nice* about it?"

He laughed, and for a moment she thought she saw a glacier glint in his eyes, sharp and hard. "What did you expect, Mari? Disgust? Anger?" He reached forward and tugged lightly at a lock of her hair. "Pity?"

Marianne jerked, so that the bed creaked. "I . . ."—she was breathless—"I don't know. Embarrassment, maybe? Annoyance?" She shook her head.

"I don't think I could be annoyed at you, sweetheart. But you should know I . . . I have nothing permanent to offer you."

"Oh, I know," she was quick to reply. "I didn't mean to . . . to care about you," she shook her head, frustrated by how inarticulate she was. "It was just kindness. It doesn't matter."

Alan made a gesture of one strong, impatient hand, but she ploughed on. Better to get it over with.

I want to go home.

She swallowed and found her throat ached. "Which is why it has to end now, you see." She smiled at him and found it wasn't so hard, after all.

"Clean break?" he asked. "Least said soonest mended?"

"Something like that." Yeah, *something* like that.

He studied her, blue eyes running over her face. For once he didn't smile—there was even a little crease of a frown on his brow. "You said you'd have dinner with me, before you left."

"Oh, I don't . . ."

He bent to take her hand, working it free of its death grip on her robe. His thumb stroked her palm lazily, and she almost cried for the gentle sweetness of it. "Your flight doesn't leave till the early morning, right?"

"Yes." His thumb still moved, making her skin tingle, making her press her knees together and sit up straight, fighting the warm languor that was creeping over her.

"Then there's still time."

"I don't think it's a good idea . . . I don't want to go out."

His eyes ran over her face, taking in her swollen eyes, no doubt. He turned her hand, and pressed a kiss into her palm, where the nerves were singing from his touch. She shivered, her breath coming faster.

Oh, God.

He waited till she lifted her eyes. "Please, Mari."

And that was it, because the simple, shameful truth was she'd do anything for him, anything he asked. Her hand lay in his, passive, accepting.

"Alright."

He smiled then, but it was not quite the blazing grin. She thought for a moment there was something anxious about it, which wasn't Alan at all, but in a second it was gone, and the blue eyes were clear and without shadows.

He strode into the bathroom, pushing aside the shower screen and turning the shower on.

"What are you doing?" Mari followed him, confused.

He caught her by the shoulders again, spinning her round and driving her stumbling before him to beside the shower. "Take a shower. Leave dinner to me. You won't have to show any face you don't want to, to any people you don't want to. Except me. I'm afraid I come with the deal."

He turned her again and laid his hands on the belt of the robe.

"Alan!" she squeaked, panicked.

"Alright," he grinned, "I'll leave that bit to you. Take all the time you want. Leave the rest to me."

He ducked his head and kissed her swiftly. "Thank you, Mari," he said, and left her in the gathering steam.

🕷 🕷 🕷

Mari emerged from the bathroom, stopped dead, and stared.

Somehow Alan had turned her small hotel room into something else. There was a table, with a gleaming white linen, candles in little coloured-glass holders, and flowers. There were sparkling glasses, delicate china, and shining silverware. Beside the table was a trolley with a number of covered dishes.

He'd even changed. And he looked good. Very good.

And she was still dripping in a robe.

"Uh, shouldn't I get dressed?"

He looked up and rose, smiling that smile that undid all her best resolutions. "Not for my sake. In fact, I would consider it a definite detraction from the evening if you did."

He moved round the table while she stood, trying to

hide her bare feet behind each other, hesitating.

"Mari," he said, holding out her chair. His voice was wonderfully calm. "Sit down. Please."

She sat.

It was another one of those magical meals. In fact, it was perhaps the most wonderful of them all. Marianne thought her memories of Morocco would always be threaded through with these moments of delicious discovery. For years to come her mouth would water when she remembered these nights. And this man.

Somewhere between the rich tagine and the iced dessert, her best intentions melted, and her instincts of self-preservation faded away. There was only Alan, talking, laughing, eating, and a need so sharp it hurt like hunger.

When they were done, and the last aromatic taste of coffee faded from her mouth, they stopped talking and sat looking at one another. She met his gaze without reserve, and held it as he rose and came round the table towards her.

"I'm going home tomorrow," she said.

"Yes."

"This . . . it's only tonight."

"Yes."

He followed the line of one lock of her hair where it rested against her cheek, watching the passage of his finger with beguiling concentration. Marianne took one great breath. She felt the fizz of it to her trembling fingertips.

His finger rested now at the corner of her jaw, infinitely lightly. "Give me one more yes, Mari."

His finger slid round, slowly, slowly, following the line of her jaw towards her mouth. "That's all. One yes. That's all I want."

His thumb brushed her mouth, tugging at her lower lip. She closed her eyes and breathed him in, took the wild scent of him inside.

She shouldn't, she couldn't . . . but then the alternative hit her. Leaving here, never having known Alan's loving? Leaving here, to go to some other man in her future, always wondering, always aching for something she had chosen not to take. Forever knowing that any man in her future would always be *some other man*.

Not possible. Not bearable.

It took an effort, but she opened her eyes. Alan was staring at her mouth with livid intensity, teasing the soft inner flesh of her lower lip with his thumb. He lifted his eyes and met her gaze.

"Mari?" he breathed.

For answer she closed her lips around his thumb, and tasted the tip of it with her tongue. His eyes burned, bright and brilliant, and his other hand was suddenly on her shoulder, gripping her hard, flexing his fingers on her flesh.

"Are you afraid of me, Mari?" he said roughly.

Unwilling to release this small part of him, she shook her head very slightly.

"Good. You've no need. And there's nothing to fear," he drew her up, onto her feet, till his breath stroked her lips. "Nothing at all."

He kissed her then, but it was not the kiss she'd expected. It was gentle, subtle, a tasting, a brushing of mouths. And he didn't stop. He held her like that, one hand cupping her head and guiding her, one now holding her hip like it was his last anchor.

It was delicious, that contrast—the convulsive tightness of his hand, and the studied lightness of his lips and tongue.

She kissed him back, following his lead, still learning. Slowly, bit by bit, she relaxed into a bone-melting, rich languor, soft pleasure rising up from her body to drug her mind.

She slumped a little, now relying on the length of his hard body to support her, turning her head to keep the kiss until her head almost rested on his shoulder, lifting her other arm to drape around his neck. He liked that. She could tell by the way the hand at his hip flexed, drawing her closer still, so she could feel all of him. All of him. She shivered.

I'm really going to do this, she thought, blown away even by the concept of it, let alone the reality.

"Yes, you are," Alan grated, lifting his head.

She stared. "Stop reading my mind!"

He grinned, a full-on, intent, wicked grin. "Not your mind, your face." But his eyes weren't on her face anymore.

He eased her four steps back until she leaned against the wall, and slid his hands up her arms to the collar of her robe. She almost moved to prevent him, then stopped herself.

"Good girl," he whispered, and slid the cotton down her arms. The material held for a moment on the slope of her breast—her breathing went out of control—and then it fell free.

Marianne closed her eyes, holding that crazy breath. In the silence she realised she couldn't hear Alan breathing either. Then he let out a long sigh.

"Oh, Mari."

"Marianne," she said automatically.

He chuckled. "Marianne then," his voice darkened to seriousness. "You are the most beautiful thing . . ."

Her eyes popped open. "What?" she gasped.

He watched her expression, smiling. He stroked a finger along her collarbone, and her neck arched of its own volition.

"You won't let me adore you with words? Pity. I'm good at that."

Without warning his large hand cupped her breast, lifting it, holding it. His thumb found her nipple, and she whimpered.

"But I am good at this, too," he whispered and bent his head.

The touch of his mouth there, his tongue sliding over her taut flesh, his teeth just nipping, was overload, almost impossible to bear. She shivered, shook, moaned, and all the time she felt the sensation growing, feeding the ache between her legs.

She throbbed, she needed. And he supplied.

She flattened her hands against the wall behind her, for what support it provided. But she still reeled.

He transferred his acute, skilful attention to her other

breast, and she gave up her grip on the wall to catch hold of his shoulders and cradle his head.

Oh, God, it was good. Better, more, than she could have imagined. She told him so, and he laughed, ripped his shirt over his head, and gathered her against him with greedy, all-encompassing hands.

"I like it," she whispered, settling her tingling mouth into the hollow above his collarbone, feeling his approbation in the bite of his hands.

She felt his chest shake. Laughter? Desire? With Alan, almost certainly both.

"Did you expect not to?"

She pressed her burning face to his shoulder, only then suddenly aware of the hand slyly easing the belt open.

"They say too often, the woman doesn't get much out of it."

He leant back from her, scanning her face, and she saw the unmistakeable incredulity in his. "Did you think I would be that kind of a man?"

His outrageous male confidence bolstered hers. "No. Not now. Not really."

There was colour in his face, too. "A challenge," he growled, eyes flashing. "For God's sake, Mari, I do know what I'm doing."

His hands made the last push against her abandoned robe and curved over her backside in a blatantly possessive gesture.

She kissed his throat, tasting. "Good." He pulsed with life and fire against her. He heated her, enlivened and drugged her in the same moment. "But I don't."

He took a breath, running his hands over every inch of flesh he could reach. She almost purred under his touch, delighted and awed by how feminine, how free she felt.

"You're here, aren't you? You do it just by being here."

She twisted against him, catching her breath when the movement teased her nipples. "But there's more isn't there? There can be more I can do?"

His voice was deep, dark, barely Alan. "There can be."

She lifted her head, and stilled at the look on his face. His eyes were wild, his nostrils flared. His mouth was clenched tight shut, and a muscle bunched in his jaw. She remembered her bold denial of fear.

She swallowed. "Show me? Alan!"

He swooped, taking her mouth, tightening her arms about her till the only breath she could take was that he granted her. It was all wild, crazy darkness, blinded by the light of his eyes.

Time passed. He lifted his head. "Mari," he said hoarsely, "you have no idea . . ."

She pushed him, shook him. "I know! That's the point! I don't want this to be something one-sided, something magnanimous! You said you'd teach me, dammit, so teach me!"

"I will," he said. And it sounded like a vow.

The rest was words. Gasped and whispered, groaned and muttered close. With Alan, it was always going to be words. Heated words, wild words, warming her just as much as each fabulous caress, each syllable, each fragmented touch pushing her higher.

"What are you? Oh."

"Here, Mari? You should feel that."

"Oh!"

"Touch me."

"Here?"

"Yes."

"Like this?"

"No, tighter . . . Mari!"

"Too tight?"

"No . . . no, gods."

"Bloody hellfire."

"What! What did I do?"

"Shhh, shh, it's okay, I'm sorry, come back, don't stop."

"But what . . ."

"Shhh. It's fine, it's . . . ah . . . Maybe another time."

"It feels . . ."

"Tell me."

"Hard . . . soft—"

"Yes."

"Slick."

"So are you."

"Alan."

"Listen. Feel. Feel this."

"Oh. Please."

"Good?"

"Incredible."

"Yeah. Trust me, Mari, go with it."

Then there were no more words, only overpowering pleasure, robbing her of breath, voice and hearing, shaking her to her soul, and breaking her heart.

Chapter Five

Alan sat on the edge of the bed, elbows on his knees, hands dangling between.

Behind him, Marianne slept in a dishevelled bed, sheets clutched to her breast, one long leg hooked over the covers. She looked abandoned, beautiful, desirable, and that last one was probably why he had his back to her.

He sighed, staring down at the intricate design on the hotel carpet. My God, what was this?

The night was still and silent, unusually so. It brooded, waiting, setting Alan even further on edge, powering this momentous night with something even more significant.

He clenched his dangling hands into fists and tried to put his mind in some sort of order.

Impossible.

How could he think clearly after that? How could he think at all after riding a storm of passion he'd never before even come close to. Bloody hellfire. It shouldn't have been like that, not like that at all.

This was about recreation, about kindness, about ending her holiday with good memories, not bitter goodbyes. It was about giving her confidence, about making reparation, about . . . Whatever it *was* about, it was *not* about changing the foundations of his life.

Too late!

He scrubbed a hand over his face and breathed deep. When had this changed, exactly? When she'd unwittingly, innocently coaxed him to a climax that drew as much from his soul as his body? When she'd quivered, panted, and accepted him generously, bravely even, while he could see the apprehension in her eyes?

No, it was earlier, wasn't it? When she'd changed her mind and offered herself anyway, when he knew, *knew* she'd been having second thoughts. Or perhaps, just maybe, it had been a lot earlier than that, even, when he'd seen a wide-eyed beauty by the pool and known, without a shadow of a doubt, that this holidaymaker was not just alone—she was lonely.

Raising his head, he slid his hand to grip the back of his neck, and that's when he saw it. His flight bag. His stomach curled, and his heart started hammering again.

That little thing, sitting there forgotten, abandoned against the wall—that was also a symbol of just how far he'd let things get out of control.

The mission has deviated from set parameters . . . That was how Stuart would phrase it. The smart card, that was loaded with the information the government wanted so badly, that men had died for. That he had removed from its safe place after finding his proposed meeting was with a dead man, planning to extricate himself from the hotel, the city, possibly even the country.

Which he had put into his flight bag and *dumped in another guest's bedroom all night.* Never mind that he'd been there with it all along. Never mind, either, that he'd been about to walk out on said guest, rationalising that it was the best way to ensure their safety.

The space between his shoulder blades prickled with sweat.

What the hell was he playing at?

What was this?

Which brought him neatly back to square one.

Alan groaned and dropped his head in his hands. It didn't matter how he looked at it, Mari had blasted her way into his life with nothing more than a shy smile and an air of tentative curiosity. Blasted into it, turned it over, and now was about to leave it in disarray.

I don't think so.

He pressed his fingers into his eyes until he saw checkerboards. It was crazy. He'd never been so scared in all his life. Correction: he'd never been so scared of something *he still wanted.*

Because he did still want her, and whatever it was between them that was throwing him so far off balance. He wanted her laughing, and smiling, and kissing him. He wanted to finish what he'd started, teach her everything he knew about sex, and then discover more with her. He needed—he didn't know why—all that Mari was, and all that she wasn't yet. And he didn't want to ask himself just how much he would be willing to sacrifice to keep all of it.

He shook his head. He had to get the smart card to safety. He had to contact Stuart, he had to . . . to act like a freaking professional. Only thing was, just how professional *was* he at the moment?

You've picked up a virgin tourist, deflowered her, and you're now trying to dream up ways of stopping her running away, Waring. Oh, and she's in love with you.

"Bloody hell."

"You should go."

He stiffened. Mari's voice was calm, a little small, but, "you should go" were not the first words he had been looking for from her. "Mmmmmmm" would have been nice. "Can we do it again?" would have been bloody nice.

Turning, he studied her. She'd tucked the sheet tighter round her and lay on her side, one hand under the pillow. That long, lasciviously displayed leg was hidden again. Her eyes were big and wary. Just how long had she been watching him?

While he cradled his head in his hands and swore.

Damn.

He closed his eyes briefly, looking for poise and the charm that she seemed to have effectively wrung out of him. He couldn't find it, so he faked it. "A man could take offence at that," he smiled, somehow, anyhow, and didn't want to think much about how it looked.

"I'm sorry," she said. But she didn't really sound it. She sounded measured. Careful. "I only meant that I have to leave soon. I need a shower and to do the last bits and pieces I need to do. Then I have to go to the airport. We should say"—her voice faltered, just a little, and her eyes flicked away, but she recovered—"we should say goodbye."

His lips twisted. "Did you change your mind?"

"What? No. I said it was just one night."

"No. About loving me."

For a heartbeat, two, three, she stared at him, her eyes too bright, her mouth flat, hurt. Then she wriggled the sheet right round her and got up. Heading for the bathroom, she shrugged. "Well, you know," she said, back straight, shoulders back. "A holiday fling, yes?" She closed the door carefully behind her. He heard the lock slide home.

Something wounded in him wanted to howl, *No!* But this was a hell of his own making after all. Being discovered groaning and swearing in apparent despair after introducing someone to the finer points of loving was not his best example of postcoital finesse.

He groaned and swore.

Then he got up and dragged on his clothes.

In the bathroom, he heard the shower start and the water hit the tiles with a smack and a rush.

When he'd finished dressing, he hesitated. He'd be damned if he'd just sidle out of the room while she locked herself in the bathroom, but . . . just what exactly was he hoping to stop her do? Dismiss him like he'd served his purpose in serving her? Anger shook him savagely by the scruff of the neck.

How dare she? He'd only wanted to *help* for God's sake. Was that such a crime?

Letting Mari go would be a crime. A crime against nature.

But that was wrong, because it was his nature to be alone, wasn't it? The ultimate loner, in the loneliest landscape in the world. Fitting and apt.

He shook his head, confused, feeling loneliness like a burden when it had used to be an escape. His eye fell on her travel wallet, on the floor by the bedside table. They must have knocked it off. He bent to retrieve it.

He stood looking at the wallet in his hand, scowling.

The shower stopped running.

Flipping it open, he pressed his lips together and tried to ignore the slightly dirty feeling he got, rummaging in her things. Breathing hard, ears straining for the sound of a hand on the door, he memorised her address, passport number, full name, and dropped the wallet back on the table.

Alan found his hands were shaking. And sweating. He wiped them on his trousers and got up.

He grabbed his flight bag from the end of the bed quickly, still watching the door, just for something to occupy his hands.

There was a small sound from the bathroom door, a tiny grating of metal on metal as the lock moved. He crossed to the door to stand near his laptop, one hand casually in his pocket, flight bag slung over his shoulder.

A split second later, the door opened and Mari emerged, wrapped in a robe. She was flushed from the shower, and her hair clung wetly to her fine-boned skull. She looked small and defenceless. Then she cast him a look carefully balanced between surprise and hauteur. Not so defenceless.

"Are you still here?" Part of him wanted to cheer the performance. Part of him wanted to shake her. She wasn't fooling him, not one bit. But this wasn't over, and he *was* going to see her again.

So why did he feel so uneasy?

Because he was putting Marianne in danger.

No. He wasn't. He'd started this with Mari, he'd thought, partly as a distraction from his sense of unease over the job. But now he thought it was the other way around.

It must be that all this unease he'd been feeling had actually arisen from the way things were going with Mari, from the attraction he'd initially felt and from how things had spiralled so far out of control so quickly. As she'd burrowed into his life and turned it over, his professional radar had gone crazy.

And the body in the passage, the blood without flies, was just your imagination, he mocked himself.

Mari was rummaging in her wash bag, applying lotion and other things.

A voice protested at the back of his mind, but he ignored it, squashed it, beat it down. It was okay.

He was off-balance, overreacting. He picked up his laptop.

She straightened and approached him, looking a little pale, but well in hand. He realised that this was about the longest he'd ever been silent in her company.

"Goodbye," she said steadily. "And thank you."

He swallowed all the words, every damn one of them, and ducked his head to kiss her on the cheek. She jumped as he moved, then stood still as a stone as he brushed his lips briefly on her warm, soft skin. She smelt sweet, flowery.

He looked down at her, at wide, dark, exotic eyes, damply elfin hair, skin that, even with its holiday tan, was still quintessentially the pink and cream complexion of an Englishwoman.

He turned and walked away.

This was not over.

It was over.

Marianne let the tears fall in the taxi, not caring, not at all, who saw her now. She sniffled her way through the short journey, paid the driver, and blew her nose in front of the airport entrance.

It had only taken one look at his stiff back when she woke, to know that she had to get out, fast. Much as she dreaded pity, regret was now her new Least Favourite Emotion in Another Person. She felt sick. It wasn't flying nerves, either. She remembered seeing him drop his head into his hands, hearing him swear, and knew, without a shadow of a doubt, that he regretted taking her to bed. Anything she took beyond that would be based on regret, pity, and embarrassment—a horrible cocktail to make yourself drunk on. And sick on.

It had been easy after he'd gone. She didn't really have to pack—with nothing to do when he'd cancelled their date, she'd packed her suitcase twice and her flight bag three times already. She called down to the front desk. When the man came up for her bags, all she had to do was pick up her travel wallet from beside the bed, check that her passport and tickets were securely inside, and follow him down to the waiting taxi.

All she wanted now was home. Home, soon. Her own home, her own bed to curl up in and remember another bed that had contained Alan, too. He'd been so . . . every time she moved, her body reminded her just how he'd been. Little tingles, little twinges of stiffness, of unaccustomed awareness.

She'd not known, never dreamed, how it could be. Now she got it. The world's obsession with sex, no, with love, because she knew, now, that for her it would not have been half so magnificent if she hadn't loved her lover.

Her lover.

Just once.

Just once.

❀ ❀ ❀

He was wasting his time. Leaving the hotel, he'd headed out into the city, meaning to try a few contacts, see what he could glean about last night's busted meeting.

To see if he could still do his job.

To forget the look in Mari's eyes.

But every mouth was closed, every face shuttered. No one knew anything, said anything, or wanted to talk about anything. Alan had the frustrating sense of an influence stronger than his, a danger greater. After an hour or so of head-to-brick-wall getting nowhere, he'd caught the bus to Mohammedia just to clear the area, and opened up his laptop on a table in a street café, defying the dust.

He was conscious all the time of Mari. He knew what time she'd have made it to the airport. Was very aware that her flight would be leaving in another half hour or so. What time it was scheduled to arrive at Heathrow. When she might make it home.

The address was in Cornwall, far, far down in the southwest among wild coasts, old folk tales, and King Arthur myths. It suited her, he thought. A little remote, a little forbidding. Very, very beautiful.

He logged in to the secure area. There was another message from Stuart. Alan resisted the urge to roll his eyes, and scanned it. Another meeting, another chance to hand the smart card over.

For God's sake.

Every instinct screamed at him to go to ground. Head out into the desert, disappear, reappear on the grid somewhere else, a month, two, from now. Then again, the faster he got this troublesome little bit of technology off his hands, the faster he could catch a plane back to England, follow Mari, see if . . .

Alan shook his head, pulling his flight bag up onto the table. He'd have to find a stash for his laptop and other gear. This time round, he'd travel light, smart card in his pocket. He unclipped the buckle and flipped the bag's top up.

And smelled Mari.

That was it. The first awareness was scent. A sweet, light, clean-smelling fragrance that was as much a part of Mari that he'd never even registered it as a perfume before. Some kind of lotion? His hands were in the bag, searching, before his mind had registered the instruction. Water bottle, two fantasy paperbacks, a pack of tissues, some paracetamol, a small tube of hand cream—there was that scent, he realised—a couple of snapshots he'd bought from a boy with a Polaroid camera, a small wash bag, a fresh T-shirt . . .

Mari's things. Mari's bag.

He flipped the photos over on the iron table. Her face stared back at him, big eyes, a little anxious, a whole lot resolute.

The bag by the bed.

The bag by the door.

"We've got the same bag."

He sank back in his chair, staring at the bag that should have been his, and was, against all reason, Mari's. He realised that beyond that first scent-laden breath he hadn't breathed again, and spent a few moments concentrating on breathing till his ears stopped roaring.

Even then, his heart thundered.

It wasn't so much of a coincidence, after all. His luggage was chosen to be unremarkable, the commonest brand, the plainest colour. And Marianne was hardly the traveller with designer luggage.

He breathed deep, replaying the switch in his mind, filled with disgust at his ineptness. But, wait . . . they wanted the smart card out of the country. They had said, hadn't they—*You are authorised to become physically separated from the package, according to your professional judgement, should the opportunity arise.*

Well, the opportunity had arisen.

No. Dear heaven, no. No way. No *way* had he used Mari as a mule deliberately. It was a slip-up, a lack of focus, a . . . lack of attention Mari regrettably fostered. That was all.

He'd used mules before, with permission and without, and none of them had ever come to harm, but still. There was no way in hell his subconscious would do this to him.

Was there?

He shook.

No. *It* was a cock-up. But *he* wasn't.

At least, he hoped he wasn't.

Shaking fingers tapped on the keys. A message to HQ, the gist of which was—*don't worry, guys. I've made alternative arrangements. Her name's Marianne Forster*—and he was free to pay the bill and take a taxi.

To the airport.

Alan got off the M25 onto the M3 and put his foot down.

After contacting HQ, getting out of the country and home had been a breeze and he was able to take a flight to London later that same day. He'd slept on the flight, thank God, because he'd had no further opportunity so far. A quick call to Stuart and authorisation to recover the smart card, and he was on his way. To Cornwall. And Mari's home.

Only . . . his premonition circuits were acting up. He had a sense of something wrong, something missing, not quite right. Most probably it was only that for the first time in his life he was going to chase down an unwilling—at least on the surface—female and offer to throw in the towel.

The one embroidered, *alone—always.*

At least for a while.

Just how long a while he had yet to analyse. Focused on getting back to England, and then on getting back to Mari, he'd had little time for more thought than that. He only knew he needed her, wanted her, and was going to get her.

But something wasn't right.

The sense of unease grew hour by hour. Buzzing down the A303 towards the south-west, Alan told himself, again and again, that everything was alright, that Mari would be quietly at home, dreaming of her wild holiday, the smart card would be still where he'd concealed it, he'd persuade her to give them a chance, and everyone would live happy ever after.

Or at least for a while.

He'd left a message on Jenny's answerphone—just to say he was home, but was visiting friends for a day or two. He'd catch up with his sister, brother-in-law, niece, and nephew soon—perhaps Mari would like to go up to Cumbria and meet them.

He consulted his directions, decided not to stop for coffee, and took the turning off to Nether Weston. Wound down through the village, the scent of honeysuckle insinuating itself into the car. Past the old pub, the ponderous vicarage and spired church. Took a left here, dipping down to the beck, through the gravel-bottomed ford and then climbing, undulating its way up on to the moor and over. There, now, the grass grew up through the tarmac in the centre of the road.

The road—it was little more than a track, really—started heading downhill in the direction of the coast, and sank down between high banks crowned with gorse and blackthorn, with the shoots of meadowsweet thick in the hedge bottom.

Then the road took an abrupt turn, levelled out, and he saw the house at its end, buffered from the world by a large garden, its broad, green, lawn framed with wild borders busy with roses and hollyhocks.

He left the car in the road, and pushed open the wrought iron gate. The house was large and granite, with little attic windows and a slated porch.

The curtains were drawn, and no lights were on.

A seagull wheeled overhead, screaming, and he stood still on the lawn, taking in the house's unmistakeably empty air.

Where the *hell* was she?

Something coldly angry took hold of his heart and squeezed.

The side door lock wasn't too difficult to pick, and although he'd have rather forced it, he forced himself to patience, and his hands to stillness. The lock gave. He pushed it open and paused, listening.

Nothing.

The bed in the main bedroom was neatly turned down as if waiting for its occupant, the blankets and sheets crisp and smooth. The carpet was newish, a pompous flecked green, but the room was old-fashioned, certainly an old gent's room, with three thrillers neatly stacked on the bedside table and a stately plant on a wooden stand near the window. Not Mari's room. No.

He found it two doors down, one of the smaller rooms, but seeing the way the place was decorated, he immediately put that down to choice. Oh, and the view. A large sash window looked down out across the rear garden to the sea. He held aside the faded velvet curtain to look. If you propped yourself on the wide sill itself, you could just see the pale sands of a tiny bay and the overgrown path that led to it.

There were two much-thumbed novels on the sill and a small fleece blanket, neatly folded. He could imagine her here, curled on the sill, listening for a call from her father. Staring out at the sea she never had the freedom to swim in.

He let the soft curtain fall and padded silently round the room. Single bed—he lifted the lilac-covered duvet and checked underneath but found no suitcase—narrow pine wardrobe, white chest of drawers, hooks behind the door. Nowhere was there any sign of any of Mari's holiday clothes, nor any suggestion that she'd been here at all in the past two weeks.

Elsewhere it was the same. The kitchen clean and untouched, the sink dry, the stove switched off at the wall. The water turned off at the stop cock under the stairs. Fridge empty, unplugged, and propped open. He looked out the glazed back door at the solitary apple tree, with its burden of small, sour fruit, and wondered why he'd even bothered to check. He'd known, as soon as he'd seen the place, that she was not here.

Perhaps he'd known before.

He locked the back door from inside and went out the front, the self-latching door locking behind him easily. He returned to his car and made his way back down the narrow lane with careful skill, then took the shortest route to the main road.

Once he hit the motorway, he put his foot down and kept it there. He headed north.

Alan stopped for coffee about three times, on a journey he would usually have spent two days on. He wanted—oh, how he wanted—to stay in the car and keep going, counting off the miles like hazards to be overcome, desperate for and yet terrified of his arrival, but he knew tired drivers were lethal, and it seemed he was learning responsibility at last.

He'd used the hands-free phone, too. Stuart was on sick leave, but there was one of his colleagues there, just junior enough to be bullied into looking for the information Alan needed, and just senior enough to get it. The answers he got were not unexpected, but when he got them he pulled off the motorway at a junction, and spent some time with his head down, breathing deeply and carefully, while his stomach turned.

Then he called HQ back. He worked his way through the layers till he reached a senior manager for his section. His requests were short and to the point.

And unceremoniously denied.

By the time he rang off, he was no longer their employee.

Alan took his last stop just outside Lancaster, pausing

this time to sluice his face with water and comb his hair, as well as take on some decent food. He didn't want to scare Jenny any more than was necessary. At the thought he paused, staring back at his stark reflection, water dripping from the comb. He was appalled at what he was contemplating, truth be told, but the alternative wasn't to be considered at all. He wished he had a razor: he needed a shave, too.

The A66 was relatively clear at seven, he pushed his luck and the speed limit, staring unblinking at the road. He passed under the ponderous mountain bulks of Blencathra and of Skiddaw and followed the road that curved round Bassenthwaite Lake and pushed across the Derwent floodplain towards Cockermouth.

The little town was just as he remembered, upright, stylish shops along a wide high street delineated by the pale green pollards. Kirkgate was the same, too—cobbled, refined and quiet, a half-forgotten street-come-square in the heart of the town, but with the feel of a tiny village in its own right. He rattled onto the cobbles in front of one three-story, black-and-white painted house and leant on the wheel.

He rubbed his eyes and then switched the engine off, and the lights, too. He sat in silence, oddly reluctant to knock on the door, after driving four hundred miles to do just that. The decision was taken from him though—the door opened, and his sister, Jenny, stood on the doorstep, her delighted smile not marred in the slightest by surprise.

He loved that—that unconditional welcome, the easy

sense of family. It helped him breathe. In blacker times it had probably been the one thing bringing him home from the desert.

He opened the door and slid from the seat, trying not to wince, conjuring up a competent counterfeit of a smile.

"Alan! How wonderful!" The smile wasn't quiet, but the voice was—ah yes, the sproglets would be in bed.

He hugged Jenny on the step of her home, lifting her clean off her feet, as he usually did.

"Put my wife down," the sardonic U.S. drawl came from the dimly if warmly lit hallway. "You don't know where she's been."

Jenny turned to aim a punch at her husband's gut, which Kier fielded effortlessly, and just as effortlessly twirled her into his arms.

And just that easily, Mari was standing in the hall with them, staring at him with reproachful eyes.

Alan shook his head sharply to clear his mind, and Kier's eyes narrowed. "You okay?"

Jenny twisted in Kier's arms to look up at her husband's face, a little frown of her own creasing her brow. Kier smiled down at her, that intent look gone in a second, and although Jenny smiled again, Alan had to remember she was family, and female, and she'd probably got it before Kier did.

"I'm fine," he said, lightly, "just the long journey."

Jenny gave Kier a shove out the door, and he held out his hand for the car keys as he went, giving Alan a quick searching look as he offered them. "I'll get the bags," he said blandly, and stepped past him.

"Where did you come from?" Jenny asked Alan.

He actually had a headache. He almost never had a headache. Jenny called him disgustingly healthy.

"Cornwall."

"Co—oh. Were the roads clear?" She moved down the hall as she spoke, towards the second door on the right, propped open with an old stone hot water bottle, offering a glimpse of neat pine kitchen cupboards and the smell of tomatoes and basil. He moved with her, the promise of decent tea suddenly mobilising.

"Yeah, mostly. It was an easy ride, just long."

She snapped the kettle on, nodding. "Alex and Kirstie are asleep—do you want me to wake them up?"

"Don't wake them. I'd like to stay the night, maybe two, if that's okay?"

She set earthenware cups on the counter and paused to smile at him, eyes open and loving. "Of course it's okay. You know that. The kids will be crazy when they find out their favourite uncle's here."

"I'm their only uncle."

She laughed, scooping tea into a pale green teapot. "You'd be their fave if there were thousands of them."

Kier ambled in and perched on a stool by the breakfast counter on the other wall of the room. "Bags are in your room."

"Cheers."

They had their tea in the conservatory. It was darkening outside, and the little solar-powered lights were coming on, highlighting roses and clematis, and an eclectic jumble of plants clustered round a small, shallow pond with a fountain. The gentle sound of moving water soothed him.

He dropped into an armchair with a sigh of fatigue, but didn't miss the worried glance Jenny threw at Kier. Damn, he was playing this badly.

"So," he said, as Jenny swirled the pot and poured the tea. "How are they?"

It was Kier who answered. "They're great. Alex is clamouring for a puppy, and Kirstie has just recovered from another ear infection, but they're not that serious."

"But . . ." said Jenny doubtfully.

Kier pulled a curl of her hair, smiling lazily at her. "No buts." He kissed her, some of the tea spilt from the teapot, and Alan was struck by a bolt of envy that shook him to the core.

He closed his eyes and sat back, working to keep his face blank. No, he was just tired, pressured, cornered. None of this was about latent family-envy in a professional lone wolf.

His head ached worse. How could he come here and break this up? How could he sit here, in Jenny and Kier's comfortable home, and make the simple request that could shatter everything?

By remembering you sent Mari home with the smart card, and that Mari has vanished off the face of the earth.

And by remembering that Kier was possibly the only man who could help him find her.

Sure, Kier McAllister was essentially retired from this sort of work, acting as a security consultant to an airline, but there had been a time when he was at the top of his field. Not exactly missing persons, more missing information, especially when that information was in someone's head.

The fact was that Kier was his brother-in-law and wasn't likely to say no. And he trusted him, like he didn't quite trust himself to do this alone.

Alone.

Never again, if he had his way.

He opened his eyes to find them both staring at him. And Kier's hand gripping Jenny's wrist like a manacle.

Jenny blinked, hard, then handed him his mug with a hand that shook ever so slightly. He took it, drank deep, savouring decent tea, and registering the need his body had of rehydration. Outside the water flickered in the wind, interrupting the steady patter of its fall.

His mouth was full of questions that tasted like sand on his tongue. All of them too hard to ask, all of them needing asking of these people, closest to him in all the world.

"Kier? How did you know when you fell in love with Jen?"

chapter six

Jenny gasped, then snapped her mouth shut. Kier reached swiftly forward and snagged a biscuit, wedging it smoothly in Jenny's mouth when it opened again. He sat back, steepling his fingers in front of him, while she made indignant crumby sounds.

Alan stared out into the darkening garden, knowing Kier was watching him carefully, quite unwilling to give him any clues from the expression on his face. But blankness was a lighted flare for a man known for smiling.

"I knew when she decided to leave me. It wasn't . . . tolerable to imagine any sort of life without her. But at that time I didn't feel like I had the right to offer or demand anything. So I let her go. It almost killed me."

Alan looked across. Jenny's hand had found its way onto Kier's thigh. Her eyes were shining, and she was smiling. He'd known a time when a discussion like this would have covered them in the shadows of past grief, but they'd come through that.

Kier flicked a look at him, and then stood, tugging Jenny with him. It was evident she wanted to stay, but a look passed between them, and she subsided.

"It's bedtime," Kier said. "Don't be long coming up—you're tired."

"No, sure," he said, knowing he wouldn't sleep. Jenny gave him a worried look, but he smiled back, as best he could, and Kier herded her into the kitchen, leaving him alone.

Please, no.

🏵 🏵 🏵

Kier found Alan in the darkened kitchen several hours later, selecting a bottled beer by touch. Jenny was right to be worried, Kier thought. Alan really was jumpy. Every third minute he looked like he was going to tell them something important—then his eyes just slid away, he conjured up a false smile and carried on as if nothing was wrong.

But something was very definitely wrong. The tension was coming off the other man in tangible waves. When he thought no one was looking. Kier had seen him close his eyes, seen his face twist into something that looked like anguished pain.

Despite that 'love' question, Jenny was convinced Alan had come over unexpectedly to tell them he had a terminal illness. And that was worrying her sick.

Which was why Kier was here. He propped a hip

against the butcher's block kitchen counter and waited.

It didn't take long. Kier saw when Alan felt his presence. He didn't turn round, but he stiffened for a moment and then quietly closed the cupboard, putting a bottle of Old Engine Oil real ale on the counter and turning around.

Which was another example of the man's cat-like awareness. Kier had never seen anything like it. Except in the mirror.

"Hi," said Alan, but it was patently obvious that he knew why Kier was there, and was just waiting for the inquisition.

"You're worrying Jenny. Spill."

Alan sighed and gripped the back of his neck with one hand. "You're a man of few words, Kier—did anyone ever get the nerve to inform you of that?"

"So you make up for it. Spill."

Alan turned to face the counter again, gripping the edge with both hands and dropping his head between knotted shoulders. Kier grimaced. This had to be bad.

Then Alan started to speak. "This is difficult, because, quite simply, I'm not supposed to reveal any of this to another person. But it's gone way beyond that now. It has to do with my second job."

"The one you do when you're not in England?" Kier stated with conviction.

Alan snapped him a look over his shoulder. "You knew?"

Kier pursed his lips and shook his head. "Nope. But

I never thought wanderlust was a good enough explanation for being away half the year at short notice. And the landscape gardening firm doesn't seem to need your input much, and certainly doesn't seem to supply the sort of money you have."

Alan nodded. "Well, you guessed right—I do have another job. I'm a courier for high-risk cargoes."

Kier stood up a little straighter. "What do you courier, Alan?" he asked quietly.

Alan faced him, arms folded over his chest. "You needn't look like that. It's nothing immoral. What do you take me for? A drug runner?"

Kier relaxed. "I'm sorry."

"Never mind. Mostly it's information, a lot of it governmental or at least from government agencies. Every client we take on is thoroughly vetted by MI5. Sometimes it's something they simply don't want in the diplomatic bag."

"So? What's gone wrong?"

"I met someone in Morocco."

Kier blinked at the apparent change in subject. Then a few things fell into place. "What's her name?"

"It doesn't matter! I mean—" he sighed. "Her name is Marianne Forster. She was just on holiday."

"So what is the problem?"

"The . . . item I was carrying was in her luggage when she went home ahead of me. She never got home." When it was time to come clean, Alan went for it with a vengeance.

"That's not good."

"Christ, Kier, do you think I don't know that?" Alan's face was wild, and Kier suddenly remembered feeling like that almost five years ago.

"Okay, okay. Don't shout—the kids are in bed."

"I'm sorry."

"How did it get there? In her luggage?"

Alan braced his arms on the counter and gave a hollow laugh. "Would you believe I mixed up our bags?"

Maybe. "So it was an accident."

"Yes. No. I—"

"*Alan . . .*"

Alan pressed the heels of his hands to his eyes. "I didn't consciously swap bags, Kier," he said, voice muffled. "But I can't help wondering if . . . if subconsciously—"

"For Christ's sake, Alan. I think you've got enough real cock-ups to deal with, without beating yourself up for the theoretical ones."

"Yeah. You're right." Alan lifted his head again, eyes dark. "I don't even know if she's still alive."

"What were you carrying?"

"I don't know. I never know—it's a security policy."

So that Alan couldn't reveal classified information in enemy hands. That made sense, even if he didn't like it. Kier knew, better than anyone, that any man would break, given time.

Years ago, he was the one who'd been breaking them.

"So I take it we have a third party wanting to intercept what you were carrying, yes?"

Alan grunted.

"So why did they take her, too? Why not just the luggage?"

Alan jerked upright again, kicking a cupboard lightly with one booted foot. Kier wished he'd stand still for a moment. "I've been thinking about this. I think they think she's me," he said shortly.

Kier frowned. "You wanna run that one by me again?"

"I'm guessing. But it's like this," Alan explained. "I've been doing this a while. I've developed a reputation for running information across North Africa and some of the Arab countries. But they don't know a name—they don't know it's me. And they don't know that I never know what I'm carrying.

"If they found Marianne with that package, they might well assume she's that courier, me, and holds all sorts of useful information in that pretty head."

Kier wisely decided not to comment on the pretty. But it sure complicated matters. And explained a lot of Alan's attitude. This went far further than guilt, in Kier's best guess. "So what are you planning to do about it?"

Alan gave him a tortured glance. "I'm going to go and see if I can find her. Get her home."

"And you have the support of your organisation?"

"No." Alan shook his head emphatically. "They . . . they didn't want to know. They told me they would be dealing with it through the proper channels, and told me to take a leave of absence."

"And?"

"And I resigned," Alan said, the words clipped. "This is strictly a 'deny all knowledge' scenario. I have no sanction for this. But it has to be done."

"And you want my help." It wasn't a question.

Alan swallowed visibly. "I've thought long and hard, trying to think who else I could ask. You have to know I wouldn't ask this of you if there was any other way. But you have the skills we're going to need."

Oh yeah.

"What skills? Need for what?" Jenny came into the room and pressed herself up against his side like she always did, given half the chance. He put an arm around her shoulders. She wasn't going to like this one bit.

"Alan has a project he would like my help with."

She looked between them. She'd never been slow on the uptake.

"A risky project," she said.

"Yes."

"You'd better tell me about it."

By dawn they were packed.

Jenny had taken it all in with a calm Alan knew cost her dearly. But she was clear that as far as she was concerned, there had never been any doubt of Kier's going.

"If he can help bring her back, he's going," she'd stated, with that fierceness that had caught many a person by surprise, coming from someone looking so delicate.

As the sun came up over the irregular rooftops, she saw them off, standing on the step. She and Kier had said their goodbyes in private—he stalked silently to the waiting Renault—they were taking Kier's car—and Alan followed him. Jenny called him back.

When he was right in front of her, she jabbed him in the chest with her finger, hissing at the same time, "That's my husband, and Alex and Kirstie's father you have there, Alan. *You bring him back.*"

He took a step back, stunned by the force of her attack, an aching lump forming in his throat, choking him. He tried to reassure her, but in the next second she had flung her arms around him and was hugging him tightly.

He hugged her back, just as scared as she was.

"And you come back, too, you idiot," she said fiercely. "Make sure you both come back. And bring Marianne with you."

His throat ached. "We will, Jen. I promise."

He set her upright on the step, trying hard to ignore the tears on her cheeks, then turned around and joined Kier.

While he buckled in, Kier turned to him, looking grim, one hand on the wheel, the other ready on the gear lever. He pushed into first. "All set?"

Alan stared ahead. *Are we really ready for this?*

"All set."

🏵 🏵 🏵

"What are you doing?" Kier asked.

"Making a list."

They were heading down the M6, Kier driving. Alan had his phone in his lap and was scribbling names on a pad.

"What's your thought?" said Kier.

"I'm thinking that it's fine enough for us to fly innocently into Morocco, but if . . . when . . . we find Marianne, I want to get her out without unnecessary contact with customs."

He looked down at the list. Four men only, and two of those he'd had no contact with in a year or more. He grimaced.

"So?" Kier asked.

"So I'm thinking a boat. Unobtrusive, quiet, quick in and out. So I need someone to pilot it, sit tight on it listening to coms, and be able to put in almost anywhere."

"How many names do you have?" Kier asked.

"Four, and two are doubtful."

Alan started phoning. "Hello? Can I speak to Jim, please? He is? Never mind. No, no message. Thank you."

"Dave! Glad I caught you. I need a favour. Or rather, I need a favour and *Clarabelle* . . . You did? That's a real shame. No, no, we need a kind of maritime mobility. Well, good luck."

He disconnected and turned to Kier. "He's sold his yacht, would you believe. He's gone into power boat racing.

His wife's going crazy."

Kier grunted, watching the road. "Can't we just hire one?"

"We could. The last two on the list we'd have to take that option. But I do need the piloting experience."

"Won't it take them a while to sail down there?"

Alan shook his head, dialling the next number. "The ones I've called have, or had, boats on the Med—hi, is Gregor there? Ah. Is he okay? Well, tell him Alan sends his regards, and said to stop being such a layabout," he laughed. "Yeah, yeah, I will. Let me know when he's home."

The signal on his phone dipped, and dropped as the broad sides of the Howgill Fells crowded in close to the motorway. He sighed and sat back in the seat, tugging up the headrest.

"Burst appendix, would you believe. What *is* it with these people? They used to be the type to fly off for something interesting at a moment's notice! For God's sake!"

"They grew up, Alan. Or grew out of it."

That was short, even for Kier.

"Kier. I really appreciate this. I know you must hate to leave Jenny and the kids."

"Forget it. Jenny will have your balls if something happens to me, but we both know she'd kill me if I refused to help, too. Besides, I need a partner for the brewery tours."

Alan snorted. An uneasy truce for Jenny's sake had matured into a much deeper friendship between him and Kier. Alan had taken it upon himself to introduce Kier, single-handedly, to the delights of British Real Ales.

All of them.

Kier passed three trucks with grave concentration. "When we're out of the hills, you might try one of my contacts."

"You never struck me as having friends in the yachting set."

Kier grinned swiftly, then resumed a frown of concentration. "Gareth's, uh, had some maritime experience."

"SEAL?"

Kier shook his head. "Royal Navy, actually. Well, originally. A diver. He's retired. He's in Gibraltar at the moment, has a yacht there."

"What retired him?"

"Hard to say. He keeps himself to himself, but he's extremely competent, and an instinctive yachtsman. If I had to guess, I'd say injury but he's perfectly active."

If Kier McAllister classed him as *keeping himself to himself,* the man must have been an out-an-out recluse. "Would he be up for it?"

"Definitely. Gareth's the type to stick with you without a word of complaint when the rest are making excuses to go home." Kier was drumming his fingers on the wheel, a sure sign he was thinking. "His name's Gareth Lacy." Kier gave him the number, and since the motorway wound its way out of the hills at that moment, Alan dialled.

"Hi. May I speak to Gareth Lacy?"

"Speaking." It was a quiet, cautious voice.

"My name is Alan Waring. I was given your name by Kier McAllister, who is sitting beside me right now. He said you might be interested in helping us out with a rather . . . specialist job."

"How specialist?"

"We need someone with a yacht to do a pickup on the North African shore, and, if all goes to plan, deliver ourselves and one other back to England."

There was silence on the other end of the line. Then: "I would need some more details."

"Of course. I'll give you more later, but we're thinking pickup sometime in the next week, our passenger will require some privacy, so a separate cabin for them would be good. All expenses covered, and we'll come to some arrangement of a fee—" Kier was trying to get his attention, shaking his head, but Gareth interrupted him first.

"No. I mean the whys and wherefores. There are some jobs I just don't do."

Alan shook his head, annoyed with himself for being dense. "I'm sorry. Of course. It's a rescue job, Mr. Lacy. A young woman has disappeared in Morocco, and we believe she's been kidnapped. We're going in to find her and bring her back."

There was that considering silence again. "Alright. I have some arrangements to make. We can talk later. The boat's ready to roll, though. She always is."

"What's she called?"

There was another pause. "*Orpheus*."

Alan remembered the tale—the Greek myth of the magically talented bard whose wife died, and who journeyed into the depths of Hades to recover her. But Orpheus had made one final mistake when they were nearly clear, and he had lost her forever.

Alan hoped to God it wasn't an omen.

❀ ❀ ❀

They caught an afternoon flight from Heathrow. There wasn't much they could do on this side of the world. He'd never get the equipment he needed on the plane without consigning the pair of them to jail for a very long time. For the first time, Alan cursed his resignation, missing the resources HQ could usually bring to bear.

But they'd refused to help him. No, they'd refused to help *her*, which mattered more. He couldn't tie himself to them after that.

Alan was still making lists as the engines powered up for flight at the end of the runway. He glanced round first class, but no one appeared to be paying them any attention. He kept his voice down, in any case. "I know someone who can sort us out with papers to cover most of North Africa. Libya might be tricky, but we'll see."

"Why wouldn't she be in Morocco still?" Kier murmured.

Alan sat back, trying to get comfortable in a seat not designed for tall men. He sighed. "I've no reason to believe she isn't. But it pays to be prepared. I rarely travel anywhere out there without the paperwork to get me in and out of at least two neighbouring countries."

Kier grunted.

"We'll need a four-by-four, whatever we can get. Or rather, whatever we can get and still get parts for. That means Toyota or Land Rover."

"Pick up a Landy. Station wagon."

Alan nodded. That would be his choice, too. "Beggars can't be choosers."

"Are we beggars?" Kier questioned, brows raised.

"Nope," Alan replied, low voiced. "I have a good deal of money with me, an account in Morocco, and one in Tunisia. Stashes in strategic locations, too."

Kier nodded, and took a few mouthfuls of spring water.

Beside him, Kier composedly closed his eyes and settled for sleep. The man had always been implacable, but marriage had added to him a calm that was more about serenity than threat. And he could sleep anywhere, the lucky bugger.

Alan held a hand out in front of him, surprised to see it wasn't shaking. He had a lot to think about, a lot to plan. He couldn't afford to be distracted by worry. But nevertheless he was surprised at the steadiness of his own hand.

He let it fall, closing his eyes with a sigh. He thought about Mari, on the beach, and the glorious idyll of that short, stolen holiday, holding life at bay for a few days. Then he thought about her in the hands of his enemies and, despite the cool of the air conditioning, he started to sweat.

It was his fault. He knew it.

That was the reality he'd had to pull over to face on the way north. When the last of his calls had come through, and he'd know that Marianne Forster had never boarded that plane in Rabat. Had never got home, safe. That the last time she'd been seen, safe, for sure, was when he'd kissed her cheek in her room, and allowed himself to be dismissed, leaving the smart card in her luggage. This was what he was facing now, and what kept him from the sleep that his brother-in-law had so effortlessly achieved beside him.

That, and the fact that he'd known, really, before he'd ever got to her home. When had he known, exactly? Before he left London? Before he left Morocco?

Before he left Mari?

Please, no.

Surely, please, he hadn't gone so far down into the darkness of a life defined by the moments he was alone, that he'd been that irresponsibly selfish.

Just at the moment, headed to Paris and a connecting flight to Rabat, he couldn't be sure.

He swallowed, hard, and deliberately closed his mind to the clawing, disabling guilt. If he was to be any good for Mari, she needed him sane, and rested, and firing on all four cylinders. And then some.

Never, in all the times he'd crossed the desert, had the stakes been so high.

⚗ ⚗ ⚗

"Look, Alan, there's nothing to be found here," said Kier, scanning the airport concourse as he spoke. "I'm going to get a drink and find a taxi."

"Yeah," he said, still reluctant to give up on their only lead. He believed she had at least made it to the airport. "I'm going to give the customs guy one last try, though."

"As you like." But Kier didn't sound all that hopeful.

They'd landed at Rabat airport at about 8:00 p.m. They'd collected their luggage, then worked their way through departures. Alan had a few copies of the Polaroid of Mari he'd found in her bag. She was smiling in it, in a blue dress embellished with gold threads. He'd showed it to a hundred people, it seemed, and only looked at it himself once.

And no one had seen her. At least, no one said they had.

As soon as he saw the customs desk his intuition came online with a vengeance. The older guy they'd questioned earlier was gone, and in his place was a younger man with a neatly trimmed moustache and a pleasant face. Alan dug the picture out yet again.

When the customs officer looked down at the photo, he knew they'd found something. The man's face stilled. He glanced up, looking faintly surprised and slightly guarded. Alan's stomach twisted, and the hairs on the back of his neck started to rise.

"Yes," said the man, matter of factly. "That lady was here, oh, two, three days ago."

He swallowed. "Did you see where she went?"

The other man paused a moment, looking at him candidly. "No. I did not see. They took her away somewhere."

"They? Who?"

"The police," he shrugged, "they were not in a uniform—how do you call it?"

"Plainclothes."

"Yes. Of course. Plainclothes policemen took her away. They told me to search her, and they took her away when they found what they were looking for." He regarded him steadily, eyes open wide and honest. "Are you a relative?"

"No."

Another shrug. "Then go home. If you do not know where she is, then you will not find her."

"You said they told you to search her. Why?"

The man frowned then and shifted his weight. Swiftly Alan slid out a few U.S. dollars and palmed them across the counter. He watched the other man take a breath, frowning, and then, reluctantly it seemed, take the money.

"They told me to search her luggage very carefully. They told me to look for a smallish package in the lining, under things, you understand? They did not say what was in it."

"Is that common? For the police to tell you to search?"

"No," he shook his head considering. "No, it is not common, Monsieur, but it is not unheard of."

There had been a tip-off then. They were pre-warned. Alan felt sweat prickle on his back, while humanity ebbed and flowed around him, barely noticed. *Dear God, where was she?*

He looked up, peeled away a few more notes. "If she was yours, where would you look for her?"

The man was silent for so long Alan thought he wasn't going to talk at all. Then he sighed, and his face twisted. "Me, I would not look in Maroc."

What? "Why?"

"There was a man whose accent was not . . . not from here. And their identification was not of the clearest, perhaps a fake. But my—my boss was here and money had changed hands. Me, I thought they were from Algerie."

Algeria? Dear heaven.

"Algeria is a big country."

"Yes. I am sorry. I do not know more." He frowned again, gazing unfocused over Alan's head. "Except . . . they mentioned a place, I think. Béchar."

"Béchar?" Alan enunciated clearly to make sure he had the word.

"Yes. A small place across the border. You cross the Middle Atlas on the road to Er Rachidia, then the P32 east to Figuig. But I do not think the English go to Algerie, no?"

"Not usually, no."

"But you will go."

Alan looked up and met the steady brown eyes of the customs officer. He had meant to lie, but there was a calm compassion in the other man's face. "Yes."

"Yes." He nodded, smiling slightly.

He still hadn't taken the money. Alan offered it again.

He shook his head ruefully. "No. She was pretty, and she was afraid. You go find her. Insha'Allah."

"If God wills it," Alan confirmed.

⚶ ⚶ ⚶

They stayed that night in a cheap hotel above a restaurant, in the heart of the city. Not for them, now, the camouflage splendour of a five-star tourist hotel.

Alan slept badly, disturbed by dreams.

They bought a long-wheel-base Landy from an avaricious dealer near the Place Lincoln. Alan found himself in charge of equipment, and spent one afternoon meeting some seriously dodgy people in seriously sinister surroundings. He got maybe half of what he wanted, but together with some good navigation aids and emergency gear he recovered from one of his safe stashes, it was enough. More than enough, under the circumstances.

He had no intention of going to war. But Algeria was still wildly unsafe. *Be prepared* was the Boy Scout motto. But he doubted any Boy Scout had ever gone to camp equipped with a brace of AK-47s, a box of grenades, and a couple of sidearms.

His own Browning 9mm was in his stash, freshly oiled and gleaming. He rarely used a gun on the job—all too often it unintentionally armed the opponent, or escalated a situation way out of control. Alan preferred to rely on his wits.

If he had to, he killed with the desert.

He'd accumulated slightly more innocuous gear, too. Tents, cooking equipment, water bottles, jerry cans of fuel, medical kit . . .

Kier had spent the time with the phone permanently glued to his ear, buried in a welter of maps, the accuracy of which, or lack thereof, made him swear with monotonous regularity.

Now Alan was working on the vehicle, in the lock up they'd hired round the corner from the hotel, doing a last check of the gear, securing everything illegal out of sight under seats and flooring. Making a safe place to hide his laptop. He was tired. His muscles ached a little.

And all the time, he closed his mind to thoughts of Mari. Where she was, what she was doing, what she was feeling.

He couldn't afford to think about it.

Except at night. At night he couldn't help himself.

She was pretty, and she was afraid.

Oh, God. The phrase haunted him then. It was written on the walls in his dreams. In waking moments, it echoed in his mind in whispers he dare not to listen to.

She was pretty, and she was afraid. Was she still afraid? Sickness soured his stomach. Was she still pretty?

Was she still alive?

Kier knocked and stepped through the metal door with the flaking paint. The sun had set an hour ago. The inspection lamp was harsh, glinting on glass and on his watch, sending shards of illumination dancing across dusty concrete walls.

"All set?"

Alan finished taping the Browning under the dash, backed out of the passenger footwell and stood, brushing his hands on his trousers. "Pretty much. You?"

"I'm done. Here."

Alan looked up to see Kier toss something across to him. He caught it, one-handed, registering something lightweight and plastic. Turning it over in his hands, he saw it looked something like a portable disk drive.

"What is it?" he asked, but he knew already.

"You said the information you were carrying was on a smart card. That's a smart card reader." Kier stood still in the doorway. "It's battery-powered, would you believe."

Alan looked down at it. Somewhere out there was a tiny plastic card, a tiny, insignificant thing—only his whole world turned on the contents. And he didn't even care what the contents were.

"I thought," Kier went on, "if we get the chance it wouldn't hurt to know what we're fighting for."

Alan turned back to the Rover, and opened up the

compartment under the passenger seat, tucking the reader down beside his laptop. "I know what I'm fighting for. And it's not that." He straightened. "Anyway, we have to find it first."

Kier shrugged. "I saw it—I bought it."

"Thanks."

"No problem. You want me to go check out?"

"Nope. We need a good night's sleep. We need to be rested. We'll set out in the morning. She's been missing three days. A few more hours can't make any difference."

Kier gave him a long look. "If you say so."

He brushed his hands on his trousers again, unnecessarily.

🏵 🏵 🏵

"Go to sleep, Alan."

Alan heaved a great sigh. "You can talk."

"I would be asleep. But there's a git in the room with me." Kier's voice drifted across the room from the other bed.

"I do apologise. I didn't realise the presence of a git induced insomnia in brothers-in-law."

This time Kier sighed, and the bed creaked. Alan levered himself up against the headboard, and stared at the light seeping through the curtains. It was only 2:00 a.m., not light outside yet, but their room faced the street, and there were lights and lighted signs to show up the spaces of the room.

"It wouldn't be so bad if you didn't keep throwing yourself around the bed and heaving great sighs. You sound like a wildebeest."

Alan's eyebrows climbed. "Could be worse. Could sound like a warthog."

"I do not snore. Jenny says so."

"Jenny wouldn't tell you. She's still in the honeymoon phase. Wait till she starts telling you your feet smell."

"Too late."

Alan grunted.

"Wanna talk about it?" asked Kier.

"Yes and no."

"Choose."

"I need to sleep. I need my wits about me if I'm going to be any use to her."

"Sure."

"But I can't. I try and doze off, and all I can do is think about where she might be, what's happening to her . . ." His voice broke off, and he swallowed.

Kier got up and turned on a bedside lamp. By its light he rummaged through his bag. "Speculation," he said, shortly.

"But that's just it. Everything's speculation. If I just knew anything . . ."

Kier disappeared into the adjoining bathroom, and reappeared with a glass, pouring a hefty slug of scotch into it from a nondescript flask.

He offered it to Alan. "God knows it's not a solution,

but it may just help you sleep tonight."

"Why do you carry it?" he asked, surprised. He'd done plenty of drinking with his brother-in-law, but never seen him as a hard drinker, or a fan of hard drink.

Kier tipped the flask and frowned down at it. "Force of habit," he said, stowed it back in the bag, and flopped down on the bed again.

"If you thought she was dead, if I said I thought she was, would you go home?"

"Do you think she's dead?" his voice was choked, but his heart felt more constricted.

"Answer the question."

He thought about it, wondering what it would take to get him to give up. "No. I'd keep looking. Till I was sure."

"And then?"

He tugged at the sheet. "And then I would do whatever . . . tidying up was necessary."

Kier grunted and threw an arm up over his eyes.

"Well, then. Get some sleep, if that's what you've decided to do. Fretting won't set her free."

"Bloody hell, Kier, I know that! I know I should sleep to be fresh, to be ready. I know a few hours can't make much difference at this stage."

Kier turned and looked at him.

"What?"

He considered Alan thoughtfully, then covered his eyes with his arm again. "Nothing."

Alan thought back over his words and started to notice

something. Was he really that cold? But he was just doing his duty, acting responsibly.

Wasn't he?

A horrible dread settled over him, an inkling that he was about to learn something about himself he wouldn't like.

"Kier," he said slowly. "What would you do if it was Jenny?" He turned quickly enough to catch Kier's wince.

"I don't think that's relevant."

"The hell it isn't. I asked you. Tell me."

"Jenny's going to kill me for this."

"She'll have to queue if you don't tell me."

"Yeah, true," Kier conceded. "Plus she's going to be too busy killing you, at this rate."

"Kier? So help me God, I'll—"

"Alan, the circumstances are different." For once, Kier sounded awkward, and Alan started to sweat.

"What would you do? If it were Jenny?"

Kier grimaced. "I wouldn't be trying to sleep."

He was right. He'd been trying to keep some sort of distance. However much he was here, however much he was working to find her, he'd been trying to keep his distance, too. He'd still been playing games.

"Look, Alan. You've been trying to keep this on one level of commitment, trying to stay professional. I respect that."

"Fuck respect." He kicked free of the covers and stalked over to his bags. He began to dress quickly, swearing at buttons, pulling on a shirt with frustrated, jerky movements.

"Let's get something straight—"

"Alan—"

He ignored Kier's placatory words and spoke as much for his own ears as for Kier's. "Whatever my *level of commitment* before, it's 100 percent now. We will find Marianne Forster. We will bring her home safe. Whatever it takes. *Whatever* it takes."

Kier's face showed no discernable expression. "And then?"

Alan stared blankly at the backlit curtains, his jacket in hand. He remembered her laughing and smiling. He remembered her poised and quiet at their parting. "And then she gets the dubious honour of hating me for the rest of her life."

Kier grunted. "Women are amazingly forgiving."

"Maybe. But I'm unforgivable."

"Well. For the record, I approve. Trying to stay cool wasn't working, and you were just looking like a prat."

"Gee, thanks," he drawled, in Kier's own voice, and got a grunt for his virtuosity.

They packed in short order. Kier was to go and fetch the vehicle from the lock up. Alan was to wake the desk and check out. And then . . .

Kier held the door open. "Er Rachidia?"

"Er Rachidia," he confirmed.

❁ ❁ ❁

It was still mostly dark when they headed out of the city. The four-wheel-drive bowled along comfortably, not sweating yet, since the road was made up here. At least, it was as made up as a Moroccan road could be.

Alan was driving, welcoming the need for concentration. Kier was studying maps beside him.

"How many days behind do you make us?" he asked, flipping an old map over to look farther east into Algeria.

Alan shook his head. "I make it three . . . a bit more. I'm losing track. Does that sound right?"

Kier grunted. "'Bout right. If they've stayed on the ground, then we've still a good chance of making headway."

"If they have."

Kier folded the map methodically, not looking at him. "We'll find her."

He took two steady breaths before asking, "Are you sure about that?"

"I am now."

chapter seven

There was a movement outside the door.

It was dark, and the sound was stealthy, and Marianne shuffled backward on the dirt floor, taking the links of the chain in her hands to muffle their clanking. No one had come to her cell for—she panicked a little—she couldn't remember how long. Wait, think . . . first night in the truck, second night the same. Then last night, here . . . and now.

Silence.

She didn't know what time it was. There was no window to this tiny room, her cell. The door opened onto a corridor, with similar rooms opening off it, and two larger rooms beyond.

She sat there, staring blindly ahead, with her bare feet stretched out in front of her, the borrowed robes covering her legs, her back against the wall.

It bothered her that she'd had to think to know how long she'd been missing. Mind you, it didn't really matter. It wasn't as if she could say to herself, *survive four days, and so-and-so will come and get you.*

Not likely.

Not possible.

There was only one person in the whole world who knew she was supposed to be home. And she'd made sure he would be the last person to come looking for her.

She'd made a rule not to think about Alan, and that idyllic time in Rabat. It was gone. Finished. And it only made her more aware of how terribly alone she felt.

Marianne wanted to cry, but she didn't dare. She couldn't waste the water. They were sparing with that, as with everything else. Except shouting. They did a lot of shouting.

Enough. Eyes closed, she bumped her head back against the wall once.

Think.

She needed to get it all straight in her head. She needed to know.

She thought back, and remembered.

⊗ ⊗ ⊗

They took her away from the airport in an unmarked black car.

She watched the world go by, the men in bright colours, tourists in sunburn and sandals, the glint of the ocean beyond.

"A problem with the papers," they said. "You must see the consulate."

She didn't like it. She worried. She knew something was wrong. But there wasn't a lot she could do in the end. A handful of men, talking mostly in Arabic, manhandled her and her luggage out of the airport and into the car.

When they left the city, she started to worry some more. "Excuse me? She leaned forward and tapped the man beside the driver on the shoulder. He swivelled round and frowned at her. "I'd like to see someone from the British Consulate, please." He eyed her up and down, and faced front again.

She tried again. "Je suis Anglais? Vous comprenez? Je Voudrais . . ." Nothing. "Are you taking me to a police station? Kissam shorta?"

The car passed on down the dusty road, past farms and small buildings, till, turning on the seat and craning her neck, she could hardly see the city at all.

There was a truck on the road ahead of them, an anonymous canvas-covered army green truck. They pulled up beside it in a cloud of dust.

There were already other men in fatigues inside the truck. They hustled and pushed her up into the back, thrust her down onto a bench seat wedged between two men clutching rifles. They pressed up either side of her, but they never looked at her.

Something was very wrong.

The truck engine started up, shaking the whole vehicle and filling the air with the reek of diesel.

She panicked. With a cry she threw herself forward,

meaning to jump out and get away somehow, anyhow, but the men beside her shouted and grabbed and pulled at her, till she was delirious with terror, half insensible. They wedged her between them, keeping her back with their elbows, surrounding her in hard restraint and the smell of sweat.

At least they hadn't shot her.

They were two nights on the road. They stopped for a few hours in the dark. The men in the truck got out, but when she tried to get out, too, they shoved her back and threw a blanket at her. So she curled up in the corner inside, and they slept outside.

She didn't sleep. She was terrified. The thought of what they might do to her sickened her. Where were they taking her? Was she being held for ransom, or were these some sort of officials and she had unwittingly done something very wrong?

Marianne wracked her brains, thinking of the things she'd seen in Morocco, where she'd gone, what she'd done. But she'd been with Alan most of the time outside the hotel, and *he* wouldn't have got her into trouble, she was sure.

The questions swirled round her head, making her sick. She shivered and cried her way through the night, huddled under the scratchy grey blanket.

In the morning, she was let out for a loo break, crouched by the side of the road. She didn't let herself think anything at all.

The roads got worse, till she was bruised and aching, suffering from sleep deprivation, hunger, and dehydration.

They gave her some water, and some dry flatbreads to chew on, but it wasn't enough. Then one afternoon they left the road completely, throwing up a huge plume of dust behind them as they creaked and swayed their way across the stony desert.

You wanted to see the desert, Marianne? Here it is.

The greener lands in the middle of Morocco had given way to stony plains, with scattered bushes and scrub. It was lonely, barren, and rough. That was all.

Once they passed a Berber woman, gathering wood. She was dressed in scarlet and royal purple, with a golden head scarf. Marianne watched that splash of colour till it disappeared.

Then, as it grew dark on the third day, they arrived at a little settlement, nothing more than a few buildings around a well. They stopped. And this time they took her out with them.

They marched her into the largest building and pushed her into a chair at a table. Everyone was talking—the bare room was full of noise. A door banged, and three men came in.

Then they shouted at her a lot. Mostly in Arabic, and they seemed surprised and disbelieving when she tried to explain she didn't understand. There were a couple of questions in English. Something about what she was carrying, and something more about information she was supposed to know.

Mostly she huddled in her chair, cringing, tired beyond reason and terrified beyond thought. Eventually they shut up, dragged her through the door the three men had entered by, down a corridor to a small empty cell, where they chained her to some old iron pipes, despite her sobbing pleas.

She didn't sleep.

They came back a long time later, dragged her out, took her to an outdoor latrine, and then back to the building. They stripped her, then, and took away her clothes, leaving her with some threadbare, greyish robes to huddle in. Then they shouted at her some more.

They kept shouting even when she was too tired to do anything but shake her head at them weakly. The big man in the photographer's waistcoat, the weasly man in the long white thing and the red skull cap, the bored man smoking a nasty cigar. They all paused when a boy came in with a tray, figs and bread and white cheese on a plate, and a tall mug of water.

He set it down on the table in front of her, and the scent of the water had just reached her when the big man swiped it off the table with a meaty hand so that the water splashed against the far wall, and the food scattered across the floor.

Watching the water dripping down the wall, turning the plaster grey, she tasted the desert, and started to hate.

The boy scuttled back in, clearing up the mess. He was crouched by a scratched cabinet, with the plate in his hands, looking at her. Something about it made her look again, and she stared. His dark, liquid eyes were fixed on her, a little crease between his brows.

He was worried.

For her? Or . . .

The big man shouted again, and the boy ducked his head and gathered up the remains of the first decent meal she'd seen in days, and hurried out the room.

Then there was a strange crackle and whine from the corner, where the cabinet was, and everyone shut up. The weasly man moved, and she saw that on the cabinet was a radio, the type that transmitted as well as received. The weasly man fiddled with the black knobs and picked up the handset.

Tired and dull as she was, it took a moment for her to realise that the man speaking on the radio was not speaking in Arabic. He was speaking in French.

Not so strange—Algeria had been French until 1960, of course, but it was oddly incongruous spoken so gutturally and in such a setting.

She caught snatches, racking her brains for her school-girl French. The man was anxious, and he was saying "no" a lot. And something else. Something about—when you come? We will wait? And tomorrow. After tomorrow we will—something—her.

Chilled as she was, her blood still ran colder. The strange tension she'd felt in her captors began to make sense, and she began to interpret looks and words differently.

Someone was coming. Tomorrow. And everything, then, was going to change.

She watched the man speaking, saw the way he stood unusually straight, feet planted square, nodding quickly, decisively, but unmistakeably subserviently.

His boss was coming tomorrow. And then maybe they weren't going to take *I don't know* as an answer.

After the radio conversation, they were more subdued. They chained her back in her cell and left her in the dark.

Then the key grated in the lock, and her throat tightened. She opened her eyes wide, but still could see nothing but shadows and deeper darkness.

What now?

The door opened slowly, and a figure backed through, carrying a lamp with the flame flickering low. It was the boy again. He poked his head round the door, smiling at her shyly. She smiled back, feeling her lips crack in the corners. He set the lamp down on the floor and pressed his finger to his lips in an unmistakeable sign for silence.

He left the room again, leaving the door wide open, and hope surged in her so suddenly she felt dizzy. But in a second he was back, carrying a tray, and pushed the door to behind him with a bony hip.

He approached her warily, crouched down, and pushed the tray towards her across the floor. Marianne sat where she was for a moment, drained by the sudden loss of the hope the open door had given her.

This was her only ally, this little lad.

The boy, he must have been fourteen or fifteen, made anxious motions between the plate and his mouth with one hand. Then the smell of the food reached her and she sat forward, examining his offering.

There was more this time, some lamb and some rice among the fruit and cheese and bread. And there was a whole pitcher of water, too. It did occur to her that some of it might be drugged, and the boy just a decoy to lull her into a false sense of security, but she was too hungry and thirsty to care. She had told them everything she knew, anyway.

She ate slowly, wary of her too long empty stomach, and drank mouthfuls of clear, blessedly cool water between bites of succulent lamb and rich, sweet figs. The cheese was crumbly and fragrant, the bread a little stale, but tasting deliciously yeasty. The rice was sticky and had little flecks of mint in it that beautifully balanced the meal. All the while the boy crouched opposite her, dusty toes in dusty sandals peeking from under his robe, watching her anxiously.

Finally she was finished, refreshed, replete and tired, as the food filled her shrunken stomach and lulled her body.

As she subsided back against the wall with a sigh, the boy smiled at her, a quick gleam of white teeth in a dark face. He chattered something at her and not for the first time she wished she understood Arabic. Some words she did know. "Thank you," she said, conjuring a smile from a reserve she hadn't known she owned.

He ducked his head at her, smiled again, and then quietly and efficiently gathered up the remains of her meal and got up to leave her. He said something, but she didn't understand him.

Marianne lifted her chains, pointed at the door and entreated him with her eyes.

He frowned, shook his head vigorously, and left.

The closing of the door seemed loud in the darkness.

She must have dozed for a while after that. When she woke, it was still dark, and she was still alone. Marianne sighed and stretched, feeling stiff and aching in every muscle.

Then saw the line of light on the floor. A soft, orange slash of light from another room, let in by the open door.

The door was open.

She surged forward, but the chains pulled at her wrists, reminding her she wasn't free yet. She sobbed a breath, tugged at the chains. Her foot knocked something, something small and silver, that spun off into the dust. A key. A padlock key.

Almost out of reach, by her foot.

Almost, *but not quite.*

The trail was easy.

Everywhere Alan and Kier stopped, *someone* had seen them. A truck. Many men. One small Western woman.

It was clear that they'd kept her in the truck, out of

sight as much as possible. But people here were friendly, and curious. They'd seen her.

They took the road for Er Rachidia and drove through the night.

☙ ☙ ☙

The two side doors in the corridor were closed. Behind one of them, someone was snoring.

Marianne had never really understood the phrase "heart in her mouth" before. Now she did. It was beating in her throat, choking her, and it was hard to swallow.

She stepped out, barefoot and tentative. No one shouted, no one came storming down the corridor to beat her back into her cage. Light seeped into the corridor from the farther end. The corridor wasn't lit, and no light showed under the two doors.

The snorer choked and snuffled. Bed springs creaked.

She had a hand on the door jamb, and it was suddenly difficult to let go. Her palm sweated, the wood felt grainy and rough where the paint was peeling. The floor was gritty, sticking to the soles of her feet. She rubbed the sole of one over the top of the other.

Marianne took a deep breath, and then another, biting hard against the shaky moan that rose up her throat.

These men, whoever they were, had been angry enough before, when she had done nothing to anger them. How angry would they be if they caught her trying to escape?

How angry would *she* be if she never tried?

She thought about Alan, then, because her mind was too taken up with the possibility of escape to block those thoughts. What was he doing safe at home? Did he think of her?

Was he lonely?

Because that was another thing, wasn't it? She had a sneaking suspicion that her aching loneliness had nothing to do with kidnap and isolation. She, who had been alone, strictly speaking, most of her life, was properly, deeply, terrifyingly lonely for the first time.

Horrible thing, loneliness. It sapped your strength and energy. It made you afraid and crippled.

Marianne clutched hard to the doorjamb of her open cell, and thought about Alan.

🜨 🜨 🜨

Sometime after midnight, Alan pulled over and woke Kier.

"Your turn. My eyesight's going." Kier's reply was a grunt. Alan slipped off the seat and used the rail on the roof to stretch out, feeling stiff muscles give and bones click. Shaking out his arms, he turned, staring down the tunnel of light the headlights beamed into blackness. Some small rodent skittered into view and froze, quivering and immobile, eyes like tiny reflectors.

Alan watched it, feeling the chill of night seeping

through his clothes, while the desert was still warm underfoot. In all the hours since the sun went down, this was the only living thing he'd seen. They might be alone in the world—he and Kier and this one, still creature.

And Marianne. Somewhere—*God, please*—somewhere out there ahead of them.

Then Kier swung into the Rover, the headlights shifted with the suspension, and the rodent sped away, the spell broken.

Alan climbed back on board and settled in. They still had a long way to go.

Marianne was getting cold. She'd actually stood there long enough to have started to chill.

She felt her chin tremble, felt the tight ache in her throat and the prickle of her eyes and knew then that if she did nothing, she would stand here and cry, and they would find her, sobbing and incoherent, clinging to the door frame. Her insides curled with self-disgust.

And then something, someone inside her head, said, quite clearly, *Sod it.*

Nothing left to lose. No one to care.

Sod it.

She dropped her aching hand, clutched the too-long robe with it, and ran, barefooted and silent down the few feet of corridor to the half-open door and the light.

Still silence. No one shouting after her. She craned slowly, carefully, round the door.

The little airless room was empty. The lamp on the table was on, stabbing the chair with hard light. The radio on the cabinet was silent. The door beyond, opposite her, was closed.

She sped across the room and laid her ear to the white-painted door, straining. She couldn't hear a thing. Which didn't mean there was no one there.

Sod it.

Carefully, silently, she laid a hand on the round handle and turned it gently. She stopped. She glanced over her shoulder at the table, then let the round handle turn back to the start slowly.

Darting across the room, she grabbed the lamp and unplugged it, wrapped the cable round it, and then gripped it tight in her right hand near the light end. The metal was warm.

Returning to the door, she twisted the handle again. She eased the door in about an inch and peered through the gap.

There was a man in the room beyond, with his head cushioned on his arms on the table. There was a plate in front of him with some scraps of bread on it, and a tin mug by his elbow.

Craning round the other way, she saw the front door open with the curtain of metal links hanging loose.

She looked at the man again. He was still. From his clothes and hair she didn't recognise him, so he was one of the background people, one of the people who hadn't asked her any questions or bothered her. His shoulders were moving, ever so slightly, moved by deep, even breaths.

Marianne eased the door open another couple of inches, watching the sleeping man for a reaction.

Nothing. She opened the door halfway and eased inside. Here the floor was half covered in rush carpeting, looking dingy and mucky. It was ever so slightly sticky under her feet.

Nothing.

She took two steps into the room and stopped. The half of the room out of her view was cluttered with packing cases and . . . crap. She couldn't get round there without tripping.

She had to pass close behind the man at the table.

Oh, God.

Sod it.

She almost choked with laughter at the little dialogue going on in her head. She was going to need professional help after this, that was sure. Any help would be nice.

She shuffled round, as quietly as possible, to get behind the table and its somnolent occupant.

Nothing.

She was directly behind him when he moved, just a sleepy shift, but his elbow struck the tin cup at his elbow, and it clanged against the plate.

And she gasped.

She couldn't help it, didn't even realise she was going

to until it happened, until the betraying little sound was out, until it had done its damage.

The man's head came up, craning round over his shoulder, looking incredulous. She tried to step out and away, towards the door, to his side, but his hand came out and he made a grab for her sleeve. Of her left arm.

The right was still free. The lamp half-hidden in the folds of that blessedly too-big robe.

In slow motion, she saw him stumble to his feet, eyes wide. Saw his mouth open to shout, to take back her freedom. Her arm came out and round, moving fast, the lamp with its heavy base in her hand. She hit him with it, hard.

⬡ ⬡ ⬡

It was dark outside—stupid thing to think, but so it was. Mari blinked blankly, clinging to the side of the doorway.

She was still shaking, and the urge just to run across the space in front of her was strong.

Think.

There were two vehicles parked in front of the building, but she couldn't drive one away and leave the other, and she didn't know how to disable the other. She choked on another stupid laugh. She couldn't drive anyway, so what was she worrying about? She'd never had the chance to learn. Her best chance lay in swift silence, but what way to run?

The first threatening of hysteria plucked at her breath,

making her sweat, making her mind run ahead wildly. What way to go? It was the Sahara out there, she didn't have a chance. What to do . . . where to go . . . what to do? She rammed her fist into her mouth and bit on it, feeling the first sobs rise.

There was another building away to the right, another single-story white house, with another closed door. But everywhere else was just . . . space. Vast openness, hinting at the expanse of unknown waste beyond.

Something moved, on the edge of vision, and the fist became a willing gag. She choked the scream back, as the lad who had fed her crept silently from beneath the first vehicle. He had a bundle over his shoulder, and a pair of boots in his hand.

He hissed at her, craning round her to look back into the room she had left. He made quick, urgent gestures with his slim brown hands—*quick, this way, come.*

Sod it.

She followed him, knowing perfectly well what he offered might not be a solution, but only a change of scene, but also perfectly aware her choices were pretty much nonexistent.

She followed him out into the dark, away from the houses, and the ground underfoot changed from smooth dirt road to sand and gravel and stone. She stumbled, reaching the end of her feet's capacity for pain. The lad ran ahead, scampering out of sight.

"Hey!" she hissed, a desperate stage whisper. "Come back! Give me the boots."

He came back, understanding the sense if not the words, and hunkered down with the boots, coaxing her feet into them, swiping at the stones that stuck to her soles. He laced them up as best he could, but they were godawful sizes too big.

But it was better than leaving a blood trail. He got up and set off again, this time clutching to her sleeve.

In the dark, with no noise in the desert but their own breath and what were probably Arabic curses, it was hard to tell how long they half-ran, half-walked into the night.

After a while the ground started to undulate, then grew steeper, the rock becoming more frequent. Outcrops loomed, overshadowing their path, then passed into the darkness behind.

He halted eventually, ushering her to the side, up a short slope to the foot of a great chunk of rock which over-hung the ground. At its base, in a jumble of smaller boulders, there was a fissure, about the height of her guide, and a couple of feet across, making a cave. The lad waved at her, and ducked inside.

Marianne hesitated. One cell for another? She gathered up the long robe and shuffled forwards. She hit her head once, then started as he caught hold of her hand, leading her forward, his other hand flapping at her head to keep it down. Then the hand on her arm stopped pulling forward and started urging up. She straightened with care, and found they were in a larger cave, the floor seeming softish and level. She could stand up easily. Reaching overhead she found the rocky roof, cold and very slightly slimy, was no more than a foot overhead. If she spread her arms, she couldn't touch the sides.

The lad let go of her hand, and she heard rustling. Then she blinked hard as light flooded the small cave. He had a lantern torch, old and scuffed. He set it down between them and busied himself with the bundle as she settled down, cross-legged.

There was water, and more of the flat breads. He gave her a square plastic container to drink from, and a corner of the bread to chew on. There was another robe, too, and a long length of cloth she took to be a head covering of a kind. There was also, God bless him, a small packet of cheap toilet tissue, and a chocolate bar.

She touched him lightly on the back of his hand and, when she had his attention, looked a question. "Why?" she asked.

He looked at her, frowning, biting his lip. He grimaced, gesturing to her, head to foot and looking anxious. And that's the best he could do. All she could suppose was that he simply cared. Why, she would probably never know, but she was grateful, stunned by the risk he'd taken for her, and she smiled for him, even though her lips cracked painfully and she felt the beginnings of a sore at the corner of her mouth.

He smiled back, lopsided and shy, then touched his chest and said, "Haris."

She smiled again, pressing a finger against her breastbone. "Marianne."

He frowned at that, mouthing it, and she repeated, quickly, "Mari. Mari?" hearing the name from her own lips with a pang.

"Mari!" he nodded and smiled.

"Mari will do," she whispered, suddenly overwhelmingly tired. She had no idea what was next, what was his plan. But for tonight, she had freedom.

Of a sort.

chapter eight

Alan was driving when the sun came up. They'd crossed the Middle Atlas, and were nearing Er Rachidia. At around six, the sun punched its way into the empty sky in all the colours of gold ever traded, and claimed the world.

Immediately the temperature started to climb, and Kier stirred beside him. "Where are we?"

"About seventy miles short of Er Rachidia, as far as I can fathom, but you'll need to check the GPS to be sure."

Kier grunted, stretching. "Can we stop?"

"Of course."

But they didn't stop long.

When Mari woke, Haris had gone.

At first she thought he might be outside, but feeling around she found the things he had bought neatly stacked as if waiting for her, and there was no reply to her tentative calls.

She scrambled outside, heartsick and daunted, and saw the tracks leading away from the cave, back the way they had come.

He'd gone back.

Had he helped her to escape only to curry favour by being the one to lead them back to her? She didn't believe it, not really, but she would be a fool to trust in his good nature, and she was done being a fool.

Marianne gathered the things together, bundling them in one of the robes as best she could. She made a scrappy job of wrapping the long cloth round her head, but the sun was already climbing the blue heavens and promised to be a greater enemy to her than any human. It took her a long time, and three tries, but finally she had it so that it covered her head and face, leaving only her eyes free, and gathered round her neck to protect her there, too.

She tried to work something to stop the boots rubbing, but she didn't want to tear up the spare robe just in case she needed it. She bit her lip, feeling the sore places on her instep and heel from last night, but there was nothing she could do about it now. Maybe she would find some sort of civilisation soon and beg some socks or other cloths or even some better fitting footwear. She had to hope. And not think about how many miles she could travel before her boots filled with blood.

She spent some time thinking about where the sun had risen, and where west might be. As far as she could tell, they must have headed east into the desert. So if she headed west that was her best chance of taking the shortest distance out.

The makeshift turban slipped a bit, and her hair itched under it. She shoved it back in place, tucking it here and there, and set out, filing one whole load of thoughts under "do not think about this" in her head.

She wasn't stupid. Her chances of getting out alive, ill-equipped and with no idea even what country she was in, were about level with a snowball's chance in hell.

And as the sun rose, and the stiff boots worked on her bare feet, she thought she might almost be there.

⚛ ⚛ ⚛

There was no sign of them in Bas-rabba. Alan swung back into the Rover and swore. Then he swore some more for good measure.

Kier finished paring his nails and put his knife away. "Not good news, then."

Alan shook his head. "Not a thing. Not a trace."

"Don't know, or not telling?"

"It's hard to judge. We'd be meeting with suspicion anyway, so what's xenophobia and what's concealment? Usually I'd be able to tell. Maybe."

"It would be hard to miss a contingent of agitated people and a reluctant Western female captive."

Alan scrubbed his hand over his mouth. "That's if she's even with them. They could . . ." He wiped his hand down his leg, picked at the hem, wiped dust from the door. *No, no, no.*

"They could have killed her and dumped the body anywhere between here and there."

He felt Kier shift in his seat to look at him clearly. There was a long pause, and he knew for a fact Kier was thinking it through, evaluating his suggestion, however emotive. He was grateful to him for it.

"Nope," Kier said, slowly. "It's easy to kill someone quickly and cleanly if you just want them dead. Especially out here. They have Mari because they want what you gave her, and what else they expect you to have. And they're taking her somewhere where they can get it. We have just as long to find it as it takes them to get it from her."

"Yes," he said, eventually, and with difficulty. And try as he might, he couldn't keep the bitter sarcasm out of his next words. "But you know, Kier, the Sahara's a fairly big place. And we do not know where she is." He punched the dash, knowing he wasn't impressing his brother-in-law, and not giving a damn.

"I know how big the damn Sahara is, Alan. I've done some work out here in my time."

Alan looked up, interested. "Yeah? Where?"

"Libya, mostly. And good fun it was, too."

"Does Jenny know about that stuff?"

"There is nothing I've done Jenny does not know about."

"You must have done a lot of talking."

"We had a very long honeymoon."

"You spent your honeymoon *talking*?" He watched the smile curve Kier's mouth and envied him to the depths of his soul.

"Amongst other things," Kier drawled.

"Hey!" Alan punched Kier in the arm. "Snap out of it. That's my sister. And bloody focus, will you?"

Kier chewed off a grin. "Okay. We have a fairly secure trail of sightings and anecdotal evidence until here, right? So. Either the townsfolk here honestly don't know Mari passed through, or they have a reason not to tell. Right?"

"Right. And so far no people have been reluctant, not really reluctant, to share. So unless these people have a connection here, it's most likely that they simply don't know they passed through. Fair enough?"

"So far. Right. Let's look at the timings. If that truck was where we know it to be *then*, then when would it get here . . ."

"We don't know if they stopped, if they detoured."

"Just work with me here. If they were doing a steady 50, 60 kph, then we'd expect them here about . . ."

"Two, three in the morning."

Kier considered it, frowning. "It's possible they simply went through at night and no one noticed. They refuelled barely fifty miles away, so they're alright for fuel for a while. What do you think?"

Alan shrugged. "It's possible, I suppose. Question is, who would be awake at that time who might know?"

Alan looked down the almost empty street.

"Goats," said Kier.

"Thanks. I've just eaten."

"Ha-bloody-ha. There was a goat-boy heading out to the other side of the town when I was asking round the market. He'd be sleeping out with his flock, most likely. Maybe he heard something. Maybe goats wake for trucks."

"Dunno. But it can't hurt to ask."

It didn't. It did hurt their pocket, but it certainly didn't hurt the lad, who was all teeth and grinning by the time he'd been loaded down with chocolate and a few dollars. Happy boy. Loquacious boy, too.

And they weren't wrong. A truck had passed through here, slowly and quietly. It had been heading east-northeast, following the P32. But half a mile or so beyond Er Rachidia, it had veered off to head east towards the Algerian border.

"I do believe we have a lead," said Alan.

"Game on," said Kier, and they boarded up.

It was a road.

Mari shaded her eyes with her hand, barely believing it. It stretched across her path, running north-south, a grey line in a dusty orange world. She didn't smile, because that *had* been a sore forming at the corner of her mouth. But she did stop and take a celebratory sip of water.

But only a sip.

There was slightly less than a pint left.

She tucked the bottle back into the sling she'd made of the spare robe, and walked forward. Carefully.

She'd given up some time that morning and torn a strip off the robe to bind her feet with. It wasn't much good, but it was better than nothing. Even so, her feet were in blazing agony.

Her mouth hurt, her eyes hurt, her head hurt. But her feet were in agony.

She went and stood on the road for a moment, ignoring the heat that rose in suffocating waves. A road had to go somewhere. Where there was a road, there must be civilisation.

What she'd do then, she had no idea. But maybe she'd find some water and food. And socks. All her fantasies were starting to centre on soft, comfortable, blister-reducing socks.

Funny, really. Without water she'd die.

But without socks she'd want to.

Stepping stiffly to the side of the road, she looked slowly in both directions. Nothing. Miles and miles of stone and sandy ground, disappearing into the haze. She stood still, concentrating on breathing easily, careful not to chew her lip, or shuffle her feet, or do any of the things she might normally have done while trying to make up her mind.

Which way to go? Because neither way was the way she wanted to go. North or south, when she wanted to go west. Wondering briefly what country she was in, Mari looked around again. In the distance, to the north, was a plume of dust.

Her heart contracted painfully. People! People who would rescue her, take her home. A little wail escaped her, and she almost sat down on the ground as her knees shook.

She watched the plume grow nearer. It was miles away, but it was coming. Should she signal it? Suppose it turned off?

People. People like the ones she'd just escaped?

The thought entered her mind without fanfare, but it laid waste to her hopes, all the same. Now her heart was racing for a different reason. This might not be rescue—it might be recapture. She swore, thickly, in a scratchy voice she didn't recognise, and desperately tried to make her choice.

When she'd made it, she swore again, then gritted her teeth and ran, *ran* to a big boulder where a stunted bush grew, twenty yards away. She lay down behind it, shielded from the road.

While she was still alive and free, she had a chance, however small. She was not giving that chance up.

Marianne lay with her face pressed into the hot stones, and she didn't cry, because she couldn't spare the water.

ࢫ ࢫ ࢫ

"Welcome to Algeria," Kier said.

Alan concentrated on driving. There wasn't anything to mark the border, wasn't anything much at all, except the tyre tracks they'd been following ever since they left the road.

"We'll stop tonight. We can't drive on this in the dark, and we can't risk an axle."

Kier nodded his agreement, put the map and GPS in the dash, and drank deep from a water bottle. Alan glanced in the mirror at the sky behind them, brilliant as a dyer's souk in Marrakesh. They'd been driving all day. "We'll stop soon," he said. "You'd better break out the rifles."

🕱 🕱 🕱

Mari slept out in the open, terrified of things that bite, and things that sting. She propped her head on her woefully empty water bottle and covered herself with what was left of the spare robe. She didn't sleep much. When she woke, her feet were numb with cold, and she was grateful.

When the dawn came, and she set off stiffly again, they weren't numb for long.

🕱 🕱 🕱

At dawn, Alan popped the bonnet of the Landy and checked the engine over. She was running well—they'd found a good one. He checked fluids, belts, and leads, and secured the bonnet again.

When he came round the front of the vehicle, Kier dropped a hand on his shoulder.

"We're getting near," he said.

"Yes."

※ ※ ※

It was hot. Such a stupid thing to say about the desert. Mari had bravado now. But the stupidity was still with her.

Her feet hurt. Every step burned. The ground burned, even the sky burned, till when she lifted her heavy head, there was no telling where the land ended and the sky began.

The horizon blurred. The line between heaven and hell blurred, so that everything blazed and everything hurt.

Somewhere, dimly, she knew this was the last of her strength. She remembered her father's graveside, with only his daughter, doctor, and vicar attending. She would be the only one at her own death. And there would be no one to bury her.

She stumbled again, a half-limp, born of exhaustion.

※ ※ ※

They hit the N6 Béchar road late in the afternoon. Alan pulled up a few yards short of it, yanked on the hand brake, and worked his hands. They were both tired, not talking much. Kier passed him the bottle, and he gulped down some water.

"Which way?" Kier asked, when he'd finished.

"I don't know."

North or south?

"Well, if we want Béchar, that's south," said Kier.

"Hmmm," said Alan, turning his head each way in turn. Bloody hellfire, south didn't feel right. Not right at all. He thumped the steering wheel with his fist, hating indecision, but unable to break free of it.

Kier was training the binoculars on the road to the north. "There's someone up there. Maybe they've seen her."

He sat back, and handed him the binoculars. Alan lifted them and refocused. There. A lone walker, a few yards to the side of the road, heading south. "Worth a try," he said, inexplicably wanting to go north anyway.

He took first and eased the Landy onto the road.

۞ ۞ ۞

When the third vehicle passed her and then stopped, Mari was just too tired to run anymore. She'd had enough of throwing herself down behind stones and in ditches. She wasn't sure she could get up again.

It was an off-road thing, more reputable than the trucks and pickups that had been passing her in clouds of exhaust and knocking engines. It backed up, raising a flurry of dust, and she just stood there, vaguely surprised she wasn't falling over.

A man jumped out of the passenger side of the car and headed towards her, moving briskly, with purpose. She tried to get a clear look at him, but the dust and her fatigue conspired against her. She had an impression of lithe bulk, of a commanding presence, a desert prince in combat gear. Then another, bulkier, darker man came round the other side of the car carrying an automatic rifle.

Her heart started thumping in slow, painful strokes, but she didn't care anymore—she didn't. They could shoot her and leave her for the birds.

She was watching the man with the gun, so she hadn't realised the other man had come so close. He stood in front of her. She could see his throat move as he swallowed, and wondered at the bittersweet pain that pierced her.

She looked up.

It was Alan.

She stood frozen, thinking herself mad, not believing it for a second. Her throat hurt. She couldn't speak. It was Alan, frowning down at her like she was a stranger. The cloth. The cloth over her face. He didn't know who she was. He would turn around and leave her, and he would never know it was her.

She tried to speak, but her throat was too dry, too painful. She stared up at him, mute and devastated.

His eyes narrowed suddenly, he made a sound. Then his hands were pulling at the material around her face, tugging it away until it loosened and fell, pooling around her shoulders, slipping to the sand.

"Mari," he said hoarsely, "Mari . . ."

His fingers were on her skin, rough and kind at the same time, shaking more than she.

She managed to force herself to swallow. "I'm sorry to be a nuisance," she whispered, "but I'm lost. Could you take me to the next town, please?"

His eyes widened, he choked, he groaned. His hands were still on her face. "Mari! We came to find you . . . we were coming after you!"

He what? The words didn't make sense after she'd worked so hard not to spend time on dreams like these.

Another burning question. "Do you have any water?"

He cursed, then shouted over his shoulder, not letting her go, "Kier! It's her! Get some water, stat!"

The other man, now with the rifle carefully shouldered, handed her a water bottle. She thanked him in a parchment voice and carefully took a few sips. Her throat didn't seem to be able to manage more.

The man called Kier said something to Alan she didn't hear, and Alan nodded. "You're right," he said. "We need to make a move."

He took her by the arm, but that was when her knees gave way, and she ended up being carried, with him muttering things under his breath she couldn't make sense of.

They set her on a seat in the back, and Kier ripped the corner off a foil pouch and handed it to her. "Drink this. It's designed to rehydrate."

She did: it tasted weird, lemony, but she drank it, and it did feel good. The dark man clambered into the driving seat, and Alan hopped up onto the seat opposite her. She should thank him. She would when her throat stopped hurting.

Alan looked at Mari sitting quietly on the bench seat. He couldn't believe it. He couldn't take it in. Her face was calm and, thank heaven, unmarked. But he didn't know whether she was hurt at all under that gear, behind that expression.

He wanted to strip her naked and check her over, every inch, with eye and with hand. Then check her again, till he stopped seeing her bruised and bleeding in his mind's eye.

Could they really have got her out of this in one piece?

They hit a big crater in the road, and the four-wheel-drive lurched madly. She almost fell off the seat, then climbed carefully back on before he could help her, hanging on to the seat and the sides. She didn't make a sound, didn't gasp, cry out—and her blank expression didn't change.

In one piece physically, perhaps, but mentally . . .

Oh, dear God.

His jaw ached—he was clenching his teeth too hard. He turned to talk to Kier through the wire mesh separating cab from back. "I don't want to go too far today. As soon as it starts to cool, I want to stop and make camp. I want her to rest."

"What about pursuers?"

He shrugged. "We don't even know if there are any yet. We don't know anything. She needs to rest, start to feel safe. She needs to talk to us."

Kier nodded. "Fair enough."

❀ ❀ ❀

They lit a fire as the sun went down. It wasn't a wise thing to do, broadcasting their position to the watching night, but Mari was still far too quiet, her movements too unsure and hesitant. A fire would warm her, reassure her. The cheer of a friendly fire could not be overestimated in the business of survival.

Alan, tight-lipped and silent, set about lighting the fire, and Kier saw fit to keep his objections to himself. They'd bought tightly bound sticks in one of the villages they passed, and it wasn't hard to start a blaze. Now Alan tended it methodically, with the vehicle looming a stone's throw away and Kier gone out scouting for more fuel. The desert here was scrubby, bushes and twisted trees hanging onto the edge of existence, alongside the banks of a dry wadi.

He'd coaxed Mari out of the back of the vehicle when the fire was well alight, and now she sat cross-legged a few feet away, her hands folded and still in her lap.

Alan threw another couple of sticks on the fire. He needed to get her talking, but he hardly knew how to begin. And never mind how afraid he was of some of the things she might say.

He got up and fetched another rehydration pouch from the bags he had brought outside. She didn't look up when he came close and settled down beside her. He ripped open the top of the pouch and offered it to her.

"C'mon," he said, "you need to keep taking on fluid."

She fumbled with the pouch and drained it, putting the empty packet carefully down on the sand in front of her.

"Mari," he said softly, ducking his head to get a look at her face. She stared at the fire, not at him. But he'd much rather she turned that look on something without a heart. If she looked at him like that—as if there was no one home, as if the little flame that was Mari had been rudely doused, he barely knew how he'd keep going.

"How long were you walking?"

She stirred slightly, as if the ground had rocked under her. But Alan didn't know anywhere else in the world as still as the Sahara at night.

Or anything as soul-destroying as waiting for bright, smiling Marianne to learn to speak to him, to share with him again. He had slept with this woman, loved her to the utmost of his ability. And he had no idea how to reach her.

She spoke then, just when he was not expecting it, in a breathy little voice that made his throat tighten.

"Not long. Two days, I think."

Two days was long enough for her. Unprepared, inexperienced. Scared and alone. Beaten?

"Do you have a headache? Any hurts that need attention? We've a first aid kit. There's no need to suffer in silence."

She shook her head slowly, then shrugged. "My feet hurt."

He looked down. They were tucked under her in those oversized boots. "Wait here," he said and rose smoothly to his feet. He grabbed the canvas satchel that was their unobtrusive first aid kit, a sleeping bag, a camp pillow he'd stuffed a couple of his jumpers into, and he headed back to her.

He hunkered down again, unzipped the sleeping bag, and spread it out behind her. "Lie down," he ordered, and when she was settled he flipped the sides of the bag back over her and started to unlace her boots.

He wondered where she'd got them from, who had owned them before. Then he stopped wondering.

He hissed a breath in through his teeth, shaking at the sight revealed. She'd been barefoot in those tough old boots, apart from strips of cloth that were half worn away. He stroked an unsteady hand down her instep, which was about the only part of her neat little feet left unscathed. Elsewhere . . . He swore, lifting her foot gently to examine it. She was way beyond blisters, now—these were sores. On the top of her toes, along her ankle, on the ball of her foot, on her heel . . . they were all burst and worn to bleeding, the blood all over in dirty russet smears. The wound on her ankle was oozing clear liquid, the one on her heel still bleeding sluggishly. They were about the worst, but her whole foot was inflamed.

"Did they do this? *Did they do this?*"

He choked as he realised. *No, you idiot, you did.*

"You must have been in agony," he said.

She was quiet so long, he thought she might have dropped off, against all the odds. "If you keep going, the pain just sort of numbs. It's when you stop it's really bad, so I didn't take the boots off. I knew I had to keep moving."

He cradled her poor foot, fighting waves of guilt. *Suck it up, mate,* he thought. *This is what you did. Deal with it.*

As gently as he knew how, he used some of their precious water to soak the ragged, scabbed strips of cloth and ease them away. Then he cleaned, dried, and bandaged, careful to put plenty of padding into the dressings. He jogged back to the Landy and fetched a clean pair of his socks, settling back down at her feet to roll them carefully over the bandages.

She started and sat up, though she made no sound even when he must have been hurting her. As he rolled the socks on, she looked down at him.

And she started to cry.

Not neatly, but with great, wailing, gasping sobs.

"Oh, God, Mari," he cried, and shuffled closer, swiping her hair back, cupping her face in his hands. "Did I hurt you?"

"The s-s-socks," she wailed, hiccupping.

He let go of her head, reaching for her feet again. "I'll take them off," he said grimly. They must be hurting her.

She skittered her feet away. "No! I wanted s-socks. In the desert. All I wanted . . . socks."

He blinked at her, open mouthed.

"I th-thought I was going to die," she wailed, and he got it then, that the socks, whatever the hell was going on there, were just a trigger, just something to break down the barrier of calm she'd erected, and let the rest of it out.

He took her in his arms, feeling her whole body shake with the sobs, feeling it shake him, too. He tucked her head under his chin and held her, aching, while she shook and snivelled and wailed out her story, piece by piece, hurt by hurt. However awful it was, there was a part of him that took some satisfaction that finally she sounded like Mari, and there was a chance she might come back. If not to him.

The words petered out, and she clambered awkwardly into his lap without a word, snuggling into his chest. He sat, stunned, so fixated on how much she would hate him when she knew that he hadn't quite realised she *didn't* know—not yet.

As far as she was concerned, now that her head was clearing, her lover had come back to rescue her. She settled against him, her bottom pushed snugly against his crotch, her breast softly full against his chest.

He'd wondered if desire was to be the first casualty of culpability. Apparently not. Marianne was limp and defeated in his arms, but it didn't matter. She felt light and infinitely fragile, but holding her loosely and gently was still a matter of control, rather than choice.

And even musing on his desire for her stirred him. He wasn't exactly rock hard and aching, but he wasn't far off.

Alan sat in the gathering dark and piled more mental stones on his own grave. What sort of a man was he? He was cradling an insensible woman, who had been distressed and hysterical as a direct result of his own selfish incompetence, and he wanted to . . . to . . . Bloody hellfire. He just wanted. And if she knew it—if she knew *any* of it, she'd hate him.

Me first, he thought. In the dark, with no one watching and no one to see, it didn't matter that his face was bitterly twisted and stark. Here, in the desert, in the dark, he didn't have to hide.

Mari's shoulders shook with a juddering breath. He slipped his left arm more securely round her and swept the hair back from her face with his right hand. She was sleeping. Her lashes were clumped together with tears, her face was streaked with them, but she still slept.

He studied the line of her throat, her jaw, the skin taut across her cheekbones. She'd lost weight. Not much, but he'd notice an ounce. That was another item owing on his account, along with the bloodied feet and the fear, and her daunted spirit.

Alan let his fingers drift through her hair, finding the angry little grit of sand here and there. He'd never dreamed she'd be hurt . . . and that wasn't true either. He was lying to himself, he acknowledged, being brutally honest now. It had occurred to him that he might be putting Mari in danger, just by spending time with her. But he hadn't wanted to acknowledge it. God help him.

He felt like weeping, but Marianne had shed tears enough for both of them.

Shifting her a little on his lap, he let her turn so that her head slipped comfortably into the crook of his elbow.

Her shoulder dug into his hip, that arm falling back across her own waist. Her other hand was curled up under her chin. She slept on, oblivious, her mouth slightly open.

He needed to move her. Settle her back into her sleeping bag, so she could be warm. He didn't want to, though.

He did it anyway, since he was going to have to get used to doing things he didn't want to. And not doing things he did.

It was a miracle she'd got this far, unaided and alone. Or, at least, not quite alone. He'd heard the gaps she'd left in her story. Gaps somewhere around man-sized. But why on earth did she need to lie to him? Even by omission?

Why not? It wasn't as if she really knew him. A few dates and hot holiday sex didn't make for beautiful relationships. He thought about Kier and Jenny's relationship, where trust and honesty were soft, tangible things between them, linking them. Then he got stuck on the hot holiday sex thing and shook himself back to the present, finding sand under his fingernails and breathing hard.

Where was he? Ah. Lies and trust. Mari had no reason to trust him. Especially when each step on this journey would only confirm how much she didn't know. How much he hadn't told her.

She hadn't woken up to it yet, but she was sharp enough to work some of it out before long. What was IT salesman Alan Waring doing coming halfway across North Africa to rescue her?

Or not rescue her. And that smarted—of course it did—that she'd already wrapped up her own escape. Never mind that she'd not have got much further, that now his task was to rescue her from the desert, that now this whole landscape was her enemy, not just some ruthless men who were after him. Never mind that. He supposed part of him had been counting on rescuing her, as a partial penance, a salve to his own guilt.

Stupid. No: bloody sinful, to think like that, even just in the back of his mind, only now acknowledged. *When* was he going to start thinking like the kind of man she deserved?

And in any case, that penance was now more to do with loving her and never showing it, holding her in the night and not kissing her, and working for a freedom she would not—not ever—want to share with him.

He shook his head, never in his life more miserable than at this moment, in this place where he was usually happy.

He zipped up her sleeping bag, tucking her hair back out of her eyes and mouth.

The sand scrunched under someone's footsteps, and Alan shifted his weight. Just a little, just so he could move fast if he needed to.

McAllister's voice came softly from the darkness. "How's Marianne?"

"Sleeping."

McAllister's grunt in response was noncommittal.

"She needs the sleep," he added, and recognised the

defensiveness in his voice only after he'd spoken.

There wasn't even a grunt in answer to that one, and Alan scowled to himself, picking the sand from under his fingernails while Kier settled down onto the ground opposite him.

"We have company."

Alan took a moment to force his shoulders to relax, listening to the steady, even sound of Mari breathing. "Where?"

"Three, four clicks back. Small camp, couple of vehicles."

"And you think they're ours?"

"No. I'm sure they are."

"Why?"

"They turned up just before sundown and set up camp. Came from the southeast. Agitated, armed, in a hurry."

"You have excellent binos."

"I have excellent sight."

Alan snorted, the twitch of his lips feeling almost alien.

The news was a problem, but it wasn't the end of the world. He stretched a foot out until his boot made gentle contact with the sleeping bag at Mari's back. Her breathing didn't stutter.

His mind whirled, making choices, evaluating options. He got up. "Let's look at the map."

They crossed over to the vehicle and pored over the map.

"I don't want to go back the way we came—it's too predictable," Alan said, indicating their original route in.

"Agreed."

Alan stared at the map. "Okay, he said softly, "we'll split up in the morning. You lay a trail with the vehicle, I'll take Mari on foot to the well at Oglat Nadja here"—he indicated on the map—"and we'll rendezvous there. It's not too far, and I'll be leaving nothing for them to follow."

Kier's mouth turned down, but he nodded. "Sounds alright. But can Mari manage it?"

He scowled, thinking about her feet. Damn the feet, what about her exhaustion? "Yes. I think so. Maybe . . . I can't . . . she'll have to. I'm thinking we might meet up with some friends. And, no offence, brother-in-law, but I want our enemies to follow you. We'll get through unseen." With luck.

Kier nodded. "Put out the fire. It's getting too dark."

Alan sighed. He was right. "Sure."

They kicked sand over the fire in silence. "I'm not happy about those men being so close," Alan said. "Perhaps we should—did you hear that?"

Kier put his head on one side, listening. "Voices."

"Scouting party?"

"Probably."

Alan scowled. "If it were only me, I'd be more proactive." He glanced over at Mari, sleeping soundly.

"You want to be proactive?" Kier asked. "Or shall I?"

The voices were louder, carrying in the still air, just noises, no words discernable. From the southeast, he judged.

Damn.

He looked across at Kier. "Watch her," he said.

Kier just smiled.

Alan crested the lip of the little canyon on his belly, looking down across the slope to the southeast. Immediately, he saw them, a hundred yards or so away.

Three men. A loose group, talking.

He scanned the area quickly, but there was no cover, no advantage. And he wanted this over fast, and quiet. The light was on his side, bleeding colour out of the landscape, casting shadows and blurring sight. And perhaps he was being overcautious after all.

But then some trick of the breeze carried words to him. *Tracks here . . . tell the others . . . take her . . . kill . . .*

The hairs on the back of his neck rose.

Take her back . . . whatever it takes.

There was more than one person here who'd do whatever it took. Whatever it took to keep her safe.

Whatever it took to bring her home.

Well, then. Speed and surprise. He breathed deep, in preparation.

One of the men, bareheaded and stockily built, put his back to the little escarpment, pointing back the way they'd come. *Bad light stops play?* The other two turned to face the same way, all three now with their backs to him.

Perfect.

Alan swung over the edge, snatching his knife from his boot, and threw himself down the slope towards them.

He was silent. They were talking. But as Alan watched, lungs burning, legs pumping, one man shifted his weight, about to turn again. He came down the last of that little slope at a flat-out sprint.

Alan's knife took the first man in the throat, but he didn't wait to see it strike. He broke the second man's neck, and he hit the deck without a sound as the third man staggered and turned.

This one was ready for him, wide-eyed and wide-stanced, shocked, surprised, and not yet reaching for the gun he must surely be carrying.

Mistake one.

The first man gurgled, down where the sand was turning black, and Alan's last opponent's eyes slid sideways towards the sound.

Mistake two.

It was all he needed. Sand in the face: fist in the throat. A kick, a tug, a knee to strike. And the man lay silent on the ground. He left that one breathing.

He recovered his blade and cleaned it with a handful of sand, quietly and neatly.

Mari woke with a gasp, stifled by the something that cocooned her, confined her. Sleeping bag.

She breathed hard, waiting for her heart rate to slow, wriggling her toes and finding them distinctly less painful. The fire was out, the night cold. One figure crouched nearby.

"Alan?"

The figure shifted, stretched, and rose. Not Alan.

"He'll be back soon," Kier said, and offered her a bottle.

She freed her arms and drank deep. "Where's he gone?"

"He's taking care of something."

Taking care of something?

Then Alan came down from the far edge of the dune, dressed in black and armed.

"Trouble?" Kier asked, but it was a rhetorical question.

"Not anymore. I've bought us some time, at least."

"Any talking?"

"Excuse me?" Mari interrupted.

Alan continued as if he hadn't heard her. "One of them. Maybe. It's possible his larynx won't be working that well. But they were looking for us. I heard them discussing it. We have to move."

"What now?" asked Kier.

"Plan B."

"There's a plan B?"

"There is now."

"Hey!" Marianne's voice broke through, and both men turned to look at her. "What is it?"

Alan exchanged a glance with Kier, grimacing. "There were some men looking for us. Now there aren't. We're going to split up—Kier will take the Land Rover and we'll go on foot. We'll meet up later on." He offered her his hand. "Come on."

She stared at him, half horrified, half stunned. Did he mean what she thought he meant?

He wasn't looking at her, but conferring with Kier. "Are you comfortable leading them off?"

"Sure," Kier said. "Do I get to play with them?"

Alan laughed and choked on it. "By all means. Try not to leave anything that might create an international incident."

Kier gave a sour little smile. "I'll do my best."

Alan nodded towards the vehicle. "We want lightweight basics. Lots of water. Small arms, first aid kit, one of the fly sheets from the tents."

"Sleeping bags?"

"No. We'll travel at night and rest up during the day."

Kier loped off silently. Alan turned to Mari.

"You killed them," she said, short, sharp, flat.

Alan stared at her. She felt it, though the oncoming darkness shadowed his face.

He paused, then said, "They would have killed you, Mari. Eventually."

She shrugged free of the sleeping bag and got to her feet without looking at him. "I know that. I would have done it myself if I could. I just didn't know *you* could."

"Well, I can. You should be glad of it." His voice was harsh, bitter.

I am. She thought, but she couldn't say it. *I am.*

Her eyes were puffy from tears. The hands she pushed through her hair found sand and grit there. There were bruises, too, but those she refused to consider. "Where are my boots?"

chapter
nine

Alan didn't let up the pace for at least an hour. The last greyness of dusk passed and the stars came out in the thousands, scattered across the vast, dark ceiling of the world.

They trudged on in silence, Alan occasionally glancing at the sky or at his watch or at a small handheld device. He didn't speak, and Mari was almost grateful for that.

Except conversation might have distracted her from the image of unknown men dying in the night.

"Alan?" She missed her footing slightly and stumbled. Her feet throbbed with a dull ache and felt like lumps of wood on the end of her legs. His hand caught her arm from behind, urged her on, then dropped her again as quickly.

"How are your feet?"

"Hurting, but bearable." There wasn't a power in the world that could make her beg him to stop.

He was silent for a few paces. "I'm sorry, Mari. We have to keep moving. They've the advantage of transport. We have to make good headway."

"Then why didn't *we* take the Land Rover?"

"Because this way we have the advantage of leaving little trace. The vehicle's our liability." His voice wasn't even breathless from effort—with the darkness masking everything, she found she was more attuned to the sounds he made. Quiet and stealthy, but sounds nonetheless. The rustle of clothes, harsh breathing from her. The occasional muffled clunk as something settled in his backpack.

She kicked a stone, getting an answering throb from her feet, but she straightened her shoulders, swung her arms, and did her best not to slow him down.

"How did they find us?" she panted.

"Hard to say. It's actually easier to hide in a city than it is in a wilderness. The desert takes tracks, when the wind is down. And soon you have to take on fuel and water.

"The fact is," he went on, "we left a trail like a big neon sign, and all they had to do was watch the roads."

They went on in silence for a while.

"Mari, stop," said Alan behind her. "Here."

She stopped and turned, reaching out blindly in the dark. She could see his looming form, but no detail of face. But his voice was sharp, tight. Angry? Worried?

"Here, take some water on."

His fingertips were fleetingly on her face, tugging cloth down, waking chilled nerve endings into shivering awareness. Then she felt the neck of a water bottle at her lips and drank thirstily, imagining she could almost feel her body absorbing the fluid like a sponge.

He took back the bottle. She heard him drink. She stood silent, not quite knowing what to say.

"I'm sorry," he said, after he'd paused long enough for her to feel the need to hug herself. He was closer, all of a sudden, his hand, cold now, on her cheek. "I wish . . . I wish I—" he broke off, and she actually heard him swallow. "I wish none of this had happened to you, Mari."

You and me both.

"I know that's a stupid thing to say, but after tonight, and what happened, what I had to do—"

"It's alright," she said awkwardly, reaching up to trap his hand against her face, wishing, *really* wishing she could see his. She wondered when roles had reversed so that it was she comforting him. "You did what you needed to."

His hand moved, half a twitch, almost a convulsion.

"I'm not so stupid as to resent you saving my life, however messy the method. I'm grateful you did."

"Don't be grateful, Marianne."

She frowned—he must have felt it, because his hand slipped away, and he did too, before she could do anything about it.

"Don't?"

"Don't be grateful." His voice was more than tight now, and the sound of it sent her over three feet of desert ground to touch his face. He stood frozen.

Sand was the first thing she felt, and she almost laughed at it. Was the desert always to be between them? Then she felt the tension, the lines, and the pain.

She almost cried again, then, with the memory of the last awful bout of tears still clogging her mind. It didn't matter—there were still tears to be shed. For him this time.

"What is it, Alan?" Her voice broke, but she didn't care. He'd held her once in anguish already.

His hands were on her shoulders. When had they got there?

"Mari," he choked, and she felt his breath warm like a blessing on her face. That looming presence was suddenly closer, blocking out everything, overwhelming her. She held her breath, caught in anticipation.

And then it was gone, her hands touched the night, and it was colder than she remembered.

"We have to go," he said. His voice was almost normal.

❀ ❀ ❀

Gradually black bled into grey, and the stars began to fade.

Looking east, Alan saw the first shimmering breath of apricot on the horizon and reached forward to bring Marianne to a halt with a gentle hand on her shoulder.

"What?"

He lifted his head in the direction of the sunrise. "Look." He couldn't say what prompted him to share this with her, not really. There was an element of defensiveness there. *Look—the desert isn't all death.* But mostly it was because he needed to watch, and he wanted to watch with her.

Marianne stood still in front of him, her hair just stirring in the early morning breeze. He wrapped an arm around her shoulder and across the top of her chest, bringing her back against him. She wrapped a hand round his forearm, but she didn't tug it away.

He looked over her head to the horizon. The apricot was gleaming gold, and where it shone strongest, the sky lightened into the palest blue. Now the faintest, wispy clouds were revealed, lying like pale dunes across the clean sky.

"Oh," Mari said, her voice faint with wonder. "It's . . . almost sacred, isn't it?"

He smiled above her, stirred again, as he was each time, by the primeval glory of it all.

"I didn't see it before. Not when I was walking. Not . . . by myself. I just . . . didn't notice."

He didn't reply. What was there to say? He knew how the business of survival blinded you. To everything.

He tightened his arm around her, trying to keep the dark memories at bay, willing her to see only the beauty he could share with her now.

"I didn't expect clouds," she said.

"They'll be gone by the time the sun really gets up."

Now the blue part of the sky was taking over the darker grey. Then the sun came up.

Light speared out from the horizon, and the land, impossibly, went darker, redder for a few seconds, like dead blood. Burning a path, all-conquering, the sun started its inexorable climb, and the temperature started to rise.

The beauty was passing. With the light came reality—a long, desperate trek with a damaged and exhausted woman, the danger they were in, the unknown, the lies, and his enemy hunting them in a land they thought their own.

They thought wrong.

He'd spent the better part of a decade travelling this quarter of the globe, in many guises. Dawn runs on hard sand. Picking fossil seashells off the Sahara's ancient seabeds. Walking old roads at night, guided by the stars.

He knew this place. And it knew him.

"We'll keep going until the heat gets too much," he said softly, into her hair. She nodded, dumb.

ꑭ ꑭ ꑭ

In the end they stopped for another reason.

Mari never saw it coming, still concentrating on that picture of a dawn, held secure in her mind's eye. Fixated on survival and death, she'd never expected the breathtaking beauty of this place. *So strange, to love what hurts you.*

It was only when Alan came to a halt, looking away to the left, that she saw the darkening haze in that direction.

"What is it?"

He sighed. "Sandstorm."

Oh, Lord. "What do we do?"

"Hunker down. Don't panic, Mari. It'll cover our tracks."

"What about Kier?"

"He'll be fine." He swung the backpack down, looking around him. "There." He pointed to a cluster of boulders, a few feet off. "We'll shelter there."

She looked. "What shelter?"

Alan grinned at her. "You'll see."

※ ※ ※

Mari watched him scooping out a hollow in the ground, a shallow depression next to the boulders. One of the stones had fallen against its fellows, and Alan dug on the shaded side of this. He worked without fuss, putting his whole body to the work. These were practised moves, experienced ones.

She watched him, desperately tired, happy just to be sitting for a moment, cross-legged on the warming ground.

It was odd that when she just wanted to sit and do nothing, not even think, that this was the moment that her brain decided to get working again.

"Alan?"

He grunted, doubled over, frowning at the ground.

"Where did you learn all this survival stuff?"

"Here."

For a man who loved his long sentences, this was not exactly forthcoming. She tried again. "But you . . . what does a salesman need survival skills for?" She remembered that strained conversation in the restaurant, under a thousand little white lights like stars. Hadn't he said he'd only been to the desert once or twice? This wasn't a man in a strange landscape—this was a man in his element.

He flicked the fly sheet from the little tent out of the backpack, spreading it out over the shallow hole, and starting to peg it out on the far side, where the rocks were. "Everyone should know how to look after themselves."

She didn't.

Marianne looked down at her feet. She'd taken her boots off. The thick socks were stretched tight over the lumpy bandages beneath. She turned her hands over in her lap, studying them, wiping dirt and dust from her skin. There was a tiny blood blister on her right hand, where the stalk of the angle lamp had closed on her hand. Her weapon had bitten back.

Her hands blurred, and her throat ached. Her heart beat fast, and her breath faltered. She shook, not meaning to, but unable to prevent it, not wanting to think, not wanting to feel.

No. Please.

She lifted her head and blinked her vision clear, fixing her eyes on the dark storm approaching, a tall line of shadowed billows, orange and red.

Alan took lengths of a slim, black rod from the rucksack. They were strung together on elastic, flexible and strong, and he pegged them out, crisscrossing across the depression he'd made, contriving with a few lengths a complicated geometric frame. He tugged the flysheet over the top, attaching it here and there, and settled himself into the scrape. He lifted the free edge and beckoned her down, between the black poles.

Mari got carefully to her feet. "You have to be kidding." It was like a tiny, almost flat, tent. There was barely room for him, let alone her.

Alan smiled at her, but tightly, and he glanced at the sky. "Come on, Mari, it'll be on us in a moment."

She looked over the stones and saw the dirty orange wall bearing down on them. *Oh, God.*

"Mari. Marianne."

She looked back at him, wide-eyed, scrubbing her palms on the robe.

"Have you ever been caught out in a sand storm before?" His face was hard. For a blinding, nauseating moment, she hated him for deliberately throwing her inexperience into relief.

"No," she whispered.

"Then you have to trust me. Get in here. Come on."

She stumbled forward, came down onto her knees, and struggled into the confined space, careful to not disturb the frame he'd made. Alan pulled her close to him, and folded the flysheet over them both, working to tuck it into place on her far side, his chin resting on her head.

The sandstorm closed over them, blocking out the light, battering the silence.

The flysheet shook and rattled, and the sand hissed against it, deafening. Marianne opened her eyes wide, seeing nothing. Alan was still against her back, his arm wrapped tight around her waist as if he half-expected her to jump up and run for it.

She thought about it.

He shifted, and she felt him, all of him. His chest against her back, his breath heating her neck, feathering across her ear, his thigh against the back of hers. She felt stifled, overwhelmed. She couldn't breathe.

"Lift your head a bit," he spoke directly into her ear, over the hiss of the sandstorm, and her head jerked away as much to escape his breath as to accommodate the arm he shuffled up against her shoulder to act as her pillow.

Every hair on her arms was standing up, every nerve strung tight. Her heart was racing.

"Stop it," he said.

"Wh-what?"

"You're tight as a drum. Relax. Put your head on my arm, and relax." He tightened his arm round her waist.

Stiffly, she laid her head on his arm, but she didn't relax. The flysheet whipped and battered at the frame.

"For God's sake, Mari." He sounded beyond exasperated, almost anxious. "I don't want to have to bully you every step of the way!"

"Well, don't."

He almost shook her. "If I didn't, you'd still be out there! We'd never have got this far! Don't make me push you!"

Twisting in his hold, she wriggled her way round to face him, grabbing handfuls of his shirt, shocking him, startling him. "Okay!"

She shook him back, two hard shoves of her tightly fisted hands, then pressed close, burying her face against his chest where the shirt parted under his throat. "Alright," she muttered. "Alright."

Breathing deep, shutting her ears to the hissing dervish outside, she forced each muscle to relax, her mind to blank. It was his turn to be rigid instead, but somewhere between the fourth breath and the fifth, his arms came round her, cradling her more tenderly than she'd ever expected.

"What did you say?"

"Nothing," he muttered into her hair. "Nothing."

And then it wasn't difficult to relax anymore. Her shoulders dropped, and her heartbeat steadied. She closed her eyes and turned her head, nuzzling a button aside, settling.

"Comfortable?" Alan asked after a while.

"I'm in a pit in the ground, in a sandstorm, in the Sahara desert. No, I'm not comfortable."

His chest shook, just a little, and she couldn't help smiling. He shifted his weight and turned her with him so he could lie on his back and tuck her up against him.

"Better?"

She wanted to say no, but he didn't deserve it. "Thanks."

"I'm choosing to believe the missing word in that sentence was 'yes'." His hand lifted and gently pushed back her fringe, one finger lingering to brush away the dust he'd left behind.

"It's too hot," she whispered. His chest was damp against her cheek. Sweat was prickling on her back under his hand.

"I know. I'm sorry—we don't have a choice. This is the best I can do."

"I wasn't complaining."

"Just making conversation?"

"Something like that."

She couldn't see, with her face pressed here, and his head above hers. But she knew he smiled.

"Try to sleep, Mari. You're tired enough, and you should be able to manage it. This won't last long. We'll move when it starts to cool."

She heaved a sigh and felt his hand tighten for a second. She *was* tired—had never been this tired in her whole life—and hot, sticky, aching, and miserable. Some of her bruises still throbbed in angry inflammation. Some were only dully aching when accidentally pressed. She was miserable.

But she was alive.

Because of Alan.

She'd thought of him, in the long empty hours between shouted questions, but never as a rescuer. Only as an image of a beautiful past to long for and remember.

At least I did this. At least I knew him.

And that made her hotter, no, warmer. A comfortable, tender warmth curling round her heart. Alan had come to rescue her. He liked her enough to care. He cared enough to risk his own life and that of his friends to make her safe.

But . . . how had he known? *How* had he found her?

"Alan? How—"

"Shh," he said, and his voice was soft with sleep. She thought about his exhaustion, remembered him sitting at her back beside a crackling fire, waking, watching over her. She subsided, grateful only to be alive, whole, here. She tucked her hand under her cheek, feeling his breathing shift her head. His heart sounding in gentle rhythm against her palm.

He moved his arm, folding it so that his hand rested, half-curled on his breastbone.

Mari took a deep breath of hot air and shifted a little. Alan's breath stirred the hair on the crown of her head, his chest rose and fell evenly. She lay still, a little thirsty, but not wanting to disturb him.

He gave one sharp breath, and his fingers twitched. She wondered what he was dreaming about. She could see his fingerprints, the whorls of grain on his skin. The lines on his knuckles were worn deep. The backs of his hands carried the gleam of long, fair hairs. His nails were pared short, but even so, there was blood under two of them.

Her breath died in her throat, caught between images of loving touches and murderous blows, each bringing a wave of bitter grief that set her throat aching. Her vision wavered, and his hand became an impression of strength and grace.

Oh, that she had somehow not been there, at the airport at that time, for those men to find. That he had never touched her, and opened her heart. That she had never loved him.

That he had never killed for her.

She blinked and focused fiercely on the dimly lit sand slope of their lair. She watched, with fierce concentration, a tiny glint of sand break loose and jump down the slope.

Ϫ Ϫ Ϫ

When the worst of the heat passed, Alan woke and sent them both up out of the pit. He checked her over with a strange impersonal approach, making her drink, asking about her feet, giving her a moment to go round the boulders and deal with the necessities while he stood with his back turned, gulping water.

When she returned, he turned away to gather their gear together.

"Is there something I can do?" she asked, hating just standing there in the late sun.

"I can manage. Cover your face." His voice seemed short, harsh, but maybe it was just the way he was bent over, gathering up the canvas.

He kept working, packing up with neat economy, kicking sand back into their dugout to disguise it. She watched, while she twined the cloth round her face, feeling awkward and useless.

"Alan." He looked up, an impatient frown on his face. He scanned the horizon before his blue eyes settled back on her.

"What?"

"Please give me something to do."

His brows snapped together. He opened his mouth to say something, thought better of it, and looked her up and down. He stared at her for a long time, sand and dust caught in the pale smile lines beside his eyes. But he wasn't smiling.

She stared back, not embarrassed now to be looked at. She'd come way too far for that.

He swallowed. She thought distantly about the way his throat moved, under its camouflage of golden stubble, desert dust, and salt. He closed his eyes briefly.

"Sort out the water bottles. Make sure they're sealing properly, put our stocks together, and bury the empty ones. We want to travel as light as possible."

She was grateful, as much for having something to occupy her as for his giving it without fuss. As she bent for the water bottles, her back protested, which set off a little chain reaction of other aches and pains clamouring for attention.

What she wouldn't give for a bed. Then she looked across at Alan, checking maps laid over the packed rucksack. And wondered if there were some things she would not exchange, for a bed or for anything else.

Which was an altogether terrifying thought.

A few hours later, she'd stopped longing for a bed, for home, for a bath, for safety.

All Marianne wanted, had wanted for the last few miles at least, was a rest.

Out of the corner of her eye, she caught Alan glancing at his watch again, and tried to quicken her slowing steps. "How are we doing?"

Alan took a couple of quick steps closer, ducked his head towards her. "Sorry?"

She cleared her throat painfully and swallowed. "How are we doing?"

"Fine," he said, with a quick smile.

Fine. It had been "fine" since the sandstorm. "Fine" when she knew she was moving more slowly now, "fine" in spite of the tight look on his face when he checked the compass, the maps, and glanced at his watch seemingly every five minutes or so.

It wasn't that Alan was a hard taskmaster. Far from it. He was kind, attentive, always careful of her. He was also impatient and deeply anxious. He never showed it when he thought she was looking. But for these last, hurting, miles, she'd known they weren't where, or maybe *when*, they were supposed to be. And no burning heat, no trembling muscles or aching bones could make her beg for a break.

She walked on, counting steps. No matter what, she knew she could walk another twenty steps, so she counted them. And when she'd counted twenty, she knew she could walk another twenty . . .

Then, almost an insult in the flat, barren, rocky landscape, there was a ridge in front of them they had to climb.

Not steep, but the burn in her legs reminded her how a gentle slope could be steep enough. She kept her head down, counting under her breath. Alan paced past her, jogging for the top.

Sixteen, seventeen—

"Mari!"

Eighteen, nineteen—

"Look." Alan's voice was laced with relief.

She raised her head, realised that she'd reached the top of the ridge and could see for what seemed like hundreds of miles of desert.

Hundreds of miles. Rock and sand and pain and effort.

She couldn't do it. She couldn't walk anymore. She couldn't do what Alan needed her to do to get them both out of here. She—

"Marianne." His voice, soft, compelling, finally got through. Alan beckoned, and she shuffled over to his side.

The set look on his face had relaxed. He stood her in front of him, pointing over her shoulder, and handed her a pair of binoculars. She focused carefully, hands shaking a little, and the hazy horizon swam into focus. There, on the edge of the world, was a cluster of low, brown tents, and groups of horses standing by.

"Oh," she breathed. "Who are they?"

"Berbers," he said, taking the binoculars back and carefully packing them away. "Our Berbers."

Our Berbers?

"Friends?"

"The best of friends, Mari."

Even without the binoculars, she could see the puffs of dust as a couple of riders wheeled away from the tents and headed in their direction.

"How do you know?"

"I recognise the horses," he said absently.

She thought about that one for a while. "Is that the well, then?"

"Nope. The well's much further on. I was hoping we'd come across these guys, though they're usually heading to the market at the well this time of year." He swung the pack up onto his back and offered his hand to help her over the first few steps of the downward slope.

"It's good, Mari. We don't have to walk anymore to meet Kier!" He grinned at her, keeping hold of her hand. "We can ride."

Oh, goody.

Mari stared up at him, dismayed. Once, just once, she wanted them to come across something she could *do*.

The Berbers stank. It wasn't a politically correct thing to notice about them, but it was true. From the toothless ancients to the beautiful youths, the horsemen she met carried with them the scent of their lives—horses, goats, spices, and smoke.

It wasn't a bad smell, not really. But she knew whenever she thought of these people again, it was the smell that would come to her first.

They sent riders out to meet them when they were within sight. Armed and cautious men, who bounced into vociferous greeting when they recognised Alan. He was hailed like a prodigal son, with cries and offers of food and drink. And ever the men came up and patted him on the chest and on the arm, on the shoulder. When they had brought forth their ancient headman he had laid his hand on Alan's head, nodding and wheezing in some sort of Arabic, well pleased, judging by the expression on his lined face.

They thought she was hilarious, this little thing their Englisher friend had brought them. They laughed at her size, at her short hair, at her paleness. But they treated her like a trophy, dressing her with their finest. At least, they tried to, until Alan explained that she needed to blend in. Then they frowned and waved their hands and shook their heads. But they laughed some more, and chattered and called orders, and veiled women with smiling eyes emerged from tents with offerings.

Here a robe like theirs, there a blanket-like thing to throw over the top. She suffered them to carefully, deftly wind a cloth around her head until only her eyes showed, patting her head lightly, almost as if for luck. There were boots, too—soft tooled leather with an odd cross design, and stiff, dark riding gloves to cover her pale, soft hands.

When the turban-thing went on, she thought for a

moment she was going to suffocate. Her head spun, but she planted her feet firmly and kept smiling so that they would see by her eyes that she was grateful. The moment passed. Although her hair was wet with sweat in a second, it was effective protection from the sun and comfortable shielding for the eyes.

Then they led her to a shaded spot, under an awning of brown and black, set down a tray with a cup and a jug of water on it, and let her rest.

Distantly, she could hear Alan talking with the Berbers. A murmur rising occasionally to a roar. She strained to listen for a while, even though she couldn't understand a word of it.

She turned to counting to twenty again, when she found she was too tired and too anxious to really sleep. She curled on the pile of rugs they'd set in the shade, surprisingly comfortable, listening to unfamiliar sounds, watching the evening sun shift shadows across the lifeless ground. People passed in the distance, trying to pretend they weren't watching her, while she pretended she couldn't see them watching.

The second time she had to start again from one, after losing her place past fifteen, she fell asleep.

It was a Berber woman who woke her, bringing water for washing, and some fruit. She helped Marianne straighten her head covering again and urged her out of her shelter. There were children laughing, running behind a line of tethered horses as she appeared. Men called greetings. Women fluttered their hands and smiled with their eyes.

There was no sign of Alan.

Then they led out a horse for her, smiling still, and her stomach turned clean over and she started to feel sick. She couldn't do this. How could she be expected to?

Alan was there, behind her, hands on her shoulders, before her blood really had a chance to race.

"It's okay. It's easy. I'm not entering you for the Olympics. I'm just going to teach you how to cheat."

"Cheat?"

"At riding. You won't have to tell the horse to do anything. You'll just have to look like you know what you're doing. It's easy if you know how, and you will know how because I am going to tell you."

She looked up into the delicate face of the pony they'd brought her. Wide nostrils flared, and long-lashed liquid brown eyes stared steadily back at her.

"This is Reesa. She's a six-year-old Arab. She's the gentlest, calmest creature they've ever bred here. They use her to train the youngsters. She's more intelligent than you think she is, and she'd have a heart attack if she ever hurt you. This love"—he smoothed a hand down the horse's nose, which blew hard into his hand, making Mari jump— "is a lady and a mother. She'll look after you probably better than I can."

Reesa ducked her head towards her, till their noses almost touched. She forgot all about Alan, still at her back, and stared. "Hi, Reesa." She tentatively lifted her hand and touched a soft lip that curled and twitched under her fingers. Reesa breathed on her again, warm and soft, and then just lipped her fingers lightly. Mari reached up and scratched at the horse's forehead, where the darker forelock fell forward, reaching under the beaded leather fringe she wore. Reesa made a rumbling sound and nudged against her hand, and there was a general taking of breaths and relaxing about her, and she realised she'd passed some sort of test.

Reesa obviously thought so, too, because she stepped back lightly, and turned on the spot to present her left side to Mari.

"Okay," said Alan, sounding pleased. "Here's how we do it."

He was right—he was teaching her to cheat. She wasn't to do anything, really, except stay in the saddle and look competent. They'd get her up there, and down again, and Reesa was apparently doing the steering.

And Mari never said a word except *okay* and *yes*. There was so much she couldn't do, so much she didn't know. But she'd be damned if she'd give in to it. She didn't know how to fight, either, and she'd done that. Kind of.

So: *yes.*

The riders around her egged her on and shouted

incomprehensible advice, laughing, and she was careful to smile under the turban, though her heart was hammering and once or twice her eyes stung with unshed tears, when she thought she couldn't do it.

She couldn't tell how well she was doing, but Reesa wasn't trying to throw her, and Alan seemed pleased. When the sun was dipping to the horizon, the scent of roast lamb was rising from the cooking fires, and Mari had collected a whole new catalogue of aches, Alan brought them to a gentle halt, and turned to face her, running a swift hand down the horse's neck. She watched the passage of that caress, the strong hand moving with a sure, knowing touch. She felt Alan's eyes on her all the time, and for a second the horse was nothing but a proxy.

"You'll do," he said, and if his voice was a little choked, he mastered it, grinning, and if her cheeks flushed hot, the turban hid it for her, too.

Others swarmed about her, patting her feet and calves, calling to her in approval. She filled her lungs, trying to recover her nerve and her balance in the same breath. Alan moved close, talking above the din. "If you're not careful, they'll adopt you."

She thought about the quiet, gabled house in the sleeping English garden, and how far she'd come. Her mind couldn't quite encompass it.

Alan pressed closer, laying his hand on the front of the saddle, a crease of worry between his sandy brows. The smiles she lived for were brief and fleeting again, and there was a darkness to him, a sadness behind the eyes. The sun was in eclipse, her world gone silent, waiting for the light to return.

"Are you okay?" he asked, but that was her line, and she didn't know how to answer him.

I am if you are.

Concentrating, she transferred the reins into her other hand, then laid her right hand on his, squeezing. Trying to tell him by touch how grateful she was, how scared, and how far out of her depth.

His blue eyes burned hotter than the scorched sky. His mouth tightened, and she thought he might have spoken, but a grinning Arab smote him a congratulatory buffet on the shoulder, and a practiced travesty of his smile slipped back over his face.

chapter ten

"Had enough to eat?"

Mari jumped, and craned over her shoulder to look up at him. "Don't creep up on me like that."

He smiled, and settled down beside her in front of the fire. "Sorry."

She looked tired, as well she might: he'd been nothing short of a slave driver in the last twenty-four hours. But he hadn't had a hell of a lot of choice. It chafed him, though, that in rescuing her, he had to treat her so badly.

"But, yes, thanks. I'm stuffed."

He looked at her pale face in the flickering firelight. She was bundled in a motley collection of blankets and robes. Despite his injunction that she must blend in, he could see at least one brand-new brightly coloured woven blanket that would otherwise have been sold at market or contributed to someone's dowry.

The fact of the matter was, the tribe loved him, and he them. They were the only collection of people in the whole world who truly knew the real Alan Waring, and they had jumped with delighted but implacable grace to the conclusion that this was Alan's woman. Which she was. And wasn't. And . . .

God. He ducked his head and closed his eyes.

And he was still lying to her, with every breath.

"Council of war over?" she asked, lightly.

He looked up to see wide, dark eyes fixed on him, and tried to force his face to relax. "Yeah. We'll go on tomorrow with a party of riders to the well. There's a market nearby, and they're taking some horses there anyway. It's not far."

"So we'll catch up with Kier there?"

"That's the plan." Here's hoping they could stick to this one. He picked an unburned twig from the edge of the fire, broke the thorns off, and used it to clean under his fingernails.

It was all a mad collection of unknowns. A horrendous hotchpotch of half-guessed tactics and second-guessed routes. He didn't even know who his enemy was. They were living moment to moment, hand to mouth, and he hated it. He hated only being one step ahead, not having the upper hand, not having a *plan*.

The headman and the elders of this tribe hadn't liked it much, either. Had liked even less the idea that an innocent woman had been involved. Kier's reaction to that news had been mild compared to theirs. But, like Kier, they hadn't hesitated to offer their unconditional help. In a quiet moment sometime soon, however, he'd have to face the idea that they might have made that offer for Marianne's sake, and not for his.

He'd told them everything he knew, which, hellfire, wasn't nearly enough. There had never been any question of lying to them—

"How do you know these people, Alan?"

He tossed the twig back to the blaze, settled to sit cross-legged. "They helped me out once, when I was lost. They take their hospitality, their kindness to strangers, very seriously."

Out of the corner of his eye, he saw Mari sitting still, watching him. Knew she recognised that tale for the incomplete half-truth it was.

The truth was they were family, in all senses but blood. They'd earned the right to scold and to frown and look dire at him for messing up—oh, colossally messing up.

The truth . . . the truth was that he'd nearly died that first mission out in the implacable Sahara. His survival training was good, his experience nonexistent. When intelligence had been lacking, and his luck had run thin, the desert had chewed him up and spat him out with the contempt he'd deserved.

But they had found what the desert spat out, and shook their head over him, bringing him back to life with rough care and tough love, showing him the reality of the desert no survival training could teach you. The barbarity and the perfection of it. Home and livelihood and tool.

And weapon.

His lips were dry. He chewed at a loose piece of skin, frowning at the fire. Out in the shadows lumps showed where men and boys were already huddled in sleep, larger patches of darkness where the tents loomed. A horse snorted, and settled again. A goat stirred, and its bell clonked softly.

"They—" he could see her struggling with the urge to demand he tell her more, and he ached for it. The firelight flickered on her face, and he couldn't be sure if it was this that made her lips appear to tremble. "They *are* kind. Everything's completely alien for me, so different . . ." She faltered, and he turned his head to watch her close her eyes for a moment.

She swallowed, and he saw the light and shade dance as her throat moved. Then she tipped up her chin and said clearly, "In spite of that, they've made me feel welcome. As if I could be happy here."

Something in the fire snapped, cracked loudly, and perhaps that was what made him suddenly breathless. Perhaps. It wasn't the fire, though, that conjured a picture of Mari laughing, relaxed, happy. With these people.

With him.

No. You don't get to have that, Waring.

He wasn't even sure he got to wish for it. He sat silent, feeling cramped and uncomfortable, when he'd frequently slept sitting up, if circumstances had called for it.

"If Granddad could only see me now," she said, and her voice was the closest to a laugh he'd heard yet. The need to hear her laugh again roared through him, stronger than desire, more elemental than fear. He shook his head at it, stunned by it, even while he tried to find something for her to laugh about. There wasn't much.

"What is it?" Her voice was soft again—and he wondered at it, knowing that despite the darkness she'd known he was preoccupied with something.

Honesty warred with pride and, wonder of wonders, honesty won. "I was trying to think of something to make you laugh."

She paused, then asked, "Why?"

"I wanted to hear you laugh again. Badly."

Her hand crept out of the night to touch his knee. "Oh, Alan." Her voice was choked, stifled.

"I said laugh, not cry," he muttered, but he covered her hand with his, twining his fingers between her cold ones and holding on for dear life.

Over to the left, one of the horses shifted, blowing contentedly. Mari sidled closer, sliding across the cooling sand to press close to his side.

He swallowed, fighting for cool while his mind howled. "Shared body heat?"

That did it. Her laugh shook her body and his mind— he slipped an arm up and over, draping it around her shoulders while she tucked her head up against him.

"Something like that." Her voice sounded muffled.

It *was* laughter, not tears, right? "Mari?"

He got a mouthful of hair for his concern, and a glimpse

of those teeth again. His heart steadied—here was laughter, certainly. His lips brushed against her brow almost before he'd recognised the impulse. Her skin was smooth, innocent of even a hint of sand. Had she washed? How?

He smelled of horse, he knew. And every movement he made scraped rough skin over roughening sand, somehow. Mercy, was she immune to the desert, too?

That one nearly made *him* laugh, but he remembered her feet, and the look in her eyes when they'd first found her, and he almost groaned instead.

"Are you tired?" he asked, sifting her hair back from her eyes.

She shrugged against him, one slim shoulder butting into his side. "Permanently. But I'm okay."

"Try to sleep."

"I don't think I can."

"Why?"

"Everything aches," she said, candidly. "And sand isn't as soft as it looks."

His lips curved, feeling stiff. "No. Neither am I, but I might do."

He shifted before she could reply, lying back in a rush, and pulling her over him. He caught hold of one knee and pulled it up a little, settling her hips flush against him, tucking her head under his chin. He dragged the blanket over them both, pinning her with it when she tried to protest.

"Sleep."

"But—"

"For God's sake, Marianne, just sleep. It's little enough to do for you."

The words, or maybe the roughness of his voice, shut her up, and before long tiredness did the rest. He felt the tension leach from her bones, felt the little shifts and settling. Her head moved, snuggling closer, till her breath warmed his throat.

What fresh new hell is this . . .

He grinned a little, not quite able to help it, while half of him welcomed the weight of her greedily, and the other half cried aloud at the agony of having her in his arms, and not having any right, any right at all, to do a damn thing about it.

❁ ❁ ❁

Marianne was dreaming. And it was a *good* dream. She didn't want to wake up. She was warm and comfortable, and just now, just this moment, nothing was aching. She felt safe. Blissful, blessed feeling. She tried to hang onto sleep, snuggling deeper into the bed beneath her.

A bed that was inexplicably harder, and colder, than her delicious dream.

Mari sniffed, snorted, and woke. She was aware of three things at once. She was sprawled inelegantly on her front, on top of a blanket, it was light, and Alan was nowhere to be seen.

She closed her eyes again, curling her fingers into the

horse—scented wool. He was there in her dream, holding her, making her feel warm and safe. He'd been her bed all night. And in spite of everything, it was embarrassment she felt first. Had she snored? Lord, had she *drooled*? She shook her head sharply and looked up. All around her she could see people going about their business: feet, ankles, robes, hooves.

There was a woman at her side, suddenly, tugging politely at her elbow. Marianne smiled, said "thank you," and got to her feet, trying to hide the sudden pain of stiff, sore muscles. The woman was trying to usher her to where she could take care of a morning routine, such as it was, but suddenly there was Alan, in front of her, blocking their path.

"Morning." He smiled at her lazily, a slow, knowing smile, and something in the vicinity of her stomach turned clean over. "Did you sleep well?" He was laughing at her, and her embarrassment snatched back her little relaxation and replaced it with tension. And a violent blush.

"Yes," she muttered, sidestepping him in the wake of her morning guide. "Thank you," and she skipped away, awkward and uncertain, leaving Alan grinning behind her.

❁ ❁ ❁

Alan smoothed a hand down a silky mane and waited for Mari.

He'd left her at dawn. He'd had to, since waking with

her in his arms was both a temptation and a penance. And had given him a bad case of morning glory. Which would have made her blush even harder than she had an hour ago. It had taken him a while to get his body under control. He wondered if she'd dealt with her blush as quickly.

There were worse ways to wake up. But substitute the hard ground for a soft bed, and get rid of the clothes, and there weren't any better—that was for sure. He sighed. Azrou kicked the ground impatiently. In his other hand, Reesa's reins were still, the gentle horse standing perfectly still, probably as much to show the younger horse up as out of natural good humour. He told the other horse to calm down in Tamazight, the Berber dialect, while his eyes searched for Mari in the bustle of the camp.

He almost missed her, his heart giving an odd thump when he refocused on the small figure moving confidently towards him in borrowed gear. They'd trussed her up in the turban again, and at this distance he couldn't even see her eyes. Sometime he would have to sit down and work out how she was more beautiful to him now, like that, than she had been completely naked in his arms, a lifetime ago, in Rabat.

She slowed when she saw him there, standing between the two horses, and Azrou flared his nostrils and flung up his head. Alan muttered into a twitching ear, and the restive horse took two steps sideways, out to the limit of the leather Alan held lightly, and stood stock-still there, muscles shivering.

Mari approached cautiously.

"It's okay," he said softly. "He hasn't seen me for a while, and he's on his dignity."

"You know him?"

"He's mine. His name is Azrou."

Her dark eyes flickered between them, and then she simply muttered, "Azrou," with a little nod.

It was probably a good thing she didn't want to pet this one—he couldn't guarantee he wouldn't bite. "Here," he said, bringing Reesa forward. "Get up."

With Reesa and him between her and Azrou, Mari relaxed a little, as he'd intended. "Where do we go after the well?" she asked.

"Pretty much straight north to the sea." Every border crossing was a risk. Now that they were *in* Algeria, he'd much rather *stay* in Algeria.

"The sea?" Mari paused, one foot in the stirrup, questioning him over her shoulder.

He nodded. "We have a yacht. The *Orpheus*. She's hanging around in the Med, but Gareth will bring her into our coordinates when we call it in."

"Who's Gareth?"

"Gareth Lacy. A friend who's helping us."

"Why is he helping us?"

"Because he can. As far I as can fathom, he lives his life on his yacht and does odd charters when he can. Kier knows him."

She dropped her foot to the sand again, soothing the

waiting horse with a soft hand. She'd come so far.

"Can I . . ." Mari interrupted his thoughts, sounding hesitant. "I mean, would there, will there be time for a swim?"

He stared at her, knowing he was doing it, not meaning to intimidate, but really, truly taken off guard by the question. "Swim?"

She shook her head, swallowing, not looking at him. "I'm sorry. It's stupid. But . . . I want to get clean." She stopped, looked up, not at him. There was a pause of a breath or two, and he watched her eyes in silence, treasuring the opportunity.

"Don't you love water?" she said, apparently apropos of nothing. "I know I do."

He wondered if she was thinking what he was—about the soft surf on a deserted beach, and softer touches under the gentle blessing of a more benevolent sun.

Her eyes crinkled at the corners, and looked unfocussed, dreamy—and he knew she was.

In spite of everything, he would have dragged the cloth from her face and kissed her then, was already taking the one step forward it would need, but someone talked, someone shouted, and she blinked into life, jerking round to face the horse again and fumble for the stirrup.

He boosted her up into the saddle and saw her well settled, with his heart pumping in his ears, while all around them his friends bounced into the saddle with bright glee, as if they were heading out on a fun excursion, not assisting in a deadly chase. He led Azrou a little away from Mari and swung up into the saddle. He let him have his head for a while, then reminded him gently who was in command, and wheeled him into line.

There was a shout from the front, an answering cry from the back, and they set off in a cloud of dust.

❀ ❀ ❀

Marianne wasn't half as jolted as she'd expected to be—not really. Reesa had a gentle, rolling stride, and her hoofs beat the sand with lulling rhythm.

She could imagine, now, how men like these learned to sleep in the saddle. Even for her, anxious with every breath to be doing this as Alan had taught her, to not be letting him down, she found she could easily slip into a half-doze if she let herself.

She didn't, though, because there was too much to think about. More than the little lessons of riding as best she could, more than what was next and whether they were safe . . . there was so much of Alan to think about.

And none of it made any sense. This businessman who wasn't a businessman. The man who had told her he'd been to the desert "once or twice" who, out in the Sahara itself looked to be in danger of going native. With his own face covered in loose swathes of white cloth against the dust, he looked like the other riders, loose-limbed and confident in the saddle. Only when he turned his head, and the sun was right, you caught the glint of shockingly bright blue eyes, all wrong, snapping you out of the illusion. Like the unexpected sapphire found in sand.

For a self-confessed loner, he seemed perfectly happy to be all but adopted into the Berber family. She couldn't work that part out. But, truth be told, she knew all about loneliness, and knew that was the real song he was singing, even if he had changed the tune.

But she'd had loneliness inflicted on her, no asking, no choice. Alan, it seemed, had chosen his lonely path. That, she didn't understand at all.

She snorted, sitting up straighter. As if she understood any of it. Except that she was still in love with him, God help her, and had acquired a whole new set of additional reasons why she could never have him.

As if simply called by her thoughts, he drew abreast of her, so damned magnificent doing the Alan-of-Arabia thing that he stole her breath without trying.

"Doing okay?"

"Yes."

"Keep your heels well down in the stirrups."

She nodded sharply, trying to ignore the way her knees were starting to ache. Her legs just didn't usually bend that way.

He edged a bit closer so that she started to be nervous about having her leg crushed. Instinctively, she leaned away. Reesa flicked one ear back at her and rolled her head.

"Easy," he said, and reached out, his hand hovering over her own, clenched on the reins.

"Sorry," she gasped, then, without meaning to, said, "you're too close!"

He flashed her a look—she saw his head jerk round, but she couldn't see the expression in his eyes—she was wholly focussed on the rough ground she could see framed by Reesa's ears. He backed off, though, shadowing her now a little behind, a couple of metres away to her right.

The Berbers were laughing and joking again, either oblivious or supremely tactful. Marianne just wanted to be not riding. Not running.

God, she wanted to be home.

No, you don't.

Alan sped past her to have a shouted conversation with the man in front on the reddish horse. It occurred to Marianne that she hadn't seen Alan this carefree since before she'd left Rabat. He laughed with the other riders, spitting something Arabic across the group that had them all laughing.

He was . . . happy. Almost.

Sometimes he would look across at her, where she was stoically riding on, and the smile would fade out of his darkening eyes and she was suddenly deaf to the laughter and the guttural words winging about in the dry, dry, dusty air. Then he didn't look happy, not really. He looked . . . troubled.

Troubled.

Marianne reset the reins in her hands again, and her stomach stirred unpleasantly. They weren't out of the woods yet, were they? They must still be in real danger, or he wouldn't be looking like that.

Would he?

It couldn't have lasted.

Alan must have been mad to think they could just waltz through and away to safety, never mind his pathetic half-plans to confuse the trail.

Well, his madness had lasted only a couple of hours. Right up to the moment he saw the dust trail of a vehicle coming close. The word whipped through the group like a dust devil. *Caution. Be at rest.*

He saw riders begin to bunch together, hemming Marianne in. He would have wheeled Azrou to join them, but suddenly there were three horses, then five, then six, between him and her, cutting him off, making him veer away.

The Land Rover pulled round ahead of them, and stopped. Two men got out the rear, and he could see both the driver and passenger seat occupied.

The riders came to a bouncing, shouting halt, calling greetings.

Ignoring the guns the men held as they began to move among the riders.

Alan caught fragments of loud exchanges. Bits of news. Things were quiet, the newcomers said. Only there'd been a theft, back at their village. They were searching for a thief.

What? Amongst us? Good humoured outrage was there

in the replies of his tribe. *Who knows the will of God,* one of the armed men replied, shrugging.

Azrou was tense under him, head down, snorting. A man beside him kicked him sharply in the ankle, and Alan forced himself to relax, desperate to stop his tension, his fear, leaching into the horse and calling attention to him. Azrou heaved a breath, annoyed, but holding it together. And there, in the middle of the group, Reesa was ... Reesa was being the placid, careful animal he knew her to be, standing relaxed, one hind leg rested, horse and rider looking equally calm and curious.

Mari was well covered up. No one was acting nervous. Maybe ... maybe ...

Azrou sidled again, and he had to loosen his grip again, hands and knees, very deliberately.

One of the men was walking among them, noticeably nervous of the horses, his AK-47 held tight across his chest. He peered closely at what he could see of the riders' faces.

Alan wanted, *needed* to be closer to Mari. To be in reach. To get to her in time, in case ... The sun was suddenly hotter. The horizon shimmered and melted in his sight. The carefully good-natured comments of his friends echoed in his ears, a long way off.

The man drew closer to Mari, looking curiously her way.

Brown eyes, Alan thought, crazily. *Brown eyes are safe.*

His own were blue. He hadn't brought the disguising contact lenses he often used. Which was why the men and horses pressed him at the edge of the little cavalcade, far from trouble.

Far from Mari.

The man was at Reesa's side now. Mari was facing the other way, nodding her swathed head at the man on her right.

Alan was so proud of her he ached with it.

The armed man laid a hand on her left boot.

She had to look round now. It would look strange if she didn't. She would look round, and although brown eyes were safe, known eyes were not, obviously feminine eyes were not, and he had to get to her, he had to, *he had to* . . .

Azrou was bunching under him, snorting, ready to rear, ready to go to a plunging gallop in one stride, but he was too late, there was movement . . .

But the movement was a horse near Mari shying suddenly, barging into the man who stood at her side. It happened so quickly even Alan, who was watching for it, could hardly follow it. The shying of the horse, distracting the armed man. The rider on the other side of Mari, who grabbed her reins and wheeled her away, covered by a sudden surging and shuffling of horses so that another was standing in Reesa's place almost at the same moment the first horse shied.

And the armed man, embarrassed and angry, backtracked quickly, clearly afraid of being trampled.

Dust and confusion. Laughter and teasing. And the men climbing back into the Land Rover and driving away.

Alan felt weak, dizzy. Unspent adrenaline pumping in

his system. The man on his right rolled his eyes disgustedly at him, and went to join the ring of riders around Mari, calling their compliments, patting her on the back. Alan wanted to be with them, but one look at his face, he knew, would magnify Mari's fear tenfold.

He stayed where he was. And Azrou, thwarted and confused, took advantage of lax hands and lapsed attention to dump him neatly in the dust on his arse.

chapter eleven

"We're early." Alan held her stirrup as she came down out of the saddle. She hit the ground hard and yelped, as much from the impact on her feet as from the burning ache of muscles and bones rearranging themselves into an attitude suitable for standing upright. Immediately Alan wrapped his free hand round her waist and held her against him. He was solid and comforting, a height, a breadth that fit her perfectly, that made him oh-so-easy to lean on. With an uneasy sense of doing something less than wise, Mari tipped her head back against his shoulder to look at his face.

Burning bright eyes, brows slanting steeply in a frown. That, and the rigidity of the arm across her back, the studied lightness of the touch of his hand at her hip, were her only clues. His face was hidden—the man was hidden.

I don't know you, she thought.

But I want you anyway.

Her heart pounded in her throat. She felt dizzy, hot.

But it was a *different* kind of dizzy and hot. This was not heat exhaustion, not dehydration.

This was not fear.

There had been fear enough when the armed men had stopped them. She'd felt out of place, felt she stuck out like a sore thumb in that crowd of competent, consummate horsemen. So she'd taken her cues from Reesa, and from the men around her, and felt nothing short of triumphant when it had worked. She'd looked around, wanting to see Alan, wanting his praise.

But he hadn't approached her.

Not till now.

"Okay?" he said, his voice muffled by something more than just the folds of dusty cloth.

"Ow," she said, with feeling, but she straightened and took a step away under her own steam, anyway. Better to concentrate on those aches. Alan passed Reesa to one of their riding companions and looked around them.

The well wasn't quite what she'd expected. A dusty road, a cluster of square, squat white buildings. Awnings and stalls, a fenced-off enclosure of moth-eaten-looking camels, and a sudden, verdant splash of lush growth, marking the well itself. There were actually date palms.

Date palms and camels.

Mari shook her head. This whole thing was unreal. "What do you mean, early?"

"If the tribe hadn't been there, we'd have had to walk a lot further. We weren't supposed to be here till tonight, so we're early. Kier isn't here yet."

Alarm pulsed through her. "You're sure it's just be-cause we're early?" She thought about Jenny and the niece and nephew he'd talked about on the ride.

And then she thought about Alan, asking his brother-in-law to walk into risk to rescue a stranger.

"Yeah, I'm sure. He'll find us tonight."

"So what now?"

"Food, shade, rest, being unobtrusive," he set off down the rough track behind a row of buildings, and she walked alongside. A woman in black, sorting beans into two bas-kets, watched them pass, busy hands not pausing.

The little track, not more than a footpath, wound into the scraggly bushes at the edge of the well, and Alan picked aside a branch of thorns to let her go ahead. The shade of the palm was fabulous.

The scent of the water hit her first. She'd forgotten that water had a smell. And there was real water here, not just a stone well or a pump, but real, open water, only a few metres wide, but there nonetheless, protected by the shade.

"Oh," said Alan. "And your first oasis."

"It's lovely," she breathed.

On the other side, one of their companions was water-ing the horses in twos and threes, at a trough fed by the oa-sis. He lifted his head and winked at them, while the horses slurped and sucked, and she inclined her head solemnly in answer, lifting her hand in a copy of the salaam gesture with-out thought. Alan gripped her shoulder lightly, something of approval, of affection, and Mari shut her eyes, her mind, and her heart, and just breathed in the scent of water.

One sweet thing at a time.

$$\text{\aa\aa\aa}$$

"Did they hurt you, Mari?" The words arrived at Alan's mouth without the apparent intervention of his brain. And only then did he acknowledge just how long he'd been carrying that question, and not daring to ask it.

He cradled Mari's left foot in his lap, just soaking the last of the bandages off with bottled water. It looked better. It was better: less dirty, less inflamed. But the sight of her wounded, hurting flesh still made him want to weep. He looked up to see Mari, sitting with her back against a date palm, water bottle arrested halfway to her mouth. When her face was covered she looked more like a native than he did—strands of hair like polished dark oak, those sweet, treacle toffee eyes.

"It took you long enough to ask me, didn't it?" And that voice wasn't Mari at all. Not at all.

"I wanted to give you some space." *Liar.* And he was still lying to her, with every breath. He put aside the old bandage, and trickled cool water over the blisters and sores.

"Me? Or you?"

God. He ducked his head and closed his eyes, fingers light on her delicate ankle, cupping her worn and damaged heel. Her foot trembled in his grasp.

"What the hell is this, Alan?" she asked, low voiced.

"What?" *Coward.*

Stop abusing yourself and engage brain, Waring.

She huffed. "You know, I always thought I was stupid—"

"You're not." He swallowed hard, took up a packet of antiseptic wipes and began cleaning, gently as he could.

"But," she enunciated clearly, "it's rapidly becoming apparent that I'm not stupid at all. And since we are agreed I am not stupid, Alan, will you please cut the crap and tell me why you know this place like you were born here, why you carry guns like you know how to use them, and why you came after me?"

"No."

Take me to the desert, Alan.

No.

He expected her to blow up. He should have known better.

"Why not?"

He took a tighter hold on her ankle, expecting her to want to retreat. Not easy, arguing with a man who set fingers to your hurting, sensitive skin. "Because this is not the time or the place. Mari, I would tell you if I could, but . . ." He sighed. "I swear I'm only trying to protect you."

He picked up a clean bandage in its sterile wrapper. "I'll have to bind them again," he said. "They could do with some air, but I daren't let the slightest speck of sand in there."

There was a pause. Then she spoke, almost conversationally. "You know, all those years I was looking after Dad, he and the doctor conspired to keep me in the dark about the progress of his illness. They 'didn't want to worry' me."

Alan winced. His hands passed round her foot, smoothly, carefully, tugging the cotton into line.

"They kept me out, sidelined me. Dad controlled everything, making plans for himself, for me. And then, when he couldn't control things anymore, the doctor took over. I was his carer, but my opinion didn't matter. My voice wasn't heard.

"Do you remember that dream I told you about, Alan, on the beach?"

He nodded, not meeting her eyes.

"That dream started before he died. Months before. Dad made plans, left strict instructions, left me with no decisions to make, or conditions to negotiate. He refused offer after offer of care and treatment for himself, never stopping to think how that might affect me. But since both of them were perfectly happy to rearrange my whole life according to that progress, that exclusion seems bloody unfair, now."

"Sorry . . ."

"Sorry isn't good enough."

He was silent. She thumped the ground with her fist.

"You hear me?" she said fiercely.

"Yes, I hear you. Mari, you have to understand—I

only have so much energy." He was finished, but he held onto her lightly for a moment more, bowed over, trying to articulate at least *some* of what drove him. "I'm used to being out here by myself, not having to concern myself with anyone else's welfare. There's a lot to tell you, I'll admit that—you *know* that, but I can't deal with that *and* get you out of here."

You. Not us.

Marianne felt the impact of the words twist sourly in her stomach. Suddenly the spurt of anger that had powered her blew away like so much insubstantial dust, leaving her tired and drooping. Her head was aching, as much from tiredness as from getting her head round the gaps and inconsistencies in everything Alan was telling her. And not telling her.

"I have to get you safe first, Mari. Then we'll talk. I promise you we'll talk."

She lifted her foot out of his lap. The fresh dressings were a comfort, but she could still feel his fingers on the soft skin above her ankle. As the palms moved in the hot breeze, the pattern of light changed—one moment his face seemed dark and shadowed, sullen, then wild and golden, bright. How could he sit there, cross-legged at her feet, physically a supplicant, while still in control, in charge? The piper who played.

Well, she would not dance.

She couldn't. Her feet hurt.

Except that wasn't right, either. She would if he asked. He had the power to make her strong when she was weak, and now, when she was stronger, he had the power to make her weak.

Lost in her thoughts, she jumped when he spoke again. "You didn't answer my question. Did they hurt you?"

She laughed. At least, she'd intended it as a laugh. "Well, that makes two of us not answering questions."

He made some gesture with his hand, or so it seemed, but then he reached for bit of stone and threw it into the pool.

But in the end, she wanted to tell him anyway. And she didn't examine that need too closely, either. "They didn't hurt me. Not really. They—it's easier with the distance, you know? I was terrified then. Every shove or hard word was magnified. They barely touched me. But I was scared. I think they were waiting for someone. They were always afraid. Even in charge, they were afraid, looking over their shoulder, hesitant all the time. I think they were waiting for someone, and they didn't dare . . . damage me until they arrived.

"They shouted at me a lot, and were cruel, as much as they could be when I didn't understand much of what they said. They tried French, and I picked up some of that, but mostly they spoke Arabic—and expected me to understand. I don't think they believed that I didn't."

"They wouldn't. They thought you were . . ." Alan

stopped, and for a moment his face seemed almost hellish. "They must have thought you had reason to know."

She heaved a sigh. "Well, I don't understand it. But we can add it to the list. I don't understand any of this."

He turned his head, and she caught the glitter of his eyes. There was barely two feet between them, but she had the odd idea that if she moved an inch either way, it would be shatteringly important. And—*oh damn*—she wanted to be closer. She drew up her knees and wrapped her arms about them.

And we can add clinging female to the list of inconvenient baggage, she thought with disgust. *Together with hysterical female, damaged female, and intractable female.*

A procession of ugly words marched through her mind, words that might not have been applied to the Marianne of old, but stuck like muck to the new reproved version. There was a lump in her throat, a hard, aching lump. If she swallowed it, it would choke her. Ducking her head, she pressed her eyes against her knees until she saw wheeling chequerboards.

There was a shuffling sound from Alan's direction, and she felt a sudden spurt of sympathy for him. There was a hell of a lot more she had no intention of telling him, too.

In her mind, she saw blood on the rush carpeting, on the desk.

She willed it away.

chapter twelve

Kier was late.

His ETA had come and gone. The sun had dipped and died. Now there were lights here and there—fires and lamps, and the purr of a generator running electric lighting in a house nearby. And Alan was struggling to keep his fears from Mari. Except . . . what had she said?

"*. . . they conspired to keep me in the dark . . .*"

He tugged the cloth down and scrubbed a hand over his face. It seemed bloody unfair, unreasonable, and inadequate to be burdening Mari with his own worries.

He hated not having a *plan*.

Turning his back on the little thoroughfare, he headed to the back of the oasis, where Mari sat leaning on a palm, half-obscured by bushes, with her feet up on the rucksack. They'd been quiet and had attracted little attention. He came close, and she tipped back her head to look up at him. He wondered what to say.

She supplied the words. "You're worried about Kier."

The rope of tension that had been coiling him tight since the sun had gone down slackened a little, and he crouched down in front of her, propping his elbows on his knees.

"Yes," he said simply.

She nodded, her eyes thoughtful. Not a hint of panic, nothing of terror. His heart swelled with a kind of pride he had no right to feel.

"How late is he?"

"About two hours."

"Okay," she said reasonably. "So what do we do now?"

Rising, he took two steps towards the water's edge. It lay utterly still, a black mirror of the night sky. His own reflection was just a shadow, a dark presence hiding the stars.

"I don't know." Since there could be nothing—nothing in the world—harder to say to her than those three little words, he wondered why he didn't just tell her the lot. In his sleeves, his hands were fists.

He heard her come to her feet. "Never mind," she said, softly, at his back. "We'll plan in the morning. There's nothing we can do just now, and you have to be tired."

Her sensible, caring words cut through him, sharper than accusations, colder than contempt. *Kick me while I'm down, why don't you?* "I don't need *sympathy*. I need to come up with a *plan!*" Even as he spat out the words, Alan knew it was unjust. She was only . . . being Mari. Sweet, kind, incurably giving.

God help him, he was going straight to hell.

He felt her hands on him and let her turn him to face her, trusting the almost-darkness to shield his face. But she still stepped back a little when she saw him, eyes wide.

"I'm sorry, Alan. I don't understand much of this— I'll admit that. But I do know you came after me, and you saved me."

She reared up on tiptoe, placing a light hand against his chest, just under his collarbone. With her face tipped up, he could see the unexpected golden flecks in her brown eyes. And the dart of a pink tongue wetting her lips. He tensed.

"Thank you," she said, and kissed him.

He turned to stone. She laid her lips tentatively on his, little more than a soft, warm touch, then drew away with her eyes lowered.

And he was standing there, breathing hard through his nose, teeth aching with the clenching of them, afraid to take one tiny step towards responding, in case . . . in case . . .

Dear heaven, he wasn't even clear what he was afraid of anymore. Now, just now, with Mari stepping away, a flush of colour in her cheeks, apparently humiliated from having had the gracious sweetness to attempt the kissing of a stone statue.

"It's okay, Alan," she said, with a twist of her lovely lips and too much brittle lightness. "I wasn't expecting you to do anything about it. You didn't have to—"

A strand of that rope of control broke, twisting free of the rest, flailing wildly, loosely. His whole body shuddered with the release of only that tiny twisted strand.

He groaned, stepping forward, grabbing hold of her as she tried to turn away, and hauling her back to him. He tipped her off balance into his arms with a hard grip on her shoulders. She tumbled against him with a cry, stumbling for balance, but he didn't let her find it. One arm went round her back, one hand under her chin, and then he had her mouth, all his, all his, feeling it blossom and move under his.

Her lips weren't soft—but then his were scratchy and chapped, too, and what did that matter? He had them, and now he had her tongue too, sweetly lifting to greet his. He bit at her lower lip, making her open wider, and thrust his tongue inside.

She tasted like everything he needed. And since he needed it, he took it, shutting his mind to his own restraint so effectively it took a few moments to register she was trying to pull away. He let her go, sharpish, then caught hold of her arm again when she stumbled. She shook him off, finding her balance, and then stood there, openmouthed, staring up at him.

She took a step back towards him, her eyes going a little unfocused, then she danced back away, dark eyes wide. "What the hell was *that*?" she all but shouted.

And it was only then that he realised he'd never kissed her that way before. Even in bed, he'd always been gentle, coaxing, courteous. She'd never experienced him . . . unleashed.

"I'm sorry," he managed, wondering whose voice he was using, since it certainly didn't sound like his.

"Sorry! I don't want an apology! I just . . . what *was* that?"

And suddenly, quite suddenly, he wanted to laugh. He remembered her breathless chorus of "why, what, how" in the Rabat hotel room. Here they were again. He was under examination.

He loved . . . the way she did that. That was all.

"I didn't mean to scare you, Mari."

"I wasn't scared. Well, not now." She licked her lip, chewed it thoughtfully. Something inside his mind whimpered.

"I liked it," she admitted, huskily.

Holy Mother of—

"I just didn't understand it."

Mari.

"I'm not sure it's that easy to explain."

She raised her eyebrows at him. "Easy? I didn't expect easy. Anyway," she shrugged. "You don't do easy."

Ain't that the truth?

"I wanted to kiss you. And you were provocative enough that I didn't care much about how you wanted to be kissed. I kissed you how *I* wanted to."

"Provocative?" There was that small, scared, *can I believe a compliment?* voice again. Damn.

"Yes. Definitely."

She looked at him a long time, and he let her, thinking it was little enough to pay under the circumstances, even if she had apparently developed the ability to read the lines off the back of his skull in the last few days.

Eventually she spoke again. "Back in Rabat, when we . . . I thought it was to help me, to be kind. That wasn't entirely true, was it?"

"That was part of it. I'll admit that. Another part was the part about feeling like I was going to die if I didn't have you."

"You wanted me." It was half statement, half question. But it was more than half wondering.

"Mari! Didn't you know what you did to me? Do to me?"

She shrugged. "How could I?"

There was that, wasn't there? "Okay. Right," he said, feeling like the hunted man at night wearing a glow-in-the-dark 'Shoot Me' T-shirt. "Let's get this clear once and for all. I want you. I wanted you from the first time I saw you—I want you still. I want you when you're a week shy of a bath, when you're pissed off, when you're downright aggravating. I want you especially bad when you look right into my eyes like you care what you see. When I can *see* you thinking about sex—"

"I don't!"

"—you do. When that happens I get hard, fast. And, no matter that you'd be showering out sand for a week, I want to take you down to the ground and get inside you. Again and again."

She was red. Then she was white. Red again.

"Clear?"

"Oh."

"Mari?"

"Oh. Yes." She fiddled with her neckline, still doing the doe-eyed thing. He wasn't being fair.

"Mari," he sighed, and flopped down cross-legged on the ground. He held up his hand to her. She made him wait, but eventually she took it, and he pulled her gently down into his lap, never mind that he'd suffer for it.

She sat there stiffly for a while, but he rubbed her back with deep, slow strokes, and slowly she curled into him.

"Mari, Mari . . . You wanted me to tell you." No, that was the wrong place to start. "It doesn't mean I'm going to jump you somewhere. Your safety and welfare are my top priority."

Better late than never, Waring.

"You're too traumatised to be trying any new intimacies."

"It's not new. We did it before."

He sighed. "You're not going to make this easy, are you?"

"Easy? No."

There it was again, the threat of laughter. He gave in, rocking her with his chuckling, reflecting that despite everything, trust was still a part of their relationship, or she wouldn't be curled up in his lap talking about sex.

But it wouldn't be too long before he would be killing that trust. Because it was based on lies. Dangerous lies.

※ ※ ※

Kier arrived barely an hour later, quite as if bowling into a Saharan oasis in the dead of night was an everyday occurrence. He dropped out of the driver's seat, nodding to Alan.

Mari watched him stretch. She got to her feet, more relieved than she cared to show. She was rather wary of this big, dark, brother-in-law of Alan's. She wondered if Jenny was an Amazon.

"Sorry I'm late," he said.

"Any trouble?" Alan asked, looking over the vehicle.

Kier shrugged. "Nothing significant." Then he fixed his eyes on her. "Hey."

She chewed her lip, and brushed dust off her seat. "Hi."

"How are you feeling now?" Kier asked, quite gently, and she was surprised. She'd thought him distant before, and only now suspected that reticence might have been the product of tact, not carelessness.

He still made her feel shy, though. "Better, thank you." Turning back to Alan, Kier asked, "Moving out now?"

"If you're okay?"

"If you'll take the wheel for a while, I'll be fine."

Alan looked across at her. "Mari? Are you rested enough?"

No, Alan, I fancy hanging around here while you two

twiddle your thumbs and get impatient. "I'm fine."

"Good," he said, and swung up into the driver's seat.

Kier helped her up into the back. He was harsher looking than Alan, close up. She preferred her golden desert-prince.

"If you wedge yourself in the footwell," he said, softly, "you might be able to get some more rest."

She blinked at his smile and wondered where in heaven he'd managed to shave. "Thank you."

"Don't mention it," he said, and shut the door.

🏵 🏵 🏵

Marianne watched Alan screw the cap back on the jerry can strapped to the back of the vehicle.

"We need more fuel. That detour cost us."

Kier leaned on the corner beside him. "Where?"

Alan sighed, wiping his hands on a rag. He stared off toward the distant mountains. "We'll have to go into El Aricha. We can get supplies there."

"Won't they be looking for her?" Kier asked.

Out of the corner of her eye, Mari saw Alan glance over to where she sat with her legs dangling off the side of the passenger seat. She pretended not to be paying attention, swinging her legs listlessly.

She'd slept fitfully through the night, waking always to whispered conversations going on over her head. Kier had been right last night: wedged into the footwell between the rucksack and a couple of blankets, she'd been held securely enough, and hardly jolted at all. At dawn they'd stopped for a breakfast of bread and water, watching the light slowly reveal the mountains ahead.

Alan moved closer to Kier and dropped his voice anyway. "We don't even know who 'they' are! But it's my guess we'll be safe there. I know a place."

"A place?"

"It's just a café. But it has a reputation as neutral ground. It's a good source of information."

"I thought we were after fuel?"

Out of the corner of her eye, Mari saw Alan shift, moving his weight to his right foot and back again. She could read the glare off the back of his covered head.

"Kier," he said, low, "have you ever known a conflict to end well when you knew absolutely nothing about your adversary? I'm sick to death of being ill-informed, unprepared, and wrong-footed. Whoever we're up against holds all the cards. I would like at least the opportunity to cheat."

"I'd have said we had at least one ace."

Marianne hid a smile. *Thanks, Kier.*

There was a scuffing sound. A boot on sand.

"Mari is not a card," Alan said. "She is the prize."

Mari held her breath. Kier grunted.

"In any case," Alan continued, "we don't have a choice, do we? The next refuelling stop is Tlemcen, and we'll never make it. El Aricha serves this whole area."

"All the more reason why our enemies might be there."

"You don't seem to be hearing me," Alan hissed. "We don't have a choice. It's refuel or walk."

Kier raised his hands. "Don't fight with me. You didn't bring me along for my blind obedience."

Alan snorted and rubbed the back of his neck.

She looked across at him now, discussing details with Kier, leaving her out again. A few days' worth of beard highlighted his jaw, catching the sun and glinting golden. He looked tired. His hair was lank and he kept sweeping it off his face until it stayed away, held by sand and salt. But he was still . . . magnificent. Still Alan.

And she still didn't have a single defence against him. "No" was not in her vocabulary for Alan.

⚹ ⚹ ⚹

They hit the town two hours later, bowling into what was, for want of a better word, the high street, throwing up dust and creating interest. It couldn't be helped—this place was way off the usual routes even for determined travellers.

Keir was driving, and he dropped them at the entrance to a narrow, awning-covered alley, then drove off in search of supplies. Alan took her by the arm and guided her into the alley, and out into a tiny square with dusty shrubs in blue pots. There, under a brighter awning, was a café, with two metal tables outside.

They passed through the door inside, and Mari blinked for a while in the gloom. Gradually she could see a few older men, sitting alone at tables, or conversing seriously. Predictably, they went quiet and stared when they went in.

"It's more likely to be a problem if we try to conceal you and someone sees through it," Alan had explained when he'd given her the expurgated version of where they were going next, and why. "Leave your head bare and ditch most of the desert gear. But keep yourself decently covered, okay?"

So now she was dressed in a weird hybrid of clothing— Kier's combat trousers, rolled up and belted, one of Alan's shirts, arms likewise rolled, and her big over robe that Alan called a burnous over the lot. It gave her an extra feeling of covering and security, however illusionary that might be.

Now in the café, she fiddled with her hair, self-conscious under the stares, but Alan guided her over to a table at the back in the corner.

"I'll get us both some coffee. No," he said, when she would have sat facing the room, "I'll sit there."

He went over to the counter, and she settled, feeling the stares on her back, and suddenly damned if she would let it get to her. She lifted her head high and sat straight, and, slowly, the low hum of conversation resumed.

Alan returned with the coffees, short, dark, and strong.

They stirred them in silence, Alan leaning his forearm across the table, and Mari watching him.

"If it's safe to be here, can't we stay here a night?" she asked eventually.

He shook his head. "Safe is a relative term. We need

to be in and out of here as soon as we can."

She tugged at her hair. "It would just be nice to have a bath, you know?"

He grinned and pulled at his own shirt distastefully. "I *do* know, believe me. But we can't Mari, I'm sorry."

She sighed. "I know. Never mind. How long will Kier be?"

"Not sure. Depends how much haggling he has to do."

"Are we going to eat here?"

"Maybe. It depends . . ." He broke off, staring past her with a frozen expression. "Bloody hellfire."

"What is—"

He slapped a hand down on hers. "Don't turn round."

"What is it?"

"Who."

"What?"

"Not what, who." He craned to see past her, half out of his chair. "It's someone who shouldn't be here."

He flicked a glance back at her, hard and assessing. "Hell."

His hand tightened on hers. "Stay here. Do no—"

"Oh no, Alan!"

"Do not move. Don't talk to anyone and do not, under any circumstances, leave this seat. Do you understand?"

She sat silent, lips pressed together.

"Mari," he pleaded, "it's important. This person . . . he might know something about this whole mess. *Please.*"

She pulled her hand away and folded it in her lap. "Go."

He hesitated, obviously torn.

"Go, Alan. I'll wait here. Just don't . . . be long."

He dropped a hand on her shoulder briefly, and was gone.

She slumped a little then, honestly scared, if only of being stuck in a café in a foreign country with no money and two coffees to pay for. Lifting the little cup, she drank a little of the hot brew, but it hit her stomach like pure acid. She set it down and clasped her fingers together in her lap.

Hating having her back to the door, she shuffled round into Alan's seat. The courtyard outside was drenched in sunlight, empty. A figure paused at the entrance to the alley, and she tensed, even though Alan had only been gone for a second. It wasn't him, anyway, but it wasn't a local, either. It was a man of medium height, with neatly cut hair that might have been fair, and might have been grey. He paused at the end of the alleyway, glancing in. Then she saw the flash of white teeth as he smiled, turned, and walked towards the café.

He was obviously Western, dressed in travel gear, very much at ease. He stepped inside, paused at the counter for an exchange she couldn't hear, then glanced across and came over.

"May I?" His accent was French, his English excellent.

"Oh. I'm not sure . . . my friend—"

"I'm sure he won't mind," he said, turning to thank

the man who came over with his coffee. "We Westerners must stick together, yes?" He stirred the cup, inhaling the fragrance with appreciation. She peered over his shoulder, desperate for a glimpse of Alan.

Pale eyes studied her with polite interest. She struggled with the urge to fidget under that smooth stare. "You seem to have been in the wars?"

She smiled noncommittally. "Things have been eventful." There was something in his manner that made her wonder what it was that was amusing him. Someone stepped into the courtyard, but it was only another local, disappearing into another door on the right.

Where was Alan? Who had he seen?

The Frenchman took a small packet out of his shirt pocket—a square shape, made of plastic, like a sim card. He waved it in front of her, then held it on its corner on the table top, rocking it with one finger.

"You have no idea what this is, do you?" he asked.

She breathed hard, nervous. "Should I?"

He pursed his lips, then smiled. "Not necessarily. But I'd be ready to swear you do not. Let me tell you."

"It is a smart card, Mademoiselle." He leant closer, staring into her eyes. "It's worth billions," he whispered.

Helplessly, her eyes fell to the little plastic square. What did he mean?

He smiled more broadly. "Sometimes life seems full of wonderful coincidences, but I believe that there are no coincidences in life, Mademoiselle, only good planning. I always plan to have people where I need them. One cannot be everywhere at once, after all." He waved a hand, and Mari strained to see past him, looking for Alan.

"A pair of eyes here, a reliable messenger there . . . and there are only so many oases, only so many towns in this part of the Sahara," he said, still smiling.

"I'm sorry. I don't know—"

He tucked the smart-card away in a pocket. "There are so few pretty young women of your appearance waltzing around Algeria, Miss Marianne Forster."

She felt cold, then hot.

After everything, it shouldn't have been a surprise when he hit her. But he was very quick, and she was not—she tried to dodge his fist, but it caught her on the cheek, up near her eye. Pain exploded, she reeled backwards, trying to cry out, but blackness slammed her down.

⊛ ⊛ ⊛

Alan raced down the side street that cut ahead of the alley.

It couldn't be. For a moment, when he'd spotted the man outside in the little square, he'd hardly believed his eyes. Stuart Bristow? Here? How? What possible purpose could his HQ contact have here? In Algeria? In this very town?

Were they looking for him?

None of the possible answers were good.

And a great deal of HQ's *edginess* and *disorganisation*

suddenly resolved itself down to one man. Stuart Bristow, who'd been on *sick leave* when Alan asked HQ to help. Who, Alan was willing to swear, was now lurking in a small town in middle-of-nowhere, Algeria.

He turned a corner and came on a small but busy market place. He scanned the crowd quickly, aware of Mari all alone in the quiet café that was, believe it or not, the best kept and fondest held secret of a number of agents active in this area.

It was, nominally, neutral. A place like that was too good to muck about with petty allegiances and power plays. So even some of his, for want of a better word, colleagues, who were active for another nation, or to the highest bidder, used that little café and kept quiet about it.

So Mari should be safe there. Unless. Unless someone wasn't playing by the rules.

And Stuart's presence here suggested the rules had been blown to kingdom come. And no one had seen fit to inform him.

Alan looked past a clutch of women, a haggling group at a corner stall, a man with a bundle over his shoulder, a small boy with some goats. Nothing.

He had to get back to Mari.

Bloody hell.

He was torn, indecisive, wanting to go back to Mari, needing to get a clue to the rules of the game they were unwittingly playing. Then Alan remembered he didn't work for HQ anymore. Didn't have any sanction to be here, or any right to know how the rules might or might not have changed. For all he knew, Stuart was the new courier in this region.

He doubted it. The man had no coolness under fire. In fact, in any other circumstances, Alan might have hesitated to trust him. But HQ knew what they were doing—it wasn't his job to query that. Except . . . there was that unease he'd felt in Rabat, that sense of things not . . . right.

He scanned the crowd again. Women, haggling group, man with bundle, boy with goats.

Man with bundle.

Man in Western dress with bundle that moved sluggishly, that, just before it disappeared from view, showed a small, pale hand emerging limply from beneath swathes of black cloth.

Dear God in heaven.

She was supposed to be safe. He had her *safe*.

Alan's vision narrowed to a bright tunnel. Other sounds blurred and faded into a low hum. He heard his own breathing as he ran, felt the angry pump of adrenaline fizz in his blood.

Not this time.

She was already free.

He was not losing her again.

He'd left his Browning 9mm taped under the dash—it not being wise to be found carrying in this brink of civilisation.

He was unarmed. But he was mad.

It was enough.

🕸 🕸 🕸

Kier drummed his fingers on the wheel and looked out at the last few scraggly dwellings on the outskirts of town. He was parked just where Alan had agreed to meet him, in the fortunate shade of a clutch of palms a stone's through from the town's limits.

And Alan wasn't here yet.

Not good.

He scanned what he could see of the town's entrances and exits—here a narrow gap between two white-painted houses, there a rutted road—and thought about relocating.

Dammit, not enough options. Alan was in charge here—which left Kier in the unaccustomed role of following orders.

Of course, his solitary detour with Marianne's enemies in pursuit had been mildly amusing.

But not nearly amusing as it might have once been.

He knew Jenny had been wondering if his life was enough for him now. Some security work, a wife, children . . . a number of fix-up projects. She'd taken to fretting again. And, truth be told, he had begun to feel restless. Which had disturbed him, because he loved Jenny with a passion that had not and would not, if he was any judge, abate. She couldn't have lived with his old, dangerous work, and he couldn't have left her. Not ever.

But it didn't matter now.

Because that detour had only been *mildly* amusing. Because when called to slip into the old mould of himself, those bounds had felt alien and restrictive. Dry and dead.

It is easier to kill a man to stop him, after all. Easier than working to disable him, distract him, misinform him. And none of the eight pursuers he had . . . discouraged from pursuit . . . were likely to suffer more than a temporary discomfort and inconvenience. Well, Kier acknowledged fairly, one of them was going to have a slightly more interesting nose now, but that couldn't be helped.

The point was—and there was a point he stressed to himself, watching a cluster of local men hop into the truck that stopped on the town's edge—the point was that there had been no temptation to resume old ways. Jenny had been with him all the time. He was a changed man—she'd changed him, not temporarily, not slightly. Permanently. And he loved it.

And he missed her constantly, deeply, like an ache in his gut.

More than that, he missed his children—their children— all the time. Little Kirstie's wide, dark, Jenny-serious eyes waiting for explanations. Alex's sturdy, frowning concentration, applying himself to some new challenge. Kirstie's wilful, deliberate disobedience, testing her boundaries. Alex's gleeful mischief, more than willing to clear up any messes he made because making them had been *so cool*.

He wanted to be home, needed to be home. With her, with them.

A man hopped out of the truck again and checked the fastenings on the tailgate. Still no Alan.

He'd achieved a new sympathy for Alan, clearly in love with Marianne, and not yet able to see that. There was pain ahead for both of them, far worse than the pain he knew being without Jenny. Because he'd get back to his family, soon, if he had his way, and all would be well. No, better, because that restlessness would be cured once and for all.

But Alan and Mari . . . God, he hardly knew how they were going to manage. Sincerely, he doubted they'd manage at all.

Certainly not if Alan couldn't work up the courage to tell her everything. And then . . . he'd hardly blame her for knocking the poor guy into next week. And he wouldn't put it past her now, either. He'd not known Marianne before. But Marianne now was someone he wouldn't mind at his side in a tight spot. Okay, so she was struggling at the moment. But Kier could clearly see past the emotional trauma she was dealing with to the new strength beneath.

He was fairly sure Alan didn't.

He heard a shout. The truck took off in a cloud of dust.

Alan came sprinting down the road, more pissed than Kier had yet seen him.

Damn.

Kier reached over and punched the passenger door open, then took first and hit the gas.

❀ ❀ ❀

Alan didn't stop running when the Rover roared towards him. He simply caught hold of the passenger door as it came level and swung inside.

"Mari!" he gasped. "They snatched her!" He reached under the dash and liberated his Browning, checking the clip was full.

Kier had the truck in sight, some two hundred yards ahead, and was keeping back. "Are we risking her? By following?"

"No. They still think she has info they need. And I think I now know who has the data she was carrying."

Kier grunted.

"A man took her, a Westerner, not a local." Alan reached over the seat and ripped up the rubber flooring in the rear footwell. "He jumped in the truck just inside town."

"They picked up two more in front of me," Kier said.

"So presumably we have snatcher, driver, and two more."

Kier grunted. "Could be more. So who has the data?"

"My guess is the one who has her is the one they were waiting for, the boss, and they will have the smart card."

He brought up the two AK-47s, checked them over, and stowed them between Kier and himself.

"And how did this man come to take Mari with you

standing by?" Kier's voice dripped sarcasm. Alan didn't blame him—he was feeling a little sarcastic towards himself, too.

"You needn't think I'm not aware your opinion of me is falling daily." The words tasted sour in his mouth. He remembered exchanges like this with Kier before they had worked out a workable friendship. Before he'd seen his sister, Jenny, happier than he had ever known her, even when their parents were alive.

He felt Kier throw a look at him, but he didn't answer.

"You cannot, in this lifetime, blame me more than I do. But this time, remarkably enough, I did have good reason."

"Yeah?" Kier's voice was mild, under the circumstances. "Check my gun over, will you?"

"Yup. I saw a man who had no business here. His name is Stuart Bristow, and he's my liaison from HQ. He's the one who told me to move the data any way possible, and he's the one who, in hindsight, has been acting unnecessarily nervous."

"Hmmm. We have a conspirator?"

"I wasn't even sure we had one, but yes, now . . . It has to be him. And I want a word with him."

"You think he's in that truck?"

"Not sure. But we'll find out."

"Plan?" Kier queried.

"Plan?" Alan settled himself facing front and dropped the window on the passenger side. "McAllister, I am more pissed off now than I can remember ever having been in my life. I have no plan. I am the plan. Get me in there."

Kier was smiling. He dropped a gear, floored the accelerator. "My pleasure."

chapter thirteen

When this was all over, Alan would invest in big, hard-toed boots for all his friends, for the purpose of kicking him with. For now, he had to be content with kicking himself.

To be fair, there wasn't much else he could have done—he *had* to react to Bristow's presence in northern Algeria. He knew, somehow, that man must be the key he was looking for.

To be fair, he'd done what he had to.

He didn't feel like being fair. He felt like being lethal.

His blood surged, heat and satisfaction.

Ahead of them the truck was bouncing and lurching on the bad road, its canvas vibrating. The wheels threw up a broad column of dust, and Alan grabbed a pair of ski goggles from behind his seat and put them on. No question they knew they were pursued. No question at all when the rear flap was shouldered aside by a man trying—and failing—to hold a rifle one-handed.

"Idiot," said Alan, evenly, transferring the Browning to his left hand and sliding that arm out the window.

"Be reasonable," said Kier. "He has to hold on to something." The man in the truck let off a couple of rounds. They missed. "He's scared of falling," Kier pointed out.

"Mostly he should be scared of missing," replied Alan. "Take me on a diagonal, will you?"

Kier spun the wheel to the right. "You're left-handed?"

"Sometimes."

Alan watched the road, read the terrain, and squeezed the trigger in the split second both vehicles were suspended at the height of a bounce. The man shouted something, clutched at the side of the truck, and pitched out.

Kier swerved to avoid hitting him as he tumbled to the ground. "One down."

"Indeed."

The Landy bounced on a rock that clanged sharply up into the wheel arch. The road took a bend round a cluster of rocks, and the truck leaned alarmingly. Alan swore.

Now the road ran alongside a small canyon that held back much rougher ground.

A second man emerged, more cautiously than the first, crouched down behind the tailgate. Alan squinted to see through the dust. He didn't appear to be armed, but he was fiddling with something in his hand . . .

Grenade.

Alan snapped a glance at the canyon on their left. "Might I suggest you—" but the words were cut off as Kier stamped hard on the brake, dropped a gear, and pulled hard left.

They went down the two-foot drop in an explosion of noise and violent motion. The whole vehicle shuddered as its belly hit the edge, but the momentum spat them down into the chasm, throwing up sand and stone. Forced to take the drop at a diagonal, it seemed for a moment that they would roll. Alan, with one shoulder thrown against the angle between the roof and the door, braced himself there with one foot, and shoved Kier back in his seat with his other foot on Kier's hip.

A split second behind them, the grenade went off.

Kier wrenched them back on course. "Tut tut," he said, entering into the spirit of things.

Alan worked his left shoulder. Stiff, but not useless. Excellent. "At least we're out of the dust."

"Does the phrase 'shooting fish in a barrel' mean anything to you?"

Alan looked ahead. The little wadi was just a foot or two wider than the Landy at base level and ran straight and true parallel to the road. They were running almost alongside the truck now. All of which made them harder to target, for sure, but gave them zero room for manoeuvre.

"I wanted to even the odds, but I think it's time to up the stakes, don't you?" he said.

Kier flicked him a glance. "There is a time and a place for extended metaphors, Waring."

Alan gave a shout of laughter, and, just like that, he was on top of the adrenaline and riding it. Oh, God, but they were in trouble.

Not them. Not Kier and himself. No. The men who had Mari were in trouble. "Keep me off the wall, if you can, please," he said, and worked his whole upper body out the window. There was a burst of automatic fire from the truck, but that only gave him somewhere to aim. Three spaced shots from him, and the shooter slumped across the tailgate. Someone inside heaved him out.

Interesting. Lightening the load, or an unexpected ally?

Bracing his boots on the seat, Alan pushed himself further out the window. One foot on the window frame, another push—he felt the wall of the canyon brush his back—and he was on the cab roof and moving. The Landy moved closer to the road for a second. The right wing mirror was wiped out.

Alan jumped.

It wasn't far, on paper. Not impossible, in a game. But this wasn't a game, and there was a distinct moment in midair where he wasn't at all certain of success, and where it occurred to him that holstering the Browning might have been helpful.

Pity, he thought, which didn't nearly cover it.

Then his left arm hit the canvas, he gripped something, twisted, and hung on. His body slammed into the side of the truck, and he used the motion to burst through the canvas at the back, hanging onto the roof strut, holding the nine milli in his right hand, yelling, "Down, Mari!"

He saw her hit the deck, then realised she was the only one moving in the interior. He stepped carefully further in and crouched down. There was only one man inside, he lay on his back with blood all over his neck from what looked distinctly like a bite on his ear. He checked quickly: unconscious.

"Once again, the lady arranges her own rescue."

She shook her head, wiping her mouth. "Hardly. I wouldn't have been able to move if you hadn't got the others."

He looked up, "Yeah, but . . ." he broke off. He pushed the goggles off and let them fall. He saw the moment Mari realised what he was staring at. She looked away, ducking her head.

"*Who did that?*"

"Alan, it doesn't even hurt, really."

"Mari, you can't see it. You're going to have the mother of a black eye, and your cheek . . ." He choked, he couldn't describe the livid bruise that was already puffing up. He felt light-headed with rage, numb with it. *Dear, sweet heaven.*

"Who did it?"

"It doesn't matter."

The hell it doesn't. He bit that one back, was opening his mouth to try a more reasonable line of questioning, because—bloody hellfire—he was going to know, when the truck lurched, throwing them both down. He got to his feet, stowed the Browning, and dragged Mari up, watching the man on the floor.

The engine was whining, the wheels spinning intermittently.

"He's off the road," Mari guessed.

"Yup," he said, and moved to the rear of the swaying vehicle. It was moving slower now, constrained by the terrain.

"Out," he said, "Jump out." He shoved Mari towards the rear of the truck, keeping an eye on the unconscious man. Unconscious he might be, but out of the picture he was not. He was taken by surprise when Mari pushed back at him.

"No!" she cried, her voice masked by effort.

"Quickly! Jump. Kier will pick you up. Don't be afraid."

"I'm not afraid," she shouted, half at him, half at the world. "I am *not*."

She turned to face him, arms still braced hard on the tailgate of the truck. Her face was wild, stubborn. And there was that mark again, the sign of another man's fist on her face. Alan went lightheaded again with the anger that pumped through his veins. He would deal with this. But not while Mari stood by watching, waiting to hate him for it.

"Do as you're told, Mari!" he yelled at her, over the noise of engine and rough travel.

Her eyes flashed. She was there, poised on the edge between leaving and staying, and she was beautiful, utterly beautiful to him, however she was marked.

"I won't!"

"Why the hell not?"

"Because you're not going!"

He stared at her, stupidly not having worked that one out, that she wouldn't want to leave him, that she was worried about him. Not when usually the only variables at work were his own feelings. *Selfish bastard.*

She'd managed to work herself round a little, not quite on the brink now—he'd have to wrestle her out to manage it, and he had no time for that nonsense.

"You're being stupid," he snarled at her, acknowledging in the same breath that this was neither the time nor the place.

"Oh? And you're here why, exactly?"

She was infuriating.

He loved her.

The truck rocked again. At least, he thought it was the truck. He grabbed hold of a strap and reeled with it, half his mind going, *huh?* and the other giving a rousing ovation for the sudden and unexpected revelation: *Oh,* timing, *Waring.*

He was in a speeding truck crewed by armed men. In hostile terrain. And, apparently, in the company of the woman he loved.

When you do a thing, you gotta do it in style.

Oh, he'd loved her for a while. He knew that now. But he'd never thought—dared—to put the name to it . . .

He didn't have a snowball's chance in hell with this woman in the long run, but, by God, he'd take every moment he had. He caught her by the collar of her shirt in both hands and dragged her to him, kissing her hard.

She didn't seem to mind. She was laughing when he

let go.

"Does this mean I can stay?"

"So help me God, Mari, if you get yourself killed I'll hunt you down in the afterlife to give you the worst spanking you've ever known."

"Promises, promises."

"Enough. C'mon, pay attention. Who's up front?"

She sobered up fast enough, clutching onto his elbow for support. "A French guy, the one who grabbed me."

"Is he the one who hit you?" he asked, as smoothly as he could manage.

"Well, I wouldn't have just wandered off with him, would I . . ." She looked up at him. "Alan!"

He smiled down at her and watched her eyes widen, knowing he looked murderous. "He and I have something to discuss."

"But, Alan . . ."

"Don't. Who else?"

"Another Western guy. I don't think he's armed—he didn't seem the type—but the Frenchman is. He said his name was Lucius. Do you know him?"

He shook his head. "No, but I think I know the other guy."

"Who is he?"

The truck swerved, throwing them down on the bench seat.

Alan got to his feet. "I've had about enough of this." He pulled his knife and attacked the canvas, cutting a long vertical slit near the cab. He sheathed the knife and looked back at her, imprinting her features on his brain, just in case.

I love you.

He pulled the Browning from the back of his trousers, took a good grip on a strut and swung out, gun in hand.

There were only the two men in the cab. Bristow hanging onto the far door and craning to see behind them, and the Frenchman driving. Alan hauled the door open and braced it with a foot, levelling the Browning. "I suggest you might like to stop."

Of course he was too close, and the Frenchman went for his gun hand, even as Bristow gave a cry of alarm and opened the door to jump out. The blow to his wrist jarred, but he kept his grip. He didn't want a death—he wanted a *conversation*.

At least at first.

The Frenchman stamped on the brake, and the door Alan was clinging to swung wide, sending him with it. He gripped hot metal and hung on, then kicked off the bonnet and swivelled back, driving his right fist through the open window, still clutching his gun. The punch connected with the Frenchman's mouth, with an extra edge courtesy of the gun, and his head snapped back, even as the impact almost crippled Alan's hand.

The Frenchman was slumped, groaning, his foot still on the brake. The truck came to a halt almost gently, and Alan rolled round the door, piling in on top of him, forcing him down across the seat. He knelt on his chest while fumbling for the ignition keys, removing them, and throwing them out the gaping door opposite.

Where was Bristow? Where was Kier? *Where was Mari?*

He backed out of the cab, dragging the Frenchman with him by his belt, and threw him down. Alan flexed his hand, studied the bloodied knuckles briefly, and transferred the Browning to his left hand, training it on the other man as he slowly pushed himself into a sitting position.

Alan stared down, feeling the sun on the back of his neck. He wondered what question to ask first. The Frenchman saved him the trouble.

"You're dying to know what they did to her, aren't you?" He smiled, showing blood on his teeth. "I suspect she has told you little. It is true she said very little to me."

He shifted against the wheel of the truck, pressing the back of his hand to his mouth and then looking at the red smears on it with apparent interest.

Alan looked down at him, conscious of the heat of battle still raging inside, knowing his fists were still ready and his heart raced for a reason.

The Frenchman tipped his face up, squinting against the sun. "Oh, how much you want to hit me! I love how the English lose control. So damn reserved and stupid most of the time, then, bam, a flash of intellect and a reversion to Neanderthal."

Alan smiled at him, felt his jaw ache with the effort, saw the way the other man's eyes widened.

And Mari still hadn't come out the back of the truck.

"Marianne," he called, with authority. "Get out here."

There was no answer. The man at his feet began to smile again. "What a pleasure it is to finally meet you."

Alan, scanning the canvas sides of the truck, snapped his head back round to stare.

"Oh, yes, I knew my men had made a mistake of the most stupid kind as soon as I heard of her. These things, as I'm sure you know, happen when one must attend business elsewhere. How is it you say?" He mimicked posh English, "'One cannot get the staff.' But that left me wondering why the girl was carrying the smart card. Unless, of course, the girl was also your girl."

Alan got a huge, thumping pump of adrenaline on that one. It fizzed under his skin and made him momentarily lightheaded.

"A long shot, of course, but worth it, I feel. After all, your cargo was waiting for me, and I had a curiosity to meet the girl, also. I wonder where she is," the man whispered, then gave a little laugh. "You make a habit of losing her."

"Mari!" he called again, supremely indifferent to the mutterings of the dead man at his feet. Where was she? Had she fallen? *C'mon, Kier, get your arse in gear.*

"I have to know," the Frenchman continued. "Did you never suspect Bristow?"

Only recently.

"Personally," the Frenchman continued, "I thought he

was becoming dangerously erratic. And stupidly stubborn. But blackmail is a poor motivator of men. He made the greatest of efforts, you know, trying to get the smart card to me, and to keep me from you. He became almost clever over that. All for nothing, of course. I don't think there was a single moment I truly *lost* her, you know. Following your trail, seeding the settlements with spies. I have no compunction, Englishman, and a great deal of money. Out here, money buys men. Helpful, informative men.

"With a knowledge of which direction you were headed in, the rest was easy. There are only so many towns where one can refuel, after all. But I bless my luck that it was to this town you came, rather than to my deputies elsewhere. I like to handle things"—he spread his palms—"hands on, you see."

"Doesn't seem to have served you," he answered shortly. Keeping him covered, he edged round towards the back of the truck. Damn. He couldn't see inside and watch him, too.

Bloody hellfire.

"*Au contraire.* I have laid eyes on the ubiquitous and much celebrated courier of North Africa. I am content."

He craned a little more, trying to see inside. No movement, no sound. *Damn it.*

"Mari?"

"And I am content to have made Ms. Forster's acquaintance also. I only wish I had been present when my men . . ." He let his voice tail off suggestively, and just like that, Alan lost it.

Completely.

He snapped the safety on and dropped the gun on the sand. There was going to be an hour's work to strip it and clean it, but, oh, he didn't care.

His peripheral vision faded—he saw the man on the ground, dirty hands on the sand, his left trouser leg cleanly torn at the shin. He saw the blood on his mouth and could have sworn he smelt it, too, especially when he stooped, caught the front of the man's jacket, and hauled him to his feet against the truck. The Frenchman's mouth thinned, his nostrils flared . . . and his hand came round from his back with a knife in it.

Alan ducked, felt the knife tug at the shoulder of his shirt, and rolled back away.

Oh, fine. That was how the game was to be played.

He was on his feet when the knife came his way again, and it was easy, in not so close quarters, to dodge back this time. His own knife was in his boot, but he left it there for the moment, frankly enjoying the dance.

Left. Right. This time striking the lunging arm down and away. Sweat seeded salt on his forehead, but as long as it didn't run in his eyes he was doing okay. Doing fine, in fact, as the Frenchman came at him again, snarling, breathing hard, stumbling when he forced an off-balance turn.

He was fading. But Alan was capable of much, much more.

He demonstrated it, when the other man tried to close with him, landing a couple of blows under the knife arm before the man had even withdrawn the lunge.

Then Bristow came round from behind the truck, with his hands on his head, and Mari behind him, covering him competently with a rifle she must have filched from the man inside.

"I think you lost something," she said, flicking a cocky smile at him. That faltered and died as her mouth fell open and shaped around a cry of alarm.

In slow motion, he saw it coming, looking down the length of the Frenchman's arm, looking at the businesslike knife point aimed at his eyes.

It was about the worst counter-move he'd ever executed, but it worked. Maybe because it was the first time it really mattered, maybe because Mari was watching, maybe because he was sick and tired of being wrong-footed.

But mostly because he was pissed.

He snapped his head back, faster than he'd ever suspected he could move, took hold of the passing wrist, and bore down. He kicked out, hard, at the side of the Frenchman's knee and felt with satisfaction the crunching connection. The leg he'd targeted crumpled, and a sharp tug on the arm he still held sent the Frenchman down into a sprawling fall. The knife spun away, in a flurry of dust and glittering steel.

He let the Frenchman get unsteadily to his feet and make one bare-fisted swing, and then he hit him.

He didn't get up again.

He nursed a stinging fist and got down on one knee

to pat the man down as he should have the first time. The smart card was in the chest pocket, still in its magnetic shielding. Well, he was right about that, anyway. He slipped it into his own pocket, getting slowly to his feet.

When he got there, he received an arm full of Mari.

He probably should have given a damn about what she was saying, and he would in a moment, but just then, an armful of Mari was more than enough to concentrate on. She was warm, giving, perfect, and he wrapped himself round her and held on while his heart steadied and his vision cleared.

He retained just enough sense to glance over her head, but Kier was there, finally, the Rover behind him. He stood over Bristow, who was on his knees now, hands still on his head.

Mari wriggled against him, burrowing closer, saying something again—he was catching snatches of it. He kissed her head, her ear, anything he could reach.

"I thought . . . I saw . . . He said . . ."

And that one snapped him out of it, because she'd been alone with Bristow and God knew what he'd told her. Well, Bristow couldn't have told her anything, because if he had, she wouldn't be in his arms, but he could start talking at any moment.

He pushed her away firmly, took hold of her shoulders, and looked into her eyes. "Go and sit in the Land Rover." Maybe it was the fight, but his voice came out rougher than he'd meant.

Her head went back, her eyes went blank.

Hello, damnation.

"But I thought . . ." she said weakly, "I brought him back."

He swallowed. "Yes. Thank you. Go and sit in the car."

She opened her mouth, colour rising to her cheeks. Then she shut it with a snap, turned on her heel, and headed out.

Alan winced, and kicked at the sand.

"That was, uh, smooth," said Kier.

"Fuck you," he swore at him. "Like you're the expert." And Kier didn't say anything to that.

"What kept you?" he snapped.

Kier gave him a level look. "Couldn't get out the canyon. It hemmed me in too tight. No way out till I ran its course."

He nodded. *I know the feeling.*

Mari threw herself into the passenger seat and fastened the seat belt. She didn't really need it, of course, but she yanked on it till it dug tight into her hips.

What the *hell* was the matter with him?

Her skin burned, fury and hurt building up in layers, one on top of the other, a careful construction designed to protect.

What did he *want* from her?

She'd seen the other guy running and brought him back, she'd taken care of one of her own captors, she'd done *everything* he could have reasonably asked. And he! When he'd kissed her in the back of the truck, when he'd looked at her like that, she'd thought . . .

And just like that the careful anger folded up inside like a card house exposed to the wind, and she found she had tears in her eyes. Not just in her eyes, either. Suddenly there were more tears, and more, tracking through the grime on her face, dripping off her chin, trickling warm into her mouth.

Gasping, she swiped at them, leaning forward, horrified at her loss of control. She'd tried so hard to not to be the old, pathetic Marianne. She'd burst free of old Marianne so completely, and he didn't seem to care.

But perhaps that was it—perhaps he didn't like the new version. She looked down at her hands, smeared with tears and dust. She choked, sobbed, and the tears made big, dark splotches on her dusty clothes.

The nauseating truth was that she didn't like the new version much, either. She was hard, and cold, and capable of things she didn't ever want to be capable of. For a moment, in her mind, she was back in the compound near Béchar and could see, quite clearly, a tin mug rolling on a wooden table.

Blood on the floor.

No.

Scrubbing her eyes with a corner of her shirt, she took deep breaths, drawing a picture in her mind's eye—a bright dawn, vibrant colours and the dark horizon coming to life.

When Alan opened the door, her face was dry and she was barely shaking at all. "This is what we are going to do now," he said, without preamble. "We've bound the Frenchman and Bristow, and the guy from the back of the truck, and loaded them all in the truck."

"They're all alive?"

"Yes."

"What did—Bristow?—say?"

There was a pause. "About what?"

She lifted a hand. "All this? Why they wanted me?"

She had to wait for an answer, and even then it wasn't one. "The Frenchman isn't talking, and I'm not listening to Bristow."

"Oh, goody. And you're not listening *or* talking to me."

He went on deliberately, as if she hadn't spoken. "Kier and I will drive the truck ahead—we're going back around El Aricha and up to Tlemcen, where we'll find a third party to take them to the authorities, or dump them in a likely spot to be found. You'll follow behind in the Rover."

"You think so?"

Alan blinked at her, still holding the door. "Mari, this is the best way to—"

"I can't drive."

She heard him take a great breath. When she looked, his eyes were closed and his head tipped back. The lines of his throat were tight, and his hand white-knuckled on the door.

"Then stay put," he said, "and Kier will come and drive

you." He shut the door unnecessarily hard, and stalked off.

In a moment he was back, opening the door with exaggerated care. "When we get home," he said, "I'll teach you to drive."

She looked into his eyes and saw an anguish she didn't understand. "You don't believe that for a second."

"A man can hope," he said, closed the door with a soft click, and left her choking on bitter incomprehension.

Kier didn't have much to say. But then, what was new?

Half irate and half miserable, she watched the sun go down, through a column of dust kicked up by the truck in front. When darkness came, she closed her eyes and pretended to be asleep.

⚜ ⚜ ⚜

Mari didn't know she'd dozed off for real until she was jolted awake by Kier swearing. The Rover swerved, skidding on loose gravel, and she cried out as something big went under the front wheels in the next instant, jolting her against the seat belt. The rear wheels bounced over it, too, and Kier hauled on the hand brake and stopped them sideways.

"What—?" she began, her voice shrill, but she was drowned out when he leant on the horn. Ahead of them, the truck's brake lights flared.

Clutching the seat belt at her chest, she craned round in her seat, but she could see nothing on the dark road behind them. "What was it? What did we hit?" *Some sort of animal?* The sound was too . . . soft to have been a rock.

Kier turned to face her. "Stay put." His voice was tight, his mouth thin.

She glanced through the windscreen and saw Alan jump out the truck, gun in hand. When she turned back to Kier, he was snapping a clip into his own firearm.

"Oh no. What was it?"

He didn't look at her. "Just stay in your seat, Mari." He slipped out the car.

The Rover's headlights illuminated the back of the truck. Alan's face was white in the darkness, his hair pale. Kier met him, and they walked back along the road together. Peering in the wing mirror in turn, she tracked them, but although she saw the light from the torch they snapped on a few car-lengths back, she couldn't see what it illuminated. Alan was on his knees, checking it out—she saw him get up slowly, wiping his hand on his trousers, and talk to Kier.

Her heart raced, high in her throat. She glanced forward.

And saw the canvas flap on the back of the truck moving.

The Englishman she'd captured stood there, pinned in the headlights, slowly raising his right arm. Holding something. Holding something he was pointing at her.

She was amazed, in a lightheaded way, that he had somehow untied himself and found a gun. She snapped free of the seat belt, throwing herself across the seats to hit the horn hard. She kept going, scrabbling at the door latch.

The door gave as the first bullets flew, and she tumbled onto the road.

☘ ☘ ☘

The Frenchman was beyond help, bloodied and broken on the tarmac. Alan's mouth curled in distaste and regret.

"You okay?" he asked Kier.

He shrugged. "Not a hell of a lot I could do about it. The first I saw, he was already falling out. He went under both wheels. He was still tied up."

"Yeah."

The Rover's horn sounded.

A great thump of adrenaline hit his bloodstream at the same time as his boot hit the tarmac. He was running, Kier's shout in his ears. He saw Mari scramble out of the Rover, rolling under it, saw—incredibly—Bristow in the back of the truck, standing clear in the headlights, aiming at her. Alan skidded to a halt, steadied the Browning in both hands, and fired three shots. Bristow crumpled, and Alan ran on, past Mari huddled down by the front wheel, keeping out the headlights, covering the downed man as he ran.

Stuart Bristow lay on his back, arms flung wide. Both hands were empty.

What?

Alan ripped the canvas aside and scanned the back of the truck. One goon, still bound and staring wide—

eyed at the Browning. He scanned the truckbed, under the truck, around Bristow on the roadway.

Bloody hellfire.

Kier approached, armed, but standing easy. "The gun?"

"There is no gun. There was no bloody gun."

"What?"

"He tricked me." Alan kicked the tailgate, which clanged loud. "Dammit, I didn't want to . . ."

A croak of a voice cut across him. "I did . . ."

Alan dropped to his knees beside Stuart. He was still alive, still bleeding, the blood soaking his shirt, spreading between his right arm and his body. Alan checked him over swiftly, but here wasn't a damn thing anyone could do that wasn't just delaying the inevitable. And extending pain.

"You did?"

Stuart spoke with difficulty, breathing shallow and slow. "Want you to kill me."

Alan was silent, stunned. He'd planned this?

There were red bubbles now, forming where the bullets had torn through the shirt. "I'm sorry . . . for all of it." Stuart coughed weakly, the pain spasming across his features. "He . . . blackmail. I shouldn't . . . couldn't—"

"Blackmail?"

"I had . . . pictures on my PC. I never touched any of them, I swear, they were just pictures. Of . . . of children."

Alan's anger chilled, fast. He heard Kier make a slight sound, and instinctively put his body between his brother-in-law and the man on the ground.

Alan laid a light hand on his shoulder. "Don't speak. It doesn't matter."

Stuart's lips twitched. "No. Not if . . ." His eyes focused with difficulty on the face over him. "He *is* dead?"

"Very."

He seemed to relax, his eyes closed. For two or three breaths, he struggled on. Then he said, softly, but quite clearly, "This "—his fingers scrabbled on the road, in blood—"not for the things I've done. For the things I might have done, if I went on. I'm sorry." His head rolled on the road, and shortly afterward the last bubbles burst.

Alan stood up and brushed off, every muscle, every bone suddenly so utterly weary he thought he was going to fall.

Kier was standing there, waiting. "I put Mari back in the Rover," he said.

"Thanks."

"Go and talk to her," Kier dropped a hand on Alan's shoulder. "I'll clear up here."

"Thanks."

He paused to talk to the man in the back, then went back to the Rover and climbed slowly inside. Mari was huddled in the passenger seat, feet tucked up under her. Her face was white, but her eyes were calm. She watched him climb in, asking not a thing. He drew his knee onto the seat and faced her, looking her straight in the eye because she deserved it.

"Stuart scraped his bonds off on a sharp bit of metal in the back of the truck. The other guy says the Frenchman had been talking to him quietly for some time. He doesn't know what he said. When he was free, he simply got up and threw the Frenchman out the back."

Her eyes, even the bruised, swollen one, went wide, and her hand crept to cover her mouth. She was trembling, her mouth, her hand. "We ran over him?"

"There was nothing Kier could do. He had no time."

"Oh, how awful for him!"

I love you, Mari. That care for someone else, in a situation she had every right to be overwhelmed by, was so quintessentially Mari . . . But then, the woman who knew to sound the horn to warn him, who knew to get out, get away, under cover, was part of the package, too. And he loved all of it.

What a twisted, horrific, godawful mess this was. All he wanted to do was love her, and they were surrounded by death. No room for beautiful feelings where there was death on his hands, and horror to bruise her spirit and her face.

"Is he—" she went on, but he finished it for her.

"Yes, sweetheart. He's dead. I'm sorry."

"And the Englishman? Stuart? How did he get a gun?"

He took a moment to swallow, and breathe deep, and be as sure as he could be that his voice would be normal and even when he spoke. "There wasn't any gun. He wanted us to think there was. He stood in full view, in the headlights, and waited."

"He committed suicide."

"Yes."

"Why?"

He shrugged. "Everything had gone wrong. The Frenchman had been blackmailing him, you see, he hadn't planned the things he'd done himself. Maybe he was just taking the easy way out."

"Maybe he was making amends."

Alan looked away, out to where Kier was digging in the darkness. "Maybe. He said he was sorry. Perhaps he was."

"And the blackmail?"

"It's not my business. I'll hand it over to Headquarters when I get back. They'll have to investigate."

There was a pause. A long pause. He thought about Bristow and wondered if he had any family.

"Headquarters?" repeated Mari, in a slow, still voice.

Oh no.

He closed his eyes. He was tired. Too tired. He'd never have slipped up like that if it hadn't been for that. The exhaustion weighed him down, and the lies were suddenly all too heavy to bear. There wasn't any point trying to protect her, to protect him. He'd proved worse than useless at that.

He let his head fall back against the headrest, and, coward that he was, he kept his eyes closed when he spoke. "Mari, I—"

The door beside him opened, letting in a drift of cool night air. His eyes snapped open to see Kier standing there, looking warily between Mari and him.

"I'm going to need some help," Kier said, baldly, and Mari turned away to look out the window at nothing.

Alan went to bury the dead.

Chapter Fourteen

"It's not what I expected," said Mari, staring out the window at the town they passed, a myriad of lights in darkness.

"What did you expect?" Alan was driving, Kier resting in the back. He'd rested himself earlier, but he'd been unable to sleep, and so had taken the wheel again.

They hadn't been long dealing with the two dead men. They'd untied the one still alive and left him the truck, with just enough fuel to get back to the town they'd just passed. He was hired muscle, Kier explained. No threat, when they themselves were that close to the sea—and to escape from Algeria.

"I don't know, exactly." She waved a hand at the view—trees, buildings, and overhead wires. "I think I was getting used to the desert. This is too much civilisation."

He was happy to talk. She was far too subdued, although he couldn't blame her—not hardly. "Far too much. I'll be happy when we're out of here. Not long now to the coast."

"Gareth will be there?"

He glanced across at her. "Yes."

Mari was silent. "Has your sister been here with you?"

"No." The hesitation that followed the one syllable was tangible. He didn't need to tell her, then, that this time he wanted to say more.

Mari waited.

Alan swallowed.

There it was finally, right in front of him. Something he could tell her, when he'd told no one else. A truth to give her, like flowers in the desert. One truth.

He checked behind him, but Kier was sleeping soundly, collapsed in the footwell.

"She's not my sister," he said, low.

He sensed her turn her head to look at him, but she didn't say a word, didn't give him any leads.

He took a breath, settled in the driving seat. "When I was fifteen, I went through a rebellious patch. I was looking through my parents' papers one day, I forget why . . . I found out they weren't my parents." He shifted his hands on the wheel, stared at the road illuminated in the headlights. "I never said anything to them. It made sense to me. It explained why I was a loner, why I didn't fit in. Eight years ago they died, and I was an executor of the will. I found more records then. I had been adopted when I was a few months old. They weren't really my parents at all. I, uh, did some research"—actually he'd abused his desk job with the intelligence services— "and found out that my birth parents were anthropologists from Norway. I guess they thought a baby would rather interfere with the travelling."

"Did you contact them?" she asked, softly.

"No. I didn't see much point." He'd lost his parents twice, struck a double blow. Suddenly, his wanderlust, his love of travel, setting him apart from the rest of his "family" made a kind of sense—was it the Viking blood?—and all at once cut off from family, he'd thought perhaps he was *meant* to be a loner. *That* was his birthright.

"You still have Jenny."

He loved Jenny, that was true, but . . . "She's not really my sister."

"You have a family," Mari's voice was sharp. "I don't."

For a second, all he felt was a species of blinding, bitter anger that she would turn his pain into a game of comparisons. But he bit back the burning words he would have thrown at her—*making progress, Waring*—and bent his mind to her words.

And looking out over his own life through her eyes, he saw things he never had before. Like the erg before dawn, seemingly flat and desolate, then the bright, pure light of first sun showing the world in relief, revealing harsh rocky crags and deep, shadowed valleys. With everything he *was* suddenly challenged, he'd distanced himself from his family and ultimately taken up a job in a vast wilderness, and a job that demanded secrecy, that ensured no one could know him, a job to hide behind.

And, bloody hell, how he'd hidden. Hidden from family, from friends, from the truth, even skulking away from the odd thoughts of his own heart. He'd buried his conscience, locked away his soul, and wrapped his whole self in an armoured loneliness that was as much about punishment as protection.

"Have mine," he said, surprising himself. "Share mine."

It was as close to a proposal as he'd come, and Mari, unhappy and exhausted, gave it the incredulous look it deserved.

He sighed. "I didn't mean it like that . . ." Mari's eyebrows climbed further. He shook his head and took a minute, trying to engage brain before he opened mouth again.

"Jenny would like you," he said, eventually, changing the subject and yet not changing the subject. "When"—*when*—"we get back, she'd like to meet you."

"What makes you think she'd like me?" *Because she'd sympathise with the urge to beat the crap out of me.*

"Because you're sweet. Because you're resourceful and capable and indomitable."

"Capable?" Trust her to latch onto that one. Incredulity had made it to her voice, turning it into something of a squeak.

He held her wide-eyed gaze. "You think you're not?"

"But I . . ."

He saw her again, triumphant behind Bristow. He saw cracked lips shape around the diffident request for a lift to the next town, if it wasn't too much bother. And earlier, another lifetime ago, he saw in her face that moment of courage, of decision, when she'd asked him to love her, and he'd left her at the door. He heard her again, asking in a tight voice for something, anything to do, needing control over some part of her life and death, like he needed her alive just to justify breathing.

"You're so damn capable, Marianne," he said deliberately, "you scare me sometimes. I worry what you're going to do if I turn my back." He let a little touch of amusement creep into his voice, and was rewarded with the flash of white teeth.

"That's easy," she said, gently. "Don't turn your back."

He swallowed, hard, and stared at the road.

⚛ ⚛ ⚛

"Wake up, Mari."

The first thing that hit her when Mari opened her eyes and breathed deep was the scent of the sea.

"Oh, my God." She struggled up from her bed on the floor in the back of the Landy, shedding clothes stiff with dust. Getting to her knees, one arm half-tangled in the straps of the rucksack, she lifted her head to look out the window. And the next words died in her throat.

The Mediterranean.

Vast, bright, beautiful, and blue, shifting like a live

thing under the morning sun. She leaned one hand on the bench seat in front of her and used the other to wipe the window.

They were parked on the edge of a steep stony slope that fell away to the shore. There was no beach, only dark, jagged rocks cutting the small waves into pieces, and surrounding the tiny bay in two, long arms. A small, pale track, nothing more than a footpath, wound down the fifty feet or so to the water's edge, where Kier stood, staring out to sea.

She looked where he looked and saw it—a bright, white shape a long way out.

"Oh, beautiful!"

"That's our transportation. The *Orpheus*," Alan said.

Twisting to face him, she saw that he was still holding the door for her, or rather, he was leaning on it, arms folded across his chest. There was a faint, tired smile on his face.

"We made it?" she asked, soft.

His eyes left her face and scanned the shoreline, east and west. "Let's just get aboard, shall we?"

She disentangled herself from the rucksack and shuffled out. The ground was rough, covered with lichen-spotted, fractured stones, and she staggered a little as she stretched. Every joint ached, but she took in the sea air gratefully, feeling like every breath soothed her desert-scratched lungs.

Alan was hovering at her elbow impatiently. "Come on."

"But—" she gestured behind her at the vehicle, stuffed

with all their equipment. "We have to unpack first, don't we?"

"We're leaving it."

She gaped at him. "What? All of it?"

"Pretty much. We've already unloaded our personal possessions. I've disabled the remaining firearms and munitions. Someone will get lucky."

Mari stared at him. There were lines on his face she hadn't noticed before. His hair was a mess. His half-soldier, half-desert-bandit clothing was . . . indescribable. But it was the ever so slightly blank look in his eyes that reminded her most clearly of the night just past.

She'd been relegated to the back of the Rover again shortly after their chat. In the dark, with nothing to see but the road in the headlights, and the lights of civilisation, and nothing to do but worry, she'd given up and wedged herself in the footwell again, wishing for sleep.

She supposed it had been exhaustion that had granted it.

She scrubbed the sleep from her eyes, wincing at the feel of her skin. She hoped to God that was grime that was rubbing off under her roughened fingers, and not the skin itself . . .

"Come on," Alan repeated, and went to take her arm.

Refusing his help, she made her way carefully down the narrow path. There was barely anywhere to stand at the water's edge. She managed to wedge one foot in a cleft, and commandeered the one flat piece of rock with the other. Alan just balanced, both feet on a knife edge of rock that ran into the sea.

When she looked up she saw the small inflatable heading their way. There was one man in it, bulky and dark.

"That's *him*?" she asked.

"Our skipper," Alan confirmed.

"How did he know where we were?"

"We radioed him in the night, en route."

She subsided. It struck her that both men were ignoring her for their own good reasons, even if she did want to jump up and down and shout in a childish bid for attention. The launch was heading in fast. Kier was scanning the horizon with constant, quick sweeps while Alan radiated impatience.

The little grey inflatable swept in close. Gareth didn't stop the engine, and couldn't get that close to the shore for all the rocks. Kier stepped into the water without hesitation, and before Mari really had a chance to wonder how she was getting out there, Alan had turned to her with a polite, "excuse me," and tipped her deftly over his shoulder.

Excuse me? she thought, upside down.

There was a splash, movement, a little spray in the face and the touch of a few impersonal hands, and suddenly she found herself right-way-up in the boat, clinging to the rope that went round the edge. Gareth twisted the throttle on the outboard, and they powered out back toward the boat.

They were crowded—Alan was beside her, arm round her, keeping her steady, Kier on the same side as Gareth— and all three of them were scanning the sea around them.

She coughed. "Excuse me?" No one looked at her. She spoke up over the engine. "What are we looking for?"

Gareth turned to look at her, just briefly, with kind eyes and the ghost of a smile. "Algerian Navy patrols."

"Oh." *Oh, goody.*

"They boarded me last night and checked my crew roster. If they catch up with us again, remember you chartered me and I picked you up in Sidia."

"Um, okay." Her voice came out a little weaker than she'd intended, and Alan's arm tightened for a moment.

They were almost at the yacht. She just had time to get a general impression of sleekness matched by bulk—more jaguar than cheetah—tall mast, a collection of hi-tech gadgetry, and a line of oval portholes running down the side before they swept up to the back, and Kier was climbing the ladder there.

Alan reached for her, but she said, "Don't you dare," and got herself up the ladder before she had time to doubt her ability or her agility. Once on deck, though, she was afraid to move. She'd never been aboard any type of sailboat, and everything looked so . . . exact. So precise.

Waiting for her to touch the wrong thing and make a mess.

There was a collection of things that looked like shining bobbins and winches round the edge of the depression where the wheel sat, gleaming wood and metal. Multicoloured ropes coiled neatly. Levers and slatted wooden seats.

All in all, this time she was grateful when Alan took

her arm, conducted her safely round the wheel, down the steep steps into the cabin. There were maps on a table, and instruments everywhere. The upholstery was dark, faded green—the handkerchief-sized curtains over the portholes checked in a similar colour. There were two recessed shelves packed with books, an old lamp hanging over another table. To her left was a miniscule kitchen area, to her right two gleaming wooden doors.

But Alan pushed her on, through the main cabin to another narrow door. They dropped down two steps, and she found herself in a tiny cabin wedged into the point of the boat.

"This is your cabin," he said.

Something whirred overhead. There was the sharp, loud flap of canvas, and the boat lurched. Mari sat down quickly on the mini double bed.

"I almost hate to ask, but what now?" she asked, looking around. There was a little hand basin next to the doorway.

"Sleep."

She looked at him blankly.

"We're as safe as we can be here. We'll get under-way. There's not really anything much for you to do." He shrugged.

"Sleep." Mari sighed, pushing her fingers through her hair and lacing them together on top of her head, letting her arms hang. "Look, Alan, I seem to have slept my way through most of Algeria. I know it makes life a lot easier for you, and you can make your nice little plans in what is, for all intents and purposes, my absence—but I am fed up with missing everything!"

She expected more of the grit-teethed temper of yesterday. Instead, she got a blank stare. He moved up close, and she tensed, but he just reached down past her to unearth a canvas tote bag from a recess under the bed.

"We brought you some gear. We'll sort food out when we make international waters. You can have a shower, if you want. It's up the other end, opposite the galley. But be sparing with the water, we only carry a hundred gallons of fresh."

She gave up. He wouldn't be provoked, and she didn't really know why she wanted to provoke him in the first place. Except for that little fact that he wasn't talking to her. Not really. Not to tell truth. Had last night been all of her quota? "Water, water everywhere, and not a drop to drink?"

His lips twitched, but it wasn't a smile. Not quite. "Something like that."

He turned to leave the small cabin, but she put a hand on his arm and stopped him. He half-turned—she got the angle of a cheekbone, the sharp edge of his jaw, a fan of sun-bleached eyelashes on a tanned cheek, the corner of his mouth . . .

"I just don't want to be an albatross, Alan."

Alan was silent.

What does it take to make the most verbose man in the world shut up? she thought. She didn't like any of the answers.

He nodded, slipped out of her grasp, and left.

Mari got to her knees and peered out the porthole. Already the coast was a dark and indistinct line. A pair of tanned, dark-haired legs went by on the deck outside, sure-footed in canvas deck shoes. Gareth, about his business.

Had they really made it? Was it over?

Unbidden, an image of Alan's blank eyes filled her mind.

No. No, it wasn't over. Not yet.

She watched till Algeria disappeared entirely, and then she went to find the shower.

🕉 🕉 🕉

"When are you going to tell her?"

Kier was lying in wait for him in the cabin.

"Shouldn't you be up on deck helping Gareth?" Alan asked.

Kier shrugged. "He didn't want any help. In fact, I'd say the offer was almost an insult."

Alan stood there, suddenly at a loss. There wasn't anything for him to do. Oh, he needed to stow his Browning and the smart card in case they were boarded, but . . . "I need to talk to Gareth," he said, uncomfortable with giving up control.

"Leave him alone. We can trust him." Kier cut to the heart of the matter effortlessly.

Passing his hand over his face, Alan dropped onto a bench.

"So," Kier said. "When are you going to tell her?"

"Keep your voice down." He felt the rush as the *Orpheus* picked up speed. "When will we be in international waters?"

"Soon. Stop changing the subject."

"You might take the hint."

"I don't do hints."

"Maybe you should start."

"Alright!" Kier flung up his hands and got to his feet. "I'll leave it to you. But listen just this once, will you?"

Alan closed his eyes and nodded. "Okay."

"The longer you leave this, the harder it will get. Every day that you keep lying to her will make it harder for her to believe you care about her. And you do care, don't you?"

Alan swallowed. His throat was dry, tight. "Yes," he grated. "More . . ." He swallowed again. "Yes."

When the silence stretched to a minute or so, he opened his eyes to find Kier looking at him with an expression of sympathy. Sympathy? He must be hallucinating.

Kier shook his head and went to the galley, ducking down to look in the tiny fridge.

"Does he have any beer?" Alan asked.

There was a pause. "Well, what do you know?"

Kier straightened, holding two dark brown bottles. "It's Sweaty Socks," he said.

"Sweaty Socks."

Kier was squinting at the label. "Winner of the 2007 Golden Rooster award for excellence in Real Ales, apparently."

"Huh."

⚛ ⚛ ⚛

Mari sat with her legs hanging over the side under the last wire of the little fence that went round the deck. She leant gingerly on the metal post in front of her and waited for the gentle waves to bathe her healing feet in spray.

The sun was warm on her back, and soon the noises of sailing—snap of lines, slap and rush of waves, and chink and rattle of metal fixings—passed through her and over her, and she was able to hear the silence behind them.

She seemed to be rushing from one wide open space to another. The great, lethal expanse of the desert, to the harsh, implacable world of water. But it was sweet to be here, with the yacht doing all the running for her, and not needing to do anything except sit in a swimsuit—a hazy blue and green one, found stuffed in the bottom of the bag Alan had given her—with her head on her arms soaking up the sun and the freedom in equal measure.

Freshly showered, she realised she had never before experienced the real sensuality of cleanliness. Her skin was smooth, soft, fresh. It felt like hers again, and it felt wonderful.

There came the slap of bare feet on the wooden deck, and she craned to see who it was. It was Alan, almost inevitably, holding a bottle of suntan lotion in his hand and a pillow under his arm. The sun was behind him, flaring round him, hurting her eyes, and she was too tired, too limp to move. She faced forward again, without a word.

He had nothing to say either, it seemed, but he settled down behind her, stretching his legs out on either side of hers. His hair-roughened thigh brushed her hip, and goose bumps rose instantly along her arms. He peeled her back from the little fence with a gentle hand on her shoulder.

"Here," he said, offering the pillow, then sliding it down the front to cushion her against the hard edges of the post when she leaned back.

Long, tanned, muscular thighs enclosed her. Her bare back brushed against his equally naked chest. She settled forward against the pillow with a long, even sigh, concentrating on the hypnotic dip and rise of the water.

"You shouldn't be out here without cream," he said, mildly. She heard the snap of the bottle top, and tensed, expecting a cold squirt of lotion. Instead his hands stroked down her back, smoothing the warmed lotion over her skin.

She buried her head in the pillow and her toes, teasing the waves, curled tight.

"It's factor forty," he said conversationally, "but don't sit out here too long."

His hand curled up round her neck and she felt like moaning. He was thorough—his fingertips now moved down and teased the edge of her swimsuit, round her ribs— and her breath caught. She wanted to let go, and lean back against him, shimmy so that his hand went further round her front to caress her breast, but she fought it, frowning.

Today, however much she wanted him to touch her, he felt like a stranger.

He started on her shoulders, long, strong fingers curving round the bones, spreading the cream and kneading the flesh. Her shoulders dropped—she'd never realised just how tense she was.

"The black eye's fading nicely," Alan said.

"Mmmm."

He wiped the residue off on his own legs. Turning her head she caught the abstracted look out of the corner of her eye. He frowned down at the sea, as if looking for inspiration.

"I'm not a businessman." He was quiet. About as quiet as she'd heard him lately. But his words weren't news, so she waited, still with nothing to say.

"I work for the British government. I am employed for the purpose of moving information, data, papers, maps, you name it, out of a country back into Britain. I can work anywhere, but my specialist field is North Africa. There's a lot of work here."

She took in a breath—it felt like the first one she'd taken since he'd sat down. The sun fractured on the waves, showering them with tiny pinpoints of light, broken diamonds.

"You're a spy."

"No. And yes. I suspect what you think of as the spies are the guys who obtain the information in the first place. I'm . . . a glorified courier—that's all. I was in Rabat waiting for orders about . . . about going home again."

So he'd been stuck in Rabat and whiled away the time with an amusing flirtation. Was that it? Was this the groundwork for a brush off? Mari's heart ached, but it didn't matter. She'd get used to it. She'd never thought Alan might actually want her in any permanent way. She was just . . . there.

"So why did you come after me?"

He picked a bit of fluff off the wire, and flicked it out to sea. "I tried to look you up when I got back to England—"

"Why?"

He laid his hands on her thighs, stroking, but she made a movement that was almost a rejection, and he removed them.

"Why?" she repeated.

"Because I wanted to see you again."

Why? "But I told you it was over. There wasn't anything to be over, was there? So why look me up?"

"I . . . God, Mari!"

His arms went round her, not to be shrugged off this time. He buried his head in the curve between neck and shoulder, and his whole body shook.

She waited, stiff and wondering, not at all clear what was going on here. Was it release of tension? Was he one of those people who went to pieces after the fact?

"Mari, Mari . . ." He muttered against her skin. "I . . . I just wanted to see you again—that's all. There's no 'why' I can give you—not yet."

"And you couldn't find me."

His lips moved on her skin. "I was frantic. You'd

disappeared."

"So you came looking."

The arms wrapped round her middle loosened slightly, and he lifted his head. His chin brushed her hair.

"I know the area. There was a chance I could find you."

She knew he wasn't telling her everything. The restraint was so obvious in him, the constraint tangible. She wanted to accuse him, but the words dried into a hot ache in her throat.

He's not the only one with secrets, remember?

He held her shoulders, lightly, as if he had already exceeded his permission to touch her. It was hard to ignore his touch, but she tried—she tried hard. The broken diamonds were harder, sharper, and the sea was like beaten, shattered silver. Everything hurt her eyes. And she couldn't stop shaking.

There was blood on the table. On the lamp.

Blood by the man's body on the floor.

She reared back from the fence, and the pillow worked loose. Alan swore and made to grab it, but missed, trying to hold her and catch that at the same time. She used the moment to lever away, twisting, scrabbling onto her knees and up.

She turned on him, seeing the dismay on his face when he turned to face her. "Whatever it is you're not telling me, Alan—" He tried to interrupt her, but she slashed a hand across the words. "I don't want to know. Don't tell me. Don't."

She spun on her heel and staggered down the deck, all but throwing herself below to her cabin. There was a lock on the door, and she used it.

⚘ ⚘ ⚘

The winds were kind and the days slipped by without incident. They sunbathed, slept, and ate when they felt like it, sometimes below deck beneath swinging lamp, sometimes above, with the wind in their hair, and their food seasoned by salt spray.

They made it clear round Spain and Portugal, to the coast of France before Gareth announced they needed to stop somewhere and take on supplies.

Somewhere was a small marina south of Biarritz. Gareth and Kier went ashore, leaving Alan to watch the boat and Marianne. Not that it made any difference, he reflected, since she hadn't looked him in the eye in days. The only person who seemed unaffected by the tension on board was Gareth, calmly getting on with it, keeping meticulous charts, and changing their papers and cover story when required.

Now, officially, they were a charter from Gibraltar, headed to Biarritz. Past Biarritz, they would be a charter from Hendaye, headed for Brittany. And so on.

Each nautical mile taking them farther and farther from any connection with North Africa. *Algeria? Never been there.*

Kier came back from shore quiet and subdued. He stowed the groceries with Gareth, working quietly and efficiently, but his face was closed and oddly sad. It was an emotion Alan didn't readily associate with his stoic brother-in-law.

He caught up with him on deck. "What are your thoughts?"

McAllister heaved a sigh, staring out at the shore. "Nothing." He nodded towards France. "You think the Frenchman worked for their government?" he nodded towards the shore.

Alan shook his head. "No, I think he was strictly on his own terms."

"They do play rough."

"They've certainly been known to. But not this. It doesn't smell right. Too much use of other people, other nationalities. The man had a private army, as far as I can tell. And anyway, I know most of their people."

There was a pause. "Why haven't you used the reader?"

Alan remembered the smart card reader Kier had bought in Rabat. So long ago, but only a few days . . . "I don't know."

Kier nodded. Then heaved another giant sigh, head bowed.

"What's wrong, Kier?"

He looked up at the coast. "I could fly out of Bordeaux and be home before tomorrow."

Alan dropped a hand on his shoulder, suddenly feeling guilty that he'd kept Kier away from his family for so long. "Put ashore. We can take it from here. I want to give Marianne time to . . . to adjust anyway. And I have to tell her when we get back."

Kier scowled at him. "Why won't you tell her till then?"

"Because I want to do it where she can get away from me if she wants to." *When she wants to.*

Turning to the glimmer of French fields and shores, Kier said, "Don't sell yourself short. You've done a lot for her."

"Too much."

"You know, guilt like that can be a kind of vanity."

Alan stared at him, not used to philosophy from that quarter. "Uh, right."

"You're sure you don't need me?"

"I think we can spare your scintillating conversation."

He was rewarded by Kier's answering grin. "I'll be seeing you soon, yeah? Jenny will want a debriefing."

"Count on it."

"Try and bring Marianne. Jenny will want to meet her."

He felt his face stiffen and an absurd tug of longing. "You know I can't promise that."

It was Kier's turn to grip his shoulder. "Just do your best. Okay?"

"Sure."

chapter fifteen

The storm came in just hours after Kier disembarked.

Mari was sitting in the cockpit, when Gareth came up from the cabin, frowning. "Problem?" she asked, since Gareth had struck her as the sort of person to whom problems were unknown.

He squinted at the sky behind them. "Yeah. Storm incoming." He glanced down at her. "Fetch Alan? Then put the kettle on and get the flasks out. After that, I'll tell you what else needs doing."

Mari stared at him. That was absolutely the first time he'd asked her to do anything on board. She looked doubtfully over her shoulder, but all she could see were a few light clouds scudding on the edges of the clear sky.

"Are you—"

He interrupted her. "Mari? Now."

She went.

Alan was in the cabin he'd been sharing with Kier. She guessed it was usually Gareth's berth, but he'd been kipping down on one of the benches in the main cabin. Although, come to think of it, she didn't know when he actually *slept*.

She knocked on the door and opened it cautiously. Alan lay on his back on the bed, on top of the covers, wearing only a pair of shorts. They'd all been in shorts, most of the time. But the guys had been wearing shirts, out of, she suspected, a kind of old-fashioned gentlemanly courtesy. She hadn't had much opportunity to feast her eyes on Alan, and now she took it, never mind that she could already tell by the movement of the *Orpheus* that the wind was getting up.

His broad chest rose and fell with deep, even breaths. He had one arm flung up, revealing the paler skin and darker blond hair under his arm. His navy canvas shorts were riding just a little low, showing the ridges of his belly and the lean arch of one hip. She remembered what it felt like to kiss him there.

She shuddered.

"Finished?" he said, muffled by his forearm.

Mari jumped, choking back a squeak. *Not nearly.* "I thought you were asleep."

Alan sat up and—*oooooh*—she couldn't drag her eyes away from the way the muscles of his chest and abdomen shifted. He scratched his belly, then tucked his thumbs into his shorts and tugged the waistband back up.

Mari dragged her eyes up to his face. He was watching her with an expression that was less than amused.

"Since that was the first time you've really looked at me for days, I thought I'd better make the most of it."

She swallowed. "Gareth wants you. There's a storm."

His brows snapped together. Snagging his shirt from the bottom of the bed, he tugged it over his head and stood, stooped. "Then we'd better batten down the hatches, sweetheart, hadn't we?" he said, and squeezed past her and up on deck.

She made coffee and sandwiches and then packed away the galley as Gareth instructed, while the men moved on deck, below deck, down in the bilges, methodically making them ready.

All the time the boat reeled harder, until she had to hang on to stand upright, and movement across the cabin was only achieved by a kind of lurching rush, throwing one-self from one hand hold to the next. When she looked out the portholes all she could see was grey sky and grey sea.

The door into the cockpit banged open, and the two men came down into the galley. Alan pushed back the hood of his coat and pushed his soaked hair back. "It's mad out there."

"It'll get worse," Gareth said, slipping out of his own jacket and throwing it in the shower. "But we've done all we need to for the moment." He wedged himself behind the chart table and checked instruments, seeming satisfied with what he found. "We'll do."

"We will?" she said, ashamed of how breathless she sounded.

Both men looked at her with comically identical expressions of surprise.

"Of course," said Alan, as if it was absurd to suggest they might be concerned. *Git.*

Gareth was a little more understanding. "We're fine, Mari. I've managed worse on my own, and as long as we do all the right things, this is exactly what this boat is designed to weather. She won't even be ruffled—you'll see."

⚜ ⚜ ⚜

Not ruffled. Right.

Mari sat on her bed with her head between her knees. She hadn't been sick—not yet—but to her mind it was only a matter of time. How long they'd been thrown about in near-darkness she had no idea.

She only knew that a fair ride was fun because it lasted for five minutes. This was lasting far longer. This was not fun.

The bow went down till she felt like she was standing on her head. Then the whole boat shuddered, and she was shifted bodily down to the foot of the bed. She was exhausted from being thrown about, and from the constant cacophony of wind and waves. Groaning, she lay down and clung to the side of the bed. Gareth has said there was webbing he could fix up if she wanted to lie down, but since Alan was actually sitting out there in the main cabin *eating sandwiches,* she didn't like to make a fuss.

The bow went down into another trough. "Oh,

God."

This time it was different, though. This time when they hit the bottom it felt different, they went up leaning over slightly. It was only slight, but it was all wrong.

Then she heard the door bang.

Her own door was fastened. What was that?

Rolling to her feet, she hung onto the door handle as they rode another wave, then wrenched it open and looked out. The little door and trapdoor to the cockpit were open, swinging, banging hard. Water rushed down the steps into the galley.

There was a plate upside down on the floor and a squashed sandwich beside it.

The cabin was empty. No Gareth. No Alan.

They were outside in *this*?

Alarm clutched at her heart and rammed it into her throat.

Mari made it down the cabin length by clinging to the furniture. The lamp struck her on the side of the head, but she punched it away and kept going. She staggered up the steps into the cockpit and reeled back, overwhelmed by the sight.

It was a confusion of noise and darkness, force and water. Craning round, she caught a glimpse of two figures in bright red waterproofs, struggling together at the bow with handfuls of white canvas. Then a huge wave crashed across the deck, obscuring her view for a moment.

The deck was awash with raging, grey and white water, throwing itself back overboard into the tempest.

Alan and Gareth were still there, miraculously, although one of them had slipped closer to the rail, a little further from the other. Then the other one straightened, hauling a last handful of canvas aboard, gestured down beyond the rail and clapped the other on the shoulder as if congratulating him.

Mari took the in breath of a huge sigh of relief, as the farther figure stood up and let go of the rail to grasp the other man's arm. Even through the dark, she saw the unmistakeable bright gleam of Alan's smile.

Then the sky came down, and it was made of water.

Mari cried out, clutching the hatchway as the giant wave deluged her, too, soaking her to the skin in an instant.

Sobbing for breath, she pushed the hair back out of her face, wiping the water from her eyes to see across the deck.

One man stood at the rail, desperately straining to reach something out of sight. The hood had been swept back from his head and showed short, dark hair. *Not Alan's.*

Mari's whole body shuddered. She cried out again, screaming something incoherent. Hours passed, or seemed to, while her clutch on the hatchway kept her upright and she stared at the water-washed place where Alan had been.

A hand came over the deck edge.

Mari was never able to remember running across the deck. She threw herself forward and out, but then it was darkness, nothing, till she felt Alan's hand grip hers, hard, and she looked down over the side of the boat into Alan's white face.

She would not let go—she would not. Her arms ached, her shoulder protested, the wire cut into her other hand, pressed against her middle. Then Gareth's arms were round her, too, and Alan was coming up out of the water, springing back to life like he had never been in danger of losing it.

The trip back across the deck was harder, mostly because they couldn't pry her off him. They tumbled down into the main cabin together, a mess of clutching hands, ripped canvas, and sodden clothing.

They started dispensing with those fast enough, but Alan stopped getting out of his to help her, since she was shaking so hard she couldn't even speak.

Gareth disappeared and reappeared in dry clothes in a moment, clutching blankets and towels, ushering them both forward into her cabin. It was about then that her hearing tuned back in, and she realised Alan had been talking to her.

"Bloody hellfire," he muttered, standing close, struggling with his own numbed fingers at the buttons of her top.

She started laughing then, adding another type of shake, not able to stop, till her knees gave way, taking Alan by surprise, so that he came down with her, and they ended up facing each other, in a tangle of legs and damp blankets.

Alan gave up on the buttons about then, and ripped the whole top over her head. She wasn't wearing anything underneath, which should have bothered her, and didn't.

Gareth made himself scarce though, slipping silently away back to the main cabin, and shutting the door behind him.

Alan was scrubbing her with a towel in one hand, and trying to get to her jeans with the other. They were too close, they were too wet, and he swore again, his voice breaking.

"I should have let go," he said.

She saw his face looking up at her out of the sea's anger, his hand holding fast to hers.

She slapped him.

His hands dropped. He sat there, stunned, staring at her like she'd suddenly turned into someone else.

Which she had, really. But not just at that moment.

"If you ever say anything like that again, *I'll* jump overboard, you hear me?" Her voice was hoarse.

"Part of the sail came loose. It was making us slew. We had to sort it."

He was still staring at her like he was stunned, and she held his eyes, willing him to see just how angry she was. He was looking pretty grim himself, it had to be said.

She shivered again, really cold this time, and he pulled a blanket up from behind her to drape over her shoulders. Carefully not looking at her.

Really carefully *not* looking at her naked breasts, with their tight, pursed nipples.

She wasn't cold anymore. Her fingers were, but not too cold to tackle his shirt buttons. He was saying something, breathing it, something in the general trend of negative, but she was well beyond listening to him.

She undid just enough buttons, then rose up on her knees against him, pulling the shirt up with her. She threw the sodden cotton away into a corner, then caught his wrists as they fell, placing his hands at the button to her jeans.

They hesitated, for a split, aching second. Then he leaned forward, just a fraction, and pressed his lips to her belly, just above his now busy hands. She moaned, shuddering, as he flicked his tongue into her belly button. She clutched at his head, feeling the strands of hair cold, wet, clinging softly.

Her heart hammered, loud enough to deafen the sounds of the storm outside, but not loud enough to drown out the harsh, fractured sound of his breathing. Her jeans, soaked and intractable, were dragged off, her underwear with them, and suddenly his hand was between her legs. She bucked, shocked by how quickly he'd zeroed in on where she ached most.

Eyes locked with hers down the length of her body. He watched her intently as he stroked her. She moaned, still shocked into immobility, utterly fixated on the sensations he was creating, that fizzed in her blood and quivered in her stomach. Turning his head, he kissed her hip, his eyes drifting closed, cheeks flushed. The sight was so erotic: his face pressed to her flesh, his large, dark hand buried between her trembling thighs. She cried out, wordless, and fell back against the bed.

Rising, he stripped out of his shorts without taking

his eyes off her, then flipped her up onto the bed and came down beside her. They rolled with the yacht, trying to find a safe place to put arms and legs and get as close as possible.

"Of all the stupid things to do," Alan gasped, and she nearly hit him again, only he took her hand and kissed it, laved the palm with his tongue, and she went boneless.

"Not that—" he said, "this! Us . . . here." The boat pitched, and he wrapped one arm round her and hung onto the bed, and she all but screamed with laughter as they slid from one end of the cramped bed to the other, throwing pillows on the floor.

"Maybe we should wait . . ."

"No."

"No."

They lost their balance, limbs flying, but Alan hit the floor first, cushioning her fall with his body. *What a body*.

While he was trying to find something to wedge his foot against, she took full advantage, running her hands down his flanks, over his hips, sliding one up his hair-roughened inner thigh to where his erection lay against his belly.

"Uh," he huffed, "you might want to loosen your grip before we hit another wave."

Laughing, she let go of him and pushed to her knees, but then another wave *did* hit, and she tumbled off balance again, to end up all but sitting on his face.

"Not that I'm complaining," he said, his voice distinctly muffled, "But you may want to slide down a bit . . ."

She shimmied down till she could brace her hands on

either side of his head. His eyes blazed with laughter and desire, and her heart sang so loud she thought it would shatter like glass.

"Hi," she said, softly, seriously.

His eyelids drooped, the grin smoothed into sensual awareness. "Hey there."

She dropped her head and kissed him, clinging when the *Orpheus* shuddered its way up the next wall of water. He tasted her chin, her throat, muttering against her skin.

"Is this sex or a wrestling match?"

"No holds barred," she breathed, and rocked against his hardness, till his lips drew back from his teeth and his hands clamped, hard, on her hips.

It was madness. But it was a wild and beautiful madness.

When she lost her balance the next time, he took advantage and rolled her beneath him, tucking one of the fallen pillows beneath her head. Mari wriggled to get comfortable, and Alan smiled down at her, smoothing the hair from her face.

He kissed her, still smiling, but the smile melted away sometime after his tongue found its way in her mouth and his thighs worked their way between hers. He was breathing hard, and so was she—she wanted him desperately, and she told him so.

He acted on it.

Mari gave a little sob when he pushed inside her. He felt so good, so right, so utterly perfect, filling her, stretching her, driving on. Their rhythm was off—the waves helped and they hindered—but they didn't care.

"The storm's fading."

"Is it? Don't stop."

"No. Never."

Mari wrapped her arms round him. She wrapped her legs round his hips and met every thrust with a demand of her own. The storm was gone. It wasn't there—it didn't matter. It only mattered that Alan was here, with her, in her, that she was his and he hers.

"Oh," she cried, "please!" caught on the crest of her own wave, shuddering, free-fall, down the other side, blissful and blind.

She dragged her eyes open when she heard the hitch in his hard breathing. She saw his face when he cried her name and came, shaking in her arms, saw what she did to him, and was awed and triumphant.

☘ ☘ ☘

Gareth hummed old Stones tunes to himself, partly out of habit, partly so that he wouldn't be eavesdropping on the happy couple, while he sat in the cabin, checking the charts. The *Orpheus* was doing her job as stoically as only she knew how, now that the loose sail was dealt with. It hadn't taken him long to lash and secure the canvas. He'd re-rig it in the morning.

It hadn't taken him long to see which way the wind blew with Alan and his Marianne, either. Not that Kier

had filled in any details, beyond those absolutely operation-
ally necessary. Not even the goddess-like Jenny could have
turned that man into a chatterer. It didn't matter. It was
in the way they looked at each other. And the way they
stiffened up in each other's company.

Gareth was glad they'd sorted some things out. And
hoped it stayed plain sailing for them from now on.

It wasn't a hope he had a lot faith in, from personal
experience.

Face grim, he pushed the charts away and sat back,
eyes closed, listening to the engines pushing them in a safe,
straight line.

🪷 🪷 🪷

The *Orpheus* rocked gently. Overhead the flap of taut
canvas testified to the fact that the storm was over, and Gareth
was well in control. Ripples of light played across the ceiling.

In the bed below, Mari stretched. Her foot pushed
between Alan's calves, one arm slid up over his head on the
pillow behind her, her backside pressed against his lap. Her
breast lifted clear of his hand, but he only slid it sleepily
down her belly and across her hip, to stroke her thigh up
and down.

Everywhere they touched there was warmth, and the
remembrance of pleasure. It was like every cell of her skin
had a memory of their night together, recalled by the touch
of him.

"Mmmmmm."

She felt the rumble of that approving sound in his chest against her back, and smiled a smile so wide it hurt. She wriggled around till she faced him, pressing close, watching his blue eyes blink open from cross-eyed proximity.

"Good morning," she breathed.

"Definitely." His hand found her bottom, cupping and squeezing lightly.

She kissed his shoulder, warm, smooth, strong.

"Mari," he said, "look at me."

Lifting her head, she met his searching look. There were lines of tiredness on his face—she loved every one. He was pale, too, and she wondered at that, and at the shadow of pain in his eyes.

"You amaze me," he said, simply. "Just when I'm sure you're at your limit, you manage more, you prove me wrong."

Smiling, she ran a finger along his collarbone, ducking her head to press that smile on his chest when he shivered. "Does that mean you want more now?" she whispered.

"God, yes," he said, frankly, but he caught her hands when they started wandering. "Mari, wait . . . there's something . . . ah, don't do that!"

She subsided, pouting, and rolled a little on her side to see his face. She felt light and free, her whole body purring with pleasure. The tiny cabin was their whole world, and she wanted no more than that. Just Alan. And a chance at a future.

He cupped her face with his hand, smoothing the hair away from her cheek. "Mari, that first day onboard, when you stopped me telling you, I—" he hesitated, but already her pleasure was crumbling and she felt cold.

"I'm sorry—"

"Don't apologise! I didn't mean that, only I wanted to tell you—"

She laid her fingers across his mouth, not looking at him. "No. Shh. I'll tell you. I should have told you before, only I—I couldn't." Her throat closed, her eyes stung, and she dropped her head to tuck it under his chin, hiding from him.

A deep breath lifted his chest. She felt his heartbeat, steady and sure under her hand. "It's difficult . . . I don't want . . ." she muttered, against his throat.

He wrapped his arms around her. She felt cocooned, safe. "I'm here," was all he said, but it was enough.

It was all she needed. It was all she would ever need.

"I killed a man," she said. And it was easy, after all. Alan didn't push her away, didn't gasp in outrage. His arms tightened, that was all, and his lips brushed her hair.

"Tell me," he said, after a moment.

"There was a boy. He felt sorry for me, I think. He left me a key, and left the door open. I went out. Well, eventually I went out, through the room they questioned me in. There was another room. A man in it. I had a lamp, you see—one of those heavy-based angle lamps. I picked it up in the first room, just in case, although I never thought I'd use it, not like that."

She turned her head, to breathe more easily, and found she couldn't quite see properly. "He was asleep with his head on a little table. But he woke up when I tried to slip by. Stupid. I made a sound and he woke up.

"And all I could think about was that I couldn't go back, that I didn't care if he hit me, or whatever, but I had to try, I couldn't just give up and go back. So I hit him. With the lamp. I was so scared, Alan."

Her voice broke, then, and she struggled to breathe, shaking badly.

He stroked her head, her back, whispering words whose sense didn't matter at all while she cried.

"Are you sure you didn't just knock him out?" he asked, when she had subsided a little.

"No! Yes, I'm sure. There was so much blood, Alan. He was so still . . ."

"And although dead men don't tend to keep bleeding, I expect there's nothing I can say that could convince you?"

Mari reared back from him, shaking him a little, trying to make him see. "No! I killed him, Alan. I murdered him. He's dead because of *me*."

Cupping her cheek again, he closed his eyes, and when he opened them again, she saw a mirror of her own pain there.

"Mari, oh, Mari. You did what you had to. No court in the world would convict you, sweetheart."

"I don't need a court to tell me I was wrong," she said.

"No." How could a voice be hard and soft at the same time? "You've already condemned yourself. Now *that's* wrong."

He tipped her chin up with his thumb. "And if you've condemned yourself for that, where's the hope for me?" he said.

Mari stared at him, seeing the care, the concern—and seeing a little of her own fear there, too. "You're a nice man, Alan," she said, with a little smile.

ዧ ዧ ዧ

As the words left Mari's mouth, something cracked inside Alan.

He let out an anguished roar, tipping his head back and raising his hands, startling her badly. He grabbed her hips and put her away from him, sliding off the bed naked, to end up on his knees at her feet.

"No!" he shouted in her face and her head went back, her mouth dropping open. "I am not a nice man! I'm the man they were looking for! The smart card was mine. I took your bag by mistake and damn near got you killed for it." He gasped for breath, torn between relief that it was out and horrified fear at what the knowledge would do to her. "It's all my fault. Everything that happened to you."

Her face went still. Her eyes were huge, blank. And then her lip trembled and tears began to well.

He shook. "Oh no," he whispered, "please." He tipped up her chin with one hand, catching the tears as they fell with the other, as if to damn the flow. "No, no, no—shout at me, hit me--don't cry, please . . . Oh, God." He was holding something beautiful, and he had taken it in his hands and broken it, wilfully, stupidly. He didn't know how to mend it. His heart ached like it had shattered with it.

"I thought . . ." Her voice wavered, and she swallowed as his fingers moved across her cheek. "I thought you came after me because you . . . because you l-liked me."

He backed up then, because the tears were coming like rain and he couldn't stop them, because being that close was torture.

"I did. I came for you because I care about you, because I . . ." What was he going to say? Because he loved her? It was hardly more than an insult in the circumstances, and it wasn't as if she would believe him, would she?

She was shaking her head slowly, that awful hurt on her face still irrigated by big tears that dripped off her chin onto her knees. Each one burned his soul.

"No," she said. "It was just because you felt responsible. I understand now. All this"—a shaky hand sketched the air between them—"was just guilt. It's why you've been behaving so oddly. Isn't it?"

Big eyes pinned him. He owed her the truth. "Yes, I felt guilty, but I . . ."

She gathered up a blanket in one hand, wrapping it round her, tugging it to her chin. "I should like you to leave now, Alan. And I want to go home."

"Mari, please . . ."

"Get out, Alan. Now."

Kier pulled the Renault up in front of his home, lulled by the reassuring lurch over the cobbles.

He hadn't phoned ahead. Probably he should have, but Jenny would have fretted more with a timetable, he knew.

He was tired. But he didn't care.

He was home.

The lights upstairs were off, kids already asleep.

The downstairs curtains were open, lights off. Usually at this time of night they'd be closed, Jenny conscientiously drawing them when the heating went on. A faint glimmer in the living room suggested a kitchen light was on.

He knew, without having to be told, that she watched for him every night.

His throat was tight. His heart raced.

The distance between the car and the front door was somehow longer than usual. The key less willing to fit the lock.

Jenny, his Jenny, his wife, was in the conservatory, watering plants. She didn't cry out, or gasp, or jump when she saw him—only she set the watering can down very carefully, and straightened slowly, looking him over.

Her eyes were huge, her face pale. "Alan?"

"He's fine. And Mari. We found her."

She wet her lips, and a little colour leached into her cheeks. "Good."

"Kirstie? Alex?"

She nodded. "Fine."

She came forward then, which was good, because his feet seemed to have stopped working. Every sense in him strained to experience the moment. The first trace of her scent blurred his vision. Her hands on his face were everything he needed. Almost.

She placed her palms on his cheeks, and he blinked his eyes clear to look down into hers.

"You're home."

This mattered, this moment. It mattered that she should understand what he'd found on this last jaunt, that everything he needed, for all of his life, was right here. "Yes," he said, holding her gaze. "I am home, Jenny."

Why did he ever worry that she wouldn't understand? Her eyes warmed, her mouth curved. He saw in her loving eyes the perfect communication of what he was unable to put into words.

He moved, then, to wrap her in his arms and bind her as close to him as he could. He felt her shoulders rise on a huge, slow breath, and felt all the tension melt out of her as she let it go, shuddering. He held her tighter, taking up the slack. And when she tipped back her face, wet with tears, he kissed her.

She showed no inclination to break away to catch her breath, or finish the kiss so they could talk.

Which was fine by him, because he didn't plan on stopping anytime soon.

Mari was still ignoring him.

Which was hard on a small boat. But she managed it.

Silent and tight-lipped as she was around him, she still spoke to Gareth. He heard them. Quiet conversations about nothing at all, that made him desperately jealous and deeply ashamed in the same breath.

Gareth tried to decide if Marianne was talking to him to piss off Alan, and came to the conclusion that it wasn't in her nature to be like that. Out of the corner of his eye he saw her come on deck, lift her face to the sun, half-closing her eyes, and watch him work through the veil of her lashes.

Nothing she and Alan had shouted at each other, nothing they'd done, had fazed him. It was their life, their business. And, more's the pity, they couldn't give each other space on the tight confines of the *Orpheus*. He was sorry there wasn't more space for them, and more time. Mostly he was sorry for their unhappiness.

He guessed Marianne found what Angela had called his calm stoicism comforting, and it was probably gratitude that moved her to talk to him more than she had since she first came aboard. He was content to listen, if that helped.

"Is it harder to sail her with more people aboard?" she

asked now. "If you usually sail alone, I mean."

He kept recoiling the line he was tidying, thinking a while before he answered. "Solo sailing's not easy, so it's easier with two, even if I do have her rigged for easy handling."

"But not so easy with three?"

He smiled. "Maybe. If you were huge."

She snorted.

"It's better without McAllister," he added.

"Yes," she smiled, or at least tried to. "He really *is* huge. How do you know Alan?" The voice was studied nonchalance. She wasn't fooling him for a second.

"I don't. Met him when you came aboard. I know McAllister through some work we did together a long time ago."

She shifted to prop her elbows on the roof. "What kind of work?"

He'd finished with this line and started redoing the one next to it, not for any need, but to keep his hands busy while he thought what it was reasonable to say. "We were sweeping for mines in a harbour. McAllister was on the intel side, I was doing the recovery and disposal."

She thought about that for a bit. "You're a diver?"

"Not anymore," he said, evenly, while the rope took on a life of its own and kinked under his hands. He twisted and eased it, worked it smooth again. And then there wasn't anything else to do, he'd done all the deck work. He could catch up with the charting, update the log.

But it was good on deck. He squatted, forearms propped on his legs, and absorbed the roll as the *Orpheus* cut through the swell.

"What stopped you being a diver?" she said.

"Pretty much what stopped you being a carer," he said, before thinking it through, and then suppressed the urge to bite out his tongue. "I'm sorry," he added quickly, sincerely, turning to look at her. But her face was serene, watchful, not hurt.

"No," she said, "I'm sorry. The end of my job," she said, her voice dropping quote marks round the word, "was a foregone conclusion, and it wasn't exactly a vocation anyway. I don't think you're talking about the kind of death that came with the job, however risky, something expected—are you?"

No, sir. No, it was not expected. And it hadn't been part of the job. "That's true. But, in any case, I just didn't want to do the diving anymore, so I bought *Orpheus* and took to the sea." He smiled at her, keeping it light, and thankfully she took the cue.

"She's lovely." Smiling, eyes drifting closed, Mari laid her head against her raised shoulder. The breeze fluffed her hair, the sun gilded her skin, and he remembered, suddenly, what made two people on board a boat so much fun.

And which person he wished were here with him.

Caught by that thought, and that longing, he wasn't sure how much time went by before she spoke again.

"Did you know what to do next?"

"I don't follow you."

"You said you bought *Orpheus*. Did you know, straight away, what you'd do with your life after you decided to give up your job?"

Not exactly the kind of giving up she was talking about. But she wasn't to know. And what she needed to know, he thought, was what she was supposed to do next. He couldn't tell her any answers. "The end of my job wasn't a sudden thing. There was the death, and then a lot of fall-out from that. Afterward, I was . . . washed out, drained." He didn't have answers for her, but maybe he had some useful questions. "I knew I needed to spend some time with myself, and I needed a project, something to do. And I knew where I felt at home."

She smiled again, the little lift of her lips coming easier now. "The sea."

He nodded, noting almost without conscious thought the slight chill as the breeze shifted to touch a different part of his face. He'd need to make an adjustment to their heading soon. "Where are you at home?"

Maybe that was the wrong question, after all, because she paled and her mouth shook for a second, before she wiped her hand across her face and cleared her throat. "I know where my home is, and I know where I feel at home," her voice was rising on the threat of tears. "But they're not the same place."

"Start where you can, Marianne," he said, gently. "The rest will come when you're ready."

She nodded, a hard, resolute movement of her head.

But her lip still trembled.

Alan cornered her in the galley one afternoon, knowing Gareth was sleeping in the berth opposite, and the exit was effectively blocked with him standing there. "You've already cleaned that stove three times in the last two days, Mari. Take a break."

For answer, she wrenched open the tiny oven door and began removing the wire shelves.

"You know, of all the reactions I expected, silence was not one of them. *Talk* to me, will you?"

"What about?" she asked, clipped, short. Not looking.

"For God's sake, Mari . . . you don't have to put on the anger face. I'll accept you're livid with me—you've got a perfectly adequate reason—but don't put on an act with me."

She slammed the oven door shut and straightened, shelves still clutched in her hand. "An *act*?" She threw the shelves in a sink full of soapy water and rounded on him. "Who the hell are you to talk about acts?"

"Keep your voice down. Gareth's asleep."

He thought for a moment she was going to hit him, even welcomed the prospect, but she backed up against the counter instead and anchored herself with two hands clutching the edge on either side of her hips.

"If we're going to talk about acts," she hissed, "What about you? With your disguises and your lies, and your

James Bond secrets. It's not a game! My life isn't a game!"

And just like that he got to see his life through another's eyes and saw the gaps. "I'm sorry," he said, stiffly. The words had never seemed so inadequate.

At least she was talking to him.

"And I am not pretending to be angry with you, Alan."

He leant back against the panelling, feeling the exhaustion all over again, despite more time in bed than any healthy man had a right to. Not that he'd been sleeping. Not for the last four days. "It's not that exactly," he said. "I meant what I said. I know you're angry with me. I expect it. But you don't look angry when you think I'm not looking at you."

And that's what was hard to bear. It was lies again, but from her to him. Everything was lies.

She was still, hardly breathing. He wasn't precisely looking at her, busy staring at the spotless floor, another victim of Mari's desperate activity. What a useless situation. How could you comfort someone suffering from your actions?

"And how do I look then?" she whispered.

"Wounded half to death," he said, clearly, as if the words themselves were penance. The last syllable fell into a grave of words, and neither of them spoke to fill it for a long time.

"At least you know, then," she said, quietly, almost, *almost* sympathetically.

He closed his eyes. "Mari, I . . ."

"Don't you dare apologise, Alan Waring," she snapped, and that brought his head up sharpish. It was the angry face again, but with the addition of wild eyes. "For a start it would take me a while to figure out which bit you were apologising for, and for seconds you . . . you—" she faltered, and spun round.

When she spoke again she was quieter, duller. "It wasn't mistakes, Alan. Not something you can easily apologise for. You were lying all the time. Every step of the way, you were eyes wide open and—and I know you just enough, in spite of everything, to realise you *knew* you were doing wrong all along. You knew how I felt about you, and you didn't walk away. You knew people were after what you were carrying, and you didn't keep clear. You— you were playing with me—"

"No—" he tried to cut across her, tried to defend himself against at least that accusation, but her voice climbed over his, and her eyes were hard.

"You were *playing* with me, from the start. You did this, Alan, and you don't get to apologise."

She had him there. There were no defences for his actions. No redemption for his soul, and no solace for his heart.

There was no grace, not for him.

Alan held the smart card in his hand, and thought about war.

With nothing to do but brood, Alan had unpacked his laptop and plugged in the reader. He'd picked his way through maps, charts, reports, and communications and uncovered the real rules of the game they'd unwittingly been playing. After an hour of it, he'd removed the smart card and come up on deck, needing air.

"He said it was worth billions."

He closed his hand and turned carefully, slowly, because, good grief, that had sounded like Mari's talking to him, and that wasn't likely. Not likely at all.

It was, though, against all the odds. In a pair of silky drawstring trousers and a green vest top, she stood on the bottom step from the cabin, and he looked down on her, thinking, *No, I should be at your feet.*

He cleared his throat. "Who said it was worth billions?"

She nodded at his left hand. "The Frenchman."

"He was right." He backed up, because she patently wasn't coming up those steps while he stood at the top. He went as far as he could go, and then sat, and she came up high enough to lean back on the canopy and watch him.

"It is worth billions," he repeated. "Billions in world trade, arms, fuels . . . It would affect billions of lives, too."

The *Orpheus* sighed across the wind, without fuss. Below, Gareth was checking the charts again.

"He said something about panning for gold, you know, when we were waiting for Bristow in the truck. I thought he meant that the smart card had details of gold somewhere

. . . for a theft, or for mining. But then he said something that made me think he meant a person."

No, it was gold. Black gold. "What else did he say?"

She wasn't looking at him, so it was safe to look at her. She was pale, but calm, her fine, rich dark hair catching the breeze and fanning across her face like a veil, hiding her lips, highlighting her gorgeous, exotic eyes. "He said he'd tried twelve streams before he found what he wanted. He screened them, he said, for opportunities. He was very cryptic. But then Bristow turned up, and the Frenchman smirked and said something about fool's gold."

Which meant . . . that Bristow was the Frenchman's gold? Alan rolled with the boat, and let his mind fit pieces together. If the Frenchman had been looking for a way into HQ, he'd have looked for a weak link, a person he could manipulate, maybe even blackmail. And he hadn't had to look at—screen—very many of HQ's quiet, serious, mostly solitary employees before finding Bristow, loaded down with his evil, guilt, and fear. Alan wondered which of HQ's contacts had been the eleven who came up clean.

"Alan?" Marianne's voice was as calm as her face. He hated it.

"Yes?"

"Are we safe now?"

He sighed, leaning back, closing his eyes for a moment. *Yes, of course. I wouldn't let anyone hurt you, Mari.*

You're safe with me.

He swallowed, cleared his throat, willed his voice to be

level. "I won't know for sure until I get back to HQ. But I'm beginning to suspect they never knew anything about this, that Bristow was feeding them false information for months." Since he'd pulled a smart card from a baked laptop somewhere in Western Sahara.

"I think he was trying to get the smart card to the Frenchman without exposing himself or betraying me." Except Bristow *had* betrayed him. The moment he started using him.

"Are you going to tell me what it is?" she said, and he had to duck his head because there was just enough hostility in her voice to wound him.

"Certainly." He swallowed. "It's about oil. It was all about oil." He held the card on his palm. He could barely feel the weight, but in all the terms that mattered it was the heaviest burden he had ever carried. "On this little card are charts, maps, reports, communications . . . from a little seismographic team that were hunting oil in the Sahara and disappeared.

"Apparently, they ended up in Western Sahara." He glanced up, but it was plain that meant nothing to her. "Western Sahara is a large area of disputed land to the south of Morocco. It's just desert. Doesn't matter much to anyone except the tribes that live there. They've fought over it before, but it's been quiet lately, even though they still can't agree—Morocco, Mauritania, and Algeria—who it belongs to, and who should govern it." He waited. He had confidence she would put two and two together soon enough.

She did. "But," she said, "if there were huge wealth

beneath the Western Sahara, it would matter a lot more."

Sighing, he turned the card over in his hand again. Such a little thing. "Yes. Matter enough to fight over, to send people to their deaths."

"Matter enough for other countries to get involved."

Alan looked up. "You catch on fast. It's a big oil field, Mari—massive." He shook his head. "It could destabilise the whole of North Africa, all the oil-producing countries . . . Can you imagine if Algeria wanted it? If another country did?"

She could. He could see from her face. She came up the last step, reaching out to touch the card, and he held his breath. Then it occurred to him if he did that, he missed out on a chance to catch her scent again—and he breathed in hard.

Lillies . . . the sea . . . *Mari*.

She heard him, looked up. He saw her pupils widen when her eyes met his . . . then she was back on the step, clutching the hatchway as if the storm was back, when in fact the gentlest of breezes sent them onward.

And then, off balance or not, she latched onto the crux of the matter, just like that. "What are you going to do with it?"

"I don't know." He pushed his hair back off his forehead.

"Don't you have to give it back to the government?"

He frowned up at her. "What?"

She flapped a hand at it. "The people you work for. You were bringing it back for them, weren't you?"

He almost laughed, but he didn't want her to disappear in a huff. Moments with Mari were precious. There were so few left. "I don't work for them anymore, Mari. I resigned."

She looked at him, looked him hard in the eye. "When?"

"I resigned when I found you missing and wanted to come looking for you. But I think I stopped being their man when I met you. From then on, I was your man."

She considered that, but her face didn't change. *Oh, please,* he thought, *do angry again. Do angry, raging, hysterical. Just don't do blank. Please.*

"So what are you going to do with it?"

Closing his eyes, he tipped his head back, listening to the little slap and rush of the waves. "What should I do, Mari?"

"You're asking me?"

"Please," he choked that one off, because that was more than likely to end up the same as his mental plea, left unchecked. He tried again. "I trust you. You decide."

He heard her step on the deck, and kept very still.

"Is there a way of getting this to safe hands?"

He could just say yes, reassure her, make it an easy decision to make. But there'd been wars over oil before, too many of them, and this one had the potential to put them all in the shade. He owed her honesty in this. "Whose hands are safe, Mari? Bristow's hands were supposed to be safe, you know. All the time he had me dancing across the desert for this thing, I thought I was working for HQ . . ."

"And you were working for him," she continued for him, when the bitterness robbed him of words. "And the Frenchman."

"Yes."

She thought about that for a while. "This could change people's lives for the better."

"Yes. But there are other ways to do that."

"Will it hurt anyone, if it never surfaces again?"

He thought about the reports on the card. The dead seismographic team, the dead agent. He thought about the dead Frenchman. About Bristow. "No."

He felt the lightest brush of her fingers on his hand, and opened his eyes. She stood over him, blocking out the sun. The breeze lifted a strand of her hair to brush against her mouth.

Marianne took the smart card from him, snapped it in two, and threw it over the side.

He didn't watch it go. He watched her, waited till she turned to look down at him again.

"I'm sorry," he said. *I'm sorry, I'm sorry, I'm sorry.*

Her eyes dropped, and she disappeared down into the cabin.

He closed his eyes again. There was no grace.

All he could hope for was a fast wind.

₰ ₰ ₰

His wish was granted. They made their destination—
a little fishing port on the south Cornwall coast—just over
a day later, early in the afternoon. The dock was quiet, the
stone arms of the sea wall almost empty. Clouds drifted in
the summer sky, running shadows over the sea and the wall,
blending the textures of stone and water to make a cool and
peaceful whole.

Mari packed with the door locked, said her goodbyes
and thank you's to Gareth with gentle sincerity, and walked
straight past him to where the granite steps led up onto
the sea wall. He turned after her, and said one of the most
stupid things he had ever said in his life, just as she was
lifting a canvas-shod foot to step off the boat. "I think I
should come with you."

She turned round, wide-eyed. "I beg your pardon?"
Wasn't that his line?

"You've been through an awful lot, Mari. I wouldn't
want people to take advantage."

What the hell was he *doing*?

Mari's mouth was open. "People?"

He gritted his teeth. "Men. I wouldn't want men to
take advantage of you." He'd been thinking about this a
lot, mostly at night. He gestured helplessly with one hand.
"There's still a lot you don't know . . ."

She dropped the bag and turned on him.

"Just because I didn't know doesn't mean I couldn't learn. Just because I didn't doesn't mean I can't. Just because you were all I wanted doesn't mean you are still all I need. And just because you were my first does *not* necessarily mean you will be my last.

"If I want to go out there"—she screamed at him, actually making him back up a second, for God's sake—"if I want to go out there and"—she gasped for breath—"and . . . have sex with half the male population of Liskeard, I can if I want to and it's *none of your business!*"

chapter sixteen

Alan realised his mouth was hanging open and shut it with a snap. Part of him wanted to cheer her, the other part wanted to lock her in his bedroom and never let her out again. Ever.

He'd created a monster. Except that wasn't strictly true. The potential of this Marianne had always been in the one he'd met in Rabat. All her experiences, drawing on her inner strength, had set her free. Free of the terrors of inexperience, the fears of the unknown. Free of not knowing what her limits were, where her boundaries were. Now she knew. The things she had survived had given her confidence.

Except the old Marianne hadn't gone, exactly. She was still there in the sparkle in her eyes, the blush on her cheeks that belied her vow of promiscuity.

He took a breath. "Okay," he said.

She stumbled forward, wrenching her arm out of his grip when he tried to steady her. "Wh-what?"

"Okay. If that's what you want, you're perfectly capable of going out and getting it. But I do dispute the 'none of my business' part."

She bristled, eyes opening wide in indignation, "I—"

"Because I love you. Maybe I shouldn't, but that's a whole other argument. The fact that I do means what you do matters to me. It becomes my business. I can't do anything about it if you don't love me, but I can't stop caring about it.

"And I'm sorry, Mari, if you haven't heard me all the other times I've apologised. I'm sorry for what I did, I'm sorry for having been a stupid, selfish, criminally reckless idiot. I'm sorry for the things I did to you, sweetheart."

He reached out and tucked her hair behind one ear. She didn't even flinch. "So," he fought to keep his voice level. "What about it? Do you love me? Can I do something about it?"

It was her turn to be catching flies. He wanted to kiss her parted lips, seal his declaration on her mouth. He was so close, so close . . . he could almost taste her. In spite of everything, for the first time, he allowed himself to picture them together, in her big house in Cornwall, weathering winter storms, lounging in a sun-drenched garden. *So close . . .*

Then she stepped away. "It doesn't matter," she said, and there was no inflection in her tone at all.

It doesn't matter. Was that a *yes*? Was it a *no*?

Something clutched at his heart with cold fingers, and suddenly Alan was shaken by a desperate fear. He couldn't go back to before. He couldn't go back to being alone, to being without Mari. It wasn't possible. He wouldn't survive. "It doesn't *matter*?"

"No." She wrapped her arms around herself, and it was so eloquent of distress, Alan wanted to howl. Oh, God, no. He couldn't hurt her more, could he?

Just by saying he loved her?

She swallowed, wet her lips. "It doesn't matter if I love you. I can't trust you. You played with me and put my life at risk. Then you slept with me when I didn't know it was your fault."

Hearing those accusations fall from her lips, hearing them in her voice was somehow far more devastating than knowing them in his own mind. He flinched, and she caught that immediately.

"What? Didn't you ever think of it all in those terms, Alan? How about this one: Did you rescue me so that you could get laid? So that I'd be grateful enough?"

No, please . . . He backed off, closing his eyes, reeling at her interpretation.

"Was it worth it, Alan?"

There wasn't an answer that wouldn't hang him. So he stared at her. Trying to commit her face to memory. Trying not to imagine how pointless his life would be without her in it.

He couldn't refute her accusations. He could see how she could interpret it that way. He'd just told her he loved her . . . and it didn't matter. He understood that now.

The feelings of his heart were nothing, were insubstantial against his betrayal. He'd given her away once. There was no second chance.

He leaned back on the railing, folding his arms. He wasn't going to cry. Not now. Later was for grieving. And whiskey.

Working his jaw loose, he spoke quietly. "If you do . . . do Liskeard, be careful."

She looked at him, blank-faced and shocked. He wondered suddenly if she'd expected a different answer. She blinked hard a few times. "I deserve better than you," she whispered.

"Yes," he said. "Yes, you do."

Not whiskey. He'd kill himself trying to numb this pain with alcohol. There wasn't enough single malt in the world.

He thought she made a sound, but the blood was pounding in his ears so hard he couldn't quite hear her. Then she swept past him up the steps, and although he didn't turn round to watch her, he could see her, head high, hair bouncing, as she walked along the wall and out of sight.

⚘ ⚘ ⚘

It had taken Gareth two days to leave port. Clean up, re-stock, fill water tanks . . . all these things had been done in a few hours. He told himself he was keen to get back to the Med. He told himself it was sensible to take a day to do repairs and get the *Orpheus* really shipshape. He told himself the squall that the forecast said might or might not swing across the Channel could make solo sailing tricky.

He told himself a lot of bullshit.

Because he was in British waters, a stone's throw from British soil, and a few hundred miles from home.

He'd stayed away a long time. He'd had good, solid reasons for that. Sound reasons, no bullshit this time. But he couldn't quite remember why they were so good.

The sun set, the boat sat lightly on the water. A small yacht chugged past at the end of a good day's sail, two people red-cheeked and grinning at the helm. Somewhere at the other side of the marina, there was a party starting up on a motor launch. Laughter and music reached him on a soft touch of breeze with a faint scent of cigarette smoke. Seagulls squealed, fighting over someone's abandoned fish and chips.

It was getting dark, and he hadn't bothered to turn any lights on. He didn't need to. It wasn't as if he was doing anything. He was just sitting, still, empty-handed, caught between the twin tugs of going home and going away. Pulled in two directions and locked solid because of it.

The ghost of Alan and Marianne's tension was still aboard. Marianne would be fine, he was sure. She'd take a time to grieve and recover, and then she'd forget all about Alan. But Alan . . . Gareth shook his head sharply and got to his feet, slipping down into the cabin and then standing between the table and the counter with nothing to do there, either.

He took a deep breath. Another.

The truth of it was this—Alan's bitter unhappiness was

the mirror of his own. He couldn't see how to solve Alan's problems, tangled and dragging with guilt and responsibility. But they made his own load of guilt and responsibility suddenly seem less overwhelming. It suddenly made him less willing to settle for the bleak existence he'd carved out for himself after he'd . . . after . . . after David had died.

It *hadn't* been his *fault*.

Maybe he'd been too indulgent of his protégé's flippant, reckless approach. Maybe he shouldn't have been distracted, even for a moment. But the police knew, the coroner knew, even Angela—for God's sake, even Angela—knew it wasn't Gareth's fault.

Staying away had been his fault, though. Putting himself in watery limbo, cutting himself off, *punishing* himself. Those had been his fault, too.

It had been a year.

A year for Angela to grieve for her fiancé. A year for Gareth to grieve, too, for a friend and a pupil. For an adventurous soul, and a terminally, tragically reckless diver.

A year for Gareth to come to terms with the fact that he wasn't guilty of killing his friend, but he *was* guilty of being in love with Angela.

Wasn't it time he took his future in his own hands and tried to make something happy out of it? Was it fair to assume what Angela would say?

Maybe there was something in this hope business, after all.

He dug his mobile out of its locker and powered it up.

Angela's number wasn't programmed in—that had always felt like he was taking too much for granted, staking a claim on a woman who wasn't his.

It didn't matter, anyway. He knew her number by heart.

HQ had that peculiar polite agitation that only showed when something had gone spectacularly wrong. People hurried to and fro in the corridors, almost, but not quite, moved to a run, and there were a higher than average number of new faces here and there.

But everyone still spoke in whispers, as if it were bad manners to interrupt the silence.

After two days in and out of meetings and nondescript interview rooms, Alan had stopped trying to remember the names of the suits who were talking to him.

He thought of the latest one as Mr. Blue for the bright tie he wore.

"The French government denies all knowledge of your Frenchman."

"He's not mine," Alan said, evenly. "I believe them, and don't we have a name for him yet?"

Blue was younger than he, but he contrived to look superior as he leafed through the file in front of him. "We have several. Take your pick." He pushed a sheet of paper across the table.

Alan scanned it. "I recognise that name—Legros, there. I heard his name among the Sahawaris a couple of times."

"Sahawaris?"

Alan rolled his eyes. "Natives of Western Sahara. They bought arms off Legros, I know. And I knew a bunch of Berbers who bought all their arms from this man," his finger stabbed the sheet.

"That sounds about right. We certainly have him as arms dealer, sometimes mercenary, and general friend to any group in conflict with authority. We haven't found any state affiliation yet."

"I don't think you will."

Blue shook his head. "You may be right there."

"Did he have any family?"

"He was married."

"Has his wife been informed?"

Blue sighed, looked up, and suddenly he *did* look older than Alan. "Which one?"

Alan stared.

"We've found three wives so far, and at least one permanent mistress. None of which are of a religion or nationality that permits bigamy."

"Huh," said Alan. "What about Bristow?"

"Not that you need to know, but as it happens he has no family. We found some . . . interesting material on his PC. Did he say anything about that?"

Alan shrugged. "Not a thing." There was nothing he could add to that debate.

"And this Marianne Forster."

Alan breathed deep. "What about her?"

"You say she knew nothing? Nothing about the smart card contents, nothing about Bristow or the Frenchman?"

"No," he said, very clearly. "Actually, I said *no one* knows anything about the smart card contents. And Forster was kept in the dark."

Blue blinked at him a few times. "And the smart card was . . . lost."

"We were caught in a storm in the Bay of Biscay. We lost some gear overboard, including my laptop. The smart card was with it."

Blue shuffled some more papers. "We'll have to bill you for that."

"You can take your bill," he said, borrowing from Kier's stock of expressions, "and shove it up your ass."

Blue shuffled.

Alan left.

ꛅ ꛅ ꛅ

Later, a distinctly more senior suit caught up with him at Alan's hotel room. They had a brief but affable conversation about the Official Secrets Act and about disciplinary action and a re-posting elsewhere.

His response was direct and to the point, and was recorded on the file euphemistically as, "Mr. Waring confirmed his resignation."

ꕮ ꕮ ꕮ

Alan turned off the TV and dropped the remote. He hadn't been watching it anyway. He padded barefoot up to his room and pulled a fleece shirt out of the wardrobe. He'd been fine just in jogging bottoms, earlier, but the night was cooling.

He pulled the shirt on like he'd done everything else recently. Like an automaton, because he had to. Leaving it unbuttoned, he trudged downstairs again and hesitated.

Which room should he brood in now?

That's how it had been, ever since he'd got home a couple of months ago. He'd moved from room to room, not sleeping, rarely eating, just thinking. And pacing. He was doing a lot of pacing.

HQ hadn't kept him long. The focus of their investigations had been on the blackmailing of Bristow and his subsequent treason. Alan had told them he'd gone back to Algeria to find the leak. He'd told them about Bristow and the Frenchman, that the smart card had been destroyed, that he had no idea what was on it.

They weren't interested in Mari. They were only interested in cleaning up and locking down. He told them he'd found her, and brought her home, and she didn't know anything, either.

They didn't tell him anything about Bristow. Until he'd asked the right questions. They didn't know how long he'd been in the Frenchman's pocket, but he'd been taking sleeping pills for two years.

Alan always remembered, though, that Bristow could have sold him, Alan, to the Frenchman at any time. Putting two and two together, he saw how the man, traitorous as he was, had tried to keep his arrangement confined to handing over *information* and not *people*.

And Alan remembered, often in the middle of the night, that Bristow had died.

When the senior suit had departed, he'd gone home and back to pacing.

He felt loss, anger, an unclassifiable, indefinable pain that almost made him double over when it hit. And it hit a lot.

There was no solace in being angry at Mari, either. It was all his fault, no getting away from it.

He ended up in the kitchen, then wondered why. He eyed a box of Crag Rat, a gift of ale from Cumbria, but discarded it as a bad idea on a forty-eight hour empty stomach. Scrubbing his face with his hands, he felt the scratch of a why-bother-shaving beard, then pushed his hair back against his skull. It stayed there, never a good sign. He needed a shower. And a shave.

And a reason for living.

He hooked a chair out from the little round table in the corner with his foot and collapsed into it.

Shit.

No kidding, Waring.

He leant forward and pressed his forehead to the cold,

polished wood, and tried, really tried. not to think about her.

How was he going to do that, exactly, when she was imprinted on his soul?

Oh, God . . . Oh, God . . . Oh, God . . . he was going to be lonely for the rest of his life. Because there was no other woman for him but Mari, and he would never earn the right to aspire to her. He had coped with being alone when it was his choice. Now . . . now he'd seen the alternative. And he honestly didn't know how to live without it.

Existence, survival, he could do. Just. But living . . . living was over.

His stomach rolled, in distress and hunger and even fear. The house was silent around him, not even creaking or sighing. Just cold, dead, quiet.

Pushing himself tiredly to his feet, Alan wandered into the dining room, propped his backside on the table, and leant there, staring at the wallpaper.

Because that was another issue, wasn't it? What was Mari going to do with herself without him? He could imagine, easily, the sort of trouble she could attract. A nice, pretty girl, with a big house and money to spend.

But that wasn't fair. She had the skills of survival now. Survival and good judgement. Strength and resilience. She would be fine. Without him. Just fine.

As a disciplinary exercise, or maybe even a punishment—he deserved it—he forced himself to imagine Marianne happily married. A stockbroker, maybe. Young, active, happy to commute. A couple of kids, a flat in

London. He imagined them together, Mari happy and smiling, laughing at her husband.

He broke out in a sweat.

He shifted off the table and went into the living room. At the back end there was bistro-style table with a lamp on it, unlit, and beside it a little cast iron chair. Beyond that, there was a set of glazed patio doors, and he stood there, looking out at the dark garden.

All he saw was his reflection.

He stared for a while, close up, leaning one arm on the glass. He'd have to clean that.

Stepping back, he picked up the cast iron chair, and with a savage snarl, swung it at the window. The glass went opaque, instantly, a small hole appeared where the iron leg caught and held. He wrenched it out, pulling more glass down in tiny, thick crystals, like giant's sugar.

He held the heavy chair in one hand, staring down at the scattered glass on the faded carpet, feeling the breath of night air on his cheek.

Then he dropped the chair and went for the phone.

Kier answered on the second ring. "McAllister."

"I just broke the patio doors."

"Excellent. Why?"

Alan didn't know. He opened his mouth to say so and heard, "Because I could see myself in them."

There was a pause. "O-kaaay." He heard Kier sigh, heard him move, and heard the creak of bed springs and Jenny's voice in the background. He leaned forward very slowly till his forehead touched the cool wall, and bit his tongue while his skin crawled with self-loathing. He swallowed. "I'm sorry to have disturbed you." His voice sounded as stiff as the words.

"Shut up." He heard a door close in the background. Kier didn't want Jenny overhearing any of this. "Alan, I hate to say this, but I think you need help."

Alan knew the impulse to lift his head and let it fall against the wall. His fingers curled on the phone and against the old, much-painted wallpaper in the effort to stay still. Damage to own property, yes. Damage to self, no.

It was mildly encouraging to note he still had some boundaries, some instincts of self-preservation.

"I don't need help," he said. "I need Mari."

It was happening again, his mouth was providing answers without the intervention of his brain. Or perhaps it was his heart. Sweat prickled between his shoulder blades.

"Well, obviously." In spite of everything, Alan's lips twitched at the volume of the unspoken *duh*.

"So what are you going to do about it?" Kier continued.

What, exactly? There wasn't anything he could do about it.

"For God's sake, McAllister, do you really think she'd waste spit on me after everything?"

"I don't know. Nor do you. But you could ask her."

Could he?

"What's the point? I asked her before—"

McAllister interrupted him. "We've been over this

before, Waring, in case you'd forgotten."

Forgotten? He barely remembered anything of the last couple of months.

Kier was continuing. "You asked her when she was shocked, angry, felt cornered and vulnerable. And, if I remember correctly, when you'd just been a twenty-four-carat jerk."

Alan thought about that. About the look on her face when he'd let her go, about the fact that she *had* admitted to loving him, a lifetime ago, back in Rabat. He let himself remember, too, what he had forbidden himself to think of since she'd walked away. Visions of Mari, naked, laughing, clutching at him, thrown around in that tiny cabin by the storm, and then rocked by the pleasure she'd found with him.

Maybe there *was* a part of her that needed him, too.

As if he'd read his mind, Kier spoke. "I believe she needs you, Alan. You should go to her."

Was she lonely, too?

"Why didn't you say this before?" he asked.

"You weren't ready to hear it. You were barely hearing anything."

His heart started pumping in strong, painful beats, shaking him. He felt breathless, started to sweat.

So this was hope. It . . . hurt. And it had been such a long time since he'd had it.

"Alan, you brought her halfway across the Sahara desert, brought her home across thousands of miles. Are you going to give up now?"

I don't think so.

❀ ❀ ❀

Alan hadn't been this afraid since Mari had stared at him like a stranger, that first time he'd found her in the desert.

He took the ford with careful precision, and drove on up the narrow lane. His hands sweated on the wheel. It occurred to him—a bit late, it had to be admitted—that she might not even be home. Might not live here anymore. God help him. God help her, because he'd scour the planet for her if she wasn't.

He'd forced himself to eat, shower, and shave before he'd set out, not willing to inflict Zombie Alan on the world. He did feel more human for it, if a bit like a human missing a soul.

A vehicle was coming. He pulled into a field gateway to let it pass—an electrician's van—and stayed parked for a moment, engine humming, steering wheel rumbling under his hands. A fault? Rewiring?

Then a red van went by with a plumbing service emblazoned on the side, closely followed by a tall, blue transit belonging to a local firm of builders.

She was moving house?

She'd *moved?*

He pulled back out onto the lane before the butcher, baker, and candlestick maker could make their entrance, and drove just a little too fast the rest of the way.

There *was* a signboard by the drive, but it was covered,

and the wrought iron stand was hardly the stuff of "for sale" signs. There were no more workmen's vans, and there was no sign of Mari. But the door stood open, and there were lights upstairs. The old sheet over the new sign rippled in the stiff onshore breeze.

He could taste the sea in it, wild and refreshing.

He didn't call. He went into the hallway, scanning, smelling new paint and plaster dust. There were new units and a new table in the kitchen, and the living room now had large French doors opening onto the brick foundations for a large conservatory.

On a small table in the hall there was an open box full of leaflets. Ears straining for any sound, Alan picked one out of the box. There were pictures of the beach, the cliffs, the scenery around Mari's home. *Ninnes House,* it said. *Respite care for the carer.* He scanned the rest of the leaflet. Mari was setting up her home as a place people could come to rest and recuperate. People who spent their lives looking after relatives without complaint, with little help.

People like her.

The leaflet said she could arrange for the relative to go into good residential care for a few days, with activities and outings if wanted, and the carer could retreat to her home and relax, eat well, and visit local sights. She'd even linked up with a local charity to run an outreach programme for the more remote rural areas, to make sure no one ever missed out. The project was supported by charities, but he knew without a shadow of a doubt she'd have sunk her own money into it, too.

The perfection of it stunned him. But in the next breath, he knew it shouldn't. How utterly Mari to apply what she had, and what she'd learned, to improving other people's lives.

She didn't need him. She'd found her place. No, she'd made her place.

He shook his head, already stepping back, reaching to drop the leaflet into the box. It turned as it fell, and landed upside down. He stopped.

Mari's picture was on the back, sitting under the apple tree. She was smiling, she looked welcoming and kind, but he saw the strain on her face, the shadows in her eyes.

He'd never know unless he asked.

🕷 🕷 🕷

Marianne was in her father's room.

Only it wasn't her father's room anymore. It was the first room she'd tackled, in a sleepless whirlwind of change. She'd redone it in neutral shades, light and airy and calm, and now she had thick, heavy, cream curtains to hang. It was light, spacious. A gentle and tranquil room.

Mari sat on the unmade bed, laid the curtains carefully across her lap, and popped open the old Quality Street chocolate tin her mother had kept the curtain hooks in. It had been a kind of grieving for her, that redecorating, while the idea for her project came together. At least, it was a

kind of farewell tinged with a freely acknowledged anger—
she paused for a moment in her counting of curtain hooks
and repeated to herself—*I am* angry *with him*—that her
father had accepted so much from her, and never valued it.

He had been lying to her when he'd said there was no
money for extra care.

And he'd been lying to her when he'd said that Grandfather hadn't left her anything.

Tipping the white plastic hooks onto the cream material on her knee, Mari slid her hand into her pocket again,
fingering the soft, thin sheets of paper, reassuring herself
that her grandfather's words were still with her.

She'd found the envelope in the attic, when she'd been
clearing out before the workmen began. A box of her dad's
bits and pieces, old school books of her mother's, even a
couple of pictures of Marianne from school. And a single,
white envelope, with her name on it, in her grandfather's
handwriting.

So much made sense now. A single letter to change the
way she saw the world.

Except that wasn't exactly true, either. Alan had begun that process.

She closed her eyes and pressed her lips together,
breathing hard against the pain. When she opened her
eyes again, it was a moment before she saw the oatmeal-
coloured walls and cream woodwork, so vivid were the
desert's russets, golds, and glowing apricots in her mind's
eye. Then four walls swam into focus and she felt again the

soft brocade under her hands and the sharp prick where she gripped a curtain hook too hard.

Mari sighed and dropped her head, determinedly threading hooks into the curtain.

Everything was smaller than before: she felt hemmed in by the gentle, familiar walls. A strange longing was born in her, a subtle, mourning ache.

And she knew what she mourned for, too. Not Alan. No, *that* grieving was a different beast, savage and untiring. That was the pain that sent her to sleep, crying, and stole her appetite and her joy. It sunk its claws into her, and tore, and Marianne doubted she'd ever heal from those wounds.

No. This one was softer, insinuating, watching.

She mourned for the wide open spaces, the grand places, the whispering darkness, and the searing light. She longed for living that felt more alive, for struggles that felt more real, for a place where she seemed to expand, her soul growing to fill the wide, magnificent horizons. She missed the feeling of only surviving by the gracious mercy of the landscape, the skill of her own heart and mind, and the strength of her body.

The longing had confused her, in those first bleak days, making her feel a little mad, as if Alan had made her dependent even on his own dreams.

Then that box discovered in the attic had revealed her grandfather's last letter to a much younger Marianne, and in that tale her longing for the desert and its wide open honesty had been explained.

But there were no words to take away the pain of loving Alan, no stories to mask the knowledge that, of all the inhospitable places in the world, in *this* theatre, her lover sought her. And found her.

And broke her.

Blinking away tears, Mari slipped the last of the hooks home, and got to her feet to hang the curtain.

Alan found her upstairs, in a bright and clean bedroom, plainly recently decorated. There were still folded dust sheets on the stripped and varnished pine floorboards, with paint tins and buckets on them. She stood on tiptoes at the window, reaching far over her head, struggling to hook the curtain onto the rail.

She wore faded, crumpled linen trousers, with a tear in the hem by her right ankle, and a pale blue T-shirt. The softness of her clothes and the stretch she was putting them to outlined the smooth curves and sleek lines of her figure in a way that made him swallow. Hard.

She looked wonderful.

Without thinking much beyond, *I missed you*, he went forward. "Let me help you with that," he said.

Marianne shrieked and spun in the confining folds of

curtain.

A sound of outrage choked in her throat.

It was Alan. He stood right in front of her. In her house. In *this room* dressed in shorts, T-shirt, and desert boots, with his hands reaching out to her.

Oh, he looks great.

That thought came out of nowhere and sent her eyebrows climbing up her forehead. Sure, he was just as tall and . . . and . . . oh, dear Lord. Desert or no desert, he was still a prince.

He saw her gawping at him, and treated her to a slow, lazy grin—twenty-four-carat Alan Special. The lines on his face creased into a pattern she knew so well, and his teeth gleamed against his tan. It was a devastating smile, and it turned her insides to water.

The months of misery had taken their toll. She was hallucinating.

That smile grew more intent, the blue eyes were hooded, his gaze dropped lower. Suddenly she realised her mouth was hanging open.

How dare *he look so great!*

Mari shrieked again and tried to step backwards, but she tripped in the fabric and snatched the curtain. The two hooks she'd managed to secure pulled free, and the curtain parachuted down, enveloping her in folds of heavy brocade, and taking her down to the floor.

Through the sounds of her struggles, she heard Alan laughing. The touch of his hand on her leg, even through the folds of curtain, shocked her into stillness.

He uncovered her face.

"Hi." He smiled down at her where she lay cocooned in curtains, slid his palm against her face, and kissed her. She almost cried at the first touch of his lips, going utterly still to preserve the sensation in her mind. She felt dizzy, breathless, half from her fight with the curtains, half from the delicious agony of having him kiss her again.

He murmured something against her mouth, touched his tongue to her lips, and that was all she needed. She twisted her mouth against his, opening her lips, inviting him in. Half sobbing, she tried to get her hands free to hold him, but they were tightly wound. His hot tongue slid into her mouth again and again, driving her senseless, claiming her . . .

"Marianne . . ." he groaned.

Oh, God.

She wriggled suddenly, miraculously wrenching a knee from the confining cloth.

She put it to good use.

While he lay gasping on the floor, curled up in a protective ball, she got herself to her feet and tried to wipe the taste of him from her lips.

"What's the matter, Waring? Do you need to tie your women up these days?"

He blinked at her from the floor, his face pained. *I'll bet it's pained.* "For pity's sake, Marianne!" he groaned.

"I don't want your pity, and you don't want mine!" she

shrieked. *Where on earth had that come from?*

She backed up when he got to his knees, then his feet, bent double, bracing his fists on his thighs. He hissed, then straightened, looking a little pale around the mouth.

"I don't pity you, Mari," he said. "I wouldn't dare."

She snorted. "What are you doing here?"

"Five minutes ago, I knew the answer to that question. Now I'm questioning my own motives." His lips twisted.

"Question them out loud," she snapped.

He looked at her properly then, taking a breath and physically wiping the scowl off his face with his hand. She wished she was wearing something that wasn't paint-splattered. Wished they weren't in a bedroom. Really, really wished he didn't make that room feel so small.

"I'm sorry. I'm not trying to keep you in the dark again. You, uh"— he winced, shifting his weight painfully from one leg to the other—"you surprised me."

"You're not the only one. Why are you here?" And why did her heart race even faster when she asked that?

"I thought . . . I hoped that we might . . ." He hesitated. She'd never heard Alan that tentative. It was scary. "I hoped we might talk."

"Talk."

"Yes."

"You were using your tongue. I suppose that's a start."

He exhaled sharply through his nose in annoyance. "Have a heart, Mari. I'm only human, and you're . . ." he tailed off, staring at her, pain that was more than physical in his eyes.

Whatever he was going to say, it wasn't what he said. She could see that in his eyes. "I like what you've done. The house . . . the project?"

"It made sense. There's nothing like it around here." She shrugged. "I wanted to do it."

"It's wonderful."

She stared. She wanted to snap at him. But his praise meant more to her than she wanted to admit. "Thank you." She bent to retrieve the curtains, but he beat her to it, lifting them, shaking them and starting to fold them loosely.

"You look unhappy," he said.

"Yeah, well."

"I've been unhappy, too, Marianne."

The use of her old name twisted her mouth and her stomach like she'd sucked on a lemon. "I was *happy* before I met you!"

"Happy?" He looked at her like she'd suddenly morphed into a frog or something. He breathed deep, two, three times, his lips a thin line. For a second or two, she thought he wasn't going to say anything else.

Then he did.

"The first time I met you, you had tears in your eyes."

She flinched, and turned her shoulder, but he was between her and the door, and there wasn't anywhere for her to go.

"And they weren't so much from being lost—"

"I was not lost!"

"—or alone, or from not finding what you were looking for, as from the fact that you knew *nothing* about yourself, or what you could do. You'd done nothing, had no life. You knew *nothing* about how to deal with life and people. And you hated it.

"By all means cast me as the villain of the piece, Mari, I'll act up with enthusiasm. But don't kid yourself you were happy before you met me." He shook his head emphatically. "You were the loneliest, unhappiest person I'd ever met."

"Apart from you," she hissed, fighting back tears.

He stared at her, hard, his mouth grim. "Alright." He swallowed. "I'll accept that. I know that now. But you saved me, Mari. You saved me from that loneliness, and you saved me from myself. I love you. I need you, I want you, and I'm sorry." He shrugged, one shoulder, suddenly boyishly awkward. "It's all I've got. If it's enough, I'll be outside."

He turned and left, and she stood there, shocked.

She'd saved him. She could be his salvation. It was a heady responsibility, that. Mari would be the first to admit that she didn't know what the hell she was doing these days. The respite care project had filled every waking hour. It was a good thing, a real thing, the right thing to do, but that didn't mean it wasn't a way to stop her thinking about Alan, to keep life at bay, to tumble her exhausted into dreamless sleep every night, too.

If she ever stopped, if she ever took a moment to think back, to think of Alan, of them, together . . . It wasn't her experiences that haunted her. It was not knowing what to do. Whether to try and find him. What she would say. *She didn't know.*

But she knew this—she had to either forgive him and tell him to get lost, or forgive him and take him in. Either way, she had to forgive him. As much for her peace of mind as for his.

She'd never been anyone's salvation before. It was crazy to think that she—*she*—could be so necessary to someone. Her dad had needed her to survive, day by day, but she wasn't so stupid she didn't know she was just a nurse. Any other nurse could have done the job.

But Alan . . . Alan needed *her*. None other. A heady responsibility indeed.

Feelings were forming, finding shape while she thought. She felt like she was on a voyage of discovery, mapping out a whole new ocean of emotions.

The truth was she didn't give a damn about Algeria anymore. Everything she knew had been put in a crucible in the last months and melted down, and she didn't know anything anymore.

Except . . .

❉ ❉ ❉

Mari found him at the top of the cliff path that led down to the bay. Gorse bloomed beside him, and at his feet the little pink heads of thrift bobbed in the breeze.

He didn't turn when she approached, but she knew he

knew she was there. He always did.

And she knew she needed to start at the wrong place, to get to the right one.

"I thought I hated you," she said, softly. Down below, the waves hissed and foamed on the shingle beach, rolling another tide's worth of round pebbles up onto the slope.

He went very still, and she remembered another time he was still, sitting cross-legged at her feet.

"You don't mean that. I know you don't."

She shook. He was right, and that was the hell of it.

"I ought to hate you," she amended, shaking her head.

"But you can't," and his smooth, lovely voice was the only living thing about him—all else was stone. "You're Marianne Forster, and even after everything, you don't have a hateful bone in your body. Not for me."

"You arrogant arse," she enunciated clearly.

He turned then, and at the sight of his face she wanted desperately to see him laughing and smiling again, not looking like this, not like this.

"I know you, Marianne," he said.

"Not anymore." She shook her head again, face twisting with distress. She didn't even know herself anymore. How could he profess to know her, to love her?

She wasn't the same!

"You fell in love with the wrong woman, Alan. She doesn't exist anymore."

"No, that's not true! You're not as changed as you think you are. You're still Mari."

She bit at her thumb, trying to stop the trembling of her lower lip. "I wasn't this . . . this hard before."

"Hard?" he stepped closer. "You mean courageous? Decisive? Independent? God, Mari—I wish you could see yourself through my eyes. You're . . . you're magnificent."

She turned a shoulder to him, leaving teeth marks in her thumb. "So do you want the credit for that, too?"

"Oh, Mari," he sounded sad, but there was something else there, too, a thread of understanding that was just as devastating to her composure as anything else could ever be.

"Don't you see? Everything you've done, everything you've survived, learned . . . the capacity was in you all the time. The Marianne I met in Rabat was as courageous as you. She just didn't know it. It was always in you. You owe me nothing."

"Except my life."

He came close, forced her head up with hard hands, pulling her punished thumb from her mouth. She saw his eyes move over her face, saw the lines of strain. Saw the need.

"But I nearly took it, too," he said, his voice shaking. "My stupid, careless, selfish actions nearly killed you." He waited, silent, swallowing.

Time beat like a broken heart, labouring for a life worth living.

What do you know?

Not so long ago, the answer to that question had been, *not a hell of a lot.*

But she wasn't the same. For the first time it occurred

to her that change like that wasn't always a bad thing. What had she said to him, that first night?

"I wanted to get away."

"Find yourself?"

"I don't think there was a myself to find. It never had a chance to grow. Create myself, maybe."

She knew, then. She knew everything she wanted, and what she was going to have to do to get it. And she was scared, more scared than she'd ever been in that dusty cell north of Béchar.

But love was like that, wasn't it? When you gathered your courage and your heart in both hands and gave it into another's keeping?

"Then perhaps," she said slowly, "we should let those two cancel each other out."

"What do you mean?"

"You put me in danger—no, it's okay, Alan—and then you risked your own life to save me."

She touched her fingers to his lips and wasn't entirely sure if the trembling was hers or his. No. It was theirs. Her lover, her hard man, the golden boy, the spy. Irrepressible, indomitable. Trembling for her.

"Shh," she said, "I love you. I can't help it."

His voice was broken. "I don't want you to love me in spite of yourself."

She smiled, knowing now, by the lightness in her spirit that this was right, was wonderful. "You said it yourself. It was always in me."

His hands cupped her face, fingers sweeping away tears she hadn't even noticed falling. "I love you, Mari. I'll spend the rest of my life putting it right."

She stepped out of his arms smartly. "Oh, no, you don't!" she snapped, but she mellowed it with a smile at the look of anguish on his face. "If we're going to do this—"

"*We are.*"

"—then it stops now. The guilt, the counting off, the recriminations. It stops now. I'm not having you paying for loving me for the rest of your life."

❦ ❦ ❦

The silence lay between them for a while, soft and gentle, while a seagull cried and Alan tried to encompass her mind-blowing generosity.

He frowned, anxious, wanting honesty about all things. "Mari, I'm not sure I did, back then . . . I can't lie to you . . ."

"Oh, hush," she laughed, and the wonderful, glorious benediction of it almost brought him to his knees. Her hands were on his chest, her eyes wide, sparkling. He forgot what he was going to say, and kissed her.

She was soft. And sweet. And *his.* It was the first time he'd touched her with any right to it, and that thought nearly destroyed him.

He pulled away, but she caught him by the hand and dragged him back from the cliff edge, went down on her knees on the sun-warmed turf, and pulled him down beside her.

"Quickly," she said, breathless, and— "please," while her hands were lifting the hem of his top. He didn't need to be asked twice.

God bless soft clothes that were easy to get into.

God bless soft clothes with naked Mari inside them.

"Beautiful," he whispered, praising her breasts with hands and lips. Then he hissed something decidedly less polite when she landed her hand inside his fly.

Then the shorts were history, and Mari made a place for him between her thighs, tugging him down to her with eager hands. He slid inside her and was torn, as he guessed he would be ever after, between the urge to move at once and the desire to stay utterly still and savour that feeling, because it was . . . So. Damn. Perfect.

He moved anyway, because she wanted him to.

She laughed and gasped and cried her way through it, radiating delight. She came with a shout, and he with her, calling her name. He was slain by her, broken apart and made whole by a combination of physical pleasure and heart's joy so acute he could barely breathe. He cradled her close, shaking, barely able to believe he deserved this. He didn't deserve it. But he'd spend the rest of his life earning it.

She rolled onto his chest, pinning him, caging his face in her hands. "Oh, no you don't," she said, smiling. "None of that. If you want a penance, I'll give you one."

He marvelled at the way she saw his soul. "You will?"

"Oh, yes." She was grinning, all mischief and enticement.

"What will it be then, oh Queen?"

She rose up, a sultry smile curving her lips. Her shifting trapped his recovering erection between their bodies, he could feel her, hot and slick, and then she rocked, humming, and he locked his jaw to stop the shout.

"You have to marry me, love me, and make me happy, for the rest of our days."

He slipped a hand behind her neck, curling his fingers in her hair, tugging her down to him.

"That," he said, against her mouth, "I can do."

"Mmmmm," she replied.

⚜ ⚜ ⚜

Later, much later, after they'd brushed each other off and slipped inside to bed, she showed him her grandfather's letter.

To my precious granddaughter, Mari.

They tell me I won't be here to see your tenth birthday. I know that when I die it will make you very sad, which is a terrible thing. I can't do anything to make you less sad, my lovely girl, but I am writing this letter because I think there are some things you should know.

I can't tell you these things now because they are grown-up things, to do with grown-up feelings and behaviour, and you are too young now to understand. But I will give this letter to your father, so that he can give it to you when you are old enough.

It all comes back to my stories. Your dark, exotic eyes were shining in the cradle, Mari, the first time I spoke of Rabat, and you used to smile so wide when I called you beloved in Tamazight. It was more than a love of my tall tales. I could see that the place was in your soul. But it's also in your dark eyes and your dark hair. It's in your blood, Mari.

Let me explain. In that picture I gave you, there is a courtyard, a cat, and a woman. The courtyard was my home for a few short years. The cat, Euphrates, adopted us when we moved there. And the woman, dear Mari, was your grandmother.

I know this will be a shock, but I know it will make sense to you, too. Your mother, God rest her soul, never knew. She accepted without question my other big story—that your grandmother was an Englishwoman, was my wife, and had died when your mother was born.

That story, and only that one, sweet Mari, was a lie.

Back then, it was hard for a young man with a young baby. It would have been harder if people had known that the mother who died in childbirth was not an Englishwoman, but an Arab, and another man's wife. So I gave your mother my name, and a tale to protect her, and everyone accepted them both.

I wrestled with myself whether to tell her when she married your father. But they were happy, and I was afraid that the truth might confuse them, and I didn't want to make them unhappy, even for a short time.

You, my Mari, are made of sterner stuff! And your heart, like mine, reaches out to the wide Sahara. So it's time, at last, for me to tell you my true story.

When I was a very young man, I went to North Africa to make maps. It was a good job, and paid well for its time, and I loved my work. I loved it far more than many of my col-leagues, who complained of the heat, and the dust and the, to them, incomprehensible Arabs. To me, the heat and dust were nothing to the beauty, and the sense of being so much closer to God in such a wide expanse of the world. I understood the Arabs who said, "Insha'Allah" all the time, because how could you not submit to God's will in a place like that?

They told me off for "going native," but I didn't care. When my job finished, I collected my last wages and looked about me for a place to stay. It was when I was in Rabat, inspecting a back-street property, that I first met your grandmother.

It's true enough to say I found her in the gutter. She was very young, about eighteen I think (I was in my twenties), but she had already been married. Her husband had cast her off (they can do that over there, quite easily), and her father was a brute who had not allowed her to come back home as is the custom. She was destitute, and desperate.

She was also the most beautiful thing I had ever seen. I hope that one day, Mari, you will understand the power of true passion and true love combined. The night I found her, I knew I should never want another woman. I gave her shelter and never for one moment expected that she might find something to like in the awkward, excitable, energetic young man I was then. But she did. Praise God and all his angels, she did.

Your grandmother and I loved each other as much as any two young people ever can. I could not marry her without her father's permission, and that was impossible. I am not at all sure that we cared a brass farthing about it. We had each other, a place to live, a little money to get by on, and that was enough.

We had lived together like that for just over a year when we found out we were going to have a baby. We were excited, and a little scared. I wondered if we ought to go back to England where there were good hospitals, but we didn't know how to get permission for my "wife" to go with me. I wish we had tried harder.

The birth wasn't so bad. She was sitting up and smiling within hours, and we held your mother together and laughed and cried over her. But a few days later your grandmother became ill, and she died when your mother was two weeks old.

I went back to England. I worked hard at bringing up your mother and making sure she was happy, healthy, and safe. But I was lost and lonely, missing my beautiful love every day. I don't think I had a single day's true, deep, total happiness in all those years, until I held you in my arms and you looked at me with your grandmother's eyes, sharing my secret and keeping it, in front of everyone else.

Your grandmother's name was Nadirah, Mari. It means "a rare and precious thing." I know she would have loved you, and been proud of you, just as much as I am.

Do, if you ever have the chance, go to Morocco and visit our home. Find out there if I was right about the place being in your heart, in your soul, and in your blood.

I suspect I am.

Your loving, story-telling grandfather.

Mari cried, watching him read those words, and Alan loved her again, promising her his love, his help, and the wide, magnificent truth of the desert.

EPILOGUE

It was a perfect picture—dark sand and dawn sun—timeless and beautiful.

There was no sound—nothing moved. The horizon was finely drawn, gently undulating, reflecting the elegant parade of clouds above. Far higher, the last stars glimmered faintly, a scattering of diamond dust on darkness.

When it came, the sun climbed into an apricot sky without warning, without a fanfare, as if it bestowed a precious gift on those who shared a secret.

Then the rider came out of the sun, sitting neat and straight in the saddle. The desert was its setting, and it was a part of that perfect picture—rider and sand and sun. The horse loped on, at a relaxed pace it could keep up for hours and miles. It tossed its mane with natural arrogance, and the new sun gilded every strand.

Alan watched them coming for a while, sitting on the edge of the muddy hole, until the dark dot with the dust plume resolved itself into a black-and-white-clad form on a sunset red mount. Then he got up stiffly, wiping grimy hands on filthy cargoes, nodding to his Berber workmates, and went to sit on the bench under the awning, taking up a bottle of water from the cool box in the shade.

The horse bounced to a halt, and the rider slipped easily from the saddle, soothing and steadying it with a word of Tamazight. The reins were flipped over the neck and held, and the rider turned to Alan, pulling the folds of white cloth from her face.

"It's all arranged!" said Mari, revealed. She swiped a hand over her face, smearing dust and sweat together without thought to her appearance. He smiled at her, soothed now that she was back after being gone for four days in Algiers. It was the longest they'd been apart since their marriage six months ago, and he'd hated every second. But he'd turned that anger to energy, and thrown himself into their project—consequently they were ahead of schedule, and life was good.

He got up and went to her, horse and all—she kissed him, he kissed her, and robes and reins and hands became inextricably tangled until she pulled back, laughing aloud, protesting she had to rub the horse down and see it fed and watered. But the boy Haris had skipped up silently to do that, nodding and smiling and gazing on Mari with a kind of hero worship. He led tired Reesa away.

It had taken a lot of time and resources to find Haris. He had disappeared so completely and so thoroughly after setting Mari free, that he might have been an angel, come down solely for that purpose. But they'd persevered, using Alan's contacts, and Mari's determination, and found him they had. Now he was fitting quietly and thoughtfully into the tribe, adopted into a large, boisterous family.

And since Mari could never rescue just one person, she'd thrown herself into helping the tribe achieve some of their plans and dearest wishes, too. A permanent well for when they weren't travelling. A school room. A meeting house.

Alan took Mari back to the shade, handing her the water bottle and watching her drink.

She's mine, he thought, and, *I'm hers.* And it was right and real and wonderful. Life was very good.

Mari pulled the cloth from her head and flopped into a canvas chair behind him. "We've got permission for another three weeks—and supplies coming next week."

"You're a genius," he said.

She shook her head, smiling. "The embassy was a huge help, and the Trust did what they could. It was easy once we had the agreement. We just had to ease the paperwork through."

"That's bloody excellent. We can do a second well for that, get the pump fixed onto this one, and start on the schoolhouse."

"Yup," she agreed, happily. Her eagerness made him laugh, on a daily basis. But her courage awed him twice as much.

"I left the Rover at the base and rode on down. They'll bring it down with the supplies next week. Reesa needed a run, and I . . . after the city, you know?"

"And you needed the desert," he said, in perfect understanding.

She put her hand in his and heaved a sigh. "Exactly."

The sky was alight with colours there were no names for, vibrant, living, and joyous.

He smiled. He'd wanted to give her luxurious relaxation for a honeymoon. Goa, perhaps, or the Bahamas. She'd asked—breathless and excited—for a trek to Tamanrasset.

"Do you miss it?" she asked. "The work, I mean?"

He shook his head. "Not at all. It was covering a void. You fill it. And I suspect you have plans for my time."

"Oh, yes."

"See? One-track mind."

"For a start, I want you to arrange activity trips for the carers who stay at Ninnes House. UK-based adventure trips for starters, but if it catches on, you could maybe take them further abroad, maybe even out here, and—"

He laughed, interrupting her, knowing she was only half joking with him. They were looking for another house in Cornwall, near Ninnes House, so Mari could keep fundraising for the project she'd started there.

He got up and dragged her to her feet, needing her close. She came without fuss, burrowing into his embrace with a sigh of happiness.

She looked up. There was dust on her face, her hair was flattened and tangled. She looked up at him, lips curving, eyes sparkling, and Alan loved her completely. He smiled at her, feeling the contentment in every corner of his soul.

The perfect dawn was forgotten—he held all the world's beauty in his arms.

He didn't know which was strongest in him, joy or amazement, to have married Marianne and found that she loved the desert just as he did.

He knew, though, that he loved her more than any land, in any world, in any lifetime.

Run Among THORNS

ANNA LOUISE LUCIA

In one crisis moment of her life, when she is taken hostage, little Jenny Waring does something exceptional. And now U.S. authorities want to know how and why she was able to single-handedly take out three armed men. Did she have special, illegal training? When Jenny steadfastly maintains her innocence, the authorities send in a specialist to break her—Kier McAllister.

Kier is very, very good at what he does. His first step is to isolate his subject, which he does by whisking Jenny away to a remote cottage in Galloway, Scotland. Then he goes to work.

But Jenny's accusing eyes are starting to hold the whole world for him, and that isn't good at all. Not when the people he works for aren't about to leave her alone. To make matters worse, Jenny is falling in love with him, too. Finally, working together instead of against each other, peeling away the layers of the onion, they find a rotten core.

And now things are about to get really interesting . . .

ISBN#9781933836331
US $7.95 / CDN $9.95
Romantic Suspense
Available Now
www.annalouiselucia.com

The Rock & Roll Queen of BEDLAM

Leggy, karaoke-singing Allegra Thome spends her days teaching dysfunctional teens and her nights with wealthy new boyfriend, Michael. The rough patch following Allegra's divorce is over, and life is grand. But when Allegra lands in the middle of a drug bust and meets Sloan, a rough-around-the edges DEA agent and, later that day, a throwaway kid from her class disappears, things quickly head south. Sloan, who has the tact of a roadside bomb, is attracted to Allegra and alienates Michael. To make matters worse, nobody seems to care that Allegra's student, Sara Stepanek, is missing.

Add to the mix a rural Washington State town under the spell of a charismatic minister who doesn't hesitate to use secrets of the rich and powerful to keep them in line, even while withholding his own dark past, and Allegra's search for Sara becomes a race against time with dead bodies piling up and her own life in peril. Under the circumstances, it's not surprising things come to a head at the WWJD (What Would Jesus Drink) Winery.

Marilee Brothers
ISBN#9781934755464
Trade Paperback / Suspense
US $15.95 / CDN $17.95
OCTOBER 2009
www.marileebrothers.com

THE PRICE OF SANCTUARY

GAYLON GREER

Shelby Cervosier murdered three men in self-defense. Brutally beaten and raped by her captors, she does what any woman would do: kill or die. To avoid manslaughter charges, one involving a sadistic immigration officer, Shelby cooperates with the Caribbean Basin Task Force, a sleazy undercover government agency. In exchange for legal amnesty and political asylum in the United States, she completes a treacherous mission in Haiti. Now the agent who hired her wants her dead. Facing a contract on her life, Shelby flees with her younger sister, Carmen, to find safe haven in America with two assassins in close pursuit.

Hank Pekins accepts the contract. Like any competent killer-for-hire, he captures Shelby and escorts her . . . to his farm in a remote part of Colorado? That wasn't part of the deal. A killer kills. A paid assassin doesn't protect an illegal immigrant and turn her into his lover.

In a coldhearted profession where ruthlessness rules and emotions obscure an annihilator's judgment, passion has no clout at the critical moment the job must be executed. But Hank knows that his own days are numbered. Money cannot buy human life. Especially not the life of the woman he adores beyond reason.

The second assassin loves no one. Vlad, known as The Impaler, intends to complete his assignment. First, he will torture Shelby in his trademark style, and then he will kill her. No one, not even Hank, will stand in this psychopath's way. For Shelby Cervosier, what will be *The Price Of Sanctuary?*

ISBN#9781605420585

US $24.95 / CDN $27.95

Thriller / Hardcover

JUNE 2009

Flight to Freedom

D.J. Wilson

I KILLED MY HUSBAND, A TOWN HERO, and then called the police and turned myself in. "He's dead as a doornail," I said to the officer and then spit on Harland Jeffers' bloody, dead body.

With my head held high, I allowed myself to be escorted to a squad car outside my house. A house which had been more of a prison than the cell I was headed for.

Cameras flashed.

"Why did you kill Harland?"

Because he needed killing. And I, Montana Ines Parsons-Jeffers did just that.

So begins the rest of what's left of Montana's life. Not that she ever really had one.

Now she's headed for prison. There's no escaping it. It was the ultimate destination in her Flight to Freedom.

But one man might be able to help . . .

ISBN# 9781933836379
Trade Paperback
US $15.95 / CDN $17.95
Available Now
www.doloresjwilson.com

LIZ WOLFE

If it's not one thing, it's a
MURDER

TWENTY-TWO YEARS OF MARRIAGE HAVE GIVEN SKYE DONOVAN a life of structure and predictability. When she discovers some women's underwear—not hers—however, she begins to suspect her husband is fooling around. And she's right, he is. But she's wrong about who the underwear belongs to. Not her husband's girlfriend, but her husband. And then she walks in on her husband . . . and his boyfriend.

Skye finds herself confronting another new reality. She needs to start life over. She needs to find a job, a place to live, break the news to her teenaged daughter and—yikes—start dating again. At least she has her best friend to help her through it all.

Not.

Corpses are turning up. And her best friend is the prime suspect.

As Skye tries to prove her friend's innocence, her own life is further complicated by a handsome detective, a sexy writer, a pagan wedding, her friend's unexpected pregnancy, and a new career. Could it get any crazier? In a word, yes. She not only must exonerate her friend, but do so before the murderer strikes even closer to home . . .

ISBN#9781933836393
Mass Market Paperback / Mystery
US $7.95 / CDN $9.95
Available Now
www.lizwolfe.net

Want to know what's going on with
your favorite author or what new releases
are coming from Medallion Press?

Now you can receive breaking news,
updates, and more from Medallion Press
straight to your cell phone, e-mail, instant
messenger, or Facebook!

twitter

Sign up now at www.twitter.com/MedallionPress
to stay on top of all the happenings in and
around Medallion Press.

For more information
about other great titles from
Medallion Press, visit

medallionpress.com